Ruby

By the same author

LIFE IS JUST A BOWL OF CHERRIES

ANNA KING

Ruby Chadwick

ARROW BOOKS

Arrow Books Limited
20 Vauxhall Bridge Road, London SW1V 2SA

An imprint of the Random Century Group

London Melbourne Sydney Auckland
Johannesburg and agencies throughout
the world

First published in Great Britain in 1991
by Barrie & Jenkins Ltd
Arrow edition 1992

1 3 5 7 9 10 8 6 4 2

© 1991 by Anna King

The right of Anna King to be identified as the
author of this work has been asserted by her in
accordance with the Copyright, Designs and Patents
Act, 1988

This book is sold subject to the condition that it shall
not, by way of trade or otherwise, be lent, resold, hired
out, or otherwise circulated without the publisher's
prior consent in any form of binding or cover other
than that in which it is published and without a
similar condition including this condition being
imposed on the subsequent purchaser

Printed and bound in Great Britain by
Cox & Wyman Ltd, Reading, Berkshire

ISBN 0 09 992600 8

In memory of my mother-in-law, Gladys Ruth King,
who gave me the idea for this novel

ACKNOWLEDGEMENTS

With thanks to my sister-in-law, Pauline Masterson, who helped with the typing of the manuscript; and to Lord McColl of Dulwich and Dr Ian Hannah for their invaluable assistance relating to medical details in this book. Thank you also to my sister, Teresa Deere, who helped me to acquire a word processor, and to my brother, Tony Masterson, who taught me how to use it. A special thank you to my niece, Claire Guntrip, for keeping my children busy while I worked; and to the staff at Welling Library, for supplying me with reference books.

PART ONE

1887

Chapter One

Beneath the pile of blankets a silent form stirred, a small leg appeared through a gap in the bed-covers, encountered the icy cold and was swiftly pulled back into the warmth. The sounds from the street carried up to her window as ten-year-old Ruby Chadwick tried to hang on to the last vestige of sleep. A woman's voice, shrill with raucous laughter, brought Ruby's head from her soft warm pillow.

'Blast!' she swore softly, her hands cupping the sides of her face as her long chestnut hair, parted into segments with cotton curling-rags, tumbled around her shoulders. Swinging her legs over the side of the bed, she shivered slightly before pulling off the coverlet and wrapping it round her slight frame. Half running, half hopping, she made her way across the cold floorboards to her bedroom window to look for the person who had so rudely awakened her.

The woman stood on the pavement, her heavily painted face illuminated by the huge wrought-iron gas lamp that hung over the pub entrance below Ruby's bedroom. On her head she wore a huge hat bedecked with multi-coloured feathers, her tattered green dress cut low at the neck revealing her soiled, much used breasts. By her side stood a seaman, his cap pushed to the back of his head, a drunken grin on his face.

As Ruby pressed closer against the window, his voice came clearly to her: 'Will sixpence do yer?'

The woman cocked her head to one side as if considering the offer, then, shrugging her shoulders, she nodded. Arm in arm, the couple walked forward towards the door directly underneath Ruby's window. She watched as the sailor tried to pull the woman in the opposite direction.

'Let's 'ave a drink first, eh, love?' wheedled the woman.

The sailor stopped in his tracks, his fuddled mind trying to come to a decision. He had docked only two hours ago after a year at sea, but

3

his pay was almost gone and he still had to find somewhere to sleep tonight, unless he could find his way home to his wife in Stepney. Pushing away the woman's arm, he stood back as if to see her more clearly, and then shuddered. His wife was no oil-painting, but at least she was clean and, more important, she didn't cost anything. 'Sorry, love, changed me mind. Got a wife an' ten kids at 'ome. I 'aven't seen 'em for over a year.'

Seeing the look that came over the woman's face, he hastily backed away, looking fearfully over his shoulder in case she had an accomplice waiting in one of the dark alleys that lined the street. He wouldn't be the first sailor to be found unconscious, a lump on his head and his pockets empty. Turning swiftly on his heel, he made off down the street, ignoring the stream of invective that followed him, anxious now to get to the safety of his home.

Still at her vantage place, Ruby watched the change in the woman. Gone now was the inviting smile; in its place came the face of an old woman, weary and drawn, a defeated look Ruby had witnessed many times from her window. Letting the lace curtains drop back, she scuttled back to her bed, muttering under her breath, 'Doxy!'

The scene Ruby had just witnessed was a common occurrence, especially on a Saturday night. She lived over the King's Arms public house in the Mile End Road and often bemoaned her misfortune at having to sleep in the bedroom directly over the bar and facing the street. If the noise from downstairs didn't disturb her sleep, the passing traffic almost certainly would. As she snuggled back down under the covers, she wondered how her two brothers managed to sleep so soundly in the boxroom next door. Yawning loudly, she settled down in the feather-tick bed, closing her eyes. Within minutes she was asleep.

'Three ha'pence of gin, Guv'nor?'

Bernard Chadwick looked into the wrinkled face of the old woman, and then down at the counter to make sure the money was there. Swiftly scooping up the coppers, he turned to the bar behind him and picking up a coloured glass from the shelf he proceeded to measure out the three-ha'pence-worth of gin from a yellow bottle. Returning to the counter, he set the drink down before moving on to his next customer.

The King's Arms was one of the many public houses that lined the Mile End Road, but Bernard Chadwick liked to think that his establishment was a cut above its fellows. The bar-room was spacious, the floor covered in clean sawdust and sand every Friday morning, the coloured drinking glasses were kept clean and well polished, as was the large looking-glass that ran the length of the bar and reflected the yellow, green and red bottles that lined the shelves beneath. At this time of the evening, just an hour from midnight, all the wooden tables and chairs were taken.

The East End women sat holding their pints of gin as they conversed about the day's events; their children, often left alone while their parents frequented the gin palaces; and the latest fashion. As most of the women present hadn't had a new dress for the past twenty years or more, this conversation piece was somewhat academic, but to these women, born to a life of poverty, the public houses were their equivalent of the gentry's drawing-rooms. And so they sat in regal supremacy, their grimy dresses showing the tattered petticoats beneath, until it was time to return to the hovels they called home.

Their menfolk stood, tankards of ale held between strong, often calloused, hands, holding forth on the topic of the day. This usually fell between two subjects, politics and religion. The arguments would rage back and forth, for the most part in good-natured camaraderie, but it would be a very dull Saturday night if the evening didn't end with a fight outside on the cobbled pavement. If the combatants were women, the entertainment was heightened considerably.

Daisy Chadwick stood at the far end of the bar counter, looking down on the dwindling plates of sandwiches and meat pies, wondering if she should replenish the food supply so vital to their trade. Raising her eyes, she looked down the length of the counter to try to catch her husband's attention, but Bernard was at that moment serving one of their more respectable customers, a costermonger and his wife from nearby Whitechapel market, their smart clothes singling them out from the rest of the crowd. Daisy could see Bernard's face wreathed in smiles, the happy face he saved for his well-to-do clientèle. She doubted if any of their regular customers had ever seen this side of his countenance, for in the past few years he had found it harder not to show the contempt he felt, had always felt, for the poverty-stricken people of the East End.

Daisy could remember clearly the first time she had seen him. She had been with her parents on a week's holiday to Southend, and they had met while walking on the promenade. She could still remember his earnest face as he'd talked about his dream of owning a hotel and public house combined. The exact location of this dream home Bernard had never quite divulged, but Daisy had always been under the impression that it would be in her beloved Essex. Even after all these years, she still thought of Essex as her home. She still missed the green fields and clean streets – streets that didn't run with filth – and clean people, especially clean people. They had married three months after their first meeting. Their short honeymoon had been a weekend in Brighton, and then he had brought her here to her new home. She had been so much in love that she had never queried where they would be living after the wedding; she had trusted him implicitly. The only thing she'd known was that they would be renting a moderately large public house from the brewery while they saved for a better place.

Her first glimpse of her new home had struck fear into her very being. As she'd walked down the pavement lined with shops and stalls of every description, she had stared in disbelief at the overcrowded tenements, the rotting refuse that littered the pavements and over-flowed on to the cobbled road already caked with horse manure, the seemingly never-ending crowd of people, beggars and pedlars that had pushed and sworn at her as she'd walked on in a daze, tightly holding Bernard's arm. The worst sight had been the children dressed in rags as they'd run back and forth, some directly in front of the horse-drawn vehicles, endangering their lives with cheerful impunity, their shouts mixing with the other street noises causing a cacophony of sound that had beaten on her eardrums. It was as the enormity of her situation had threatened to overwhelm her that she had looked up into Bernard's white, strained, face. The sight of the silent plea in his blue eyes had filled her with love and shame. She had taken his arm and walked on, her back straight and her step firm.

That had been fourteen years back, and although housing con-ditions hadn't changed much, at least the homeless waifs that roamed the streets had found a benefactor in Thomas J. Barnardo. Many orphaned children destined for a life of crime and prostitution had found their way to the Barnardo's Home in Stepney Causeway, lured there by the notice that hung over the building door: 'NO DESTITUTE CHILD IS REFUSED ADMISSION.'

The sound of the piano-player returning to his seat brought Daisy back to the present. Moving away from the food counter to attend a customer, she forced a smile to her lips. Bernard's dream of one day owning a posh hotel had never materialized, and it never would. They both knew that, but it was never discussed aloud: it was always 'one day'. That kept her going; that and her children. She was thirty-five years old and it looked as if she would be spending the rest of her life in this god-forsaken place.

'Thank you, sir,' she smiled brightly as she handed the man his tankard of ale, then watched as he joined the crowd around the piano-player who was valiantly trying to make his music heard above the boisterous, bawdy songs that resounded to the rafters.

Looking down the bar again, Daisy regarded her husband as he worked. His slim body was clothed in fawn trousers and matching waistcoat. The white shirt she had ironed that morning was buttoned high to his neck, the starched collar biting into his Adam's apple. Not for him the casual open-necked shirts and rolled-up sleeves adopted by his neighbouring landlords. Oh, no, appearances were very important to Bernard, and he insisted that his wife and children follow his example.

Daisy turned to face the looking-glass. Glancing swiftly over her shoulder to make sure no one was watching her, she returned her gaze to the mirror. Frowning, she leaned forward, her hands going to the back of her head where the braids she had plaited to the nape of her neck were in danger of coming loose. Her fingers worked deftly, and within seconds her black hair was firmly back in place, secured once again with her favourite tortoise-shell combs. Giving the braids one last pat with her hand, she turned to face the tap-room once more. It looked as though the heavy trade was over for the night. Those customers who still had a drink would nurse it for as long as possible before buying another to see them through to the early hours of the morning. Others would leave the bar to return later with the price of a drink and a meat pie. Where the extra money came from Daisy didn't know, and she would rather keep it that way.

'Are you staying all night, Mrs Chadwick? I can manage if you want to get off to bed. Proper tired you look.'

Lily Watkins stood before Daisy, her arms full of dirty glasses she had collected from the nearby tables. She was paid a shilling a night during the week, and one and sixpence at the weekend.

Looking at the seventeen-year-old's grimy but nevertheless pretty face, Daisy wondered if collecting the glasses and helping behind the bar was the only type of work the blond girl occupied herself with, once she herself had left the bar. Not that she was unduly worried. She still loved Bernard, but these last few years, given a choice between a bit of loving and a good cup of tea, she would choose the latter. She derived more pleasure from it, and it lasted longer. Shrugging off the thought, she answered, 'Thank you, Lily. I am tired. I'll just have a word with Mr Chadwick and then I'll be off to bed.'

Lily grinned at her mistress, then hurried over to the barrel that stood beside the large black spittoon and plunged the dirty glasses into the already murky water. It was part of her duties to keep the water in the barrel clean. Biting on her lip, she wondered if it was worth all the trouble of getting the barrel outside into the yard and emptying it, then the agonizing wait for it to fill up from the old brass tap that seemed to reliniquish its precious water, drip by drip. Shaking her head, she decided against such a drastic measure, then crossing her fingers she sent up a silent prayer that her employer wouldn't come down this end of the bar and check up on her. If he did, and found the dirty water she was using to wash the glasses, he would sack her, she had no illusions about that.

He was a fussy sod, but good-looking with it. Dreamily she stared down the room at Bernard, her blue eyes travelling over his clean-shaven face, the dark hair parted in the middle glistening with pomade and the gleaming near-white teeth that were a rare occurrence in a man who must be nearing his fortieth birthday. Most men, or women for that matter, had lost most of their teeth by the time they were thirty and those that remained were often yellow, decaying into black stumps in later years.

Lily's eyes moved to Daisy, her keen glance taking in the details of the dress she wore. A dark maroon colour, the skirt was cut full and heavily pleated into the waist, the three petticoats underneath giving it a hooped effect, which was as near to the current fashion as a working woman could get. The face above the white lace collar was plain, the features too large to be called attractive until she smiled, and then they would soften, giving the impression of a handsome woman.

Lily's own dress was dirty and torn. Once a pale blue, it was now an indescribable colour, the cloth stained with years of neglect that no amount of washing would remove. For a moment she felt envy and a touch of hatred for her mistress. As a child, she had watched her mother work her life away, crouched over what had seemed to Lily a mountain of material. Her earliest recollection of her mother was of a woman with eyes red-rimmed from lack of sleep, fingers often bleeding from the continual plying of her needle. Of her father she knew nothing, that erstwhile gentleman having absconded one night, taking with him his wife's hard-earned money. Lily felt her eyes begin to smart as she recalled her mum sitting her on her lap and singing to her a song written by someone called Thomas Hood. It was called 'The Song of the Shirt', and Lily remembered it vividly.

> With fingers weary and worn,
> With eyelids heavy and red,

8

A woman sat, in unwomanly rage,
Plying her needle and thread –
Stitch! stitch! stitch!
In poverty, hunger and dirt,
And still with a voice of dolorous pitch,
She sang the 'Song of the shirt'.
Work – work – work,
My labour never flags,
And what are its wages? A bed of straw,
A crust of bread – and rags –
That shattered roof – and this naked floor –
A table – a broken chair –
And a wall so blank, my shadow I thank
For sometimes falling there.

Humming the song softly under her breath, Lily rinsed the glasses
vigorously before putting them upside down to drain under the bar
counter. A man pushed by her, squeezing her backside as he passed.
Lily glared after him, hatred in her eyes. After her mum had died six
years ago, two men from the workhouse had come to the one-roomed
flat she and her mum had called home. She remembered them both.
One had given her a lecture about how fortunate she was to be given a
place in the already overcrowded workhouse. He had made it sound
as if an honour was being bestowed upon her, while the small man had
just stared, a lecherous look in his eyes. Children grew up quickly in
the East End. They had to; it was a matter of survival. When the men
had left, the neighbours had closed ranks around her, taking it in turns
to feed and shelter her. For nearly three years Lily had dodged from
one stinking, overcrowded, home to the next, always one step ahead of
the men from the workhouse.

When she reached the age of fourteen, she had come to the King's
Arms looking for a job. It had been New Year's Day 1885 when she
had walked into the chaos of upturned tables and broken chairs in the
tap-room. Smashed glasses covered the floor, while a dark-haired
woman had valiantly tried to bring some kind of order to the place.
Tentatively, Lily had stepped forward to offer her services, and when
the woman had asked her age, she had quickly added an extra two
years. After what had seemed an interminable wait, the woman had
nodded her head, whereupon Lily had immediately rolled up her
sleeves and waded into the mess. That had been over two years ago,
and she had been here ever since.

'I'll be going up to bed now, Lily. I'll see you in the morning.'

Lily jumped. She hadn't heard Daisy come up behind her. 'All right, Mrs Chadwick. Good night.'

Daisy smiled tiredly, then turned away, her feet taking her through the heavy door that led to the upstairs bedrooms. Picking up the lantern from the hall table, she began climbing the stairs slowly, watching her shadow dance in front of her from the light of the flickering candle. When she reached the top of the stairs, she came to a halt outside Ruby's room. Pushing the door open, she looked in on the silent figure. Satisfied that she was asleep, she went to the room next door. The two boys were huddled together in a heap, their arms and legs flung wide, the blankets barely covering their small bodies. The patchwork quilt she'd made herself lay in a heap on the floor. Shaking her head, she backed out of the room. It would be a senseless exercise to cover them up, as the offending blankets would be thrown off as soon as she'd left the room. Walking softly, she opened the door to her own bedroom, wondering why she was trying to be quiet. The noise from downstairs drowned out any movement she might make. Luckily, the children were used to the noise, not knowing any different way of life.

Closing her bedroom door, she leaned against it for a moment, her body slumped with fatigue, then, making a supreme effort, she moved towards the bed. This room was the largest in the entire building, which was just as well, as most of it was taken up by the enormous four-poster bed that Bernard had acquired some years before at a public auction, the previous owners having fallen on hard times. Placing the lantern on the bedside table, she began to undress. Her tired fingers undid the buttons on her blouse while her weary mind went over the day's events. She had been awake since six-thirty, and between doing the washing and ironing, she had made the children their breakfast before settling them down with their school work for the morning in the small study next to the kitchen that they used as a classroom.

She herself had been taught in much the same way by her mother in the small but comfortable cottage in Essex. Her parents had never been well off in a financial sense, but they had been determined to instil knowledge into their only daughter. To this end they had spent every spare penny they had on books in the hope that if she were properly educated, she would have a better chance in life. The young Daisy had absorbed any new knowledge like a sponge, her keen mind soaking up the printed words in the books her father was forever bringing home. By the time she was twelve, she had no longer needed any help with her learning, but rather than make her mother feel inadequate, had continued to ask for help with her lessons. Thinking back to those days brought a tired smile to her lips. All that education her parents had crammed into her for the sole purpose of ensuring that she have a good start in life – which to them meant her having the chance to marry well – and where had she ended up? Slaving away from morning to night in a pub in the East End of London. Sighing heavily, she removed her blouse, laying it carefully over the end of the bed. That her parents had been disappointed at their daughter's choice of a husband would be an understatement, but once they'd assured themselves that Daisy was happy, they had let her go without further protests.

Despite her circumstances, Daisy had never regretted her choice, and the years of self-education had enabled her to teach her own children. She had taught them to read with the aid of the enormous Bible she'd had since a small child. She had brought all her books with her when she'd left home, and such works as Dickens, Thackeray and Sir Walter Scott played an important part in the children's education.

Ruby in particular loved reading, especially *Vanity Fair*, a book she had herself enjoyed as a child, but would try all sorts of tricks to get out of her arithmetic lessons. Daisy had a strong suspicion that her recent improvement in fractions and long division was mainly due to the help she received from her brothers, who excelled in the maths lessons she set out for them each day.

Once the children were settled with their morning's work, she would begin to make the piles of sandwiches and pies that the customers expected to greet them when they entered the bar. It was customary in most public houses to feed the working man on his way to work and provide supper for him on his journey home. Stifling a yawn, she pulled her nightdress over her head. She wished they could afford to hire more staff to help out in the pub, so that she would be able to spend more time in the home and with the children. She was so tired, her feet ached from standing in the bar all evening, and her head throbbed from the noise and smoke of the tap-room. As she reached out to dim the lantern, she wondered how other publicans' wives had coped before the law stating that pubs be closed daily from the hours of one until four in the afternoon had come into effect nearly twenty years earlier. God knows it was hard enough now. Those few hours were the only times she could spend with the children; the rest of the day they were on their own.

Go to sleep, she chided herself. Stop worrying about things you're powerless to alter. Go to sleep; you need as much rest as you can get. Obeying her inner voice, she laid her head back on her pillows and slept.

Chapter Two

Ruby shut her eyes tight against the harsh morning sunshine that streamed through her thin curtains, and burrowing under the covers, attempted to get back to sleep. A sudden loud clatter brought her eyes wide open. Resisting the temptation to stay where she was, she swung her legs over the side of the bed, shivering as her feet touched the icy floor. Pulling the blanket round her shoulders, she made her way down the thinly carpeted stairs into the kitchen and hurried over to sit by the roaring fire, thankful that neither of her two brothers had beaten her to the comfortable armchair as they normally did.

'Morning, Mum,' she called into the scullery, where she could see the back of her mother busying herself over the huge black cauldron full of porridge for the family's breakfast.

Stifling a yawn with the back of her hand, she wriggled uncomfortably as the morning pressure on her bladder increased. Not yet able to face the trip to the outside lavatory on such a cold October morning, she tucked her legs under her bottom so that her mother wouldn't see her fidgeting.

Daisy watched Ruby from the doorway of the scullery, noticing straight away the absence of the curling-rags she had painstakingly wound round her daughter's hair the night before. Giving vent to a long sigh, she came into the kitchen, wrapping Bernard's old overcoat around her, her long black hair, still braided, hanging in a plait down the middle of her back.

As she set the table for breakfast, she cast a quick look at Ruby and felt the wonder she always felt when looking at this child of hers. How, she asked herself, did I give birth to such a beautiful child? Her eyes took in Ruby's long wavy chestnut hair and the large blue eyes always filled with laughter. She was the joy of her life. That the girl was a beauty there was no denying, but Ruby's outward appearance belied her character. There was nothing girlish about her. Ruby scorned the frilly dresses Daisy loved to see her in, preferring to wear a pair of her brother's trousers whenever she could. Her hair tucked up under an old cap, she would run with the boys in the street, her brothers trailing after her in case she got into trouble. Ruby ruled her two brothers with a velvet glove, inciting them to mischief when they would have preferred to sit quietly and study their books.

A sudden clatter on the stairs heralded the boys' arrival. Bursting into the kitchen, their faces fell when they saw Ruby firmly ensconced in the treasured chair by the fire. George, the younger at nine years of age, gave his sister a watery smile and was rewarded by a large pink tongue poking out at him. Being of a placid nature, he decided to let the insult pass, but twelve-year-old Bertie was made of sterner stuff.

'Mother, she poked her tongue out at us,' he cried in a plaintive tone.

Daisy sighed. It was the same every morning. Turning to the two boys standing before her clad only in their nightshirts, she answered tersely, 'Can't you ever be in the same room without arguing?' And before either had time to answer, she marched them from the room, issuing orders as she propelled them forward. 'Upstairs, and get washed and dressed. You'll catch your death of cold, and before you say it' – here she held up her hand – 'your sister will be joining you in a minute. Go on, away with you!'

George's face fell, his plump baby features taking on a mulish look, then, shaking his mop of black curls, he turned and headed for the stairs. Bertie hesitated for a minute longer, and Daisy, seeing his dark eyes drawn together with anger, the lean features of his face working as if trying to say something in retaliation, could see what Bernard must have looked like at the same age. His face suddenly relaxed, and Daisy could actually feel the tension leaving his body. This was yet another way in which he took after his father. Quick to anger, that same anger just as quickly forgotten. Turning to Ruby, he gave her a wide grin and bent over in an exaggerated bow, then turned and left the room.

Daisy then walked over to the large wooden table and started laying the breakfast dishes. 'You'd better get out of that chair now, Ruby. Your father will be down soon.'

At the mention of her father, Ruby slowly uncurled herself from the warm chair. She wasn't afraid of her dad, but on the other hand there was no need to go looking for trouble. As she stood up, the urgent need to visit the lavatory overcame her, and now heedless of the cold, she pulled the blanket tighter round her shoulders and ran outside into the yard, telling herself that tomorrow she would use the chamber-pot under her bed before coming downstairs. Her brothers always used theirs, but she could never get used to it.

Back in the kitchen, Daisy's eyes wandered around the room lingering on the much-fought-over chair. 'Just for a minute,' she told herself as she eased herself into the warm comfort of the old armchair.

She glanced fondly around her private domain, her glance taking in the large round table and the four wooden chairs, all solidly made, that housed them all for their meals. Bernard had demanded good furniture, and this table and chairs would surely last their lifetime. On the opposite side of the room, a large window let in the morning light, and from her chair she could see the stables where the two horses, Lady and Nobby, were kept, together with the smart carriage that Bernard had said was a must for business folk. Leading off from the large kitchen, which also served as a dining-room, lay the scullery where all the cooking, washing and ironing were done. The smaller room next to it was used as a study for the children's lessons and also as a store-room for the many books, papers and writing implements needed in their small private classroom. She bent down to pick up the heavy flat-iron she'd left there after pressing the children's clothes and Bernard's shirt the night before. Reaching up, she set it on top of the stone-built mantelpiece that surrounded the fire, the actual fire being contained in the middle with iron bars to stop the coal from falling on the hearthrug. The sound of the kettle whistling made her jump. As she picked it up from the hearth, she heard heavy footsteps coming down the stairs.

Bernard entered the now warm and cosy kitchen, his eyes searching for and finding his wife. Having made sure of her presence, he walked to the armchair, and as he sat down in the newly vacated seat, he wasn't surprised to find it warm, and not from the heat of the fire alone. He watched Daisy disappear into the scullery, her clothes clutched under her arm, and smiled fondly.

When Daisy came back, she had divested herself of the overcoat and was now dressed in what she called her day clothes. This outfit comprised a navy skirt and matching blouse, together with a rusty brown shawl fringed with black, which she wore over her shoulders, as was the custom. Her hair was now done neatly and tucked into a white cotton cap.

'Good morning, Bernard,' she welcomed her husband, a smile taking the plainness from her face. 'I've got some nice bacon from old Mrs Jessop. Would you like some with an egg for your breakfast?'

'That would be very nice, dear,' he answered, as she busied herself getting the heavy black frying-pan down from the shelf in the scullery, all the while her eyes darting back and forth to Bernard's face.

She noticed that his hair was still wet from his morning wash. It was his custom to wash from the pewter jug and bowl that stood on the dresser in their bedroom before descending the stairs in the morning. In all their married life, Daisy had only ever seen him in his nightshirt when he went to bed in the evening. He never wore it outside the bedroom. She, on the other hand, always laid her clothes out in the kitchen at night. In the morning, while she was preparing the breakfast, she would place the garments in front of the fire to warm, and as soon as she heard Bernard's footsteps on the stairs she would dash into the scullery to put them on. Her morning wash also took place in front of the fire in warm water; she liked her comfort. As she made her way across the room, she was nearly bowled over by her daughter rushing to get back into the warmth.

'Ruby, how many times must I tell you: walk, don't run.'

'Sorry, Mum! It's freezing out there. Why can't we have a lavatory in the house like the nobs do?'

'Ruby!' The stern voice caused her to jump. She hadn't seen her father sitting there. 'We do not talk about such matters in public, girl. And why are you still in your nightclothes?' Leaning forward in the chair, he pointed to the stairs. 'Go to your room and get dressed immediately.' He took his gold watch from his pocket and looked at it intently. 'If you are not back in this room, washed, dressed and ready in ten minutes, you will forfeit your outing to the park today. Do you understand me, girl?'

Clutching the blanket tighter round her neck, Ruby nodded and made for the stairs. 'Sorry, Dad,' she began, her words suddenly cut off by the sound of her father bringing his fist down on the arm of his chair.

Rising to his feet, he strode over to where his daughter stood, her face showing signs of apprehension, but not fear. No, never fear. For a moment Bernard was caught by the admiration he had for his daughter. If it had been one of the boys standing before him, it would have been a different story. Ignoring these thoughts, he shot his hand out and grabbed her arm. 'Dad? What common talk is that? I am your father, and you will address me as Father at all times.' For the second time he said, 'Do you understand me, girl?'

'Yes, Father.'

Removing his hand from her arm, he gave her a push towards the stairs. As she ran lightly up to her room, Bernard returned to the chair by the fire.

'There was no need for that,' Daisy said as she placed his mug of strong tea by his side. Yet, as she had said the words, she knew why he behaved as he did.

It was his own sense of failure that made him the way he was. The way he dressed and spoke, always trying to ape his betters, his insistence that the children be taught at home because he didn't want them mixing with those from the poorer areas. He had never asked if Daisy minded taking on the task of teaching them; he had just assumed she would. Then there was the four-poster bed he had spent a small fortune on. It had cost more to hire the men to get it safely installed than it had to buy. She recalled the day it had been delivered, the looks of envy on the neighbours' faces as they had watched the huge monstrosity being carried into the pub, and Bernard had watched and exulted in their envy. Then of course there were the two horses and the smart carriage, another expense they could have done without. She herself had been out riding in it only three times, preferring to walk. His rule that the children must not on any account mix with the children from the nearby tenements she heartily agreed with. The parents they had to deal with were poor, shabbily dressed creatures who would have been better off spending their money on food and clothes for their families instead of pouring it down their throats. At this thought, Daisy felt a sharp pang of guilt.

She was no better than Bernard, for deep down she too felt distaste for her neighbours and customers. But if it wasn't for the likes of the people they looked down on, what would become of them? If the brewery decided to revoke their licence, where would they go? Her parents had died ten years earlier in a fire that had destroyed the beautiful cottage she had grown up in and Bernard had been estranged from his father for many years. The bitter quarrel that had parted them long ago had driven a wedge between them that was never to be mended. She had only met Bernard's father once – at their wedding – and she had a memory of a tall rather forbidding man, stern in his manner, a family trait Bernard had inherited. His mother she had never met, the unfortunate woman having died giving birth to Bernard's younger brother David, now the apple of his father's eye.

Shaking her head, she turned her attention to the frying-pan, laying two strips of bacon and one egg to the sizzling fat. She had just censured Bernard for his treatment of Ruby, but she was no better herself. If only Bernard had bought the pub outright instead of renting from the brewery, they could sell up and move to a better area, or if they had managed to save some money instead of throwing it away to keep up their pretentious style of living, they might have been able to escape from the squalor that surrounded them. Not for her own sake, but for that of the children. She didn't want them growing up in this place, not that they minded. Why, only last week, George had brought a boy of his own age home with him, a filthy half-naked urchin from the gutter. Daisy had recoiled in horror at seeing the child sitting in her clean kitchen. Luckily he had sat on one of the wooden chairs, easily washed with carbolic after he had departed. If it had been the armchair, she would have insisted on it being burnt, for the boy had been crawling with lice. If it had been Ruby who had invited the boy home she would have thought it was out of devilment, but George was different. Any action on his part had stemmed from kindness. They were also picking up the local idiom, although they were careful not to use any Cockney slang while their father was present. Just for a moment, Daisy wondered if Ruby had deliberately called her father 'Dad' just to antagonize him. But, no, not even Ruby was that brave.

'There was every need for "that", as you term it. Do you want your children growing up like the poor unfortunates that cram the tenements around us?' Bernard was out of the chair again. Walking round the room, his hands clasped behind his back, he continued talking. 'Do you blame me for trying to keep us apart from the riff-raff that surround us?' He stopped pacing for a moment, his face red from either the heat of the fire or shame, Daisy didn't know, but she knew better than to interrupt him. 'The people I look down on are our bread and butter, yet even that knowledge doesn't stop me from despising them. I know it's wrong of me, but I can't help the way I feel, and even . . .'

His words were cut off by the sound of footsteps clattering down the stairs as Ruby, George and Bertie all reached the bottom seemingly at the same time. Remembering the bacon and egg she had left in the pan, Daisy ran into the scullery, swiftly lifting it from the cooking range. Putting the food on a plate, she returned to the kitchen and placed it on the table before Bernard, who was now seated and waiting for his breakfast. Minutes later, the children were slowly spooning their thick porridge, their gaze directed at their father's plate.

As Bernard forked a piece of bacon into his mouth, he became aware of their envious looks. At his sharp bang on the table with his knife, they all jumped and began to gulp down their porridge, their gaze downcast. When they had finished, they waited patiently for permission to leave the table. After what seemed an age, Bernard laid down his knife and fork and rose, inclining his head towards them, indicating that they might get down. Taking a penny from his pocket, he held it out to Bertie.

'Run down to the corner and get me a copy of *The Times*, and don't take all day about it.'

Bertie held out his hand for the money, his fingers curling round the smooth shiny coin. 'I won't, Father. I'll run there and back.'

Pulling down his cloth cap over the dark curly hair, he put the penny into the pocket of his grey flannel trousers, the feel of them around his ankles instead of his knees making him feel like a man, as befitted his twelve years. Turning sharply, he opened the kitchen door that led out on to the street and made his way down to the corner where the newspaper boy could be found.

Ruby and George watched him go, then sat down again to wait for his return. As soon as he got back, the children would make their way to Victoria Park, as they did every Sunday, weather permitting. In the scullery, Daisy was busy making cheese and pickle sandwiches for their lunch. When she had finished, she put them, together with three apples and a large slice of cake, into a big wicker hamper. Glancing out of the window, she was relieved to see that the sun was shining, and although the day was chilly, it seemed pleasant enough for the park. She was always glad when Sunday came round. That was the one day she had to herself, as the children would spend the morning and most of the afternoon at the park. Bernard and Lily, together with Jack the cellar-man and barman, would take over the running of the pub while she got on with household tasks. Giving the hamper a final inspection, she picked it up and came back into the kitchen just as Bertie was entering the room, the newspaper tucked under his arm.

'Here you are, Father,' he said, slightly out of breath, as he handed the paper to Bernard. When the paper was pulled from his grasp he turned to where Daisy was standing. 'May we go now, Mother?'

'Let's have a look at you first,' Daisy replied, as they lined up for her inspection. First George, his face scrubbed and shining, beamed up at her. Bending down, she straightened his new blue jersey jumper and pulled up his grey knee-length trousers. Then she passed to Ruby, whose hair spilled around her shoulders and over the top of her white frilly blouse, over which she wore a plaid pinafore. Daisy looked at the long white stockings, and sighed; they wouldn't remain that colour for long. It was a pity that women and girls didn't wear trousers – well, not women of breeding. 'Off you go, and mind you get back by three o'clock. It's roast beef for dinner today,' Daisy laughed as their faces lit up in anticipation, and then gently shooed them out of the house.

Closing the door behind them, she looked at the clock on the mantelpiece which showed eight-thirty. Jack and Lily were already in the bar waiting for the first customers of the day, she could hear their voices laughing as they shared a joke. Anxious to get on with the new dress she was making for Ruby, she began to clear the table.

'Oh, come on, George! Just for a minute.'

'No, Ruby, you know Father doesn't allow us to visit the horses unless he's with us.'

Putting her hands on her hips in a gesture George knew only too well, Ruby faced him, her head set on one side as she waited for him to capitulate.

George's heart sank. He wished he had the strength to say no to his sister, but he knew he would give in as he always did. He reluctantly nodded. 'All right, but just for a minute. I want to get to the park.'

Ruby's face split into a wide grin. Reaching out, she grabbed his hand and ran with him to the stables. Bertie had already walked on, not wishing to be included in his sister's madcap schemes. Entering the stables, they walked over to where the two horses were tethered.

'Hello, Lady.' Ruby put her hand up to the horse's neck, stroking it affectionately. Then, putting her hand into her pocket, she pulled out a slice of bread and jam she had made in the scullery while her mother's back had been turned. 'There's a good girl.' Lady sniffed at the outstretched hand, then quickly gulped at the offered delicacy.

George, standing by the door, stiffened as he heard the sound of footsteps approaching. 'Ruby, quick,' he whispered urgently, his eyes wide with fright. 'Someone's coming!'

Ruby turned quickly, and it was as she made to move from the confines of the stallbox that she tripped. As she fell she reached out and grabbed Lady's tail, causing the startled horse to rear and lash out with her back legs. Stifling a scream, Ruby fell to the straw-covered floor as an agonizing pain shot through her left leg.

Seeing his sister fall, George covered the distance between them in three long strides. Pulling Ruby away from the horse's flaying hooves, they both fell into a corner, gasping for breath. The footsteps paused outside the stable and he watched the door slowly open, his mouth agape, his heart fluttering. As the familiar figure of his brother strode towards them, George felt his body go limp with relief. For one awful moment he had thought it was his father. Seeing the look on Bertie's face, George raised his hand to him.

'Don't start, Bertie! Ruby's hurt, Lady kicked her in the leg.'

Bertie's head snapped back, the words of censure dying on his lips. His eyes grave with concern, he dropped to his knees beside his sister, his arms going round her shoulders to pull her clear from the stalls. 'Are you all right, Ruby? Where does it hurt?'

Her head cradled against her brother's chest, Ruby fought down a wave of nausea. Her leg did hurt. Oh, it hurt really bad! The sound of her crying brought the two boys' eyes upon her. They had never seen her cry before. They had seen her in a temper tantrum where she had shed tears of rage and frustration, but never tears brought about by grief or pain.

Thoroughly alarmed now, George rose to his feet. 'I'd better go and get Father.'

'No, don't. I'll be all right in a minute." Ruby grabbed at his sleeve. 'We'll all get into trouble if Dad finds out.' Putting out her hands, she attempted to pull herself up from the floor, and immediately the two boys were beside her, helping her to her feet. 'It doesn't hurt so much now,' she lied bravely, as she wrapped an arm around each of their necks. Over the top of her head, the boys looked at each other, neither knowing what to do. 'Hurry up! Dad will be coming in soon to feed the horses.' Her voice was muffled, her head hung low to prevent the boys from seeing the tears that were coursing down her cheeks.

Following her lead, George bent down and picked up the hamper, then, tightening his grip on his sister, he helped Bertie to half carry her from the stables. Once outside, they looked quickly to either side of them, then, seeing the coast was clear, they made their way to the park with Ruby limping as she clung on to their arms.

Chapter Three

Victoria Park, or 'Vicky Park' as the East Enders called it, was one of the few places where the public could listen to music on a Sunday. Men in high hats played their instruments at the bandstand, affording great pleasure to their appreciative audience. Mothers rested beneath the trees, their babies laid out on blankets placed under the large leafy branches that protected the new-born infants from any strong sunlight. Boys ran wild playing their favourite games of football and rounders, while the young girls happily bowled their hoops, their high childish laughter ringing out loud and clear. The men drew on their pipes and chatted with their friends and wives, determined to enjoy this one day of freedom, the only day of the week they could call their own.

As they passed through the open wrought-iron gates, Ruby breathed a silent sob of relief. Soon she would be able to sit down on the inviting green grass that stretched as far as the eye could see. She had thought they would never get there. The weekly journey that normally took half an hour, their young legs running and jumping, eating up the miles, had taken over an hour as the boys had half dragged and carried her. George's face was red with exertion, and tiny drops of sweat ran down his cheeks. For a moment Ruby forgot the pain in her leg as a pang of guilt ran through her. Poor George! Throughout the nightmare journey he had uttered no word of complaint, no censure about her latest escapade that had landed them, once again, in trouble. They were on the grass now, walking past the shimmering water of the large circular lake where the smaller children sailed their home-made wooden boats under the watchful eyes of their mothers.

'Can't we stop now, Bertie?' Ruby pleaded, trying desperately to keep the quiver from her voice.

'Yes, please, Bertie? I'm so tired.' George added his voice to Ruby's.

Bertie looked at Ruby's white pinched face and felt again a tremor of fear. They should have gone back home, no matter what punishment would be meted out. It would have been better than this awful predicament they had landed themselves in. His arms ached from holding Ruby steady, and poor George was breathing so hard he looked as if his chest would burst.

'Just a bit further,' he answered, his voice faltering as he tried to catch his breath. Ignoring their protests, he urged them on towards the centre of the park where the drinking fountain stood. He wanted to make sure Ruby didn't have to walk too far to get a drink. 'All right, we can stop now,' he said, as he eased Ruby's arm from round his aching neck, and as if of one body, they sank slowly on to the clean-smelling grass.

The three figures stretched themselves out, their arms flung wide, their eyes closed, as they waited for their breathing to return to normality. Bertie was the first to recover. Pulling himself up into a sitting position, he looked down at his brother and sister and suddenly grinned.

He playfully punched George on the arm, chiding him, 'Come on, weakling, get up. Don't tell me a little stroll like that has tired you out.'

Goerge looked up at his brother and, taking his cue, gave a watery grin. Lifting himself on one elbow he said, 'How about something to eat? I'm starving!' Turning to his sister, who was still lying on the grass, he nudged her gently in her side. 'You all right, Ruby? How's your leg? Is it still hurting?'

Ruby swallowed hard, fighting down the sick feeling in her throat. Her leg was still throbbing something awful, but the shivery faint feeling had gone. With a supreme effort she raised herself and gave what passed for a smile. 'It's not so bad now. Pass me one of the sandwiches, please.'

Upon hearing their sister speak in her normal tone, both boys gave an audible sigh of relief. Neither of them had relished the same hazardous journey home.

Soon the three of them were tucking in, and it was as Ruby bit into the last sandwich that she looked up and stared at her brothers as if seeing them for the first time. A feeling unfamiliar to her flooded through her body. Then in a voice totally different to her usual strident tone, she said quietly, 'Thanks.'

Both George and Bertie bowed their heads in embarrassment, not knowing how to answer her. Then the tension was broken by a large rubber ball bouncing into their midst, followed quickly by its owner.

'Sorry, mate!' A boy about Bertie's age, shabbily dressed but clean, stood before them.

Bertie jumped to his feet, the ball under his arm. Grateful for the diversion, he handed it back, saying cheerfully, 'That's all right,' then, looking over to where a small group of boys stood waiting, he asked hopefully, 'Can we play?'

The owner of the ball looked at Bertie doubtfully. He didn't speak like a Cockney, but he wasn't a toff. They didn't come to the park on a Sunday. It was an unspoken rule that this day was reserved solely for the working classes. No, he wasn't a toff, but he did talk nice, sort of posh. Looking into Bertie's eager face, he made up his mind. 'Come on, then, and your mate if he wants to,' he added, looking at George. Taking his ball, he ran off, calling over his shoulder, 'Well, come on then.'

Bertie looked at George, a wide grin on his face, then, giving a whoop of delight, he bounded after his new-found friend with George close behind. They had covered only a short distance before coming to an abrupt halt. Looking back to where Ruby was still sitting, they both felt a twinge of guilt. For the first time that day they had forgotten all about her, and with dragging feet they started walking back.

Ruby saw them coming, and immediately called out, 'Go on! I'm all right, really. I feel like a nap anyway.'

The lie stuck in her throat, causing her voice to break, but, taking a deep breath, she forced a smile to her lips. She watched as her brothers were torn between a sense of loyalty binding them to stay with her and the burning desire to leave and take the unexpected chance to play football. Moving her hands in a dismissive gesture, she watched with envy as they ran off. If she hadn't hurt her leg, she would have gone with them, and woe betide any mere boy who objected to a girl intruding on their male territory!

Getting slowly to her feet, she was relieved to find she could put her foot to the ground, and gingerly limped over to the drinking fountain, blessing Bertie for his foresight in making them walk that extra few feet. Ignoring the metal cup that hung by a linked chain to the side of the fountain, she cupped her hands under the gushing stream of water and then ran her wet hands over her face. It wasn't a very warm day, but she still felt clammy. She limped back to the hamper and sat down beside it, plucked a blade of grass and began chewing on it, her mind working furiously. Her leg was definitely not hurting as much as it had been, but she'd probably have an enormous bruise in a couple of days and she wondered how to explain it to her parents. She would just have to make sure she wore her stockings all the time until the bruise faded. She could hear the boys shouting above the music from the bandstand, and wondered why it sounded so far away. Slowly her eyelids drooped, and to the sounds of chirping sparrows perched in the tree above her, she fell asleep.

Daisy looked out of the kitchen window for the fourth time in as many minutes. Where were they? It was well past their usual time of coming home from the park. Bernard had refused to wait for his dinner and had insisted she eat with him. The children's plates, filled with beef and roast potatoes, were in the oven keeping warm, the boiled cabbage stewed in a saucepan on the range. At first, when they hadn't put in an appearance, she had been angry, but that anger had long since faded and in its place was fear. Just as she was about to let go of the net curtain and fetch Bernard from the pub, she saw the three of them coming down the road. With a sigh of relief she dropped the curtain and hurried to the door.

'Come in, come in! Where on earth have you been? I've been so worried, I was just about to get your father.' Bustling round, she ushered them all into the kitchen, the angry words forgotten in the relief of seeing them back safe and sound. Soon their dinner was before them on the table, with Daisy sitting in the armchair watching them eat.

When they had finished and had asked one by one for permission to leave the table, she laid down her sewing and, turning to Bertie, said, 'Well now, are any of you going to tell me why you're so late, or do I have to call your father?'

Before either of the boys could speak, Ruby said quietly, 'It was my fault, Mum.'

'Well, wonders will never cease! Your fault, you say, and what was it this time, madam?' The words were delivered in a bantering fashion as Bertie and George waited with bated breath for Ruby's answer.

'I was skipping along a wall on the way home and slipped and hurt my leg,' Ruby said quickly. 'It really hurt, and . . . and I couldn't stand up for ages. Bertie and George had to carry me most of the way home. That's why we're so late. It's not their fault, Mum. Bertie told me not to climb the wall, but . . . but I didn't take any notice. I'm sorry if you were worried.'

As she uttered the words, she felt a deep sense of shame. She might be many things, but she wasn't a liar. If it had just been herself who would get into trouble she would have owned up to her misdeed that morning, but it was too late for the truth. If she came clean now, Bertie and George would also suffer, and she couldn't let that happen, not after the way they'd been so good to her all day. They had argued all the way home as to the best solution to adopt. The boys had been all for telling the truth and taking their punishment. She had seen the determined look on Bertie's face as he'd faced their mother, and had spoken quickly before he could get the damning words out.

'Let me see. Here, over here by the fire so I can see better.' Pushing Ruby gently before her, Daisy went back to the armchair and pressed her into the seat. Ruby slowly rolled down her dirty stocking, unable to look for fear of what she might see. 'Well, it's a bit red and slightly swollen, but nothing a cold flannel won't cure,' Daisy said brightly. 'You go on up to your room and I'll bring some cold water and bathe it for you after I've cleared away the dinner plates.' She stood back and looked at the guilty faces of the three of them, and laughed. 'Well, that's two shocks you've given me today, and if your father was here, you wouldn't be getting off so lightly! But seeing as he isn't, we'll say no more about it. Now, go to your rooms and study the work I've left out for you on your beds for tomorrow. And, Ruby, you pay extra attention to your spelling.'

Glad of the excuse to leave the room, the children filed past Daisy, kissing her on the cheek one by one. Daisy watched them climb the stairs, her mouth open in surprise. They usually set up a howl of protest when told to study on a Sunday evening, believing that they, like the children of well-to-do parents, should be exempt from any form of work on a Sunday.

As Ruby climbed the stairs, Daisy noticed that she was limping, and made a mental note to check on her leg in the morning. Turning back to the table and dirty plates, she gave a long sigh. It seemed as if she spent most of her life washing up after her family. Then, telling herself not to be so lazy, she rolled up her sleeves and set to work.

Chapter Four

'**M**orning, Lily.'

'Morning, Alf. Any letters for the pub?' Lily pulled her shawl tighter round her shoulders while stamping her feet against the cold November morning.

'Just the one, for the Guv'nor,' Alf answered, holding out the long white envelope. 'I'll see you, Lily. Keep smiling.'

Lily watched the postman skirt round the old tenement from which she had just come, his round taking him on to the row of open-fronted shops to deliver the rest of his mail. Turning the envelope over, she saw the fine italic writing and felt a sense of pride at being able to read her employer's name and address. It would be more truthful to say she recognized the collection of letters that made up the wording on the envelope, for Lily had never had the chance to go to school. But on one occasion when she had been sent to fetch Mrs Chadwick from the study where she was teaching the children their lessons, Daisy had asked her if she could read or write. Hanging her head, Lily had admitted that she could do neither, whereupon Daisy had offered to teach her in her spare time. It was then she had shown Lily a similar envelope and told her what the words were. Lily's dreams of being educated were cut short, however. When Mr Chadwick had found out, he had immediately forbidden his wife to have any personal arrangement with Lily, adding that it would be a waste of time with someone of her class. Pushing open the heavy doors, Lily entered the tap-room.

'Good morning, Lily.'

'Good morning, Mr Chadwick. There's a letter for you,' Lily answered, holding out the envelope. Bernard waited until it was laid down on the counter before picking it up carefully. Lily noted the movement and turned away before he could see her look of scorn. He could just have easily taken it from her hand, but no, the point must be seen to be made: he was the employer, she was merely the hired help.

'Miserable old bugger,' she muttered furiously as she settled herself behind the bar.

Looking up, she saw Jack standing behind Bernard, his head held to one side, his tongue protruding while holding his hand high in the air, imitating a man being hanged. Lily quickly ducked her head, afraid she would burst into laughter and give Jack away, and then the sudden clatter of footsteps overhead told her that the children were already up and about.

'I have to go out for a while, Jack. If Mrs Chadwick should enquire as to my whereabouts, tell her I had to step out and will be back presently,' Bernard said, forcing Lily to step back as he swept by her, shrugging himself into his thick warm overcoat, a satisfied look on his normally dour face.

'He must have got some good news in that letter you gave him, Lily. Maybe you've brought him good luck,' Jack said, smiling.

'The only luck I'd give 'im is bad,' Lily turned to face him. 'The way 'e's treated those children this last few weeks is awful, poor little mites. Shut in their rooms, only letting them come out for their meals and to use the lav, it's terrible. 'E's only 'appy when 'e's throwing 'is weight abaht. I'd leave today if it wasn't for Mrs Chadwick, poor cow. If I left, it'd be another worry for 'er, 'cos 'e wouldn't lower 'imself to 'ire a new girl; finks the likes of me are beneath 'im.' Stopping for breath, she thought about what she'd just said, then grinned. ''E should be so lucky, eh, Jack?'

The conversation was halted by the arrival of three young students from the nearby London Hospital. As Jack hurried forward to serve them, Lily began to lay out the food Daisy had brought into the pub earlier that morning. While she busied herself, her thoughts returned to the children. Just over three weeks ago the accident had happened, and she had heard all about it from Mrs Chadwick as they had been preparing the food for the evening trade. It was as Lily had been taking a batch of meat pies from the oven that Daisy had started to talk, desperate for someone to confide in. She had told Lily about the story Ruby had concocted in order to save her brothers from punishment and how she had contrived to keep out of her father's way the following morning. However, Bernard had noticed her limping and had demanded to know what had happened. Ruby had tried to stick to her story, but under Bernard's insistent questioning she had broken down and admitted the truth. Bernard had been all for using the belt on all three of the children, and it was only Daisy's frantic pleading that had saved them from a beating. Lily's train of thought was cut short as one of the students detached himself from his friends and made his way down to where she stood.

'Hello, Lily. Could I have one of your meat pies, please?' the young man said shyly.

Lily snapped out of her daydream to serve the young man. Aware of his admiring glance, a smile came to her lips, and for a while the children were forgotten.

'May I have some more bread please, Mother?'

Daisy looked at Ruby's white, pinched, face, her normally lively personality dampened by Bernard's presence, and felt anger bubble to the surface. Casting a reassuring smile at Ruby as she handed over the plate of bread and butter, Daisy shot a look of pure venom in Bernard's direction, but the gesture was wasted. Ever since he had returned from his mysterious walk that morning, he had been going around with a self-satisfied look on his face. When she had enquired the reason for the sudden miraculous transformation, he had merely shrugged and told her to bide her time, he would tell her when he was ready. Rising from the table, she walked into the scullery on the pretext of fetching some more bread, but, once outside, she leaned over the sink and rinsed her face in cold water. She must stand up to him; she must.

All their married life she had done what he had told her to do without complaint; up to a point, for she wasn't a servile woman, no, never servile. She shook her head at the notion. She wasn't afraid to stand up to him about certain matters, but she had always relied on him to make the decisions about the children's welfare and discipline. When they had first married, he had assumed responsibility for their financial matters without consulting her, and she had been only too pleased to find she had married a strong man, someone who would look after her and shield her from the unpleasantness of the world. Then, when Bertie had been born, Bernard had taken responsibility for him, instructing Daisy as to when she should pick him up and when he should be left to cry, and Daisy had complied because she thought he knew best, even though it had torn at her heart to hear Bertie screaming for attention. She would make to rise, and then, catching Bernard's disapproving look, would slowly sit down again, her eyes filling with tears. It had been the same with Ruby and George, but she was no longer the dewy-eyed girl he had married fourteen years ago. The last few years had seen a marked change in her character, so that no longer would she meekly do as she was told without question. The time had come to make a stand.

The first thing she must do was to insist that a doctor be brought in to look at Ruby's leg. Although Ruby claimed that the leg didn't hurt, she knew better. The child had been listless for the past week, picking at her food and falling asleep at odd moments during the day, which was totally unlike her. Passing a hand over her forehead, Daisy experienced a moment of physical weakness. How had she let matters come to such a pass? She should have put her foot down on that same day she had fought with Bernard for the belt, and she should have sent for the doctor immediately, but the years of bowing to Bernard's decisions without question had held her in check. But no more, definitely no more! Straightening her back, she walked into the kitchen, a determined look on her face. The children were waiting patiently for Bernard to finish his dinner so that they could leave the table, he in his turn making them wait as long as possible.

'If you've finished your dinner you may leave the table,' she said firmly, her eyes directed at the children. Three pairs of eyes looked at her in amazement, but nobody moved. 'I said you may leave the table, children.' Her voice brooked no argument, but still they hesitated, their eyes going to where Bernard was sitting reading his daily paper.

The air was filled with tension until Ruby pushed her chair away from the table and stood up, her hands resting on the table so that she shouldn't have to put pressure on her bad leg. Bertie and George looked at each other, not knowing what to do, the atmosphere charged with an emotion they were as yet too young to understand. Then, very slowly, Bertie rose and stood by Ruby's side, his hand going out to steady her. George remained sitting, his blue eyes filling with tears, his young mind unable to take in what was happening. The room was deathly quiet except for the sound of George softly crying. Daisy came round to his side and gently helped him up from his chair.

Bernard sat still, his face showing no sign of the anger that was building in him. How dared she usurp his authority in front of the children in this way! What had come over the woman? Well, he would soon put a stop to it; no one was going to make him look a fool, especially not his wife. Lifting his head, he looked at the children standing together in a cluster, and then at Daisy, who had aligned herself with them, and for a moment he felt a pang of shame that they should be so afraid of him, but the moment didn't last. Without moving, he said quietly but firmly, 'Sit down. You will wait until I give you permission to leave the table and not before.'

'No, Mother said we could leave.'

Bernard looked up in amazement at Ruby, with her face flushed, her eyes challenging him, and for a moment he wavered. For the first time in many a long year he felt himself at a disadvantage. He couldn't forcibly push them back into their seats without losing dignity, but this open show of defiance was not to be tolerated. Getting to his feet, he faced them again, his face filled with anger. 'I said *sit down*. I am your father, and you will obey me.'

Still nobody moved until Daisy moved forward, her body shielding the children from his rage. 'Go to your rooms, children. I will be up presently,' she said quietly, her eyes never leaving Bernard's face.

Ruby let go of the table and caught hold of Bertie's arm as he led her from the room, with George following them, still crying. Bernard watched them go, his face filled with disbelief that they had so openly defied him and sided with their mother. He was about to spring forward, but the look on Daisy's face stopped him in mid-flight. He could only watch helplessly as the children ascended the stairs with Ruby still hanging on to Bertie's arm to take the weight off her bad leg. As she hopped up the stairs, Bernard felt a stab of fear run through his body. She was really hurt; her leg must be much worse than she had let on or she wouldn't be hobbling like that, for Ruby would never try to elicit sympathy, it wasn't in her nature.

'Sit down, Bernard. It's time we had a long talk; a talk, I may add, that's long overdue.' Daisy was now seated, her face calm but determined.

With as much dignity as he could muster, he replied stiffly, 'I'll stand, if you don't mind.'

'Oh, I don't mind, Bernard, but you may be grateful for the armchair by the time I've finished what I have to say.'

Bernard tried one more time to regain control of the situation. Squaring his shoulders, he jutted his chin, his faced suffused with colour. 'Now look here, Daisy, I won't have . . .'

'Sit down, Bernard.'

Bernard sat.

'First of all I am calling in a doctor to see Ruby. I should have done it when the accident first happened, and it *was* an accident, Bernard, not a deliberate attempt to flout your authority as you seem to think. I would ask you to go to the children and apologize for the unnecessary harsh treatment they have had to endure over the past three weeks, but I know you would never admit to being wrong.' Daisy sat forward in her chair, her eyes never leaving Bernard's face. 'Why can't you unbend a little, Bernard? I know from the little you've told me about your childhood that your father was a very hard man and that he was often cruel to you. That being the case, surely you of all people should know what it's like to live in fear of your own father?'

At the mention of his father, Bernard started, the muscles in his face twitching nervously as he tried to regain his composure. Rising from the armchair, he stared down at Daisy, and in a voice that was devoid of any emotion, said coldly, 'That will be enough, Daisy. If you insist on getting a doctor in to Ruby, then do so. I don't see the necessity for such an action. If I had, I would have done so myself. Ruby has told us that the kick barely caught her leg, but I can see it's no good arguing with you in your present state of mind. I would also ask you to refrain from talking about my father: that part of my life is over and I have no wish to be reminded of it. Now, if you will excuse me, I have business to see to.'

As he walked from the room, Daisy slumped with relief. Her whole body was trembling and she felt sick, but she had won the first round. She would ask Lily to go for the doctor in the morning. Maybe Bernard was right and she was worrying unnecessarily, but she had to make sure. Rising shakily from the table, she began to collect the dishes. Yes, the first round had gone to her, but there were many still to go, and she would face them one at a time.

Chapter Five

'**E**vening, Guv'nor. Got any meat pies going? I've just finished work an' I could eat an 'orse!' The shabbily-dressed man smiled at Bernard, eager to strike up a conversation, but his hopes were quickly dashed.

'Go down to the end of the bar and ask the girl serving there,' Bernard answered curtly. He was still seething with rage at the loss of face he had suffered. It had been nearly four hours since his altercation with Daisy and the children, but the humiliation still rankled.

The smile dropped swiftly from the man's face, and as he walked away he called over his shoulder, 'A little bit of kindness never 'urt nobody. You should remember that, you miserable sod!'

Resisting the urge to throw the man out, Bernard called Jack over. 'I'm taking a short break, Jack. If things get too busy, I'll be in the hallway.'

Without waiting for an answer, Bernard made his way down the bar and out of the side door that led to the small square hallway. Conscious that Daisy was only a few feet away behind the kitchen door, he sat down on the chair by the hall table and took from his pocket the letter he had been carrying around since that morning. Pulling the lamp nearer to him, he smoothed the crumpled paper and re-read the words he had memorized by heart.

Dear Bernard,

It is with great sadness that I write to inform you that our father is dying. I am sure that under the circumstances you will put all the bitterness behind you and make your peace with Father before it is too late.

Your affectionate brother,
David

Reading the last few words, Bernard gave a 'Huh' of a laugh. 'Affectionate brother', indeed! Where had he been the last fourteen years? The anger that had long been simmering inside him rose to the surface, and he crushed the letter into a tight ball.

He could remember the exact circumstances that had led to the estrangement. It had been on his wedding day, when he had taken his father to one side and told him about the pub he had leased from the brewery, and the career he had marked out for himself. The plans he had kept so secret, wanting to impress his father with his initiative, had come tumbling out as he had earnestly explained that it was only a start, that within a few years he would have made enough money to move to a bigger and better establishment. He had spoken the same words to his father as he had to Daisy, but the reactions had been vastly different. Whereas Daisy had clung to his every word, her eyes shining with love and admiration, the look in his father's eyes had chilled him to the bone. He could still see the veiled look of contempt on his face, hear the disparaging note in his voice. 'You, make a success of anything?' he had said quietly, making Bernard's stomach lurch with fear and apprehension. He had remembered as a small boy running for his father's approval, only to be met with the same contemptuous reception. He had stared at his father for a long time before turning on his heel and marching back to the wedding party, where Daisy was waiting for him. His father and David had left shortly afterwards, and he had never seen either of them since.

There had been no communication for nearly two years, and then Bertie had been born. As he'd looked down on his first-born son and felt him grip his finger, all the hate he had felt for his father had vanished. Eagerly he had written to inform him of his new grandson and sent a beautifully embossed invitation to the christening. On the day, he had stood outside the church waiting for a sign of his father's coach and horses, nervous at the prospect of meeting him again. His eyes had scanned the road until Daisy had come out from the church and led him gently back inside. Since then there had been nothing, not even from his brother. 'Your affectionate brother, David.' He said the words quietly. That his brother was a weak man he had always known, but he had hoped that he would have had enough backbone to stand up to their father and visit him and his family.

Shaking his head, he tried to wipe the memories from his mind, only to experience a great desire to cry, weep and shout at the utter futility of it all. During the intermittent years, he had forced himself not to think of his father, telling himself he hated him. Even when he had read the letter he had felt no sadness, only wondered what there would be in it for him. For his father was a wealthy man. Thirty years of dealing in stocks and shares had paid off. Laying the letter down on the table, he put his head in his hands; he could ignore the truth no longer.

He still loved his father, and above all else he wanted to see him before he died so that he could tell him so. He sat for a long time, examining his own character, and what he saw didn't please him. The confrontation with Daisy had left him feeling angry. It had also set off a chain of thoughts in his mind. For the first time he had seen himself as Daisy and the children saw him, and again he felt a sudden desire to weep. Getting to his feet, he put his hand on the knob of the kitchen door and hesitated for a moment, his pride not allowing him to admit he was in the wrong, but the need for Daisy's comforting presence was stronger. Silently he twisted the handle and walked into the room.

Daisy looked up at him from her sewing, and the uncertain words died on her lips as she saw the anguished look on his face. Putting her sewing down on the hearthrug, she hurried over to him. 'What is it, Bernard? What's happened?'

When he made no answer but continued to look at her in a dazed fashion, she became frightened. She had never seen him look like this. Taking his arm, she led him to the armchair, and when he was seated beside the blazing fire, she dropped to her knees and took hold of both his hands.

Bernard gulped twice before he said quietly, 'All I could think of was the money he might leave me. All day that's all I've thought about: the money, and what was in it for me. Never once did I think about him, that he was dying; just about how I would benefit. God!'

The contempt for himself in his voice made Daisy wince. Gently tightening her grip on his hands, she raised her eyes to his, all the anger she had felt for him earlier vanishing in the face of his distress. She had no need to ask who he was talking about: she could read it in his face. The anger and the fear she could cope with, but the look of sheer loathing made her cry out, 'Don't, Bernard! Don't!' And then she was in his arms, her head resting on his shoulder, listening to the spate of words that tumbled from his lips. When at last he quietened, she pulled herself away, saying, 'Why don't you go to bed, dear? I'll take your place in the bar, and we'll talk more tomorrow.'

'No, I want you with me tonight. Go and tell Jack to lock up early and go home, Lily too.'

'But, Bernard, it's only ten o'clock; the night trade is just starting,' Daisy protested. It was unheard of to shut a public house at this time of the evening.

'Daisy, please. I want the house to ourselves. I don't want to hear the laughter and music; not tonight.'

'But what shall I tell Jack and Lily? They'll wonder what's wrong, and they'll have to give the customers a reason. They could turn ugly if they're deprived of their drink.'

Turning swiftly round, he faced her, shouting, 'Tell them there's been a death in the family.'

Daisy jumped back, startled, and then walked towards the door, where she paused as she heard him say again, but more quietly this time, 'Yes, tell them there's been a death in the family.'

Bowing her head, she left the room.

Jack and Lily pushed the last protesting customers through the heavy doors and then quickly bolted them, ignoring the hammering that started up almost immediately. When they were certain the doors were secure, they looked at each other and grinned.

'Bloody 'ell, I was a bit worried for a while! It could 'ave turned nasty. Do you know what's going on?' Jack asked, leaning towards Lily.

She moved away from him, saying, 'No, no idea. Must be something up, though. 'E's never done it before; too fond of making money.'

An awkward silence then fell between them. Although they had worked together for several years, this was the first time they had ever been alone together. The silence was broken by Jack clearing his throat, then, with much shuffling of feet, he blurted out, 'Look, Lily, 'ow about tidying up and then going down the Nag's 'Ead for a drink and maybe a bite to eat?'

Lily looked up, the surprise she felt clearly showing. This was a turn-up for the book! Fancy Jack asking her out. She had never thought of him that way before. But why not? She was in no hurry to return to her dingy little room where the only company was mice and cockroaches. She looked up into his face, now red with embarrassment, and thought again, 'Why not?' All right, he might be overweight and his hair was thinning on top, but his nature was kind, and Lily craved kindness.

Before she could answer, he turned from her, muttering, 'It's all right, no need to feel awkward. It was just an idea.'

The tone of his voice brought a feeling of sadness to her. He was as lonely as she was. 'Jack, I'd love to go for a drink, but how –' and she pointed towards the doors they had just barred – 'are we going to get out? Mr Chadwick usually locks up after us, and I don't fancy going into the house to ask him, do you?'

Jack looked to where Lily was pointing, his mouth agape. He hadn't thought of that. Raising his eyes to the ceiling, he immediately dismissed the idea of calling his employer; whatever was going on up there, he wanted no part of it.

''Ang on a minute,' Lily cried. 'We can leave through the yard. Lock the back door from the outside, then push the key under the door.'

Now that the problem of leaving had been solved, they set to work to clear up the empty glasses and plates, both looking forward to the evening ahead.

Chapter Six

The dawn was just breaking as Ruby opened her eyes and began to stir. Outside her window she could hear the sounds of another day beginning. Turning over on her pillows, she gave a gasp of surprise as her eyes took in the dim figure of her father sitting on the chair by her bed.

Seeing she was awake, Bernard leaned over to the night table and turned the lamp up so that he could see her more clearly. 'Good morning, Ruby. How is your leg today?' he enquired kindly.

Ruby lay back, dumbstruck. The shock of finding him by her bedside had been frightening enough, but this sudden change in his character was bewildering. What was going on? Apart from the day he had caught her out in the lie, he had barely mentioned the accident, and then it had been in an accusing tone as if daring her to complain of any pain she might be suffering. For a sick moment she wondered if he was drunk. She couldn't think of any other reason for this complete change in his attitude, but her father never drank. He had seen too much of the effects on those that did. Her eyes still wide, she continued to stare at him, not knowing how to deal with this stranger that was her father.

Bernard looked at her frightened face, and felt once again a stab of shame. He had done this to her, to all his family, had made them fear him when all he wanted was their love. Pray God it wasn't too late to make amends! Leaning forward, he caught hold of her cold hand and said quietly, 'Your mother is sending Lily for the doctor as soon as she comes to work, and we'll see what he has to say.'

Startled, Ruby sat up, the sudden movement making her wince as a sharp pain tore through her leg. 'He won't make me go to the hospital, will he, Father?'

The terror in her voice was not lost on Bernard. The London Hospital was much feared among the poorer people and they would have to be very sick indeed to go willingly, for it was said that many men, women and children who had entered the gates had never returned. It held the same terror as the workhouse, to such an extent that it had had the same motto attached to it: 'Abandon hope all ye who enter here.'

Swallowing hard, Bernard forced a smile to his lips. 'No, Ruby, you won't have to go to the London. If the doctor says you have to visit a hospital, I'll make sure you go to a different one; a good one, I promise.' Now at a loss for words, he rose to leave, saying softly, 'I'll tell your mother you're awake. She'll be up presently.'

Ruby watched her father leave the room, her mind a jumble of confused thoughts. He had acted so differently, seemed so kind, that she had nearly blurted out the truth about how she was feeling. She couldn't explain exactly how she felt, just that she didn't feel well. Carefully pushing back the sheets, she looked down fearfully at her leg. The knee-joint was red and swollen, but what frightened her most was the yellow stuff that kept coming from it. She had managed to keep her mum from seeing it by always being up and dressed before coming down to breakfast, and by telling her that she was bathing it every day, but now she was getting really frightened. Every night for the past week she had had to wet her stocking before she could peel it from her leg. She always washed the yellow stuff away, but in the morning it was back again. Biting down on her lip, she pulled the sheets back over her trembling body. She wished she could tell her mum, but she was afraid of getting into trouble again. Lying back against the pillows, she tried to stop the tears from falling as she waited fearfully for the doctor to arrive.

It was two hours later when the sixpenny doctor arrived. A grey-haired old man who stank of beer came into her room, and without any preliminaries began to grope and pull at her leg through the long flannel nightdress she always wore to bed. So rough was he that she screamed loudly, for the pain made her feel sick. Within minutes her father burst into the room, grabbed the unfortunate man by the scruff of the neck and bundled him unceremoniously out.

The two boys stood in Ruby's doorway, their eyes wide as they saw their father return to the bed and gather Ruby in his arms, all the while muttering endearments as he rocked her back and forth. Bertie raised an eyebrow at George as if asking him to explain the sudden change in their father, but George was just as bewildered. It wasn't that Bernard had ever been cruel to them, except on the occasions when they had felt his hand, but none of them had ever received open affection from him, although they all knew he loved them.

Bernard laid Ruby back on the bed and strode past the waiting boys, saying curtly, 'See to your sister; she is very distressed.'

Taking the stairs two at a time, he flew into the kitchen where Daisy sat, her hand clutching the front of her blouse, her face troubled. 'That drunken old sot!' he exploded. 'We would have been better off getting the horse-doctor in to see her! He would at least have been gentler.' Sinking on to a chair, he put out his hands to Daisy and said, 'What shall we do? We can't take her to the London; the place is no better than an abattoir.'

Daisy thought for a moment and then said quietly, 'When are you going to see your father?'

'My father?' Bernard repeated sharply. 'I'm more concerned with Ruby at the moment. As – as soon as I'm sure she's all right, I'll go and visit my father, but first let's get Ruby seen to.'

As if she hadn't heard him, Daisy continued, 'If your father is as bad as David says, then you must go as soon as possible. No, listen, Bernard,' she said quickly as he made to interrupt. 'I've been giving it a lot of thought. Guy's Hospital isn't too far from Brixton. What I suggest is that you go to see your father today and take Ruby with you. It would do her good to get out of the house, and once you've seen him and found out just how ill he really is, you could drive on to the hospital. I've heard good reports about Guy's. I only hope we haven't left it too late.'

Bernard heard the unmistakable censure in her voice, and bowed his head. What had he been thinking of to let Ruby suffer these past weeks? But then, he defended himself, I hadn't known how much pain she was in. But you should have known, his inner voice told him. You should have made it your business to find out. Rising from the table, he appealed to Daisy. 'I was hoping you would come with me. You know how much I'm dreading seeing my father again after all this time.' Clearing his throat, he said softly, 'I could do with you by my side, Daisy. I need you with me when I see him again.'

Daisy knew how much those words had cost him and felt a warmness for him she hadn't felt in a long time. But it wasn't his father she was frightened of meeting, it was hearing what the hospital doctor would say when he examined Ruby's leg. Pushing down the compassion she felt for Bernard, she answered firmly, 'We've been over this already, Bernard. We can't both leave the pub for the day. Lily and Jack can't possibly cope with just the two of them. You'll have to go on your own.'

Realizing that further argument would prove futile, he spread his hands wide, saying, 'You'd better get Ruby ready. I'll go and saddle the horses.'

Ruby heard her mother coming up the stairs and carefully pulled herself up into a sitting position.

'How do you feel, dear?' Daisy asked solicitously, then, before Ruby could answer, she sat down on the bed and taking Ruby's hand in hers, she said gently, 'Listen, dear, your father is going to visit your grandfather today. How would you like to go with him?'

Ruby's bottom lip dropped in surprise. She knew she had a grandfather, and an uncle, but she also knew that her father didn't talk to them any more, and that's why none of them had ever visited his house. She had asked her mum a long time ago why she and Bertie and George couldn't visit their grandfather, and had been told that their father would explain the situation to them one day, but that at present they were too young to understand. 'But, Mum, I thought we weren't allowed to visit Grandfather?' she said in bewilderment.

'Ruby, I . . .' Daisy began, then tightening her hold on the small hand, she said, 'Look, dear, I haven't time to explain properly, but your grandfather is very ill, and your father wants to go and see him. And – and afterwards, your father is going to take you to a hospital called Guy's, so that a proper doctor can look at your leg.' She felt the hand beneath hers jerk suddenly and hastened to reassure the small tense figure. 'It's going to be all right, Ruby, I promise. The doctor at the hospital won't be anything like the one that's just been, and you want your leg to get better, don't you?'

Ruby looked up at her mother with fear and anxiety. 'Yes, of course I do, but, Mum – I feel scared. Mum, are you going to come with us?'

Daisy lowered her eyes guiltily. 'I'm sorry, dear, but I have to stay here and look after the pub, but look . . . Listen,' she hurried on, anxious to dispel the frightened look from her daughter's eyes. 'Your father is getting the carriage ready, so we'd better hurry and get you dressed. And just think while you're out with your father, your brothers will be stuck here doing their lessons! Now, up you get, dear. The sooner you get started, the sooner you'll be back home.'

Slightly mollified at the thought of her brothers having to miss out on a ride in the carriage, Ruby threw back the bedclothes and then painfully swung her legs over the side of the bed. With Daisy's help, she washed her hands and face in the pewter basin, then pulled her underclothes on carefully. Gently Daisy slipped over Ruby's head the new white blouse with the frills at the neck and cuffs she had so

41

lovingly sewed on by hand. This was followed by an equally new pink pinafore she had finished only yesterday, the hem of which fell around Ruby's calves. When she was finally ready, Ruby looked down at herself, pleased with what she saw. Ordinarily she would scorn such fripperies, but if she was going to see her grandfather for the first time, then she wanted to look her best. What would happen after the visit, she carefully blocked from her mind.

'There,' Daisy said proudly as she stepped back to admire her handiwork. 'Now you wait there while I fetch your father to help you down the stairs.'

'But, Mum,' Ruby protested, 'I don't need help down the stairs! Well, not much. I can lean on your arm.'

'No, dear, I'd rather you waited for your father, and anyway, you don't look very well to me. Your face is flushed, I think you may be coming down with a cold.' Placing her hand against Ruby's forehead, she was alarmed to feel the heat coming from the dry skin. Careful not to worry Ruby, she smiled brightly and said, 'Now be a good girl and do what I tell you,' before leaving the room to attend to the two boys who had gone back to bed.

Once Daisy had left the room, Ruby sat back further on the bed, trying to make herself comfortable while she waited for her dad to come and fetch her. A sudden wave of dizziness came over her and, resisting the strong impulse to lie down, she opened her eyes wide and straightened her back, trying to concentrate on the day ahead. Now that she had had time to get over the shock of the plans, she was quite looking forward to it. Anything was better than staying at home doing lessons. She wished her dad would hurry up. Eh, she'd have to stop thinking of him as 'Dad'. He got so angry when she forgot, and she'd have to be specially nice to him today because his dad – no, his father – wasn't very well and he was worried about him. Folding her hands in her lap, she waited patiently for her father to come.

Bernard finished feeding the horses and hurried back into the house. As he climbed the stairs, he saw Daisy leave Ruby's room and then bang on the boys' door before disappearing into their room. In his bedroom, he sat down heavily, wondering if he could change her mind about accompanying him on his journey today. He felt in dire need of moral support. Even though he had recovered from the emotional trauma he had suffered the day before, there still remained a feeling of dread at the prospect of coming face to face with his father after all these years. Well, at least he would have Ruby by his side, and he only wished the reason for her coming with him were due to different circumstances. With heavy steps he walked over to his wardrobe and took out his black morning coat and black high hat, both of which he very rarely had the opportunity to wear. Laying them on the bed, he made his way to Ruby's room, where she was waiting patiently for him.

Dressed in the pink pinafore and white blouse, her newly-washed auburn hair was tied back from her forehead, leaving the rest of her abundant curls to fall softly around her shoulders. He smiled gently, taking in the loveliness of her. Coming to sit beside her, he asked kindly, 'Is your leg paining you, Ruby?' at the same time realizing the stupidity of the question.

'It is a bit, Father. Do you think the doctor at the hospital will give me some ointment to put on it, to make it better? I miss running with Bertie and Geo –' Her words trailed off miserably as she realized she had let the cat out of the bag.

Bernard watched her face fall, and turned his head away. He knew that the three of them played in the street whenever the opportunity presented itself, with Ruby often dressed in a pair of Bertie's trousers as she raced up and down the dirty streets. He didn't approve of their playtime activities, or of their companions, but what could he do? He could hardly forbid them to play outside, even though he was ever fearful of their picking up some dreadful disease from the manure-laden roads or their lice-ridden friends. As Daisy often pointed out when he raised an objection, children needed their playtime, needed to run and shout and let off steam. Oh, yes, he knew the situation full well, but could never openly condone it, nor could he in all fairness forbid them the streets, and so he turned a blind eye, thus preserving his authority. Maybe he should relent and let them attend school. There was nothing the children would like better, and it would ease the burden on Daisy. Slapping his hands on his knees, he stood up, the sudden movement causing Ruby to sway for a moment, her face troubled.

Bernard saw the look and said, 'We'll say no more about your leisure time now. I've more important worries to think about at the moment. We'll talk again at a later date.'

Walking to his room, he came back with his morning coat draped over his arm, his shiny high hat in his hand. 'I'll help you down to the kitchen, and while you're having your breakfast, I'll be getting the horses saddled to the carriage.' Already he was putting his coat on, ready to leave.

'Well now, don't you look a smart couple?' Daisy beamed from the doorway, her smile hiding her anxiety. On either side of her stood Bertie and George, both rubbing the sleep from their eyes. Pushing them behind her, she said, 'Go and have your wash, both of you. I've put warm water in your jug, and make a good job of it. I'll be checking ears and necks after you're dressed. Get along now.'

Bertie came into the room, his eyes fixed firmly on Ruby's face. 'I want to say goodbye to Ruby,' he said quietly, walking towards the bed.

'Goodbye? Where do you think she's going? On her holidays? She'll be back this evening. Now go on, and get yourselves ready.' She could hear her voice rising, and struggled to control the fear within her – the fear that was preventing her from accompanying Bernard. It wasn't fear of meeting her father-in-law. No, it was the fear of walking through the hospital gates with Ruby and coming out without her. Stop it, stop it! she told herself fiercely, but her mind refused to stop working. Down on her knees, she began to button Ruby's ankle-length black boots, careful not to hurt her, while her mind went back to the past.

She remembered the Crimean War. Remembered a man who had returned from a place called Sebastopol. She remembered him sitting drinking tea in her mother's kitchen while he told the story of the charge of the Light Brigade in Balaclava. Her father had sat rapt in silence listening to the man's tales of heroism. He himself had been declared unfit for service because of his poor eyesight and weak chest, much to her mother's relief. Daisy couldn't remember the man's name, or his face, but she could remember the man's wooden leg and being chastised by her mother for staring at it.

The man had laughed loudly, and pulled Daisy to his side, pointing to the artificial limb. Knocking his pipe against it, he had said cheerfully, 'I'd like a penny for every three-legged table and chair in the country this day! Why, I'd never have to worry about money again.'

At Daisy's bewildered look, he had explained that the common soldiers coming back from the war with an empty trouser-leg had had to improvise, and what better than a leg from an old table or chair?

Daisy had fought a mixture of fascination and revulsion as she'd asked timidly, 'Were you shot, sir?'

The man had thrown back his head and let out another roar of laughter. 'Why, bless you, child, nothing so grand. I was kicked by a horse!'

Long after she had waved Bernard and Ruby off in the carriage and returned to the house, the words kept echoing in her mind. Words from long ago. 'Why, bless you, child, nothing so grand. I was kicked by a horse!'

'Kicked by a horse'
'Kicked by a horse'
'Kicked by a horse'

Chapter Seven

Ruby sat upright on the comfortable leather seat, her eyes darting from left to right, taking in the sights around her, the weakness that pervaded her body temporarily forgotten as she entered a different world. The greatest thrill was when they passed over London Bridge. Her mouth hung open as she stared at the huge expanse of the Thames, which seemed to stretch as far as her eyes could see. Soon they were entering Brixton, and again her eyes widened at the sight of the large villas partly obscured by the huge trees that lined the road. Opening her mouth wide, she breathed in the sweet-smelling air, and for the first time understood why her dad was so desperate to leave the East End. She understood, too, his concern about their playing in the dirty streets and mixing with the dirty urchins that hung around the pub waiting for their parents to come through the heavy doors and take them home. And if by chance the parents had a few pennies left and were in a good mood, the children would be sent to the fish-man that stood on the corner in all weathers to purchase a bag of jellied eels for their dinner. All too often the waiting children were rewarded for their diligence by a hard blow to the side of the head that would send them tumbling on to the cobblestones, while the mother or father stumbled off down the road without a backward glance. Ruby had often witnessed such scenes, and had been filled with a deep sadness.

'Nearly there, Ruby. What do you think of Brixton? A far cry from the home I've provided for you, isn't it?' Unable to keep the bitterness from his voice, Bernard fell silent, not trusting himself to say any more.

The familiar streets had evoked memories he had thought long buried. Images of himself as a young boy holding David's hand as their little legs tried valiantly to keep up with their father on the weekly visit to morning service. The delicious roast dinner that had awaited them on their return, cooked by Hannah the housekeeper, who had tried to fill the place of their dead mother. Again the bitterness rose within him. Hannah had died at the grand old age of eighty-one more than six years ago, and if it had been left to his father or David to impart the news, Bernard would never have found out. It was by chance that a servant from one of the villas in the same road had wandered into the pub and, recognizing Bernard, had brought him up to date about the happenings in the house he had once called home. He remembered his sadness at hearing of Hannah's death, and then the anger at not being informed. Good God! Would it have killed his father or David to have written a short note and sent it by the penny post? He had been only five years old when his mother had died. Dim visions of a tall lady immaculately dressed, smelling of flowers, were the only recollections left to him of the woman who had given him life. Hannah he could remember clearly: a small plump woman with white curly hair kept in place by a sheer fine net. Her face always wearing a kindly smile, her arms ever open to the two small boys, she would pull them on to her ample lap as they buried their heads into her comforting breasts after their father had berated them for some small misdemeanour. The visions of days gone by caused a lump to settle in his throat and he was relieved when he reined in the horses outside 15, Acre Lane.

Turning his head towards Ruby, seeing the beautiful young face before him, he felt the bitterness seep away, and vowed that whatever it took he would get his family out of the hell-hole in which they lived. Coming back here, seeing the beauty of the street and the cleanliness that surrounded them, reinforced the goal he had set for them years ago. He no longer cared about a posh public house and hotel – that dream would never materialize - but he could try to get another pub in a nicer area, somewhere decent. Tonight he would talk it over with Daisy. As he looked at the large villa, he wondered if the solution he longed for lay within the house he would soon be entering for the first time in fourteen years. Jumping nimbly down from the carriage, he tethered the reins to the iron railings in front of the villa, then walked round to where Ruby was sitting, her eyes still glued in front of her.

'Do you think you can walk, Ruby?' he enquired, and she replied by putting her arms out. Resting her hands on his shoulders, she then winced as he swung her to the ground, immediately lifting her leg to relieve the pressure on it.

Bernard saw the look of pain cross her face and the small beads of perspiration on her forehead, and cursed himself for being such an obstinate fool. If his pride hadn't prevented him from running to his father's side as soon as he'd received David's letter, if he hadn't been so annoyed at the accident, so preoccupied with playing the big man, he would have taken Ruby to the hospital as soon as he had known about it. Pulling her close, he noticed her flushed face and hoped it was only a cold she was getting. Pray God the delay hadn't caused any serious damage. Bending his head down, he said kindly, 'Not long now, Ruby, unless you are feeling unwell. In that case we can drive straight to the hospital. We can always visit your grandfather another time when you're feeling better.'

'No, Father, I feel fine. Mother says I have a cold; that's why I feel hot and shaky. I'll be all right, honest!'

Tucking her arm into his elbow, Bernard helped her up the path, coming to a stop outside the solid oak door. He lifted the brass handle and banged it down twice. While he waited, he straightened his back, then ran his finger nervously round the top of his tight collar, moving his head from side to side in an effort to calm himself.

'Yes, sir, can I help you?' The girl who stood in the doorway looked no older than Ruby, while her floor-length dress of dark navy, over which lay a white starched bib and apron, denoted her position as housemaid.

'Mr Bernard Chadwick to see my father,' Bernard answered in an unnaturally loud voice as he stepped into the hall, handing the girl his hat. Then, divesting Ruby of her thick red coat, he held it out for the girl to take.

Her coat disposed of, Ruby stared at her surroundings, unable to believe her eyes. The carpet she was standing on was of a deep shade of red and so thick that her boots seemed to be sinking into the pile. The hall was bigger than the whole upstairs of their house, but what impressed her most was the curved stairwell that seemed to curl round and up to the very top of the house. This too was covered in the same rich carpet, and on the white and gold embossed walls hung small pictures in gold frames, the like of which she'd never seen before.

'Bernard, how wonderful to see you!' A dark-haired man was coming down the thick carpeted stairs, his pudgy hand, heavily laden with gold rings, holding the wooden banister, as he beamed down at them. Even to Ruby, at her tender years, the smile seemed false.

Bernard moved towards his younger brother, taking the outstretched hand, noting his corpulent frame, and derived a childlike pleasure from the fact that he had run to fat.

'And this must be your daughter? You must be very proud, Bernard. She's beautiful.'

Ruby blushed, and averted her gaze from her uncle's pale, watery blue eyes. Why, he doesn't look anything like Dad! she thought in surprise, disappointed at the first glimpse of him.

Bernard fidgeted impatiently. He was eager to see his father and unable to return David's show of enthusiasm. They had never been close, and he saw no reason for subterfuge at this late date. Clearing his throat, he released his hand, and said, 'I would like to see Father, David. Where is he?' Seeing the serious look that passed over David's face, he felt his stomach lurch painfully. 'I'm not too late, am I, David? He's not dead?' he asked fearfully. To have come this far for nothing would be more than he could bear.

'No! Good heavens, no,' David replied quickly. 'But he's very weak just now; his heart, you know. Dr Benson's with him now. Good fellow, only the best for Father. But I don't think he'll last for much longer, that's why I wrote to you. He knows, you see, or at least he suspects, and he wants to make his peace with you. Old age seems to have mellowed him, what!'

Bernard looked with distaste at his brother. He showed not the slightest sadness at the thought of his father dying. In fact, his whole attitude spoke of indifference. He was saved from answering by the sudden appearance of Dr Benson.

William Benson was a medium-sized man, his posture giving the lie to his sixty-eight years. His silvery-white hair lay smoothly close to his head, and as he came down the stairs, a genuine smile upon seeing them caused his face to dissolve into a morass of wrinkles. But what impressed themselves most on Ruby were the twinkling blue eyes that seemed to laugh at her from behind the gold-rimmed pince-nez perched precariously on his nose.

'Bernard, my dear fellow, it's good to see you again,' he exclaimed loudly, putting his hand out.

'Dr Benson,' Bernard answered stiffly, still unsure of himself. 'I'm pleased that my father is receiving such good medical attention.'

Dr Benson stood back as though to see him more clearly. His eyes flickered briefly to where David stood nervously behind Bernard, and noted the fact that he looked uncomfortable. 'And well he might,' he thought grimly. It was hard to believe he had been in attendance at the births of both these men. He suddenly felt very old. Turning back to Bernard, he pumped his hand vigorously. 'I would very much like you to drop the title and call me "William", Bernard. Yes, I'd like that very much indeed.'

At the warmth of his tone, Bernard began to relax, a smile coming to his lips for the first time that day. Behind him, David stiffened, a dark hue spreading over his face. Clenching his fists by his sides he thought savagely, 'Damn him!'

Once, many years ago, fortified by port, he had made the mistake of crossing the borders of familiarity. Upon hearing David address him by his Christian name, Dr Benson had rebuked him sharply, and now here he was asking Bernard, whom he hadn't seen for well over fourteen years, to call him 'William'. 'Damn him to hell!' That the affront had been deliberate, David had no doubt. It was yet another attempt to put him in his place. He was looking forward to the day when he would have the authority to boot him from the house, and that day wouldn't be long now.

'I'd like to see my father, Doctor, I mean William,' Bernard said quietly.

'Of course, of course, although I must warn you that you will find a marked change in him. But I supposed you will be expecting that.' Extending his arm, Dr Benson gestured towards the stairs, his head slightly bowed.

Straightening his shoulders, Bernard pulled at the front of his coat before walking forward, his steps steady as he mounted the stairs. As Ruby made to follow, she felt her arm grasped gently, and turning slightly, looked in surprise at the doctor standing by her side.

'I think it would be best, Bernard, if you were to see your father alone. He is very ill, so I don't want him upset or agitated in any way.'

Bernard nodded curtly. Now he was here, he no longer felt the need for moral support. Anxious to see his father, he continued up the stairs, acutely aware of a sense of urgency. When he reached the landing, he stopped for a moment to collect his thoughts. Looking down, he saw Dr Benson leading Ruby towards the library, while of David there was no sign. Taking a deep breath, he knocked once on his father's bedroom door, then, grasping the knob firmly, he opened it.

He didn't know what he had expected to see, but certainly not a frail old man propped up on a mountain of pillows. Bernard's breath caught in his throat. He had never seen his father in bed before. All memories of him had been of a proud stern man going about his business, always smartly dressed, his clothes immaculate. He had taken a great pride in his appearance.

'Who is it? Is that you, William?' the voice said querulously.

Moving forward into the dimly-lit room, Bernard approached the four-poster bed and took a chair beside it. 'It's me, Father – Bernard,' he answered, his voice husky with emotion.

'Bernard?' The name came out as a question. Then, in a stronger tone, he added, 'You came, then. I didn't think you would.'

Bernard felt his earlier uneasiness return, and sitting upright, he said stiffly, 'I can always go if I'm not welcome.' The sudden laugh made him jump.

Pushing himself up on his pillows, Charles Chadwick studied his elder son. 'Still on your high horse, eh, Bernard? You always were a stiff bugger.' Seeing Bernard's eyes widen in surprise, he went on, 'Surprised at my language, are you? Well, things have changed since you saw me last, and no, I don't want you to leave. I need to talk to you. But first open those blasted curtains. It's like a tomb in here. I'm not dead yet.'

Bernard rose hurriedly to do his father's bidding. Pulling back the heavy velvet to let in the morning light, he took a moment to take in the situation. According to David's letter and Dr Benson's words, his father was supposedly at death's door, but the last few minutes had given the lie to that. Turning from the window, he faced his father once more.

Charles Chadwick was sitting upright against his pillows. His body might have given up on him, but the shrewdness in his watery eyes gave evidence that his brain was in no way impaired by the illness that had confined him to his bed. 'Well, don't just stand there gawping! Come and sit by the bed,' he barked, patting the coverlet impatiently.

When Bernard was once again sitting, his hands on his knees, his father gave a long sigh and then began to speak. 'We have fourteen years to catch up on, Bernard and it cannot be done in half an hour. That is as long as we'll have before that old fool Benson comes in like a fussy old hen and orders me to rest.'

'I think you're being unjust, Father. Dr Benson is an excellent physician, and I . . .'

'Be quiet, boy,' Charles ordered imperiously, waving his hand at his son.

Bernard felt his face redden, and with considerable restraint stopped himself from uttering the angry words that sprang to his lips.

Charles Chadwick looked at his son struggling to contain his anger, and chuckled softly. 'Oh, I know, Bernard! I know what you're thinking, but bear with me until I've finished what I have to say.'

'Very well, Father. I'm listening.'

'Good. As I said before, we have a lot of years to fill in, but the important parts, the reasons for the lost years, I can explain in one word, "David".' Bernard's mouth opened in surprise, but before he could say anything, his father had begun speaking again. 'But first let me explain why I acted as I did on the day you came to me to tell me of your ambitions. Although I was cold to you, there was no malice in my behaviour. I acted as I did for a specific purpose. I wanted to see if my rejection of you would change your plans in any way. You see, I couldn't be sure that you intended to stand on your own two feet or whether you hoped I would finance you towards your ultimate goal. To manage a hotel and public house, as you described, needed a great deal of enterprise and determination and, of course, money. The trust fund you inherited on your twenty-first birthday would have been adequate enough for the small public house you intended to buy, but for the rest, well, that would require a great deal more: intuitive business acumen, but, most important of all, strength of character. If I had offered to finance you at the start, there would have been no incentive for you to succeed, and so I set you a test. It may have seemed cruel, but I have always believed that there is no telling what a human character is capable of until it is tested. To most of us the test comes early in life. A man is confronted quite soon with the necessity to stand on his own feet, to face dangers and difficulties and find his own way of dealing with them without expecting others to shoulder his responsibilities. Whichever road it is, a man usually learns early in life just what he is made of. For your sake as well as mine, I had to act as I did.' The voice faltered, his strength momentarily deserting him.

Bernard sat quietly, his mind in a turmoil. Had he made this journey just to hear his father tell him what he already knew – that he was a failure? But his next words brought his head up sharply.

'I'm proud of you, Bernard,' he said, his voice softer now.

'But, Father,' Bernard stuttered, 'I haven't succeeded in life. I never realized the goals I set myself. I didn't even buy the pub. Instead, I leased it from the brewery in an attempt to save some money, but it all went on fripperies. I'm still where I was fourteen years ago – in a small public house, surrounded by the dregs of humanity. Oh, not all the people are dirty and lazy and most of them try to raise themselves out of the squalor in which they live, but it's an insurmountable task, and most just give up and make the best of what they have, like I have,' he ended miserably.

'Bernard, look at me.' The command was weak, but firm. 'You have a home, a good wife and three healthy children. Many never achieve that particular goal. To my mind, that does not constitute failure.' The words were cut off by a bout of coughing.

'Father,' Bernard rushed to help his father, 'enough now, rest yourself, we will talk later.'

'Wasn't a good father, too hard on you, knocked the stuffing out of me when your mother died, didn't mean to be cruel, didn't mean . . .'

Thoroughly alarmed now, Bernard took one last look at his father lying ashen-faced on the bed, and fled from the room in search of Dr Benson.

Ruby watched in silence as her father paced the floor, his footsteps muffled by the thickness of the carpet. Her eyes wandered, taking in the huge walnut desk that stood in the centre of the room and the large black leather armchairs. She hoped her grandfather wouldn't die before she had had a chance to see him. Careful not to disturb her father, she limped over to the large cabinet that took up nearly all the main wall, which was crammed full of books. Large books, small books, thick and thin books – Ruby had never seen such a collection in one place at the same time. Carefully she extracted one of the smaller ones and read the title on the front. The sound of the door opening made her jump, so that she nearly dropped the book.

'How is he, William?' Bernard bounded across the room as Dr Benson entered.

'Calm yourself, Bernard. He's resting now. The excitement of seeing you again tired him, but there's no need for immediate concern.' Looking over at Ruby sitting in one of the large leather chairs that threatened to envelop her, he smiled kindly, and said, 'What is that you're reading, Ruby?' As he took it from her hands, a wide smile spread across his face. 'Well now, Voltaire's *Candide*! I think perhaps you had better wait until you are a bit older before you embark on this. I myself have read it twice and still fail to comprehend it fully.'

'Yes, sir,' Ruby answered obediently.

Dr Benson took the book and returned it to its rightful place, and then pulled on a thick tasselled rope that hung down on the side of the cabinet. 'Would you like to sit in the kitchen with Mary, Ruby? I'm sure she'd like the opportunity to talk with someone near her own age.'

Ruby looked to Bernard for guidance, and when the answer was given as an impatient nod, she stood up slowly, taking the weight on her good leg. There was a discreet knock on the door before it was opened slowly to reveal the young maid who had admitted them to the house.

'Ah Mary,' Dr Benson boomed heartily. 'Take Miss Ruby into the kitchen and ask Cook to give her something nice to eat.'

Upon hearing herself addressed as 'Miss', Ruby's small body swelled with importance and with a tentative smile at Bernard, she limped from the room saying, 'Thank you, Doctor, for looking at my leg.'

When the door had closed behind them, Dr Benson's face assumed a look of grave concern, and turning to Bernard, he said gruffly, 'You'd better sit down.'

'What is it? Is it something about my father you couldn't tell me in Ruby's presence, and what did he mean when he said David was responsible for the rift between us?' Bernard was now seated in the chair Ruby had just vacated. He was trying hard to control his impatience with Dr Benson, and wished he would sit down and finish the conversation his father had started. If there were any secrets to be told, the man standing in front of him would know the answers.

'David?' Dr Benson said, looking puzzled for a moment. 'Ah, yes. David.'

Walking to the chair opposite Bernard, he sat down, carefully adjusting the coat-tails of his morning suit. He was in no hurry to impart the bad news he would eventually have to tell Bernard: for the moment he had a reprieve. Making himself more comfortable, he said, 'To put it bluntly, Bernard, your younger brother has tried to do you out of your rightful inheritance. No, hear me out,' he added hastily as Bernard made to speak. 'This won't take long, and there are more important things that I have to speak to you about.' Leaning back in the chair, he continued, 'You remember when your first son was born and you sent an invitation to your father and David to attend the christening?' Bernard nodded, wondering where this was leading to. Dr Benson went on, 'Well, your father never received it, neither did he receive any of the letters your wife wrote to him in an attempt to end the estrangement between you.'

Unable to contain himself any longer, Bernard leaned forward. 'Daisy wrote to my father? When? How often?'

'A great number of times, I believe, but like the invitation, your father never received them. They were carefully intercepted and destroyed, just as the letters your father wrote to you were never sent. It was in David's best interests to keep the feud between you and your father going, but he wasn't quite clever enough.'

Dr Benson paused for a moment, then, seeing he had Bernard's full attention, he leaned back in the armchair. 'Ten days ago I had an unexpected visitor. The housemaid who was in service here before Mary came to see me at my home. It seems that she and David had been on,

54

shall we say for propriety's sake, friendly terms for some time. He persuaded her to intercept any letters addressed to your father. She was quite willing to do anything he asked without question, for the silly girl actually believed David would marry her some day. Then your father's condition worsened and it was at that point that David made his first mistake. He told the girl their relationship was over, adding that he would soon be the heir to his father's home and business and, as such, would be expected to maintain a certain standing in the community. In plain terms, she was no longer of any use to him. When the girl refused to accept the situation and threatened to tell your father what had been occurring, David immediately dismissed her. At the same time, he warned her to keep her mouth shut, adding that nobody would believe the word of a servant against that of a gentleman.' Here Dr Benson paused in his narration to utter a scornful 'Huh!' 'Well, Bernard, that seems to sum up the whole sorry business. Like many a man before him, David made the mistake of underestimating a woman scorned. It is fortunate for you that the girl wasn't so easily intimidated.'

He looked at Bernard sitting in the leather chair opposite, and wondered what was going through his mind. He had received a tremendous shock, but what he would be forced to tell him next would make the last half-hour pale into insignificance. He fervently hoped that Bernard had inherited some of his father's strength to fortify him against the terrible blow that was about to descend.

'Does David know his deception has been found out?' The words were spoken quietly, but the anger beneath the calm tone was unmistakable.

Dr Benson looked at Bernard, his keen glance taking in the silent battle that was being fought beneath the calm façade. He could sense the anger of betrayal, but also the elation at the knowledge that his father had not deserted him. He jumped as Bernard sprang from his chair.

'The swine! The miserable conniving swine! Does he know the game's up? I asked you. Answer me, man.'

'No, Bernard, no. He suspects something's wrong,' Dr Benson stuttered, 'or else he would never have sent that letter even at my insistence. He feels safe in the knowledge that he is named as sole beneficiary in your father's will. What he doesn't know is that your father changed his will as soon as I informed him of what David had done.' He broke off as Bernard headed for the door, his face like thunder. Rising swiftly, he called out desperately, 'Bernard, please! David can wait. I must speak to you on a matter of grave importance, please.'

The plea in Dr Benson's voice stopped Bernard in his tracks. Turning slowly from the door, he said in a voice as cold as ice, 'What could be more important than wringing that miserable bastard's neck?'

Dr Benson swallowed twice, then, taking his courage in both hands, he replied, 'Your daughter's life.'

The words hung heavily in the air as the two men stared at each other. Bernard was the first to speak. 'Ruby?' he whispered. 'Ruby's life in danger?' His voice held an incredulous note. Then shaking his head, he said more firmly, 'What are you talking about, man? Ruby is in excellent health. Why, she's never had a day's illness in her life.' He began to walk towards Dr Benson, his hands held out, palms upward.

'Please, Bernard? This is very difficult for me. Won't you sit down and let me explain?'

With an impatient shake of his head, Bernard strode swiftly to the armchair, his mind in a whirl. 'The man's in his dotage,' he thought angrily. 'He should have retired years ago. He can't possibly be allowed to tend to Father any longer.' He had recovered from the initial shock at the doctor's words, and had already dismissed them from his mind. He was eager to leave the room and tackle David, but the doctor was old and deserved some respect. He would hear him out and humour him. David could wait a little longer. He leaned back more comfortably, an indulgent smile on his lips, but as he looked into the kindly intelligent eyes he felt a qualm of doubt as he waited to hear what Dr Benson had to say.

The old man sat down slowly, trying to formulate in his mind the words that would soften the blow, but there were none. Taking a deep breath, he said quietly, 'I took the liberty of examining Ruby's leg while you were with your father. I believe Ruby has a condition called osteomyelitis.' Here he paused for a moment to wipe his brow with a large white handkerchief, then plunged swiftly on. 'There is evidence of severe bruising to the knee joint. In plain language, the bruise is eating away at the bone, and unless immediate surgery is carried out to stop the spread of the disease, it could poison her entire body.'

The indulgent smile had vanished from Bernard's lips. He felt the sweat break out on his face and his heart beat painfully. Running his tongue over his dry lips, he struggled to speak. 'What kind of surgery are you talking about?'

As the messengers of ancient Rome must have feared and dreaded their inevitable task, so did Dr Benson feel now, but he did not shirk his duty. 'Amputation.' He watched in pity as Bernard's eyes stretched in horror and made to go to his side to offer what little comfort he could, but before he could rise from his chair, Bernard waved him back.

'No, leave me,' he shouted fiercely. 'I don't want your sympathy! I want you to tell me you may be mistaken. How can you be so sure? You're not a surgeon.'

Bernard's voice had risen in anger, but Dr Benson was not afraid. He had seen this reaction of rage and bewilderment so many times. He waited patiently for Bernard's tirade to abate and then answered, his voice compassionate and weary. 'I'm truly sorry, Bernard, but I know what I'm talking about. I was stationed in a medical field hospital during the Crimean War and I've seen too many cases to be mistaken.'

'It can't be true! She only slightly bruised her leg. Surely there must be an alternative?'

Bernard's distress made Dr Benson bow his head in the face of such abject misery. The truth was that Ruby's life was in no immediate danger unless blood poisoning had already set in, but if he told Bernard that, he would never agree to the operation. In the meantime, the infection would steadily spread, causing bacteria to build up in the wound until the very stench of the festering wound would drive the unlucky victim into the arms of the nearest surgeon. It was in times such as these that he felt, like so many of his colleagues, the inadequacy of his profession. There was something badly wrong when the only solution to problems of this kind was the drastic step of amputation and mutilation. Shaking himself out of his reverie, he spoke briskly. Loath as he was to add to Bernard's pain, there were plans to be made. The sooner Ruby was admitted to hospital, the better.

'I think you should call Ruby from the kitchen, and I shall come with you to Guy's. That is, if you are agreeable? I know an excellent surgeon there who will do everything in his power to make Ruby as comfortable as possible.'

'Are you absolutely sure there is no chance her leg can be saved, no cure to be obtained? I'm clutching at straws here, William. Please help me?' The look on the doctor's face was an answer in itself. Shaken to the core, Bernard threw his hands up and began to rock back and forth. Presently he dropped his hands and asked quietly, 'How am I going to tell Ruby? I mean, how do you tell a ten-year-old child she has to have her leg taken away? Can you answer me that, William?'

'She mustn't be told; not yet. Wait until she is settled into hospital, and then we shall discuss the best way to break the news.'

'Wait?' Bernard was on his feet, his face dark with anger. 'Wait until before or after the operation? She's a bright child. I think she'll notice something's wrong when she wakes up and finds her leg missing!'

Neither man heard the door open as a scared-looking Ruby entered, followed closely by Mary, the housemaid. Ruby looked at her father's strained face and then at the nice doctor who seemed to be perspiring heavily, his ruddy cheeks glistening with sweat. The atmosphere in the room was heavily charged with a tension she couldn't identify.

Suddenly aware of her presence, Bernard swung round. In two long strides he was across the room, his hands firmly on her shoulders as he demanded fearfully, 'How long have you been standing there, girl? Answer me – what have you heard?' His hands increased their pressure; he was oblivious of Ruby's gasp of pain as his fingers bit cruelly into her flesh.

'Please, Father, you're hurting me! Let me go – please . . .' The last word came out on a sob.

As if he'd been stung, Bernard dropped his hands, only immediately to envelop Ruby in his arms in the first real cuddle he had ever given her. Gently he led her over to the armchair, his arms still wrapped round her shivering body. When they were both seated, with Ruby on his lap, her face buried in his neck, Bernard raised his eyes to Dr Benson, the appeal in them stronger than any words.

Motioning the wide-eyed Mary from the room, Dr Benson seated himself once more, but before he could speak, Ruby raised her head from Bernard's neck. Her eyes bright with unshed tears, she looked her father full in the face, and said tremulously, 'It isn't true is it, Father? You won't let them cut my leg off, will you?'

'Oh, Ruby, my dear child!' Fighting back his own tears, Bernard searched for the words to still the rising panic emanating from the small body pressed close to his chest. 'Listen to me, child,' he said gently. 'Your injury is far worse than any of us realized. If you don't let the doctors remove . . .' 'Dear God,' he prayed fervently. 'Give me strength and wisdom to say the terrible words! Give us both the strength to face and conquer this awful burden you have forced upon us.' He could feel Ruby's frantic struggling to extricate herself from his arms, saw her hands go up to cover her ears. Holding her wrists firmly with one hand, he lifted her chin, forcing her to look at him. 'You must be brave, Ruby. If your leg is not removed, you will die.'

'I don't care,' cried Ruby. 'I'd rather be dead!' Her scream tore through the air and then was swiftly muffled as Bernard pulled her into his arms once more.

Neither of them noticed Dr Benson rise quietly from his chair and head for the door. He paused for a moment, wondering if there was anything he could do to alleviate the suffering of the two figures locked together in the chair. Shaking his head sadly, he opened the door. There was nothing anyone could do for them now, except pray. From the other side of the room he heard Ruby sob, 'Don't let them hurt me, Father! I'll be good, I promise! Just don't let them hurt me!' before shutting the door quietly behind him.

Chapter Eight

The night had turned bitterly cold, but Bernard, still clothed in his morning coat, scarcely noticed the icy wind that blasted his body, a body that felt as numb as his mind. Acutely conscious of the empty seat beside him, he urged the horses on, part of him longing to get home to Daisy, the other part wanting to whip the horses into a gallop and drive into the darkness of the night until they dropped with exhaustion.

Releasing one hand from the reins, he drew his arm over his tired stinging eyes, trying to wipe out the memory of Ruby fighting to get out of the arms of the two nurses who had kindly but firmly stripped her before placing her in the narrow wooden bed. If Dr Benson hadn't been by his side, he would have caught her up in his arms and carried her home to Daisy. As Daisy came to mind, he could imagine her clearly sitting by the open fire, her glance going to the clock on the mantelpiece, wondering where they were, worrying in case they had been involved in an accident, her brow furrowing as it always did when she was anxious. He hoped the boys would be in bed by the time he got home. It was going to be bad enough telling Daisy without the presence of his two sons, both of whom adored their sister. Flicking the reins sharply, he shouted, 'Get up there, Nobby, good boy,' ignoring Lady's presence completely. As the horses picked up speed, the memory of the last few hours came flooding back. Wearily he tried to block them out, but it was no good, he was back in the library once more.

He had sat holding Ruby until she had cried herself to sleep, while the thought had come to him, sadly, that this was the closest he had ever been to her, and this brought about only by a tragedy. Dr Benson had wisely left them alone for an hour before coming back into the room, but now he could wait no longer.

'Bernard, it's time to go.' The words were kindly said, his sympathy coming through in the tone of his voice. Easing himself from the chair,

Bernard held on to Ruby tightly, fearful of waking her. 'It would be better if we took my coach, Bernard. It will be more comfortable for Ruby.'

Gathering Ruby's still sleeping body in his arms, Bernard whispered, 'Look, William, I've been thinking about what you said, and the more I try to imagine . . . well, what you suggested . . . I can hardly believe it. And as for rushing her to some hospital this minute before I have had a chance to confer with Daisy, it's out of the question. I know you mean well, William, but such a drastic step cannot be taken lightly, as I'm sure you can appreciate.'

Dr Benson looked with pity and concern at Bernard's flushed anxious face, and shook his head. 'And what will happen when you get home?' Nodding towards the sleeping form, he added, 'How do you imagine she will be once she wakes up and remembers what she heard in this room? Are you prepared to lie to her, tell her it was all a mistake, when you know in your heart I'm telling the truth? And what about tomorrow and the day after – are you going to wait until she is in so much pain that she can no longer bear to put her foot to the ground? Think, Bernard, think. What you are suggesting is understandable, but it's also incredibly foolish. You are no longer a child who believes that an unpleasant thought can be made to disappear simply by going to bed and pulling the covers over your eyes, and when you wake up in the morning the troubles will be over, gone.' His voice held a desperate note as he tried to convey the urgency of the situation to the man who now stood, a mulish look on his face, refusing to face the truth. No, not refusing, simply afraid to. As Bernard made to move past him, he searched frantically for the right words, words to penetrate the deliberate shutter that Bernard had pulled over his mind. Catching him by his arm, he whispered fiercely, 'And how will you explain to Ruby why her skin is putrefying, turning bad, and the smell from the useless rotting bone? What explanation will you give her then, Bernard?'

'Shut up, man! Shut up!' Bernard hissed furiously, his face twisted in anger. The face before him showed no fear, only compassion, and his anger melted as quickly as it had come.

'Come, Bernard, my coachman is waiting.'

With head bowed, Bernard carried the sleeping Ruby from the house.

The afternoon light was slowly fading when the coach turned into the large iron gates of Guy's Hospital. Telling the coachman to wait, Dr

Benson watched as Bernard stepped awkwardly down, trying desperately not to wake Ruby, but his efforts were in vain. As soon as the cold air hit her face she opened her eyes slowly, a smile coming to her lips before she became aware of the strange surroundings. The smile faded, and with a cold feeling in the pit of his stomach, Bernard saw her eyes grow round with terror as she looked up at the huge grim buildings that surrounded them. Like a wild animal caught in a trap, she suddenly realized the horror of her situation, and as Bernard tried to control her flailing arms, she struggled to free herself from his grasp, opened her mouth wide and emitted a piercing scream that reverberated round the courtyard. With Dr Benson urging him on, Bernard ran into the building, ignoring the startled looks from the doctors, students and visitors who thronged the courtyard. Ignored, too, the frantic pleading of Ruby to be taken home. Keeping his eyes fixed firmly on Dr Benson's back, he followed the elderly man through a maze of long bleak corridors until he stopped by a brown wooden door and, without hesitating, banged sharply on the door panel twice before entering, leaving Bernard standing in the corridor.

Within minutes, Dr Benson re-emerged, a tall middle-aged distinguished gentleman dressed in a three-quarter-length coat and black pinstriped trousers following him closely. 'This is Mr Davis, Bernard. He's the man I told you about.' He spoke in a casual way, the word 'surgeon' carefully omitted for Ruby's sake. The introductions over, Dr Benson stood to one side, clearly relieved that the responsibility for Ruby was now out of his hands. At the sight of the stranger, Ruby let out yet another frightened wail, burying her hot face in Bernard's shoulder, her arms clasped firmly round his neck.

'If you would care to follow me to my ward, Mr Chadwick, I would like to examine your daughter's leg.'

Unable to make any kind of reply, Bernard simply nodded; the fear he could feel radiating from the small body in his arms having now violently transferred itself to him. His steps felt leaden as he walked behind the two doctors now deeply engrossed in conversation, all the horror stories he had ever heard now replayed over and over in his tortured mind. Stories he had dismissed as hysterical nonsense came flooding back. Grim tales of death and mutilation, unsanitary conditions, children herded together in tiny stone cells tended only when the gin-sodden so-called nurses remembered them. 'Not my Ruby,' he vowed silently. 'If she has to die, then she will die between clean sheets, nursed by people who love her.' Gripping her tightly, he continued to walk, urgently seeking a way out of this nightmare. He could hardly believe that only a short while ago his sole concern had been for the wealth and property he had so nearly been denied. Even the hatred he had felt for David had vanished, even the thought that his father might only have a short while to live no longer caused him pain. All that mattered was that his child be spared. His father was old, his life nearly over, and as for David – well, let him have the money and position he had coveted; he no longer cared. 'Please, God, don't let my Ruby die! I'll do anything, anything at all, but please don't let her die.'

The age-old act of bargaining with the Almighty completed, Bernard quickened his steps to catch up with the two men who were now waiting for him outside a large room, at the sight of which his eyes widened in astonishment. The ward was large and airy, the rows of beds lined up neatly along the walls leaving the middle free for the patients who were well enough to walk to do so. Around each bed was an iron rail to which dark green curtains were attached, to provide privacy for the patients being examined. He noticed also that some of the beds had iron rails at the sides, much similar in design to a baby's cot, and these obviously were for children.

A youngish woman dressed in an ankle-length pale blue gown, a white bib covering the front, was handing out drinks to a group of children dressed in their night-clothes, and the scene was so unexpected that Bernard felt his body slacken with relief. Maybe there was a chance, after all. Maybe William had been wrong in his diagnosis, but if he hadn't, well at least Ruby would have a good chance of surviving the dreaded operation, wouldn't she?

'Would you lay your daughter on the bed, please, Mr Chadwick? I need to examine the injured leg.' Bernard felt Ruby's arms tighten as he tried to prise them from his neck. 'Ruby – hello, my dear.' Mr Davis had moved round to behind Bernard, his face now on a level with the still terrified Ruby. 'My name is Mr Davis. I'm a doctor, and I'm going to try to make you better. The first thing I'm going to do is give you something to make the pain go away. Will you let me look at your leg?'

Bernard held his breath as he felt her hands loosen on his aching neck, then he watched in amazement as Ruby trustingly put her arms out to the stranger. Mr Davis picked her up and carried her to one of the railed beds and gently laid her down.

'Now then, let's see what's what, shall we?' he asked kindly. 'Can you answer some questions for me, Ruby?' The small head nodded, her eyes never leaving his face. 'Do you feel hot and unwell?' Again the small nod, this time her eyes travelling to where Bernard was standing, his face anxious.

He saw the look and felt his stomach lurch. She was afraid to admit that she was feeling ill in case he would somehow blame her for her condition. All the times she had insisted that she was all right had been a lie; she must have been feeling unwell for a long while and been too afraid to admit it. The knowledge hit him forcibly, causing him to stagger away from the bed. Was he such a bad father, was he so terrifying that his own child was afraid to seek help from him? Closing his eyes tightly, he remembered how, the day after the accident, he had gone for the children with the belt and how Daisy had fought to get them safely away from him. He remembered, too, the coldness he had shown to her, and like a child crying out for forgiveness, he cried silently, 'I didn't mean it! Oh, God, I didn't mean it!'

'Mr Chadwick, are you feeling all right?'

No, he was not feeling all right! He felt like hell, but now was not the time to admit his failing. Forcing himself to remain calm, he answered, 'I'm quite all right, thank you. I'm more concerned with my daughter's condition.' Even to his own ears the words sounded stiff and formal, but the surgeon merely nodded, then turned back to Ruby.

'Does your leg hurt very much? Have you been able to walk on it?'

'No, Doctor.' The words were spoken so softly that Mr Davis had to lean forward to hear her. 'I mean, I haven't been able to walk properly for a long time. It hurts too much.'

'I see. Well, don't worry. As soon as the ward sister arrives, I'll look at your leg and then give you something to make the pain go away as I promised. Ah, talk of the devil! Ahem . . . Sister Anne, this is Ruby. She's not been feeling very well. I'm just going to take a quick look at her leg. She was kicked by a horse, you know.'

A small stout woman dressed in the same manner as the younger nurses had come to stand by the bed, the dark navy uniform denoting her rank as a Sister. 'Kicked by a horse, were you? And what were you doing, that a lovely kind animal like a horse should want to kick you?'

Bernard listened to the kindly banter, his mind telling him that it wasn't fair on Ruby to behave like this. Already she had relaxed, lulled into a false sense of security by the attention she was receiving. He looked at the Sister, judging her to be in her late fifties, her hair, already grey, caught up in a solid bun at the nape of her neck, leaving the top of her head free for the frilled white cap she wore.

'Would you draw the curtains, please, Sister. We can't expect a young lady to undress in front of complete strangers, can we?'

'Indeed we can't, Doctor,' she answered, her face beaming down on the now calm Ruby.

'Would you wait outside please, sir.' She turned to face Bernard, the smile still in evidence, but not bright enough to hide the concern in her dark brown eyes.

'No, Father, don't leave me!' Ruby cried, and she attempted to sit up, but Mr Davis held her firmly.

'I'll just be outside the curtains, my dear. I won't leave you, I promise.' Bernard said quickly, the new form of endearment sounding hollow to his ears before the faded curtains were pulled around the bed, shutting Ruby from his view.

Left alone, he became aware of the curious eyes surveying him. Grimly determined not to make eye-contact with any of the women and children that filled the clean but cheerless beds, he fixed his gaze firmly on the varnished wooden floor, lifting them only to stare at the large gas-lamps that hung from the grey ceiling, their soft light giving the ward a soothing effect that would vanish in the light of day. A sudden bout of coughing startled him and, without thinking, he looked towards the bed from which the sound had emanated. A woman as old as his father was leaning over the side of her bed, her face suffused with blood as she tried to catch her breath. Watching her struggles, Bernard felt a pang of sympathy, a feeling that changed to one of disgust as the unfortunate woman promptly began to retch violently over herself and the bedclothes. Nauseated, he turned his head away, unable to witness such a spectacle, then stepped quickly to one side as a young nurse pushed by to get to her patient, the look of compassion on her fresh face shaming him.

The swish of the curtains being drawn back brought his head round sharply to where Ruby lay quietly, the elderly Sister holding her hand, her soothing words too soft for Bernard to catch. Eagerly he raised his eyes to Mr Davis, but his hopes were cruelly dashed at the bleak expression on his face. With a slight shake of his head he motioned to Bernard to remain silent. A moment later, the smile was back on his face as he turned to Ruby.

'I'm going to have a talk to your father, Ruby. We shall both come back presently. Sister Anne will look after you until then.'

'You're not going to cut my leg off, are you?' Ruby whispered fearfully. 'Dr Benson said you were going to cut my leg off! You're not going to, are you?'

Bernard felt his breath quicken as he waited for the surgeon to answer. 'There now, don't you go getting yourself upset,' Sister Anne interrupted quickly. 'Tell me all about your family. Have you any brothers and sisters?'

Taking the chance to get away, Mr Davis walked off quickly, with Dr Benson and Bernard close behind him.

'But he's not going to cut my leg off, is he? Father! Father . . .'

'I'm sorry, Mr. Chadwick, but the condition of your daughter's leg leaves me no other choice but to amputate.' Mr Davis's voice seemed to be coming from a long way off as Bernard fought down the feeling of nausea. 'It is unfortunate that she should have overheard your conversation. In the circumstances, there is no alternative but to operate as soon as possible. It would be unbearably cruel to leave her contemplating her fate any longer than is absolutely necessary.' Pulling open his desk drawer, he extracted a large sheet of printed paper resembling a document. 'I shall need your permission to operate, Mr Chadwick. Mr Chadwick?'

Bernard raised his head slowly, his hand going to the form in front of him. As if to gain some time, he tried in vain to study the black print that seemed to jump and blur in front of his eyes. 'I'm sorry, I . . .' Clearing his throat noisily, he tried again. 'What exactly shall I be signing?'

'It's a standard procedure, Mr Chadwick, exonerating myself and the hospital from any liability should sudden death occur. Not that that is likely in your daughter's case,' he added hurriedly, as Bernard made to rise from his chair. 'Medical science has come a long way since the days of strapping patients fully conscious to the operating table with a gag in their mouths to stop them from screaming out in their agony. Twenty years ago it was found that one out of every three successful amputation patients died later from septicaemia, or a similar type of infection. Now, thank heavens, we have chloroform to render patients unconscious while we perform surgery, and the risk of death by infection has been almost ruled out thanks to Joseph Lister's development of antiseptic methods.' Warming to his theme, Mr Davis seemed to have forgotten the presence of Bernard and Dr Benson. 'He realized that by sterilizing the surgical instruments during the operation and also the wounds afterwards, he was saving more lives than hitherto had been deemed possible. Did you know that in 1871 he operated successfully on the Queen?' The question was rhetorical, and he swept on, 'Yes, we all have a lot to thank Joseph Lister for. I met him once at King's College. A remarkable man!'

The feeling of lethargy momentarily left Bernard. Yes, he kept abreast of current affairs. He prided himself on his knowledge of world events, and yes, he had heard of Lister and read about his amazing techniques. He had also read that until very recently, although surgeons were grateful for the invention of chloroform, the majority of London's doctors and surgeons had ridiculed and scorned his revolutionary methods, even though their Scottish counterparts had been using them successfully for years. At any other time Bernard would have taken great pleasure in demonstrating his knowledge to the man sitting before him, but not now.

'Oh, yes, I've no doubt that he is a great man. It's a pity he hasn't applied his brilliant mind to the curing of disease rather than the simpler method of removing it.' Bernard's voice was bitter. 'Perhaps you would like to inform my ten-year-old daughter how lucky she is to have had her accident in such an enlightened age?'

Mr Davis looked at Dr Benson, then back to Bernard. He could feel the anger, sense the grief that was consuming the man sitting dejectedly in the chair facing him. His keen eyes took in the clenched white fists that Bernard held on his knees, and knew the man was near breaking-point. 'Mr Chadwick, I suggest that you sign the form, say goodnight to Ruby and then go home to your wife. I intend to operate at ten o'clock tomorrow morning. It means having to rearrange my schedule, but I'm fully prepared to do so on your daughter's behalf.'

'That's good of you,' said Bernard dully.

Knowing that any further conversation would be futile, Mr Davis once more pushed the offending piece of paper across the desk. Bernard stared at it while both men held their breath, then slowly released it as he picked up a pen and carelessly scrawled his name at the bottom of the form before flinging the pen down with such force it rebounded off the desk and on to the polished floor.

Without a word, Mr Davis leant over and retrieved the pen, placing it back in its rightful place on the table before saying, 'Would you like to say goodnight to your daughter? I think it would be best to get her settled. Obviously I shall give her something to make her sleep, so you need have no worries about her lying awake in torment and distress all night.'

Bernard scraped back his chair and walked towards the door without answering. The time for words was long past. He was about to wrench open the door when Mr Davis spoke again.

'We are very proud here at Guy's, Mr Chadwick. I know there are many hospitals in London where I wouldn't send a sick animal for treatment, let alone a loved one, so whatever you may have heard about the medical profession, please believe me when I say that I and the rest of my staff will do everything in our power to comfort and re-assure Ruby and will try to the best of our ability to ease her suffering, both in mind and body.'

Anxious to leave before he broke down, Bernard gave a curt nod, then swiftly left the room.

'Now listen to me, Ruby. I have to go home and tell your mother what has happened. You know how she worries. And what about the boys? They will be anxious too.'

'But, Father, I don't like it here. I'm frightened! Please take me home? My leg feels much better now, honest it does! Please, Father, take me home! Don't leave me here!'

Gently disentangling his hand, Bernard looked to the Sister for help. Taking her cue from the beseeching look in the smartly dressed man's eyes, Sister Anne broke into the conversation. She had witnessed this painful scene so many times, but it never got any easier. 'Now, then, Ruby, let your father go. The doctor will be here soon to give you something to stop your leg hurting and to make you sleep, and when you wake up, your mother will be here.'

Tearing his eyes away from Ruby's terrified face, Bernard got unsteadily to his feet. His forehead broke out into a sweat and the floor seemed to come up and smack him right between the eyes. Shaking his head helplessly, he stumbled from the bedside and staggered drunkenly down the ward with Ruby's screams ringing in his ears.

'No, Father, don't go! Oh, please don't leave me here. I'll be good, I promise. Father, Father, oh please!'

He was at the entrance to the ward now, the tears spilling down his white shirt. He heard a last agonized cry behind him.

'Father! Father, come back! Come back, Dad! Dad . . .'

'Oy, look where you're going, mate! You nearly ran me over. You drunk or summink?'

Bernard sat up sharply, his hands tightening on the slack reins, his mumbled apology lost above the noise coming from behind the brightly lit windows of the King's Arms. Pulling the horses to an abrupt stop, he sat for a moment longer, then brought the whip down lightly on the horses' backs, guiding them towards the stables at the back of the pub. Jumping down from the wooden seat, he caught hold of their bridles and led them into the straw-covered stalls before sinking wearily to the ground. He wished now he had accepted William's offer to come home with him to break the news to Daisy. After he had left the hospital, with the concerned doctor by his side, he had slunk down in the corner of the plush carriage, staring through the small window into the dark. No words had been spoken until they had arrived back at his father's house, where William had broached the subject of accompanying him home, but Bernard had been in no mood for company. He hadn't even bothered to enter the house to see his father, merely shrugging off William's offer of help and ignoring the doctor's genuine concern. He could hardly wait for the servants to saddle up his horses so that he could be gone.

The sounds of nearby drunken laughter brought his head up slowly. He must go in to Daisy. She would have heard the horses enter the yard and would be waiting for him . . . for them. And still he sat, outwardly calm, his mind seething with suppressed anger, until the soft nuzzling of a horse's face against his own brought him back to reality. Raising his red-rimmed eyes, he gazed at the cause of his misery. Still calm, he gently released Nobby from the shafts of the carriage, ignoring Lady, who stood waiting patiently for her turn. Free of his shackles, Nobby trotted off to the bale of hay in the corner of his stall. The soft whinny behind him caused Bernard to clench his fists, then, as if touching something loathsome, he began to free Lady from the carriage. The anger was burning fiercely now, he could feel it travelling through his body from the tightening of his stomach to the red mist that slowly dropped over his eyes. He grabbed the whip he had earlier thrown down on to the straw, then, looking into the soft trusting brown eyes only inches from his face, he brought his arm up high in the air.

At the sound of the horses entering the yard, Daisy's head came up from her sewing, her face relaxing into a smile of relief. Thank God they were home! Turning to where the two boys sat at the kitchen table listlessly playing with their red and blue soldiers, she said lightly, 'There, you see, they're home. I told you not to worry, didn't I?' Her voice trembled slightly as she laid her sewing down and got to her feet. 'Now, put those toys away. I don't want any arguments when Ruby comes in, for you know she doesn't like you playing with her soldiers,' she said, indicating the line of red soldiers that George was lining up for combat.

'That's not fair, Mother! She always has the English soldiers. Me and Bertie always have to play with the French soldiers, and they always lose!'

But Daisy was already at the kitchen door, now wide open, as she anxiously scanned the dark alley towards the stables. Why were they taking so long to come in? She knew Bernard had to untether the horses and settle them down for the night, but where was Ruby? She shivered in the cold night air and hugged herself to try to get some warmth into her body.

'Shall I go and see what's keeping them, Mother?' Bertie stood beside her, his face mirroring her concern.

Daisy nodded, but before he could move, they both jumped as the shrill scream rent the air. 'Oh my God!' Clutching her throat, she stood transfixed, the sound of the horse's agony cutting through her brain. Suddenly she knew. Knew what had happened to make them so late, knew for certain that Ruby wasn't in the stable with Bernard, and knew with sickening certainty what was happening in the stables. Picking up her skirt, she ran towards the sounds of the screams with Bertie close behind. Pulling the door wide, she looked into the gloom and put her hand out to stop Bertie from coming any nearer. 'Go and get Jack. Quickly, now!'

Bertie looked at his mother, his eyes wide with fright, and then at another piercing scream he screwed up his eyes as if in pain and ran hell for leather towards the pub. 'Jack! Jack, come quickly! Something awful's happening. Mother says to come quickly!'

Jack and Lily looked at Bertie in amazement, his body trembling, his head barely reaching the top of the bar counter.

'What is it? What's wrong? 'Ere, turn the noise down, you lot! The little lad's in trouble and I can't 'ear what 'e's saying. Come on, shut yer noise!' Jack bellowed, his voice cutting through the laughter and singing.

Heads began to turn towards the smartly dressed young boy, his face red from running, his eyes staring from his head in fright and anxiety. The noise abated as the customers, sensing a drama unfolding, craned their necks to see what was going on.

'That's better,' Jack shouted into the now quietened room. 'Now then, me lad, what seems to be the trouble?' Bertie was saved from answering as Lady's terrified screams carried through to the packed bar. 'Bloody 'ell! What was that?'

'It's Father, Jack! He's hurting one of the horses. Oh, come and help! Please!' His errand completed, Bertie turned and began to force his way back through the crowd, his young mind in a turmoil. He had just told a room full of strangers that his father was hurting a helpless animal, but it was true – he had seen him beating Lady before Daisy had pushed him away.

'Stay here, Lily. I'd better see what's going on,' Jack ordered, his face worried. As he raced from the pub he was aware of a handful of men following him and was grateful for the company. He didn't fancy tackling the Guv'nor on his own, whatever the reason.

Within seconds, the men were standing in front of the open stable doors, and what they saw made them stop dead in their tracks. The woman and young boy were struggling with the tall man whom most of the men present recognized as the toffee-nosed owner of the pub they had just left. But this man before them bore no resemblance to the publican who stood behind the bar, serving them drinks as if he were doing them a favour. None of Bernard's customers had any love for him, and the anger they had felt over the years now boiled over at the sight of the helpless horse now lying still on the dirty straw, its body covered in blood. As one man they burst into the stable, gently pulling Daisy and Bertie to one side, prising their hands from Bernard's arms as he continued to beat the unconscious horse.

'Bastard!' spat one of the men as he grabbed the whip from Bernard.

The man's action sounded like a signal, and the rest of them poured into the stall, punching and kicking at Bernard as he cowered against the wall. Offering no sign of resistance, his eyes clouded, he looked from one angry face to another before sliding down the wall while the blows continued to rain down upon him.

'Stop it! Stop it! Leave him alone!' Daisy's voice was joined to Bertie's as they rushed to his aid. Shielding his body with their own, they glared up at the men through tear-filled eyes. 'Get out!' she screamed at them. 'Get out, or I'll set the constables on you! You've nearly killed him! There was no need, no need . . .' Her voice broke off into sobs as the men, quiet now, shambled back from the three people lying huddled together on the floor. One by one they backed away until only Jack and the man who had wrenched the whip from Bernard's hand remained.

'No need, missus,' the man said angrily. 'No need, you say? What about that poor beast lying there beaten half to death? Your husband got what he deserved – a taste of his own medicine – and if you ask me, it's been long overdue!'

'You don't understand,' Daisy sobbed brokenly. 'You don't understand.'

'No, I reckon you're right there, missus. I don't understand. If you want to tell the constables, well, Jack here knows where to find me.' So saying, the man turned sharply on his heel and disappeared into the night.

'Come on, Mrs Chadwick, let's get the Guv'nor into the house.' Jack was kneeling by their side, his big red face displaying mixed signs of bewilderment and worry. He didn't like the Guv'nor, but would never have thought him a cruel man, not this kind of cruelty, anyway. Reaching out, he helped Daisy to her feet, then with her assistance managed to get Bernard standing, his face still bearing a look of puzzlement. With Daisy and Jack on either side of him, he stumbled into the dark night towards the house.

Left alone, Bertie dropped to his knees beside the now still horse. His eyes were blind with tears as he gently put his arms round the bloodied body. 'Why, Father? Why did you do it? Lady never hurt anybody,' he sobbed wildly, his body shaking with emotion and fear, and then his eyes widened as comprehension dawned upon him. 'Ruby?' Jumping quickly to his feet, he desperately scanned the empty space. 'Ruby, where are you?'

Miles away in a darkened ward, the night sister looked down at the sleeping man sprawled in the uncomfortable chair beside the narrow bed. Tentatively she reached out a hand and touched his shoulder.

'Mr Davis, sir?'

The surgeon jumped, startled from his light sleep.

'You should get some proper rest, sir. You've a long day tomorrow.' She spoke in a hushed, almost apologetic tone.

'Yes, you're quite right, Sister, I have a long day tomorrow. Thank you.' The words were kind but dismissive and the sister took the hint, creeping back silently into the dark.

Looking down at the sleeping child, Mr Davis gently stroked her soft cheek, feeling the dried tears that lay upon it.

'And how will you face tomorrow, you poor little mite? Sleep soundly, Ruby, and pray to your God for strength to see you through the rest of your life.'

Chapter Nine

The small group of students made their way across the hospital courtyard, their cumbersome textbooks hugged closely to their chests. As they reached the dark green door that led to the operating theatre, they were joined by four of their colleagues. Pairing off, they climbed the stairs, the older, more experienced, ones deep in conversation while the younger few chattered excitedly, their voices high and over-bright as they tried to disguise their nervousness at the prospect of witnessing their first operation. Upon entering the theatre, the young men became separated as they pushed and shoved through the throng of students already present, each one desperately trying to get the best possible position in the already overcrowded gallery.

The theatre had a semi-circular floor, on which stood a small operating table screwed down by angle irons. The table was covered with a blanket, over which lay a large sheet of brown oilcloth. Placed at the foot of the table was a wooden box filled with sawdust, its purpose to catch the rivulets of blood that ran off the oilcloth during the operation. Another table stood nearby, the rows of instruments laid neatly out in readiness for the surgeon of the day. Against the wall in the far corner was a small basin, about the size of a large soup-plate, in which the surgeons washed their hands after operating. Some of the younger surgeons, like Mr Davis, took the trouble to wash before operating as well. Above the basin hung a board bearing the inscription: *'Miseratione non mercede'* (From compassion, not for gain). Alongside the basin was a row of pegs bearing the operating frock-coats, stiff and stinking with pus and blood. Next to these hung three grocers' bib-and-aprons, fashioned of non-absorbent material, for the more advanced surgeons.

The operating floor was separated by a partition from the rising stand places. The first two rows of benches were reserved for the surgeons, dressers and assistants. Behind the second partition stood the students, packed like herrings in a barrel, but not nearly as quiet, as those behind continually pressed forward to get a glimpse of what was going on. The semi-circular standings rose in tiers that nearly reached the large skylight which lighted the theatre.

The babble suddenly ceased as the door to the left of the theatre opened to admit Mr Davis and his assistants, followed closely by two porters carrying a small child on a stretcher. While the porters placed the patient on the operating table, Mr Davis and his assistants donned the bib-and-aprons. Ignoring the gasps of sympathy that came from the student gallery at the sight of the auburn-haired girl lying still and vulnerable, they proceeded to wash their hands.

'Gentlemen, may I have your attention, please?' Mr Davis was forced to raise his voice to make himself heard as the voices grew louder in the stands. 'Thank you,' he said more quietly, as the noise abated. 'The patient is ten years of age. She received a severe blow to her left leg some three weeks ago, but was brought into the hospital only yesterday. Upon examining her, I discovered she had a very high temperature and was feeling generally unwell. Further examination of the leg showed an area of swelling that was hot and tender to the touch; the said area was also dripping pus. This observation led me to believe that bacteria had settled in the wound, causing dead tissue and inflammation. My diagnosis is a condition called osteomyelitis, and unless immediate surgery is carried out, infection will set in, causing blood poisoning. In short, gentlemen, unless I amputate the infected leg, she will undoubtably die.'

He paused to let the students digest this information before continuing. 'One of my assistants will hold the leg above the knee, the other will hold the foot below the calf. I shall then use a curved knife designed to permit an incision called the "Tour de Maître". This is a movement by which a rapid circular division of skin and muscle can be made. I shall then use the saw to complete the amputation.'

He broke off his speech. Reluctant as always to perform this kind of surgery on any child, he had deliberately avoided looking at Ruby since she had been carried into the theatre. Acutely aware of the sympathy, and in some quarters abject horror, throughout his audience, he addressed the gallery once more. 'I am fully aware of the tragedy in having to amputate on one so young. This is something that each and every one of you will, in all probability, encounter, should you decide at the end of your studies to become surgeons. I would ask you in the meantime to call to mind the words of that grand lady, Florence Nightingale. She said, and I quote: "The very first requirement in a hospital is that it should do the sick no harm."' Then, turning to his assistant, he held out his hand for the knife.

'She's waking up! Quick, Bertie, run and fetch the Sister!' Daisy rose from the hard bench, her face clearly showing her distress. Bending over the bed, she said softly, 'Ruby dear, can you hear me? It's me, Mother. Are you awake?'

'Mum . . .' The word came out as a whisper.

'It's all right, dear. Don't try and talk, everything's going to be all right,' Daisy said tenderly, her hand brushing away a damp tendril of hair from the flushed forehead.

'I don't feel well, Mum, and my leg hurts. It hurts really bad,' Ruby cried piteously, her face screwed up in pain.

Daisy looked quickly round to where Bernard was sitting silently on the bench, his bruised face drawn and haggard, and at this moment she was hard put to decide whom she felt sorrier for. Apart from telling her what had happened to Ruby, he hadn't uttered a word since last night when, together with Jack, she had laid him down on the four-poster bed before the constables had arrived. They had listened gravely as she had explained the circumstances of the situation, and had asked her if Bernard would be pressing charges against the men responsible for the violent assault. She had told them they had no wish for revenge, and had asked them to see to Lady. All through the long discourse Bernard had remained mute, his pain-filled eyes staring sightlessly in front of him. Not even when some hours after the constables had left and the sudden loud retort of a gun from the stables had woken her from an uneasy sleep did he make any sign of movement. And the boys: dear God, the boys!

George stood at the foot of the bed, his eyes filled with tears, holding the small pot of mignonette he had insisted on buying from the flower-lady outside the hospital. Then Bertie came hurrying down the ward, the Sister walking sedately behind him. He reached the bed first, and going immediately to George's side, his arm went round his brother's shoulder before he looked down at Ruby.

Closing her eyes for a moment, Daisy felt her body sway with fatigue. She was going to have her hands full over the next few months, for not only would she have to look after Ruby, she would also have the extra burden of the three men in her life, who at this moment were dependent on her to smooth the way for them. Ruby was in for a rough time, but she would pull through. It would take a while, but Ruby was a fighter, she wouldn't give in easily. As for Bernard; she lifted her shoulders in despair. He was no longer the Bernard she knew, not this silent, withdrawn man sitting beside her. Ruby might have lost a limb, but it was Bernard who had become a cripple – an emotional cripple.

So deep in thought was she that the Sister had to speak twice before Daisy heard her. 'I'm going to give Ruby some medicine to ease the pain, Mrs Chadwick. It will also make her sleep. And, if you don't mind me saying so, you look as if you could do with some sleep yourself, and your husband.' Then she poured out some liquid into a spoon.

'What is that?' Daisy asked, more from a desire to talk than a genuine need to know.

'It's laudanum, Mrs Chadwick. Ruby will be taking this for a few days until she gets over the worst. Then we will give her tincture of opium for the pain for as long as she needs it.'

Daisy nodded dumbly. For as long as she needs it. Pray to God that wouldn't be for too long.

'It's all right, Mum,' Ruby said weakly, trying to give Daisy a feeble grin. 'I don't mind the taste of the medicine, and I don't mind my leg hurting any more, honest, Mum. And, Mum,' she added, quieter now as the laudanum began to take effect, 'I was so frightened, Mum! I thought the doctor was going to cut my leg off, but he hasn't. I know he hasn't because I can still feel it . . .' Her voice trailed off, and then her head lolled to one side, the smile still on her face.

Daisy's hands flew to her face in despair. Oh, God, she didn't know! She thought she still had her leg! Oh, no, no! Pressing her hand to her mouth, she tried valiantly to stop the sobs that were tearing at her throat, but in vain. She heard the loud keening sound in her head, but was completely unaware that the animal sounds were coming from her own throat.

'Mrs Chadwick, please! You are distressing the other patients. And look at your sons! For their sakes, if not your own, calm yourself.' The Sister was pulling Daisy's hand from her mouth while at the same time trying to push her from the bedside and the ward.

Daisy felt the urgent hands pulling at her and cast them off impatiently as she tried to get back to Ruby's side. The only thought in her mind was to get her daughter home, to be with her when she discovered the truth. She had to be told by someone who cared, not somebody who did the loathsome task every day because they were paid to. She felt hands come out and grasp her arm, and the rage built inside her body. All the fear, anger and despair she had bottled up during the past hours now came bubbling up. She wanted to hit out, to shout and kick, to hurt somebody. Anybody would do! She had to find release from this feeling burning inside her.

What would have happened next she never knew, for it was at that point that Bernard rose to his feet, the curtain lifting from his eyes as he said firmly, 'Take your hands off my wife. I will see to her.'

The sound of the familiar voice brought Daisy back to reality and her body slumped with relief. She had been one step away from madness! If she had released the scream that had been spiralling inside her body until it had seemed to fill her very brain, she would have been doomed. For once that scream had been released, she would have been unable to stop. Leaning against Bernard's firm body, she allowed herself to be led sobbing from the ward.

Bertie reluctantly detached himself from the foot of the bed and went to his mother, his arm going tenderly round her waist. Left alone, George placed the pot of mignonette by the bed, then, making sure no one was watching, he crept round and kissed Ruby's forehead. 'I love you, Ruby. Get better soon,' he whispered before running after his family.

Chapter Ten

Ruby sat quietly in her chair by the window, the book open on her lap, forgotten, as she tried to put her thoughts in order. The hot sun caressed her face. It was nearly eight months since her leg had been amputated, six of which had been spent in a convalescent home where she had been among people like herself: men, women and children who for some reason had had to endure the same terrible agony. It hadn't been so bad then, she hadn't felt different, and with the help and care she'd received from the doctors and nurses had even come to accept what had happened to her. It was while she was there that she had learned of the death of her grandfather and the news that, when she came home, it would be to this house, the house she had been in only once, on that fateful day that seemed so long ago. This had come as a great shock, for not only had she lost a grandfather, a grandfather she had never had the chance to meet, but she had also been deprived of her home, a home she had loved despite her parents' feelings about it.

She still could not take in the size and grandeur of her bedroom. She had a double bed all to herself, a large walnut writing-desk where she took her lessons, and in the far corner lay the washbasin and dressing-table, something she had always longed for. The wardrobe against the main wall contained a dozen new dresses and outfits, but the bottom shelf, used as a storage-place for shoes and boots, was bare. Thinking about the matter of footwear brought a sad smile to her face. Would her mum try to find a cobbler to make only one shoe for her, or would she have to buy them in pairs and throw one away? It was an interesting problem and one she'd have to put to her mum some time, but not just yet. At the moment she was quite happy to remain bare-footed.

When her mother's voice floated up to her, she leaned forward to look out of the window. Daisy was talking to the new gardener, her outstretched hand indicating the large flower-bed that had become her pride and joy. Ruby watched her mother's animated face and felt a sudden surge of love for her; she looked so pretty in her new colourful dresses, and the one she was wearing was a particular favourite of Ruby's. It was a lovely shade of violet and white, the bodice being tucked in at the waist with tiny pleats before falling to the ground in soft folds. Daisy's insistence on not wearing bustles, as was the current fashion, had Ruby's wholehearted approval, but not her dad's. Ruby remembered one night when they had received an invitation from one of Bernard's new-found friends, a banker in the City, and he had tried to persuade Daisy to have a new dress made for the occasion. Still unsure of himself, he had tentatively asked if she would be following the mode of the day, by which he meant having a bustle at the back of the dress. Ruby found a smile coming to her face as she recalled her mother saying that if the *men* had to restrict their bodies in a whalebone corset to keep them upright and then have to don a garment that seemed to walk two steps behind them all day, they wouldn't be so keen on fashions and trends! Bernard had capitulated, as he often did nowadays, and because he did so, Daisy then, with perfect woman's logic, ordered a new blue dress to be made; with bustle. She had worn it only once, and then put it away in her wardrobe, ready to be taken out and dusted down for the next social engagement.

Thinking about her dad and the way in which he had changed caused the smile to slip from Ruby's lips. Since the accident he had bent over backwards trying to please her as if somehow he blamed himself, and it was strange what had happened to Lady. Her mother had told her that both Nobby and Lady had been taken to a farm in the country because they couldn't afford to keep them any more; but that couldn't be true because they had more money now than they'd ever had. It was after this incident that her dad had redoubled his efforts to please her, and she wasn't sure if she liked him this way. She had often wished he would unbend a little and be more attentive to her, and now that it had happened, she should be feeling very happy. At long last he was the kind of father she had always wanted, but the price she'd had to pay was too high; much too high.

Giving a long sad sigh, she turned her eyes again to the book on her lap, but for once the trials and tribulations of *Jane Eyre* held no excitement. She wished she had gone down to the garden as her mother had wanted, but the thought of the new gardener staring at her had prevented her from leaving her room, where she felt safe, away from prying eyes and sympathetic stares. She couldn't abide sympathy; she didn't need it, she told herself fiercely. Suddenly she caught a glimpse of the wooden leg propped up by the side of her bed, and quickly averted her eyes. It looked grotesque, seemingly suspended by the heavy mesh corset and belt necessary to keep it in place. She had tried it on only once, and that had been enough. In spite of Daisy putting a soft sock over the stump to stop any chafing, it had still hurt when she put her weight on it. That had been over a month ago, and she hadn't tried it again and didn't see the need: she could get around the house quite well on her crutches.

Giving yet another protracted sigh, she turned once again to the window. She was so bored! If only Bertie and George were here instead of at the stuffy old boarding school her dad had insisted on. His purpose had been to make educated men of them in the hope that one day they might join him in the business he had taken over on his father's death. Tapping her finger on the side of her chair, she pondered on what to do next. She could call her mother up for a chat, but she would only start persuading her to try the leg on again, and she didn't want to; it was horrible. Maybe her next governess would have some spirit, unlike the miserable creatures she had had to endure so far. Her education had greatly improved but she needed more; she needed a friend, someone not afraid to talk back, someone who wouldn't suck up to her, but, more imporant, someone who could make her laugh again. Someone like Lily from the pub.

At this thought, her hands stopped their fidgeting and a smile came to her lips. Imagine someone like Lily coming here! It would be like a breath of fresh air, but how could she arrange it? Certainly not as a governess, since poor Lily couldn't even write her own name, but maybe as her personal maid. Yes, that was an idea. Now that it had taken root, she thought frantically for a way to get Lily here. It wasn't going to be easy, for she knew how her dad viewed common people, especially now that he was a proper gent and no longer just pretending. There must be a way; there must be! If she were to get her own way in this matter, she would first have to put her parents in a good frame of mind, and what better way than to pretend to accept the hateful leg and learn to walk on it? Chewing on her bottom lip, she looked again at the polished leg, and shivered. Deep down, she wanted to walk again, to get out of this room, this house, and live again. She had had her eleventh birthday while at the convalescent home, but she felt much older. She wanted someone who would treat her as an equal, not as an object of pity or guilt. This thought was quickly banished: why should anyone feel guilty? What had happened had been her fault, no one else's. As her mother kept telling her, no one would know she had a wooden leg. Her clothes would cover it for the most part, and if she worked really hard, she would learn to walk without too much of a limp.

Quickly, before she could change her mind, she leaned out of the window and called, 'Mum, could you come up here a minute, please?' She felt a pang of remorse when she saw the smile that lit up her mother's face, but quickly dismissed it. There was no time to waste on guilt, she had her life to live. Getting up from the chair, she hopped over to the bed and sat down next to the leg as she waited for Daisy to come up the stairs.

Daisy alighted from the train at Liverpool Street station and immediately cursed herself for a fool. That Ruby had manipulated her into this venture she hadn't the slightest doubt, and she had fallen for it, promising her anything if she would only learn to walk on the false leg that Bernard had paid fifty pounds for. Quickly hailing a cab, she settled back, taking in the sights around her, her mind working furiously.

After Ruby had left the hospital, she had been sent to a convalescent home in Surrey. She had been there only a week when Bernard had received news of his father's death. The news couldn't have come at a worse time for him. He was just getting over his narrow escape from a nervous breakdown, and the visits to his father had helped to lift him out of his depression. At the funeral, she had watched him anxiously, fearing this latest blow would send him plummeting back into the dark gloom, but he had remained impassive. Although he had become closer to his father during the last few weeks of his life than ever before, the reconciliation had come too late for him to feel any deep sorrow. After the funeral, they had gone back to the house for the reading of the will, and Daisy had sat open-mouthed as the small wizened solicitor had told them that Bernard had been left the house and several thousand pounds-worth of stocks and shares, together with the wish of his father that he, Bernard, should leave the pub and take over his position in the City. His brother David, whom she had disliked on sight, had sat silently throughout the reading, only the dark red flush on his heavy features indicating his anger.

Bernard should have been suspicious at the way his brother had accepted the provisions of the will and been on his guard, but his mind had been so full of Ruby and the death of his father that he hadn't noticed anything out of the ordinary. It was only when they had taken up residence in the house that the valuable items of ornaments and paintings had been missed. After a hurried inventory, it had been discovered that David had made off with some four thousand pounds-worth of goods. He hadn't been heard of since. There was a whisper among the servants that he had gone to America, but it was dismissed as idle rumour. She for one was glad he was gone; she wouldn't have known a moment's peace if he had stayed in the house. Of course the loss of the valuables had come as a blow, but they still had been left with more than enough to live on.

''Ere we are, lady!'

Daisy's head jolted back sharply as the cab came to a halt. Getting down on to the familiar cobbled pavement, she paid the cabbie his money before looking around her in dismay. God, she had forgotten just how dirty the streets were in this part of London! She should have taken heed of Bernard. He had been livid when she'd told him of Ruby's request, dismissing it as utter nonsense that she should even consider bringing a girl like Lily into the house. However, Daisy had been quick to point out that although Lily might be uneducated, she was clean, hard-working, honest and bright. But it was Ruby's insistence that had worn him down as she had hobbled bravely into the room wearing the artificial leg, her eyes filled with unshed tears. Shrugging his shoulders, he had remarked that it was up to the pair of them, and he wanted no part in such a madcap scheme.

And now, standing here in the dirty cluttered street surrounded by the hotchpotch of people that made up the East End, she was beginning to agree with him. She looked up at the window behind which she had slept for fourteen years and then to the open door of the pub. The noise and laughter that had for so long been a part of her life now sounded threatening, and instinctively she stepped back, her breath coming in short puffs. She could always go back home and tell Ruby that she hadn't been able to find Lily, but she dismissed the idea as quickly as it had come. She would never do such a thing, and Ruby wouldn't let it rest there: she would keep on until Lily was found. Squaring her shoulders, she lifted her chin and sailed bravely through the door.

'Any work going, Guv'nor?'

The landlord of the Four Feathers looked disdainfully at the poorly-dressed dirty young girl standing in front of him before shaking his head. 'Sorry, love, I'm fully staffed. Try down at the Nag's Head.'

When no response came, he shrugged his shoulders and went to serve one of his customers. This was the third time she'd been in this week, but by the looks of her she wouldn't be bothering him for much longer; she looked as if she could snuff it at any moment. Pity – underneath all that dirt she could be a real looker. Well, it wasn't his problem, there were always the streets, but he doubted she would get many customers in her condition. Out of the corner of his eye he watched her leave the pub and breathed a sigh of relief. People like her were bad for business. 'Yes, sir, and what can I get you?'

Lily stumbled out on to the pavement, her eyes blurred with tears. That had been her last chance. She'd been in all the pubs this side of London, there was nowhere else for her to go. Her footsteps dragging, she made her way back to the tenement building. This would be her last night, as the rent man had warned her that if no rent was forthcoming tomorrow, she would have to clear out. Where she would go tomorrow she didn't know, and what's more she didn't care, not any more. She dragged herself up the stairs, pushed open her door and staggered over to the bed. Throwing herself down on the dirty-smelling sheets, she began to cry; deep heart-wrenching sobs that racked her frail body. She was going to die – she was only seventeen – but she was going to die alone and frightened in this dirty little room, and when she was gone, there wasn't a single person in the world who would miss her or mourn for her. She had no money, no job, and tomorrow she would have no home. When she could cry no more, she turned over on her back and stared at the bug-infested ceiling.

She couldn't believe that just a few months earlier she had been so happy, so full of optimism for the future. She'd had her job at the pub and she'd had Jack. When Mr Chadwick had told them he and the family would be leaving the pub, she had been overjoyed at the prospect of getting a new employer, someone who wouldn't treat her like dirt. She had been sorry to say goodbye to Mrs Chadwick and the two boys, but not to see the back of him. She had asked Daisy to let her know how Ruby got on, but of course she never expected to hear from her again. They lived in a different world now, a world she would never know or be a part of.

The new Guv'nor, Cyril Jackson, had turned out to be a small oily individual, a man who never tired of trying to get her into dark corners for a quick feel, despite her angry protests. Things had come to a head when his missus had caught them out in the yard. He had been trying it on as usual and she had been struggling to get him off her. Mrs Jackson, a stout woman as unpleasant as her husband, had ordered her from the pub and Lily had been only too happy to leave, confident that she would get another job the next day, but it hadn't been that easy. Word had been passed along the pub grapevine that she was a trouble-maker, and the landlords had closed ranks.

It hadn't been so bad at first with Jack bringing round pies and bottles of ale after he finished his shift at the pub. When he'd asked if he could move in with her, she had gratefully agreed, especially as he'd undertaken to pay the rent until she got fixed up. Wearily she closed her eyes. She had really thought that Jack had loved her and had envisaged wedding bells, whereas he had still looked on her as a companion, someone he could have a laugh and a joke with, nothing more. She could see him now, standing here in this room, his face smiling, expecting her to be pleased at his sudden stroke of good fortune. An old aunt whom he hadn't seen for years had died and left him fifty pounds. She'd watched silently as he'd packed his few belongings, all the while chattering excitedly as he told her his plans. Off to see the world, he'd said, his round face alight with excitement, with no word or thought as to how she'd manage without his support. But that wasn't quite true: he had given her five pounds to tide her over until she found a job. She had managed to keep smiling until the door had closed behind him for the last time, before collapsing on the floor in grief and despair. Maybe, if she'd told him about the baby she was carrying, he would have stayed – Jack wasn't the type of man who would desert his own child – but she had said nothing, merely wished him luck and sent him on his way. The money he had left her had soon run out and she had walked the streets looking for work. Pubs, shops and factories, the story had been the same: they were all fully staffed. There were always the streets, but she could never have brought herself to that level. Maybe if she hadn't lost the baby, lost it right here in this room, maybe the child would have given her something to strive for, a reason to keep on trying, a reason to live.

She had relived that night in her mind every day since it had happened. The sudden cramps before the agonizing pains had hit her, bringing her to her knees. In desperation she had clamped her hands over her stomach, as if by this action she could prevent the unborn child from leaving her body. She had watched in horror as the lifeblood of her baby had seeped from her womb over her shaking fingers. The scream she had emitted had brought no running of feet, no offers of help from her neighbours. How she had endured that terrible night, she didn't know. For days afterwards she had lain on her bed, still clothed in the blood-soaked dress, too weak to clean herself or try to get help. Finally, when the hunger pangs had become too hard to ignore, she had dragged herself once more out on to the streets for one last desperate search for work, but it was over now. The only place left to her was the workhouse, and she doubted whether even they would take her in in her condition: you were fed and clothed only if you could work for your keep. The only thing left to do was to lie down and wait for death to come. Turning over on her stomach, she finally slept.

Daisy emerged from the King's Arms, the place she had once called home, a bemused look on her face. She had expected to walk in and find Lily behind the bar; what she would have said to her she didn't know – she had planned to play it by ear – but now her carefully-laid plans were blown. The new owner, a smarmy little man, had told her importantly that he'd had to sack Lily on account of her laziness. Daisy had resisted the temptation to call the man a liar and had swept grandly out, leaving the customers staring curiously after her.

Once out on the pavement, she looked wildly around, at a loss for what to do next. She knew where Lily lived, but she couldn't go there, could she? Perhaps she was entertaining a gentleman. Immediately Daisy felt her cheeks redden with shame at the thought: Lily wasn't like that. Maybe it was she herself who had changed? Did she think she was superior now that she lived in a nice house in pleasant surroundings with servants to wait on her? She couldn't believe that she had once lived here in this street, alongside these people who now frightened and repelled her. 'Well, you did, and pleased to have a roof over your head! So don't start coming the grand madam now; it doesn't suit you,' her inner voice rebuked her sharply.

Her eyes strayed towards the tenement where, as far as she knew, Lily still lived. Well, she could only ask, couldn't she, and once she had done that, she could go home with a clear conscience. Now that she was actually here, the whole idea seemed utterly hopeless. Lily must have another job by now. How could she think that a lively happy-go-lucky person such as Lily would throw away her job in a noisy friendly pub to come and work as maid to a crippled child? Furthermore, could anyone who knew Lily picture her in a maid's uniform going about her duties quietly and bending her knee to visitors? To them, the whole idea would be laughable! Still, she was here now, so she must pluck up courage to enter that grim building and enquire after her former employee. Straightening her back, she jutted her chin out and marched towards the tenement.

Carefully stepping over the two drunks huddled in the doorway, Daisy picked her way through the piles of rubbish and filth that littered what passed for a hallway. Holding her handkerchief to her nose, she grimly made her way up the rickety planks that served for stairs, noticing the rags and papers that covered the smashed windows, the paper that hung in strips from the peeling walls, her eyes growing wider as she beheld the terrible sights. Dear God, how could anyone live in a place like this? she asked herself silently. If Lily did indeed live here, how could she take her home with her? What did they really know about the girl, except that she was cheerful and hardworking? Blast you, Ruby, and more fool me for agreeing to come here! Inching her way along the darkened corridor, she came to an open door.

'Excuse me, is there anyone at home?' she called out hesitantly, and jumped back fearfully as a woman appeared in the open doorway.

'What d'ya want, ducks?' the woman asked, showing black rotten stumps in her grin.

Daisy recoiled from the odour that was wafting from the woman. Lord, she stank! Then, taking a deep breath, she said, 'I'm looking for a girl called Lily Watkins. Does she still live here by any chance?' She was acutely aware of the fear in her voice and tried to keep it steady. It wouldn't do for the woman to know just how afraid and vulnerable she was feeling.

'Lily. Lily, you say? Now what would a fine gentlewoman like you be wanting with the likes of 'er?' the old crone cackled loudly.

'That is my business!' Daisy licked her lips nervously while at the same time backing away.

'Don't be so 'oity toity, ducks! If it's Lily you wants, she's three doors down – that's if she 'asn't gone to the Bastille. Not seen 'ide nor 'air of 'er for days.'

About to walk away, Daisy stopped and turned back, her face screwed up in bewilderment. 'The Bastille?' she asked, thinking she had misheard the woman.

'That's right, ducks. Not from round 'ere, are you? The workhouse is what you'd know it by, and that's where your friend's 'eading if she ain't already popped 'er clogs.' Then the door was shut rudely in Daisy's face.

Deeply troubled, Daisy continued down the hall. Upon reaching the third door down she hesitated before knocking, then brought her fist sharply on the peeling panelled door, calling out clearly, 'Lily, are you in there? It's Daisy Chadwick, I've come to see how you're getting on.'

The inaneness of her words echoed in her ears. Aware of other doors opening and the curious gazes, she took her courage in both hands and pushed open the door, only to come to a full stop at the sight of the young girl lying motionless on the filthy bed. Adopting the attitude she always did when distressed, she raised her hand to her mouth, biting down on her knuckles. What was she to do now? She couldn't just walk away and leave her, but if Lily were dead, or seriously ill, what could she do then? Oh dear, what a predicament to land herself in! But she was here, and it had taken courage she didn't know she possessed to get her this far. She wasn't running away now.

Striding over to the bed, she gingerly touched the thin shoulder. 'Lily? Lily, it's Daisy Chadwick. You remember me, surely? Lily, dear, are you ill?'

Lily heard the familiar voice and closed her eyes again. She must be in a worse state than she'd thought. Fancy thinking that Mrs Chadwick would come to this hole to find her! When the white-lace-gloved hand started to wipe the hair from her brow, she opened her eyes warily. One of the girls had been found knifed in her bed a couple of years back, and they still hadn't found out who'd done it. On recognizing the smiling face of Daisy bending over her, her eyes widened in disbelief. It wasn't a dream then; she was really here, but why?

Before Daisy could say anything else, Lily flung her arms round Daisy's waist, her sad tale bursting from her trembling lips in a torrent of woe. Forcing herself to sit on the grimy bed, Daisy pulled her into her arms and listened silently. When Lily came to the part about the baby, she gripped her hand tightly, feeling the tears come into her own eyes. The poor girl, to lose a child in that way, alone and frightened! The pain she must have endured didn't bear thinking about. She would like to bet that this was the first real cry she'd had since that awful night. Looking round the bare, dark, dirty room, Daisy shuddered. Well, the decision had been made for her. She couldn't leave her here. She wouldn't leave a stray dog in this hovel! When she got up, her foot came into contact with something soft, and, lifting her skirt, she let out a scream at the sight of the large black rat that lay at her feet.

'Oh, Mrs Chadwick, it's all right, it's dead. I killed it a couple of days ago. It's all right, it can't hurt you.' Lily was babbling fearfully, now desperate to keep Daisy with her for as long as possible, for the minute she walked out of this room her last chance to live would vanish. Weak with hunger, she suddenly bent over in agony as the cramps hit her stomach.

Still shuddering with revulsion, Daisy spoke sharply. 'Quickly, Lily, get your things together; I'm taking you home with me. You'll be looked after, but quickly, dear. I won't breathe easily until we're out of this place.'

Lily looked at her in wonderment, unable to believe her ears before saying, shamefaced, 'I don't have anyfink to pack. It's all in the pawn. I even 'ad to pawn me knife and fork to buy food. Everyfink's gone. I never 'ad much, but what I did 'ave is gorn.'

Ignoring Lily's woeful tone, Daisy bundled her from the room in her anxiety to be gone and within minutes they were in the street. Daisy raised her face to the sun, thankful to have escaped from the grimy building in one piece. Tucking Lily's arm through hers, she marched her down the street, looking for a cab. Conscious that the girl beside her was in a bad way, she went so far as to shout after one that was disappearing down the road. Bernard would have been horrified to hear her yell, 'Hey you, cabbie, wait a minute, please!' but this was no time for niceties. Soon they were seated in the comfortable interior, and patting Lily's hand reassuringly, Daisy settled back, her eyes closed in relief that they were on their way home.

Two hours later Daisy was lying in a steaming hot bath, having told Mary the maid to burn the clothes she'd come home in, along with Lily's. Even now, lying in the clean soapy water, she still felt dirty, as though the squalor of the tenement had permeated the very pores of her skin. When she rang the bell, it brought Mary running in with a large towel for her mistress to wrap herself in.

'How is Lily, Mary? Has she been given a bath and something to eat?'

'Yes, ma'am,' Mary answered, her head averted from Daisy's gaze.

'What is it, Mary? Are you annoyed about Lily being here? If so, there is no need to worry. Your job is safe for as long as you want it. Lily has come to help look after Miss Ruby and she won't interfere with any of your duties,' Daisy told the flushed girl kindly.

'It's not that, ma'am.'

'Well, what is it, girl? Speak up,' Daisy replied while taking a quick look at the clock on the mantelpiece. Bernard would be home in less than an hour, and she wanted Lily to be bathed and dressed in one of her old gowns before he returned. If he had seen them when they had come home, he would have been horrified.

She could still see the startled look on Mary's face when she'd opened the door to the pair of them. Having had neither the time nor the patience to explain the situation to the open-mouthed maid, she had simply asked her to fetch Mrs Mason, the cook, to help take care of Lily, and told her to fill a bath for the girl as quickly as possible. While she waited for Mary to speak, Daisy reflected ruefully that she still couldn't get used to being waited on, but it wasn't as if the house was teeming with servants. Apart from Mary, there were two under-maids for the heavy work, the cook, and the gardener who came in twice a week. There had been two stable-boys, but Bernard had dismissed them after he had sold his father's two horses. He could no longer bear to have a horse near him for any length of time, and instead of the smart carriage he had been so proud to ride in, he now used either the train to get to work, or he walked.

By some standards, theirs would be considered a small household, but it suited her. Although they weren't rich like some of Bernard's new friends, they were comfortable and, more important, Bernard was happy in his new position. Under the expert guidance of his father's old business associates, he had quickly stepped into his father's shoes, although, by his own admission, it would be many a long year before he developed the razor-sharp judgment of his father but he was content to continue taking advice until he could take over the reins himself.

'Ma'am!' Mary's voice brought Daisy back to the present. 'Ma'am, it's Miss Maybury. She's proper put out about Lily sleeping in Miss Ruby's bed, and Miss Ruby said that Lily is going to have her lessons with her from now on.' Mary's face was flushed with excitement.

Pulling her dressing-gown round her still wet body, Daisy strode to Ruby's room, intending to make the position firm and clear. Lily must have no illusions about her position here. She had already issued orders for the attic room to be cleaned and aired for her, and compared with what she had just left, it must seem like heaven. But as for sleeping in Ruby's bed even for a moment – well, the idea was intolerable! She only hoped that Lily had taken a bath as instructed.

As she neared Ruby's room, she was met by an irate Miss Maybury. 'Mrs Chadwick, I must protest, I really must!' The woman stood before her, her hands joined beneath her ample bosom, which at that moment was heaving with indignation.

Daisy groaned. Was she to get no peace today? She didn't want to upset the new governess, despite her already having shown an iron hand when dealing with her troublesome daughter, so that there was no danger that she would ever be reduced to tears like her predecessors. Taking a deep breath, Daisy said firmly, 'Now, Miss Maybury, Mary has told me about Lily, and I can assure you that she will be moving to her own room in the attic just as soon as Mary has made her bed ready. As for her taking lessons with Miss Ruby, of course that is out of the question.'

'I'm glad you think that way, Mrs Chadwick,' she said, more calmly.

Daisy, however, was quick to detect a note of triumph in her tone, and couldn't resist adding, 'I'm sure that even a woman of your experience would find it impossible to impart any knowledge to a girl of Lily's intelligence.' Smiling gently at the governess's startled face, she swept past her into Ruby's room.

At the scene that met her eyes, the carefully planned speech she had rehearsed died on her lips. There in Ruby's bed, lying between clean sheets, lay Lily, her face scrubbed clean, wearing one of her own nightdresses, the shining blonde hair lying in plaits over her chest, her eyes firmly closed as she slept her first carefree sleep in a long time. Beside her sat Ruby, keeping watch over her new maid.

As she made to creep away, Lily's eyes opened and, pulling herself upright, she called out softly, 'Thank you, Mrs Chadwick. Thank you ever so much, you've save my life!'

Daisy blinked as she heard the trembling words, then said firmly, 'Don't talk nonsense, Lily! You are being over-dramatic. You've been ill, so you may rest until you feel well enough to take up your duties. You are here to look after Miss Ruby. Do you think you will be able to manage that task?' She heard the sharpness of her own voice, and relaxed her face into a smile, the effect taking the sting from her words.

Weakly stretching out her arm, Lily clasped Ruby's hand in hers and, looking at her new charge, said fiercely, 'Oh, yes, Mrs Chadwick, I'll look after Ruby. I mean . . . Miss Ruby. I'll never leave her unless she wants me to. And I'll learn to speak proper so you won't be ashamed of me. I can if I want to, honest!'

Daisy looked at the earnest face and felt a lump come to her throat. In an effort to hide her emotion, she turned her attention to Ruby, and was met with the same look of gratitude.

'Thanks, Mum,' Ruby said, smiling broadly, her eyes alight with her new-found interest.

Not trusting herself to speak, Daisy merely nodded and backed from the room. Closing the door behind her, she leaned against it for a moment. She hadn't seen Ruby look so animated in a long time. It was as though new life had been breathed into her, and if that were true, all the fears and discomfort she had suffered that day would have been worth it. Walking slowly back to her own room, she reflected on what Lily had said about never leaving Ruby. Of course the poor girl was feeling grateful now – who in her position wouldn't? But once she had recovered her strength and saved a bit of money, she would in all probability become bored and leave to find a position more suited to her natural temperament.

But only time would tell. She would have to wait and see what the future held.

PART TWO

1895–1906

Chapter Eleven

The sound of a door closing brought Ruby out of an uneasy sleep. Forcing her eyes open, she listened intently for any other noises to explain what had disturbed her, but the house remained silent. Peering at her bedside clock, she could just make out the time from the watery grey light that was seeping through her open window – five o'clock. That could only mean that the noise must have been made by Bertie returning from his night shift. Hitching herself up on her pillow to prevent herself from falling back to sleep, she yawned loudly as she waited for her brother to pass her door. Minutes passed, and her eyelids began to droop, so she sat up straighter, opening her eyes as wide as she could manage. For her, this was the best time of the day when Bertie worked the night shift. He would always knock softly to see if she was awake before coming in, his face tired but animated as he told her about the evening he had had. Sometimes there was nothing much to tell, but Bertie could make even the most trivial incident sound exciting. When ten minutes had passed with no sign of him, she gave a sigh of disappointment and snuggled back into the warm bed. Maybe he had gone into the kitchen to make himself something to eat; he was always starving whenever he came off duty. But still, she told herself rebelliously, he could have forgone his hunger today of all days. He couldn't have forgotten her birthday, could he? Not Bertie!

Suddenly wide awake, she sat up again, all thought of sleep banished as she contemplated what the day had in store for her. There would be a party, of course, a dull affair as they usually were, but still a party, nevertheless. Dr Benson and his wife would attend, as they had done every year since they'd moved into this house, and then there would be a few of her dad's friends and their wives to make up the numbers. The tables in the drawing-room would be groaning under the weight of the food Cook would have spent all day preparing, most of which would end up back in the kitchen for the staff to enjoy at the end of the evening. She would put on her new dress and smile brightly for the guests, who in their turn would tell each other how marvellous it was that a girl of her tender years could be so brave in the face of such a terrible handicap. Biting down hard on her bottom lip, Ruby tried to banish the depressing picture from her mind.

Ever since the accident all those years ago she had had to endure such gatherings, and for her parents' sakes she had bitten her tongue many a time to stop herself from screaming at the stupid insensitive people who tended to treat her as a curiosity, rather than as a person in her own right. Dr Benson and his wife were the only people outside her immediate family that she had any time for, and it was these two whom she planned to waylay that night to try to enlist their help in persuading her dad to let her find employment. For a moment her courage wavered as she imagined his reaction when she informed him of her intentions, but she must do something; she couldn't remain forever tied to her family's side. They had protected and cosseted her for nearly eight years and she was grateful, but lately she had begun to feel stifled, trapped as surely as if she were imprisoned in a cage. Some young women in her position would probably relish such a sense of security and be content to spend the rest of their days safely cocooned in the bosom of their family, but Ruby wasn't made that way. Her character was too strong for her to remain dependent on others, no matter how good their intentions or how much she loved them. She had no idea as to how she would accomplish her independence, but that didn't worry her overmuch; there was always a way. She firmly believed that if you wanted something badly enough and were prepared to fight for it, any obstacle could be overcome.

Reassured, she settled herself down in the bed once more, as she had a long day ahead and, more important, a battle to win. Wondering vaguely why Bertie hadn't knocked on her door, she gave an impatient shrug followed by an enormous yawn before closing her eyes. She would no doubt find out later. Maybe he was too tired to talk this morning, or maybe . . . All thoughts were cut off as sleep finally overcame her.

Holding a glass of milk in one hand and a large sandwich in the other, Bertie crept silently past Ruby's bedroom, careful to avoid the loose floorboard that always emitted a loud creak when stepped on. Normally there was nothing he enjoyed more than to talk to his sister in the early hours of the morning, when, despite his numbing tiredness, the desire to talk about his work overcame the need to get some much-needed sleep, but not tonight. Safely inside his room, he put his breakfast down on the round polished table that stood by his bed and began to undress. Wearily he took off his heavy serge jacket, making a mental note to polish the silver buttons before he went back on duty. When he was fully undressed, he laid the navy uniform he was so proud of over the wicker chair alongside the tall round police helmet. Then, sitting down on his bed, he held his head in his hands as he tried to keep back the tears that had been threatening ever since he had found the small body several hours earlier, but the effort to keep his emotions in check proved futile. Slowly the tears began to fall, bringing with them some small measure of relief from the tension that had been tearing at his body. Filled with shame at his weakness, he got unsteadily to his feet while wiping a hand angrily across his red-rimmed eyes. Stop it! he told himself savagely. Pull yourself together, man! You're a police officer – you can't fall to pieces every time you see a dead body.

Pacing the carpeted floor, he tried to put the picture that had been tormenting him from his mind, but to no avail. Walking over to the window, he cooled his head against the glass, and as if looking into a mirror, he saw again the tiny blue body of the baby he had found lying in a shop doorway as he had made his rounds. He wouldn't have noticed it but for the two stray cats sitting beside it pulling at the dirty piece of blanket that partly covered the naked body. He had put the tiny scrap of humanity inside his jacket, in the vain hope that if he could get some warmth into the child he could bring it back to life. Then, running as if his own life depended on it, he had arrived back at the police station breathless and agitated to be met by the scathing comments of his desk sergeant.

Red-faced with humiliation, he had stood silent while the sergeant had berated him for reacting like a young schoolboy to a sight which, although tragic, was no excuse to forget his position as an officer of the law. These things happened all the time: young girls got themselves pregnant, women, already burdened with too many mouths to feed, often abandoned their babies in the side streets and alleys. Only last week two newborn infants had been fished out of the river. Bertie had listened to the tirade, not trusting himself to speak, and now at home in his warm comfortable room a world away from the streets he had just left, he wondered bitterly if he was cut out for the job he had dreamed about since a young boy. More to the point, was it worth it? To say that his father had been disappointed in his choice of profession would be an understatement.

When, two years earlier, he had informed Bernard of his intention to join the police force, his father had at first tried to talk him out of the idea, thinking it just a whim on the part of a young impressionable man, but when he had finally realized that Bertie was deadly serious, he had been furious. He had reminded him of the expensive education he had paid for him and George, an education that would be wasted as a lowly police constable, and the people he would be forced to mix with. Bertie had fought back, telling his father that he wouldn't always be a constable; he meant to rise in the ranks and would make good use of his education to achieve that goal. The argument had raged for hours until finally Bernard had stormed from the room, shouting that he would give him six months to come to his senses, and if at the end of that time he still refused to change his mind, he could find somewhere else to live. At the end of the allotted time, when Bertie showed no signs of leaving the constabulary, Bernard had relented on condition that he change out of uniform as soon as he entered the house, preferably by the back entrance.

Rubbing his eyes tiredly, Bertie walked back to his bed. The fact that his father was ashamed of the job that he himself loved was deeply upsetting, and he had only been allowed to remain at home through the tearful intervention of his mother. He had been more than willing to leave and find lodgings, for at that time the atmosphere in the house had been unbearable. Now, nearly two years on, the tension had eased somewhat, although his father still insisted that he should on no account wear uniform in the house for fear of his friends seeing his eldest son dressed in such a lowly garb. His mother, bless her, after the initial shock, had given him her blessing, but he knew she suffered agonies every time he went out of the house, fearing that some dreadful fate would befall him as he walked the crime-ravaged streets of the East End.

George, at the tender age of sixteen, had taken his place working alongside his father in the salubrious stockbroker building in the city. Bertie knew that George had no love for the daily business of buying stocks and shares, finding it dull in the extreme, but George had always been complacent as a child, and the years hadn't changed him. He still wanted to please everyone, to be everyone's friend, and to achieve that purpose he would always take the line of least resistance. Whether he was happy with his life, none of the family could ever really tell, for George always kept his feelings close to his chest, preferring to say and do what people expected of him rather than what he wanted for himself.

Picking up the sandwich, Bertie looked at it for a moment before returning it to the plate in disgust. He was no longer hungry; all he wanted to do now was to sleep, to banish the picture of the tiny blue body from his mind. If only he could go to his father, to talk to him about his work, to be able to unburden himself and so relieve the tension that seemed to be tearing at his very soul. But that luxury would always be denied him. Not only was he forbidden to wear his uniform proudly, he was also under strict instructions never on any account to talk about his work in the presence of the family. Only Ruby was interested in his job, and when they were alone, she would ask, no demand, to be told all about the people he met in the line of duty.

As she came to mind, he opened his heavy eyes briefly. God, it was her eighteenth birthday today, and he would bet all the money he had in his pockets that she had been waiting for him to come to her room. Again he felt the prickle of tears start to form behind his closed eyelids. Poor Ruby, stuck here in this house all day, never venturing further than the shops in the West End, and then by private carriage, always accompanied by either his mother or Lily. She never complained, but Bertie knew what agonies of mind she must be suffering to have to live a life full of restrictions. His beautiful little sister who had loved nothing more than to run and jump, play leap-frog and rounders, who had been forever getting into mischief and loving every minute of it, her blue eyes always sparkling with laughter. He was sure that she had come to terms with her disability, but it was difficult to know for certain as she rarely spoke about it. She had worked hard over the years to manage her false leg, and was now so adept at walking that no one would ever know of its existence. She limped, of course, that was only to be expected, and some days were worse than others, but at least the need to be measured and fitted periodically for a new leg was no longer there, as she would be unlikely to grow any more now.

He hoped she wasn't waiting for him to visit her – he couldn't face anyone at the moment, and he would never be able to tell her about the baby, that horror was something he would have to bear alone. He was thankful that he had two days' leave, for he was in no hurry to return to the station and face his sergeant. He was still feeling ashamed and humiliated at the way he had behaved but, being the man he was, he couldn't have reacted in any other way. How the sergeant could remain unmoved at the sight of such a pathetic scrap of humanity was beyond him. He could hear him now, bellowing at him, as he'd stood mutely with the baby still cuddled close to his chest.

'You'd better toughen up, Chadwick! You'll get used to it, and a sight worse, before you're much older. Now clear off home. You're no good to me in the state you're in.' The words echoed in Bertie's brain as he silently punched his pillow. He'd never get used to it, never. And if the day ever came when he could be as hard faced as his sergeant, he would give up the job, but until then he would struggle on the best he could. Giving his pillow one final punch he settled himself down in the bed, but it was a long time before he finally succumbed to sleep.

Chapter Twelve

'Oh, you look lovely, Miss Ruby! That colour blue really suits you,' Lily said happily as she piled the long chestnut hair on top of Ruby's head.

Ruby smiled back faintly as she inspected her reflection in the ornate dressing-table mirror. Yes, she had to agree she did look nice, but to what purpose? No one was going to see her – that was, no one who would really appreciate her in the way she craved to be noticed. When Lily had finished her hair and stood back to get a better look at the whole effect, Ruby leaned forward, her elbows resting on the dressing-table, her face cupped in her hands as she stared at herself in the mirror. She saw a young woman clothed in an expensive dress of midnight blue, the top of which was cut decorously to cover her breasts but left the wide expanse of her neck and throat bare, framing perfectly the diamond necklace she had received from her father for her birthday. She fingered it nervously and then moved her hand to the matching earrings that hung heavily from her lobes. The set had belonged to her grandmother, and had escaped her Uncle David's clutches only by chance. At the time he had been busily collecting as many valuables as he could while he could, but these had been safely stored in a vault at her grandfather's bank to await re-evaluation. She had protested strongly that the precious jewels should be given to her mother, but Daisy had smiled and said they would look much better on a younger neck, and besides, they had been saving them for her for years. The pride and happiness on her parents' faces had stopped any further protests she might have made, but why did she feel so uncomfortable about taking the expensive presents they insisted on showering upon her? Suddenly, inexplicably, she began to shake, and rose clumsily to her feet.

'What's wrong, Miss Ruby? Don't you feel well?' Lily asked anxiously.

'Yes, I'm fine, Lily, don't worry yourself. I'm just excited about my birthday, I suppose.' She saw the doubtful look that passed over Lily's face. 'As a matter of fact, I do feel a little faint. it must be this dreadful corset you've strapped me into. I'm not used to being so restricted. Now I know why Mother refuses to wear one except on special occasions.' But the words were spoken quickly, too quickly to hold any real conviction.

Lily looked down at the bowed head of the girl she had looked after for nearly eight years and felt a pang of apprehension. The blatant lie about the corset was merely an excuse to fob off any probing questions, but Lily wasn't going to be put off. Walking quickly across the room, she made sure the door was closed before returning to Ruby's side, and then in a clear voice she asked firmly, 'What's the matter, Miss Ruby? And don't give me that old flannel about your corset being too tight. It's not the first time you've worn one, so don't try to con me. I know you too well!'

Ruby looked up into the face of her dearest friend and wondered how she could explain something she herself didn't understand. Swallowing twice, she wetted her lips, then, her voice low and soft, she said, 'I don't belong here, Lily. Not in this house, in these fancy clothes and especially not decked out in diamonds. It's hard to explain, but I feel out of place, somehow.' Raising her eyes to Lily's, she ended simply, 'I belong in the East End, among the people I grew up with. I don't know why I feel this way, but I always have. I thought I'd get used to living this life, but the older I get the more uncomfortable I am. Bertie feels the same way; that's why he does the job he does. I know it's difficult for you to understand as I don't really understand it myself. The only thing I'm sure of is that if I live to be a hundred I'll never be comfortable living in the lap of luxury, and neither will Bertie. He stays only because of Mother . . . and me, of course. If it weren't for us, he'd have left years ago. George is the only one who has settled into his new life; maybe because he's younger than Bertie and me. Oh, I don't know. I only know I can't stay here much longer. I have to be free to make my own way in life.'

Her words trailed off miserably as she looked into Lily's worried face. It was impossible. Lily would never understand how anyone could want to leave a life such as they had now, but the reason was quite simple. Ruby was the product of her early environment, she would always be, inside, what her early years had made her. The rest was a façade, a pleasing façade that gave pleasure to her parents and made her life a misery. She had long ago realized the meaning of the words 'A bird in a gilded cage', and that's just what she likened herself to. She must break free; her rebellious spirit would not allow her to continue in this way of life for much longer. She planned to speak to her dad after the guests had gone, but before that she would endeavour to enlist the help of Dr Benson and his wife. She felt sure that they alone knew how she felt; no words had ever been spoken on the subject, but it was something about their attitude to her. They had never treated her as an invalid, and for that she was grateful. Maybe she was wrong, but if so, she would tackle her dad by herself. He would be deeply hurt, as would her mum, and for that she was truly sorry, but if she didn't speak out now she would go mad. So wrapped up in her thoughts was she that she had forgotten about Lily until she spoke.

'And what do you intend to do, Ruby?' The 'Miss' had been dropped, as it frequently was when Lily was upset or agitated. 'Pack a few things and hurry back to the East End, and what then? Get yourself a job in a pub, like I did? Or maybe you intend getting started in one of the sweatshops? Oh, that would be an education for you, that would really make you feel you were among the people of the East End you talk so grandly about! And where do you propose to live, eh? You might be lucky and get my old room; you'd like that. No fear of any luxury there, and you'd have plenty of company: why, the rats and cockroaches would hurry out to meet you – and the neighbours, well, you wouldn't believe the reception they'd give you.'

Ruby's eyes widened at the bitterness in her friend's voice. 'Lily, why are you so angry?' she asked hesitantly; she had never seen Lily like this before.

'Angry? Angry, you say? Yes, I'm angry, bloody angry, and amazed that you could be so stupid. There's a world of difference between the East End you knew and the East End I was forced to grow up in. You moan that you're cosseted – well, let me tell you, madam, you've always been protected, only you never knew it.'

Amazed at the unexpected outburst, Ruby could only sit and stare, her mouth agape as Lily ranted on. Fearful that someone would hear the altercation, she got to her feet, putting out her hands to her friend, this girl she had come to love as she would a sister, and said gently, 'Lily, Lily, calm down, please! I have no intention of packing my bags and scooting back to the seedy streets of Whitechapel. I'd have a hard time to scoot anywhere, wouldn't I?' Ruby smiled, trying to inject some humour into the tense atmosphere, but Lily refused to be mollified.

'You don't know you're born!' she answered back, her voice still tinged with bitterness and anger, and her next words wiped the smile from Ruby's face and made her head jerk back as if she'd been slapped. 'You seem to be forgetting about your disability. God knows it's hard enough to survive in this world, but what chance do you think you'd have with your handicap?'

As the damning word came from her mouth, Lily clapped her hand over her face in dismay, and when Ruby's face reddened with anger she knew she had overstepped her position: too late she realized that she had gone too far. In all the years she'd worked in this house she had never heard Ruby moan about her misfortune; even when the stump was hurting, she never complained. She remembered the first few months when Ruby would call out in the night, and she would rush into her room to find her frantically scratching and scrabbling at the sheets in a vain attempt to relieve the itching in an ankle that was no longer there. At these times Lily would hold her young mistress in her arms, speaking to her softly until she fell back to sleep, the tears still wet upon her face. But Ruby was no longer a young girl; she was a woman now, a woman with a strong character and a sharp tongue. Now she watched in alarm and apprehension as Ruby walked towards her, her head held high, the tiny spots of anger still evident on her cheeks.

'How dare you talk to me like that, Lily? You forget yourself!' Ruby the friend was gone, and in her place stood a woman of breeding, a woman too proud to accept that her disability would in any way prevent her from carrying out her plans, whatever they might be.

She was forced to step back as Ruby advanced upon her. 'Ruby, please, I'm sorry . . .'

'*Miss* Ruby to you, Lily. You are in danger of crossing the line of familiarity, I will not be spoken to in such an insolent manner, especially by a servant!' Ruby's voice was deceptively soft, only the glint in her bright blue eyes showing her anger.

Lily was forced to back away, her hands nervously smoothing down her white starched apron, and then in a placating voice she said quietly, 'Look, Miss Ruby, I didn't mean any harm. I'm only thinking of you. I know how you feel . . .'

'You *don't* know how I feel. You have no idea how I feel. Nobody does!' Ruby hissed between clenched teeth, her face only inches from Lily's. 'Do *you* know what it's like to be mutilated? To feel disgust at the sight of your own body? Have you any idea what it's like to be set apart from other people, so-called "normal" people? And what about the shame I feel when I see people staring and smiling at me while

102

their minds' eyes try to penetrate my clothing to see beneath, to the severed stump. Oh, I've seen them, Lily, the so-called friends who call to pay their respects. I'm an object of curiosity to them, and they try to salve their consciences by proclaiming "What a brave girl you are" while trying to hide the revulsion they feel if I get too close to them. I'm a cripple, Lily. That's what they call me behind my back: a *cripple*! Well, let me tell you – my handicap, as you so delicately put it, is not going to stop me from leading a normal life. I'm going to succeed on my own, and by doing so maybe I'll recapture something I lost a long time ago: my self respect.' She was about to say more, but to her horror she felt her lips begin to tremble and tears spring to her eyes. As if she'd been caught in a shameful act, she covered her face and turned away from Lily, her head bowed.

As Ruby walked unsteadily to the bed, Lily began to breathe easier as the fear left her body and compassion took its place. Uncertain of Ruby's reaction, she tentatively put out her hand, resting it on Ruby's shoulder ready to pull it away quickly if she met with a rebuff. When no movement came, she said gently, 'God, Ruby, I never dreamed you were suffering so much. Why didn't you ever let on how you were feeling?'

Taking a shuddering breath, Ruby turned to face Lily. 'I couldn't. I've always felt this way, but I could never bring myself to put it into words.' Her speech was jerky as she fought for self-control.

'I'm so sorry, Ruby, I don't know what to say. And you were right: I don't know how you feel, but this much I do know, that if you really want to leave here and get a job, if it means that much to you, I'll come with you. I wouldn't want to stay on here if you left, and you will leave, I know that now.'

A loud knock on the door turned both their heads round in alarm. 'Are you decent, girls?' Bertie's voice called out cheerfully.

Ruby clutched at Lily's arm, whispering urgently, 'Go and tell him I'm not ready yet. I don't want him to see me like this. Hurry, Lily, before he comes in.'

Pushing Lily away, she stumbled to the small bathroom that led off from her room. Her breathing still coming in painful jerks, she listened intently as Lily told Bertie to come back in ten minutes as 'Miss Ruby' wasn't quite ready yet. When she heard her bedroom door close, she quickly washed her tear-stained face in cold water.

'It's all right, he's gone. Look, if you don't feel up to facing anyone tonight, I can always say you're not well,' Lily said anxiously.

'What, and have my Mum and Dad fussing over me all evening?

No, thank you! If you could lend me some of your face-powder to cover the redness round my eyes, I'm sure no one will know I've been crying.'

Lily hurried from the room, reappearing moments later with the box of face-powder she had bought over six months ago and had never used. Following Ruby back into the bedroom, she sat her down in front of the dressing-table and deftly set about repairing her complexion. 'There, not a bad job, if I do say so myself! Maybe we could get a job in the theatre; they're always looking for make-up girls.'

Ruby said nothing for a moment, then, gently laying her hand on Lily's arm, she whispered, 'What I said, Lily . . . I didn't mean to take my feelings out on you. You've always been so good to me, you didn't deserve to be treated like that. I'm sorry, it'll never happen again, I promise.' As Lily made to answer, Ruby held up her hand. 'No, don't say anything, not yet. What you said before, about me packing a bag and making my way back to the East End, well you were right to ridicule me. I wouldn't last five minutes, and deep down I always knew it.'

'Does that mean you've changed your mind about leaving?' Lily asked hopefully.

Ruby was quick to see the relief that passed over Lily's face, and laughed out loud, her good humour restored once more. 'No, I haven't changed my mind about leaving. Let's just say I'll have to re-think my original plans.'

It was at this fortuitous moment that Bertie returned. Knocking sharply on the door, this time he didn't wait for permission, but walked into the room, his hand covering his eyes, a wide grin on his face. 'All right, ladies! Ready or not, here I come.' Ruby and Lily smiled at each other, the last fifteen minutes forgiven, if not forgotten. Bertie lowered his hand and looked from one to the other before declaring, 'Well now, I don't know which of you is the prettiest! I'm spoilt for choice.' Leaning towards Lily, he said in a mock whisper, 'I suppose I'll have to choose Ruby, seeing as it's her birthday, but another time, Lily, another time!' Then, giving her a broad wink, he held out his arm to Ruby.

Lily looked on happily as they stood arm in arm. Oh, they did make a lovely couple. Ruby all decked out in her new finery and Mister Bertie dressed in smart black tails and trousers and a crisp white shirt instead of that hateful uniform he left the house in each day. Daisy and Ruby weren't the only ones who worried about his choice of profession. Lifting her eyes slightly, she looked at his clean-shaven smiling face and felt the familiar tug at her insides that she experienced whenever she saw him. Aware that Ruby was watching her, she quickly dropped her gaze, saying, 'Your cravat's crooked, Mister Bertie.'

Ruby turned to face him, saying cheerfully, 'Here, let me straighten it. We don't want to let Father down in front of his friends, do we?' The simple task completed, she turned back to Lily and, taking her hand in hers, she said softly, 'We'll talk more later.' Then, ignoring Bertie's curious look at the tender action he had just witnessed, she marched him from the room.

As the door closed behind them, the smile slowly dropped from Lily's face. Picking up the yellow dress that Ruby had discarded earlier, she rolled it in a tight ball, together with the underwear that littered the bed. Putting the bundle of clothes by the door ready to be taken down to the laundry, she set about tidying up. When she had finished, she stood back to study her handiwork, then satisfied that everything was in order, she made her way to her own room that was situated beside the bathroom she shared with Ruby. It wasn't as large or as luxurious as Ruby's, of course, but it was a far cry from the tiny attic she had originally been allocated. Seating herself in the wicker chair by the window, she gazed into the night, her eyes misty with unshed tears.

Despite the controlled front she had displayed for the benefit of Mister Bertie, she was still feeling shaken by the confrontation she'd had with Ruby, added to which was the worry about what would happen to her once Ruby left the house. The position she held now would obviously not exist any more, so she, like Ruby, must begin to make plans for her future. Finding another job shouldn't prove too difficult. After all, she was no longer the ignorant illiterate girl who had arrived here dirty and near to death from starvation all those years ago, and she had Ruby and Mrs Chadwick to thank for that.

It was Ruby who had pleaded for her to be allowed to sit in on her lessons and Mrs Chadwick had heartily endorsed this plea, much to the horrified disapproval of that old dragon Miss Maybury, but even she had been grudgingly surprised at the speed and natural ability that Lily had shown in her efforts to achieve an education. The Cockney idiom and poor grammar she had once used had almost entirely disappeared, although she often lapsed back into the old way of speaking when upset or excited. She was certain that Mrs Chadwick would give her a good reference, so why did she feel so desolate? A smiling face winking at her suddenly appeared in front of her closed eyes, and impatiently she brushed the mental image away; there was no future for her in that quarter.

Then her mind started to take in the individual objects in her room, as if storing them away safely in her memory where they could never be taken from her. A few feet away stood her single bed draped in a warm brown coverlet, and there beside it rested her very own wardrobe containing her three dresses for her afternoons off and the two navy house-dresses and aprons. Beside these hung her grey dress with the white collar and cuffs, which was used only when she was called upon to take over the role of housekeeper on special occasions when Mr Chadwick held business lunches for his associates from the City. Over in the far corner were the writing-table and chair that Ruby had presented her with on her twentieth birthday five years ago, and which she now used as a receptacle for her weekly magazines and the occasional book she would borrow from the library downstairs.

The room seemed to dip and blur as she tried to hang on to the familiar images, and silently she cried out, 'Don't go, Ruby! Please don't leave, because I don't want to. This is my home now. Please don't make me have to start all over again. I'm frightened, Ruby! Please see how afraid I am and stay! Please, Ruby, please!'

Chapter Thirteen

'**H**appy birthday, dear. I hope our small gift will afford you some pleasure.'

Ruby took the gaily wrapped parcel from the outstretched hand, her mind searching frantically to remember the woman's name. 'Thank you, I'm sure I will,' she answered brightly, hoping the omission of the elusive name would go unnoticed. Pulling off the red ribbon, she unwrapped the present, her heart sinking as she saw the contents. 'Another lot of poxy handkerchiefs.' She must have a drawer full of them by now! 'Oh, they're lovely; thank you again. It was very kind of you to think of me.'

'Dearie me, Ruby, it was my pleasure! I only wish I'd had more time to visit the West End stores for something more original,' gushed the oversized nameless person sitting beside her.

'So do I,' thought Ruby, the smile still fixed firmly on her face.

'I was only saying to Vanessa the other day how difficult it is to buy a present for someone one isn't fully acquainted with, and she said . . .'

Ruby's concentration wandered as she found herself nodding and smiling, adding a 'Really' and 'That's very interesting' in what she hoped were suitable rejoinders in the woman's conversation while her gaze wandered round the long dining-table before settling on her brothers.

To her right sat Bertie and George, a young blonde-haired, rather insipid-looking girl sandwiched between them. This no doubt was Vanessa, who seemed to Ruby's keen eyes to be running the emotional gamut between embarrassment and excitement as the two young men vied for her attention. She watched with amusement as Bertie leaned closer to the girl, whispering something into her ear that caused the already pink complexion to redden into an unbecoming blush. As for her younger brother, poor George seemed to be struggling to compete with Bertie to impress the now giggling Vanessa, but his valiant efforts to attract the girl's attention were in vain. As far as charm and personality went, George was no match for Bertie! George eventually gave up the struggle and returned his attention to the half-empty wine glass on the table in front of him, while his hand played nervously with the hem of the white tablecloth.

Looking at him sitting so miserable and out of his depth, Ruby was reminded strongly of her uncle David. George had inherited the same heavy features, and his young body, already broad and stocky, suggested the likelihood of his running to fat in later years, but thankfully the resemblance was merely outward; there was nothing, as yet, to suggest that George had inherited any of uncle David's traits, and she thanked God for it. She had met her uncle only once and had taken an immediate dislike to the man, and had been as relieved as Daisy to hear of his sudden departure, even if he had taken half his father's treasures with him.

A sudden loud laugh made her look towards the head of the table, where Bernard and Daisy sat, their faces wreathed in smiles as they listened to Dr Benson telling some tale, his small thin wife sitting beside him also seeming to be hanging on his every word, her face alight with merriment. As another loud laugh split the air, Ruby found herself grinning as though she too were in on the joke that was causing so much amusement.

At that moment Bernard lifted his glass of port and raised it in her direction. The unexpected action brought a lump to Ruby's throat. He looked so happy, so proud. How could she spoil the evening for him by telling him she was leaving the house to find work, to make a life of her own, a life that would no longer include him? But she must; she couldn't change her mind now, not after confiding in Dr Benson and extracting his promise to intercede on her behalf. When she was sure her father was no longer watching her, she began to study him. He was still handsome, despite his forty-eight years, and although the once lean frame had filled out, there wasn't an ounce of spare fat on his body. The only concession to the years was a sprinkling of grey in his dark hair and the neat moustache that now adorned his upper lip. Her eyes softened. It was hard to believe that this same man had once ruled them all with a rod of iron.

Turning her eyes from him, she looked at her mother, and felt a thrill of pride run through her body. The black satin dress she was wearing suited her to perfection, as did the string of gleaming pearls round her bare neck. Unlike her dad, no grey had yet invaded the mass of shiny black hair that was piled softly round the crown of her head.

A touch on her arm brought her rudely from her reverie. 'Ruby, are you unwell? You look flushed.'

She reluctantly returned her attention to the woman sitting beside her, and replied, 'I'm quite well, thank you, although it is a little stuffy in here, don't you think?' while thinking, 'What *is* the woman's name?'

'Yes, yes, I was thinking that myself. Would you be so kind as to ask one of the maids to show me to the ladies' room. I would like to wash my hands.'

'Of course,' Ruby answered, raising her hand in the direction of Mary, who imdiately came to her side. 'Mary, would you show Mrs . . . um, Mrs . . . er . . .' Oh, Lord, this was embarrassing!

Bertie, who had been listening to the exchange with amusement, decided to come to Ruby's rescue. Leaning over the table, he said gaily, 'You must forgive my sister, Mrs Stacey. She has an appalling memory for names.'

Ruby glared at him. He could have phrased it in a better way! Turning from his smiling face she said sweetly, 'Do forgive me, Mrs Stacey, and take no notice of my dear brother. His favourite pastime is in teasing me.' Then, addressing Mary, she said, 'Show Mrs Stacey to the ladies' cloakroom, Mary, she wishes to wash her hands.'

When the woman had left the table, Ruby turned on Bertie. 'Did you have to show me up like that? You could have found an easier way to tell me her name instead of embarrassing me.'

Bertie threw back his head and laughed loudly. 'Embarrass you, Ruby, impossible! The only person embarrassed was Mrs Stacey. "Wash her hands", indeed! Why can't women just say they need to use the lavatory. We all have to, it's nothing to be ashamed of.'

Still angry with him, Ruby relied stiffly, 'Ladies don't refer to such matters in male company. There is such a thing as etiquette.'

Bertie stared at her in amazement, for this wasn't the Ruby he knew and loved. She was on her high horse, and no mistake. 'Etiquette', for God's sake! She was the last person to worry about the social refinements of life. Stifling the desire to laugh again, he took her trembling hands. 'What is it, Ruby? What's up? And don't insult my intelligence by saying nothing's wrong, I know you too well. Have you had a row with Lily? Is that it? Is that why you said you'd talk to her later?' When Ruby remained silent, he pulled his chair out from under the table and moved closer to her, much to the chagrin of the young Vanessa, who was now looking very put out at being ignored. 'Look, Ruby, we've never had any secrets, have we? So come on, spill the beans before that old trout comes back,' he whispered urgently.

Ruby wavered for a moment. She would rather have waited until Dr Benson had had a chance to talk to her dad, but the desire to tell Bertie her plans was too strong. Turning to face him, she said simply, 'I'm going to leave home and get a job.'

If she had announced she was going to run off with the coalman, Bertie couldn't have been more stunned. Surprised, no. He had always known that one day she would tire of the dullness and inactivity of her life, but not yet; she'd just turned eighteen, and where would she go, what would she do? Looking at her set face, he felt the first stirrings of fear run up his spine. He had seen that same look many times, and if he attempted to dissuade her by pointing out the obvious, she would only shut him out completely. So, jerking his head in the direction of Bernard, he said quietly, 'He'll never agree.'

With a confidence she was far from feeling, Ruby lifted her head and said firmly, 'Dr Benson agrees that I should have my independence, and he's going to have a word with Dad when the other guests have left. Besides, you're too hard on him. I know he was strict with us when we were children, but he's changed. He's much kinder now, he'll understand.'

Bertie closed his eyes in disbelief. Surely she didn't think their father would let her leave this house without argument, and as for him changing his ways . . . 'Huh!'

Seeing the expression on his face, Ruby said earnestly, 'He *has* changed, Bertie. He's nowhere near as strict as he used to be.'

'Maybe not to you, but he's still wielding the whip as far as George and I are concerned.' Bertie's face became grim and bitter, forcing her to look away, but she couldn't shut out his words. 'Have you forgotten the uproar when I announced my decision to join the police? How he ranted and raved like a madman? He would have thrown me out on to the streets but for Mother intervening on my behalf. Even now, I have to creep in and out of the house like a common criminal because the sight of my uniform both infuriates and shames him!'

'He worries about you, Bertie. We all do,' Ruby whispered lamely.

'Rubbish! He doesn't care a fig about me. And what about George, forced into a job he hates just to keep the old man happy? Oh, he's never said anything, but then George wouldn't. He'll always be content to let someone run his life for him. I only hope for his sake he marries a strong-minded woman; he'd be as helpless as a child without someone to make his decisions for him. He's not like us, he doesn't have our strength of character . . .' Too late he realized what he'd said, and when he saw the triumphant smile light up Ruby's face, his heart sank.

'You're right, Bertie. George is weak, but we're not. We'll always get what we want because we're prepared to fight for the right to live our own lives. You've already fought your battle, and won. My fight is just beginning.' Clasping his hand, she said urgently, 'Help me, Bertie? Come with me when I face Father.'

The fact that she had used the term 'Father' conveyed to Bertie the extent of her feelings. For as long as he could remember Ruby had always referred to their parents as 'Mum and Dad', and this familiarity was just another example of how she differed from George and himself. He could no more think of calling his father 'Dad' than he could of addressing the queen as 'Vicky'. Not that he was ever likely to meet that grand lady, but the thought was the same. He felt Ruby increase the pressure on his hand and shifted in his chair uncomfortably; then, without raising his head, he muttered thickly, 'I'm sorry, Ruby, I can't.'

He felt her loosen her grip on his hand and tentatively raised his eyes to look at her, but such was the look of hurt and accusation she gave him that he was compelled to bow his head once more. It was with great relief that he saw Mrs Stacey bearing down on them and quickly took the opportunity to return his attention to the waiting Vanessa.

He listened with only half an ear to the girl's ramblings while his mind continued to mull over Ruby's startling revelations, his active brain already formulating a plan to escape from the house as soon as the party was over. He didn't want to be around when his father heard the news from Dr Benson. Contrary to Ruby's insistence that their father had mellowed, he knew differently. He wondered if her opinion of her 'dad', as she called him, would change if she were ever to find out the truth about Lady and how Bernard had beaten the unfortunate horse so severely she had had to be put down. But, wait a minute, he must be fair: his father had been half out of his mind with grief when he had laid into Lady with the riding-whip. Any man would have reacted likewise in similar circumstances.

Bertie could still remember vividly that day they had returned from the hospital and had watched with tears in their young, bewildered, eyes as their strong and capable father had stumbled from the room like a man twice his age. It was then that their mother had sat them down gently and elicited a promise that they would never tell Ruby what had happened to her beloved horse. They must stand by the story that both Lady and Nobby had been taken to a farm in the country because they could no longer afford to keep them. She had stressed the importance of keeping to this story, and had apologized for making them accessories to a lie. Then she had added, sadly, that it would be only half a lie, because their father would probably send Nobby away as soon as possible. After what had happened, for quite some time he wouldn't be able to stand the thought of any horse being dependent on him. Bertie remembered also how Ruby's eyes had clouded over when their mother had repeated this lie in their presence before turning her back on the three of them to stare fixedly out of the window of her new bedroom; she had never mentioned Lady again. Shrugging his shoulders impatiently, he glanced over at the mantelpiece to the gold and marble clock that rested grandly on the wide ledge. Nine-thirty. Good! With any luck, the party would break up soon, and the moment the last guest had left the house he intended to grab George and make for the nearest pub. Brushing aside his feelings of guilt and shame, he gave a bewildered-looking George a broad wink and moved closer to Vanessa.

'Goodnight, and thank you for coming,' Ruby said pleasantly to Mr and Mrs Stacey and the simpering Vanessa, her jaws aching from the effort to keep the smile on her tired face. The Staceys were the last guests to leave, and Ruby, her duties over, left her parents to see them to their coaches and limped tiredly along the hall to the parlour where Dr Benson and his wife were waiting for her. They looked up as she entered the room, and Ruby was quick to see the look that passed between them. Sinking into a soft leather chair, she waited for a moment before Mrs Benson spoke.

'Are you absolutely sure about this, Ruby?' Her face was full of concern as she bent towards her.

Ruby gazed softly into the kind face, and then in a clear voice she answered, 'I've never been more sure of anything in my entire life.'

The determination in her voice brought Dr Benson to his feet. Crossing the short space that separated them, he placed his hand gently on her shoulder. 'Fair enough, my dear, fair enough. I'll do what I can, but it won't be easy. No, it won't be easy,' he repeated thoughtfully.

Ruby flashed him a grateful smile, then turned to the doorway as Bernard and Daisy entered the room arm in arm.

'Well, I think everything went off very well. Very well indeed,' Bernard said heartily. Then, disengaging himself from Daisy, he walked jauntily to the sideboard, calling over his shoulder, 'A glass of brandy, William?'

'Thank you, Bernard, that would be most welcome.'

Picking up the heavy glass decanter, Bernard poured out two liberal helpings, then, handing one of the glasses to Dr Benson, he addressed the ladies. 'And what can I get you, ladies? A glass of wine, or maybe you'd prefer port?'

'A drop of port would do nicely, thank you, Bernard,' Mrs Benson answered, her eyes moving to her husband, who was standing awkwardly by her side.

'I'll have a glass of wine, please, Dad. What about you, Mum?'

Daisy looked at Ruby sharply. There was something going on here that didn't include her. She had noticed the air of tension as soon as she'd entered the room. And now, looking at Ruby's flushed face and hearing the brightness of her voice, her eyes narrowed as she wondered what her daughter was up to. It was also evident that the Bensons knew what was going on, and she experienced a sharp feeling of hurt at being excluded from the secret the three of them were sharing.

Her suspicions were confirmed when, some minutes later, William first looked at his wife and then at Ruby, and then said, 'Could I have a word, Bernard? In private.'

Bernard looked at his old friend in surprise before answering, 'Of course, William. We'll take our drinks into the library. If you'll excuse us, ladies.'

When the door had closed behind the two men, Daisy walked swiftly to the sideboard and replenished her drink. Then, her fingers plucking nervously at the fold in her dress, she said sharply, 'What's going on, Ruby?'

Ruby's head jerked back on her shoulders. She was now wishing wholeheartedly that she had confided in her mum. It was going to be bad enough telling her why Dr Benson had asked to speak to her dad without confessing that she had gone to the Bensons with her troubles instead of to her own mother. Added to which, she had also told Lily and Bertie. Cursing herself for her thoughtlessness, she faced a now grim Daisy and said between trembling lips, 'I'm sorry, Mum, really I am,' and then, drawing in a deep breath, she told her.

'She wants to do *what?*' Bernard roared, his face stretched wide in disbelief.

'Now, Bernard, calm yourself, it's not as bad as it would first appear.'

'Not as bad as it appears?' Bernard rose from his chair and began to pace up and down, his hands clasped firmly behind his back, then spinning round on his heel, he shouted, 'You tell me that my eighteen-year-old daughter wishes to leave home and find work. You also add that she speaks nostalgically of her old home in the East End, a home I might add I spent years trying to get my family away from . . . and you tell me to keep calm? How do you expect me to react? Did you imagine I'd beam with delight, call Ruby in here and say fondly, "I understand you want to find employment, preferably among the people you grew up with. Here's two hundred pounds, go and open a soup kitchen in Whitechapel, and I hope you'll be very happy?" Pshaw!'

William looked at his friend's angry face, and sighed. Well, as he'd told Ruby, it wasn't going to be easy.

'Bernard, please, come and sit down. I have an idea that might solve the problem for all concerned. Please, Bernard, I beg you, sit down and listen,' William pleaded, fearful that he would rush from the room and confront an already nervous Ruby. He held his breath as Bernard, his body taut with anger and hurt, fought silently with his confused emotions before dropping heavily into the chair opposite him. William heaved a sigh of relief, then, leaning forward in his chair, he began to speak. 'I've been expecting something like this to happen. Ruby is a very strong-minded young woman; moreover, she is fiercely independent, and that being the case, she will never be happy unless she can prove to herself that she's useful, that despite her disability she can and will live a normal life. It's very important to her, Bernard, and unless you agree to her wishes, you may wake up one morning and find her gone.'

As Bernard listened to William, he felt a great tiredness steal over him. The man was right, of course. He had always known that one day Ruby would leave, but had secretly hoped that her handicap would bind her to him for ever. Her disability had only strengthened her resolve to prove to herself and others that she was not prepared to be dependent all her life, and secretly he admired her for her fortitude and felt some small measure of relief that the need for subterfuge was at an end. 'What do you suggest, William?' he asked.

William heard the note of resignation and defeat in Bernard's voice, and was reminded of that day long ago when he had been forced to impart bad news. Briskly now he began to talk. 'I've been giving the matter a great deal of thought all evening, and as I've already said, I think I may have the answer. There is a patient of mine, Lady Caldworthy, who is looking for a companion, and what I suggest is that Ruby applies for the post. Her duties won't entail any strenuous work, merely reading to the old lady and writing letters for her. In general, she would be just what the position implies: a companion. Also she wouldn't be too far from home, as the house where she'll be working is in Islington. Not that she'd be able to pop home any time she feels like it, because if she agrees to this idea I shall make it quite clear that she will be treated like any other young woman in the role of companion. Her days or afternoons off will be decided by Lady Caldworthy; there will be no question of her receiving special treatment. I must also mention that the lady in question is quite a formidable character and has had numerous companions, none of whom has lasted longer than a month, but I'm confident that Ruby will be able to handle her. Don't you see, Bernard? Ruby will get her wish – she'll be working for a living, she'll have her independence – and at the same time you and Daisy can rest assured that she's safe and sound. And, as Lady Caldworthy's physician, I'll be able to keep an eye on Ruby when I make my visits. Well, what do you say?'

Bernard's mind was working furiously. He would be perfectly within his rights as a father to forbid Ruby to leave home until she came of age, but that was not for another three years, and knowing his daughter as he did, he was forced to admit that William was right. If Ruby didn't get her own way, she would simply vanish one day. Furthermore, if she left in anger, it could be years before he saw her again, and he couldn't bear the thought of that.

'Does Ruby know about this patient of yours requiring a companion?' The question was barked at William.

William drew himself up in his chair, and with quiet dignity replied, 'Of course not. No plans have been made behind your back, Bernard. You should know me well enough to know I would never do anything underhand. As I've already explained, I only suspected what Ruby was thinking, and was completely unaware she was planning to leave home until a few hours ago when she asked me to talk to you. That's all I promised her: that I would talk to you.'

Rubbing his hand over his face, Bernard muttered, 'I'm sorry, William. It seems to be your misfortune in life to be the bearer of bad news. Are you sure this woman will take Ruby on? I don't want to tell her she has been found a place and then have to tell her that it's fallen through. She'd think I was stalling for time.'

'I think it's safe to say that Lady Caldworthy will be agreeable to taking Ruby on. She's a lonely old woman in spite of her sharp tongue, and with my recommendation I don't foresee any difficulty.'

With a tremendous effort, Bernard slapped his knees in a jovial fashion and exclaimed, 'Well, then, I think it's time we had the person in question in here. I'm sure she's waiting anxiously for my answer.' Getting to his feet, he walked towards the door.

'Lily, Lily, wake up!'

Lily jumped, then winced as the muscles in her neck sent a shooting pain up to her head. Rubbing the back of her neck gingerly, she carefully turned her head and peered through the dimness of the room to where Ruby was standing by the door.

'Do you mind if I turn the lamp up, Lily?' she asked, her hand already on its knob.

As the warm light flooded the room, Lily looked at Ruby's flushed happy face and felt a sinking feeling in the pit of her stomach. So she'd got her own way, but she'd never supposed otherwise. Fighting down the sick feeling that was now creeping up into her throat, she forced a smile to her tight lips and said brightly, 'Well, don't stand there grinning like someone just let out of Bedlam! Tell me what happened.'

'Will you come into my room, Lily? We can talk when I'm in bed. To tell the truth, I don't know what's hurting more at the moment, my corsets or my stump.'

Without a word, Lily followed Ruby past the bathroom and into her room, and when fifteen minutes later Ruby had been divested of her clothes and jewellery, her face washed and her hair combed out and falling round her shoulders, she sat propped up on her pillows and, taking hold of Lily's hand, began to talk. 'It's all settled. Well, nearly. Dr Benson has a woman patient who's looking for a companion, and he's going to make a special trip out to Islington tomorrow to see her and tell her about me. He's certain she'll give me the job, although he did warn me she's a bit of a tartar; but who cares? I'll be working for a living, doing a real job and getting paid for it. Oh, Lily, I can't tell you what this means to me! It's as if I'm about to be set free. I know that sounds ungrateful, and I'll miss Mum, Dad, Bertie and George – and you, of course – but for years I've resented everyone in the house because every single one of you had something to do, while I just sat and watched and envied you all your normality. That's all over now. Now I'll be able to talk about what I did and the people I met. I'll be just like anyone else – normal – and that's all I've ever wanted.'

Lily could feel the lump settling in her throat as she continued to nod and smile, and knew she must speak and appear to be glad for

Ruby. 'A companion' was it? Well, to her mind, the doctor and the master must have put their heads together to find Ruby a cushy job, and somewhere not too far from home either. The way she saw it, this so-called job had been created merely for the purpose of keeping Ruby happy, just as any doting parent would buy a new toy for their child, a toy the child had whined and cried for, only to watch the child tire of it and discard it before turning its attention to something else. Ruby obviously didn't realize what her father had done, and she wasn't about to enlighten her. Instead, she patted Ruby's hand and said in what she hoped was an enthusiastic voice, 'I'm glad for you, Ruby. I hope you get on with the old girl, whoever she is, but I'll miss you.'

'Oh, and I'll miss you, Lily. But as soon as I get my first day off we'll go up to the West End and I'll treat you to the best meal you've ever had, even if it does take all my pay! I'll enjoy it all the more because it'll be *my* money: money I've earned.'

Now Lily was forced to pull her hand away. The smile slipped from her face as she said flatly, 'I won't be here. I'll be long gone before you get the chance to come back home.'

Ruby's face stretched wide in astonishment. 'What do you mean – you won't be here? Oh, Lily, I know you don't want me to go, but surely you wouldn't leave here just to spite me?'

Now it was Lily's turn to look amazed. 'Spite you? You think I'd leave my home, and it is my home, just to spite you? Good God, Ruby, don't you realize that, once you've gone, there'll be no need for my services? Your father isn't going to pay my wages to sit around waiting for you to come back on your odd afternoons and days off.' She was on her feet now, her face turned away so that Ruby couldn't see the pain she was suffering.

Ruby stared at the stiff back of her best friend, her thoughts galloping wildly. Lord, what a fool she'd been! So wrapped up in her own private thoughts and desires that she hadn't realized that if she left, Lily would automatically be put out of a job. She couldn't let that happen. 'Lily, I'm sorry I've been selfish. I always assumed you'd be here for me. But don't worry, I'll have a word with Mum, you'll see! She'll find another position for you, I know she will. She's as fond of you as I am, as we all are. You're like one of the family, Lily, nobody's going to make you leave!'

Lily heard the earnest appeal in Ruby's voice, and shuddered. Would she really be kept on? She'd do anything, anything at all as long as she was allowed to stay here. Although for now she must put her best face on, she mustn't spoil this evening for Ruby. 'We'll see,

Ruby. But don't you worry about me. I can look after myself, so you just concentrate on getting that job, eh?' Tucking the bedclothes in round Ruby, she turned down the lamp and left the room hurriedly.

As she watched the door close, Ruby felt the air leave her body. She felt deflated now, all the excitement of the day had gone. Lying against her pillows, she stared into the darkness and thought fiercely, 'If Mum won't keep Lily on, then I'll stay. I will! I'll stay here rather than see Lily thrown out of her home.' Then, turning her face into the pillows, she wept.

Ten days later Ruby stood beside Daisy, two suitcases on the ground in front of them as they stared up at the four-storey house that was to be Ruby's new home. Ruby could feel her body trembling with excitement and apprehension, and for a wild, brief moment she was tempted to take her mum's hand and say, 'I've changed my mind, Mum, take me home', but of course she would do no such thing. She wasn't going to give in before she'd even started. Swallowing the sick feeling in her throat, she turned to Daisy and said brightly, 'Well, this is it, Mum! Now don't forget what you promised. You'll keep Lily on for at least six months, just in case I don't like the job or Lady Caldworthy doesn't take to me.'

Daisy looked at the dear face before her, and nodded reassuringly. 'I have no intention of letting Lily go, she's far too valuable. There's plenty for her to do around the house, so you just worry about yourself. Dr Benson will fetch you home on your first afternoon off, and he's promised to take you back again in the evening. If for any reason he can't, then Bertie will hire a cab and see you safely back here. And, Ruby, if at any time you feel you want to come home, don't let pride stand in your way. Promise me.'

'I promise, Mum. Look, you'd better go, the cabbie is waiting. I can manage from here.' The next minute, she was in her mother's arms, both of them fighting to hold back their tears. Then Ruby felt herself being pushed gently away and watched as Daisy climbed into the carriage, her handkerchief dabbing at her eyes.

Ruby watched until the cab had disappeared from sight before returning her gaze to the house. The words of Dr Benson came back to her, words he had said last night when he'd found her alone in the library selecting a few books to take with her to her new employment.

'I know you don't like your handicap being referred to,' he started awkwardly, 'but you must realize that here, in this house, you've been sheltered and loved. It will be different once you leave.

People can be cruel, Ruby. You must prepare yourself for unsavoury curiosity and unpleasant comments. Just remember, you are a beautiful and intelligent young woman, and your strength of character will stand you in good stead. Remember that the majority of people are ignorant and treat them as such; it's the only way you'll survive.'

She paused for a moment longer, then, jutting out her chin, she picked up her cases and began to walk towards the house.

Chapter Fourteen

L ady Mabel Caldworthy had been a legend in her day. She had been married four times, each of her husbands younger than his predecessor. There had even, at one time, been talk concerning the Prince of Wales – whether there had been any truth in it, no one knew for sure – but it was interesting to note that her second husband had petitioned for divorce shortly after the rumours had started flying. Now in her seventieth year, she no longer bore any resemblance to the young beautiful woman who had set London alight with speculation. The once raven-black hair was now pure white and twisted up into a wispy knot at the back of her head, and the beautiful face that had driven men mad with desire was now buried for ever beneath a morass of deep lines and wrinkles. But if time had been cruel to her outward appearance, it had compensated by leaving her remarkably shrewd brain intact. Shifting slightly in her favourite armchair, she settled her large bulk into a more comfortable position as she continued to appraise the young girl standing awkwardly in front of her. William had said she was a beauty, and he was right – not that it would do the poor girl any good saddled as she was by a peg-leg. If she were entertaining any thoughts of finding a husband, she would have to seek one from the lower classes; but then, one never knew, men were strange creatures, as she herself knew only too well. Clearing her throat loudly, she addressed the girl.

'I trust Dr Benson has acquainted you with your duties?'

Ruby jerked nervously at the sound of the strident voice. 'Yes, Lady Caldworthy. I hope you will find me satisfactory.'

Twisting the top of her gilt-topped walking-stick, Lady Caldworthy reflected for a moment before answering. 'That remains to be seen, young woman. Now, let me go over your duties so there will be no misunderstanding. You will be required to be at hand whenever I need you, day or night. For that purpose, I have arranged for the room adjoining this bedroom to be prepared for you.' Ruby's eyes followed the wavering hand in the direction of the closed door over in the far left corner. 'Furthermore, you will be required to attend to the running of the household. My staff are loyal and trustworthy and many of them have been with me for many years, but, like most servants, they tend to become lazy if the opportunity presents itself. I would expect you to keep an eye on them, make yourself known. It won't make you very popular, but then I'm not paying you to make yourself agreeable. The last young woman I employed was totally inadequate – boring, futile, creature that she was, she nearly drove me mad with her inanity, as did her two predecessors! Of course, most ladies' companions seek this type of employment only because they are fit for nothing better. It needs a certain type of woman to run a household smoothly: she must be able to keep the servants happy, to eliminate the everyday petty quarrels and grievances, while at the same time commanding respect. Servants expect to be given orders; it is the manner in which they are given that is important.'

Closing her eyes, she reflected on what William had told her about the girl who stood nervously before her. She had been fascinated by the story of a young girl bravely battling to adjust to the horror that had befallen her, and had silently applauded her decision to seek employment rather than live out her days always dependent upon others. Mabel Caldworthy had always had a great deal of respect for courage, and it was this reason, and a certain amount of curiosity, that had prompted her to offer the girl the chance to prove herself. But now she was suffering severe misgivings. Servants stayed with their employers for only one of two reasons: money, or loyalty. Since the monetary aspect was of no importance, the girl would be free to walk out of the house at any time knowing she had a secure and comfortable home to return to. Maybe she was sincere in her thinking, but words were cheap. Deeds were what mattered. Settling herself deeper into the armchair she thought about the course of action she should take, leaving Ruby to stare self-consciously around the large overcrowded bedroom cum drawing-room.

It reminded her somewhat of the bedroom her parents had shared over the King's Arms. It contained an enormous four-poster bed, the head of which was piled high with pillows. The heavy damask curtains that surrounded it were tied back and fastened with wide sashes to the bed-posts. Ruby took in the walnut dressing-table covered with trinkets and velvet boxes, and the jewels scattered carelessly over its surface that were reflected brilliantly in the brass-framed bevelled mirror. Beside the dressing-table stood a mahogany bureau, much the same as her dad had in the library, but this one was much older and not nearly as tidy as her dad kept his. The flap had been pulled down to reveal the pigeonholes crammed with letters and documents, some of which had spilled over on to the wooden flap. Over to the right hand side of the room stood an oval table, the white chenille tablecloth that covered it beautifully embroidered with tiny coloured flowers. Arranged round the table were four sturdy chairs, their high backs covered with antimacassars to protect them from the sunlight that streamed into the room from the large bay window that seemed to take up most of the right-hand wall. A few feet away was an old horsehair sofa with two matching armchairs that had at one time been a deep green but were now faded with the years, leaving it at variance with the brightly patterned carpet that covered the whole of the floor. Her curiosity sated, Ruby turned to the old woman again, noting with annoyance and dismay that her heavy eyelids remained closed, and wondered if she should waken her: she might sleep for hours. Almost immediately she rejected the idea and, carefully shifting her position, leaned her weight on her right leg to relieve the pressure on her stump and propped her hand on the back of an armchair to steady herself. Then, taking a deep breath, she resigned herself for a long wait.

Mabel Caldworthy peered through half-closed lids, noting the slight movement before closing her eyes once more. Dear! Oh, dear, this wasn't going to work. The girl had been standing only a short while, and already she seemed tired. Whatever had she been thinking of when she had allowed William to talk her into offering a time-consuming, responsible position to this inexperienced young girl? Even without her handicap, the work would prove too much for her, but with a peg-leg to contend with – well, the situation was impossible. The problem now was how to tell the girl her services would not after all be required. William would be furious, for it was obvious he was very fond of Ruby. Maybe she could force her into leaving of her own accord – but how?

A germ of an idea began to form in her mind, and opening her eyes slowly, she said sharply, 'Well, girl, I dare say Dr Benson has painted you a rosy picture about a companion's life. But as I've already explained, it's not simply a question of reading a few books to an old lady in her dotage – which I am far from being yet, I may add. It's hard work with very little time for yourself, so do you honestly think you are up to the work? If not, then speak up now. It will save us both a lot of time.'

Ruby stared into the bright gimlet eyes and fought to hold down the rising feeling of panic that was making her limbs weak. She hadn't expected this catalogue of work. The duties described seemed more in keeping with a housekeeper's than a companion's, but maybe the two were combined. Dr Benson should have prepared her, but perhaps he hadn't known. Well, she wasn't about to give up before she'd even started, and so, wetting her lips nervously, she answered with a confidence she was far from feeling, 'I'm sure, if you give me a chance, I will be able to be of service to you, ma'am.'

'That's as may be, girl,' Lady Caldworthy snapped back, her gnarled fingers gripping her walking-cane tighter. It was obvious that the girl wasn't going to be frightened off easily, so she would have to try other tactics. She didn't like having to resort to this measure, but it would be kinder in the long run. Clearing her throat noisily, she said, 'I'm sorry to have to say this, but I'm a blunt woman. I speak my mind, always have done. I agreed to take you on because I felt sorry for you, but now you are here, I'm experiencing grave misgivings for my hasty decision. The plain truth of the matter is that you are severely handicapped, and with the best will in the world you would find it extremely difficult to cope with the day-to-day work routine of a normal person. Furthermore, I need someone to converse with on an intellectual level: not to read from books and newspapers in a parrot-like fashion, but to be able to understand what she's reading and be prepared to discuss current events in an intelligent and articulate manner. Well, I've had my say. If you still wish to accept the post, I shall give you a month's trial. I can't say fairer than that, so, girl, what's your answer to be?'

Ruby felt the blood rush to her face as she heard the disparaging tone of the old lady's voice. She felt sick with disappointment and fear. How could anyone be so cruel as to offer employment and then to snatch it away again on a whim? For that's what the old lady wanted. She'd deliberately spoken in the way she had in the hope that she, Ruby, would burst into a flood of tears and rush back home! Any other young girl in her position would have reacted in such a manner, but not Ruby Chadwick. Removing her hand from the back of the chair, she stood up straight and, looking down on the waiting Lady Caldworthy, she said coolly, 'You were already aware of my condition when you agreed to employ me. That being the case, I see no reason why you should change your mind at this late stage.' Ruby's voice remained steady as she battled to control the anger she was feeling. 'You have painted a dismal picture of a companion's duties, but the prospect of hard work doesn't alarm me; it never has. As for my intellect, I think you will find me reasonably intelligent. Fortunately I had an excellent surgeon who was able to remove my leg without tampering with my brain. You have said that you are prepared to give me a month's trial, and I accept. There is one point that worries me, however, and that is you don't appear to know my name. It's "Ruby", not "girl", and I would appreciate being addressed as such in the future.' She finished speaking, her breaths coming in small gasps as she realized what she had said, but she wasn't sorry. No, her temperament wouldn't allow her to be ridiculed without hitting back in some form. Now she stood stiffly, her gaze directed unwaveringly upon the old woman, awaiting the result of her outburst.

The minutes passed slowly, and the only sound came from the marble clock, the soft ticking sounding to Ruby's strained nerves like gunshots. Then an extraordinary thing happened. Lady Caldworthy slapped her knee soundly, her loud earthy laughter cutting into the silence like a knife.

'You'll do, girl! You'll do!' she roared, her face crinkled up in merriment. 'Pull up that chair beside you and sit down before you fall.'

Ruby felt the tension seep from her taut body as she quickly complied. When she was seated, she carefully placed her trembling hands in her lap in an effort to bury them in the folds of her skirt. Lady Caldworthy waited a minute longer before she spoke, and in doing so gave Ruby precious moments to compose herself. She felt dangerously close to tears, and prayed fervently that she would be able to contain her overwrought emotions until she was alone.

'Well, now, girl, you have spirit, I'll say that for you. As for addressing you as "Ruby", you'll have to wait for that privilege. I don't feel comfortable with Christian names unless I know the person well. But that's a minor point, so we'll forget it for now. I have a few pertinent questions I wish to ask. Is that agreeable to you?' Dumbly Ruby nodded, knowing the questions would be asked with or without her permission. 'Good, good. Are stairs a problem? Because your duties will entail you having to use them frequently during the course of the day.'

Ruby considered the question carefully, then with a wry smile she said, 'I can't run up and down as I used to, but I can manage them well enough.'

'Excellent! That was one of my main concerns. As to the rest, you know what is expected of you; let us take one day at a time.' Lady Caldworthy leaned back in her chair, a satisfied look on her face. 'You will no doubt be wanting to see your room and settle yourself in, but before you do I may as well tell you now what your salary will be, and the arrangements for your time off. You will be paid one pound five shillings per week, to include your food and board. You will be allowed one whole day a month free from any duties, and also one half-day fortnightly. These arrangements will, of course, vary, and you may have to alter your day, or half-day, if I happen to need you. Have you anything you wish to ask before you leave?'

Ruby shook her head. 'No, ma'am.'

'Very well, you may leave me. If I need you, I shall ring the bell. Take the rest of the day to acclimatize yourself to your new surroundings. Tomorrow will be time enough to acquaint yourself with the rest of the staff.' Waving her hand imperiously as a dismissal, she once again closed her eyes and fell almost immediately into a light sleep.

Ruby waited a few minutes before rising from her chair, then, picking up her case, she walked heavily over to the door Lady Caldworthy had mentioned. Twisting the brass knob, she pushed gently and found herself in a room much the same as Lily occupied at home. Dropping her case on the thinly carpeted floor, she walked over to the single bed and sat down. Then, staring sightlessly at the large dark brown wardrobe that seemed to take up the entire wall, she thought wildly, 'What have I let myself in for?' before dropping her face in her hands and releasing her pent-up emotions in a flood of tears.

It was nearly two months before Ruby had her first day's leave. Despite Dr Benson's indignant efforts on Ruby's behalf, Lady Caldworthy had steadfastly refused to allow her new companion to return home, insisting that her health was waning and that Ruby's presence was essential to her well-being. Dr Benson had stoutly refuted this statement, declaring that she was as strong as a horse and would in all probability outlive them all, upon which the autocratic lady had told him, if that were the case, she would dispense with his services and save herself the guinea a week for his visits. The plain truth was simply that she didn't want to let Ruby visit her parents for fear she wouldn't return. The speed at which Ruby had become so dear to her had surprised Mabel Caldworthy, for she had seldom formed any lasting friendship with any of her own sex, always preferring the company of men. But this young crippled girl had found a way into her cynical heart, and it was with deep foreboding that she had reluctantly agreed to grant Ruby her Sunday off.

In her room Ruby was busily making her bed, her eyes anxiously darting to the small clock she kept by her bedside. Dr Benson was due to visit Lady Caldworthy at nine o'clock, after which he had promised to drive her back to Brixton. Pumping up her solitary pillow, she sent up a silent plea that Lady Caldworthy wouldn't suddenly get another attack of the vapours, for Ruby was missing her family more than she would have thought possible, and if she were prevented from seeing them for much longer she wouldn't be accountable for her actions. The bed made, she sat down and waited for Dr Benson to arrive. She had already attended to Lady Caldworthy some forty minutes earlier, and had purposefully turned a deaf ear to the old lady's complaints.

Despite Ruby's efforts to make sure her employer could find no reason to cancel her day off again, the old lady had found fault with everything. Her bed hadn't been made properly, causing her a sleepless night. The egg Ruby had boiled, timing it to perfection, had been too hard, the bacon under-cooked and the toast soggy. In spite of these gastronomical disasters she had managed to clear her plate, after which she had lain back on her pillows, declaring that she would probably suffer from indigestion all day. Ruby had escaped from the room as soon as was decently possible, expecting at any moment to be summoned back on some pretext or other, but the room next door remained blissfully quiet.

At five minutes to nine Dr Benson arrived, and without stopping to be divested of his overcoat and hat he mounted the circular staircase, wondering as he always did if Ruby was continuing to manage the steps. He had kept a close eye on her progress over the weeks, and had been amazed but not unduly surprised at the speed with which she had adapted to her new life. He had worried that the work would prove too much for her, and had secretly asked Mrs Rodgers, a grand old lady who had worked in the house for over thirty years as cook and substitute housekeeper, to keep an eye on his young friend. She had been wary at first, for being aware of Ruby's background she had expected the young woman to try to lord it over the staff. When Ruby had first appeared in her kitchen, she had viewed her with a mixture of distrust and grudging respect due to her class, and had been immensely relieved to find the girl pleasant and eager to please, and completely free from any airs and pretensions. From that moment Mrs Rodgers had taken the young girl under her wing, endeavouring to lighten her load whenever possible. Dr Benson had been delighted that Ruby had endeared herself to the staff so quickly, for without their help, the work would indeed have proved too much for her. What he hadn't expected was the irrational possessive effect she would have on his old friend Mabel Caldworthy, a proud woman who had always scorned close friendships, declaring that she had no need for the troubles they invariably brought with them.

Upon entering the familiar bedroom, he suppressed a smile at the sight of his patient lying back on the mountain of pillows, one hand placed dramatically across her heart. 'Now, then, Mabel,' he cried heartily. 'All's well with you, I trust?'

Lady Caldworthy opened one eye, saying tersely, 'Not planning on stopping, I see.'

Paying no heed to the waspish tone, Dr Benson pulled up a chair and sat down, then, taking hold of her liver-spotted hand, he said gently, 'I hope you're not intending to renege on your promise, Mabel. Ruby is entitled to her time off, as is any servant. She would have been perfectly within her rights to demand her leave over the past weeks, and another young woman in her circumstances almost certainly would have. To my mind, it is a testament to her character and loyalty to you that she has kept by your side when she could have been with her family. But don't push her too far, Mabel. That same strength of character could work against you, and result in Ruby leaving for good.' When the hand was snatched away from his grasp, Dr Benson sighed heavily before rising to his feet. Looking down at the figure feigning sleep he added firmly, 'We've known each other for many years, Mabel, so I feel I can say freely that you are without doubt the most cantankerous, insufferable and downright aggravating woman I have ever met! But, for all that, I'm fond of you, though heaven only knows why.'

Opening her eyes, Lady Caldworthy looked at him intently before saying, 'There was a time, William, when you were more than just fond of me.'

Dr Benson looked at the now grinning face and smiled back fondly. 'You're a wicked old lady, Mabel, and what happened between us was a long time ago and best forgotten!'

'At my age, William, memories are all I have left.' Then, waving her hand at him, she said irritably, 'Oh, go away, you old fool! Ruby will be waiting for you, and I want her back here at six o'clock sharp! Not a minute later.'

Then Dr Benson did a surprising thing: he leaned over the large body and planted a kiss on her wrinkled forehead. 'Six o'clock, Mabel; never fear,' he said gently before crossing the room to Ruby's door.

Ruby stood on the doorstep under the front porch, tapping her foot impatiently as she waited for Dr Benson to rejoin her. They had already left the house when he had suddenly clapped his hand to his forehead and exclaimed he'd forgotten to give Lady Caldworthy her new bottle of medicine, before disappearing back indoors. Ruby stared in dismay at the torrential rain that was beating down on the pavement. She had taken great care with her appearance and was wearing the new dark green coat and matching bonnet her mother had bought her as an extra birthday present, but now, even walking the few feet to where the carriage was waiting would soak the hem of her coat. Forgetting her own troubles for a moment, she looked with pity upon the coachman who sat outside the carriage, the relentless rain beating on his unprotected head, and the men and women who scurried past the house. The women especially were suffering the worst from the unexpected downpour as they struggled to walk, hampered as they were by their mud-soaked skirts.

Tearing her eyes from the depressing spectacle, she looked anxiously past the open doorway into the long, wide hall and then up to the curving stairway, scanning the deep red carpeted stairs, willing the small, slim grey-haired figure to come into view, but to no avail. He had only been gone a few minutes, but, to Ruby, her nerves tingling with anxiety, it seemed like hours. A sudden gust of wind blew a stream of rain into the porch and she hurriedly stepped back further into the doorway. Common sense told her to wait inside the house, but she had an irrational fear that if she so much as stepped back over the threshold, something would happen to make her stay. As another gust of wind and rain swept over her she muttered angrily, 'Oh, hurry up, Dr Benson, please!'

Such was her preoccupation that she failed to see the tall figure of the man, his head bent low against the rain, jumping up the stone steps leading to the house. As his heavy body cannoned into her, she cried out in alarm, grabbing at the man's sodden sleeve to stop herself from falling.

'Bejasus, sweetheart, I didn't see you standing there! It's a clumsy oaf I am and no mistake! Are ye all right?'

About to make a sharp retort, Ruby stopped as she found herself looking into a pair of the bluest eyes she had ever seen. A strange lethargic feeling came over her body, and the desire to step further into the circle of the stranger's arms was so strong that she stepped back awkwardly. Trying to overcome her confusion, she made a great play of adjusting her already secure bonnet and mumbled, 'I'm all right, but thank you for your concern.' When the man made no move to leave, she wetted her lips nervously before saying, 'I hope you won't take offence, but it would be better if you moved on. The lady of the house is a bit of a tartar, and, well . . .' Here her words trailed off miserably. How could she tell this nice, shabbily dressed man that tradesmen and people of the lower classes were not welcome at the front of the house? Not knowing what else to say, she stared fixedly at the driving rain, willing the stranger to leave her side before Dr Benson came back.

Her hopes were dashed as the man moved nearer to her, and in a voice filled with laughter said gaily, 'Ah, now, don't you be worrying about hurting me feelings. Me skin's as thick as me skull, so me dear sainted mother was forever telling me! Tell me now, are you waiting for somebody, or is it just sheltering from the rain you are?'

'The young lady is waiting for me,sir, and kindly remove yourself from these premises. This is private property.' Both Ruby and the man turned their heads as Dr Benson appeared in the open doorway.

The smile slid from the man's face as he answered coolly, 'I have an appointment to see Mr Masters, the butler of the house, concerning the post of gardener and odd-job man . . . sir.'

Although the man had addressed him as 'sir', Dr Benson was quick to note that the word held no respect for this man standing before him. In fact his whole demeanour smacked of insolence. Placing his arm protectively round Ruby's shoulders he said stiffly, 'Tradesmen's entrance is down below. If you go down the stairs at the side of the house, you will be seen to. Come along, Ruby, your parents and brothers are anxious to see you.'

Taking hold of her arm, Dr Benson steered her quickly down the stone-flagged steps, leaving her just long enough to open the carriage door. 'Quickly, Ruby,' he called out urgently as the rain continued to fall, the large drops of water hitting the top of his high hat and trickling down the back of his neck.

Conscious of the stranger's stare, Ruby endeavoured to walk as normally as possible. As she put her right foot on to the carriage step, she quickly lifted her left leg so that her dress covered the tip of her wooden leg. For some unknown reason she didn't want the stranger to be aware of her deformity. Once seated inside the carriage, she stole a last look at the bedraggled figure still standing resolutely in the porch, flanked by the two stone pillars. As the coachman whipped up the horses, she saw the man doff his sodden cap to her and felt a ridiculous surge of pleasure before the carriage moved away from the house.

Michael O'Brien watched the carriage drive away, his eyes narrowed in anger. 'Jumped-up English bastard!' he muttered furiously, his teeth clenched with rage. 'Talking to me as if I were the dirt beneath his feet. We'll see who's the better man, me foine Englishman! Maybe the little colleen will be more appreciative of me charms than you were. Now wouldn't that make your stiff upper lip tremble?' This pleasing thought had the desired effect, and running lightly down the steps leading to the servants' quarters, he whistled happily.

Chapter Fifteen

Lily knocked once on the parlour door, then, without waiting for the command to enter as she normally did, she pushed it open and announced in a high excited voice, 'Miss Ruby's just arrived with Dr Benson, Mrs Chadwick. Shall I answer the door, or would you prefer to do the honours?'

Daisy laid down her embroidery, her face alight with happiness and relief. 'Oh, thank heavens! Have they just driven up? I was afraid that dreadful woman would change her mind again at the last moment.'

As she rose to her feet, Bernard, who was sitting in his favourite armchair pretending to read his *Sunday Times*, said sharply, 'Sit down, Daisy. I'm sure Lily can open the door by herself, she's done it often enough. Besides, it's not seemly for the mistress of the house to admit visitors.'

'Stuff and nonsense, Bernard! You can hardly consider our daughter a visitor!' She was already walking towards the door. Looking over her shoulder, she saw him shake the newspaper outwards and his solemn expression, and burst into laughter. 'Really, Bernard, you know you're as excited as I am at the prospect of seeing Ruby. Why do you have to pretend indifference? It doesn't fool anyone, least of all me!' The resounding of the heavy brass knocker against the front door cut off Daisy's remonstrances, and before Bernard could answer, she had already left the room.

Ruby was about to knock again when the door was flung open wide to reveal her mother and Lily standing side by side, their faces stretched into wide smiles.

'Come in, dear, and let me look at you. Oh, it's lovely to see you again!' Daisy was already trying to pull off Ruby's coat before she was properly into the hall.

'Mum, give me a chance to get in the door!' Ruby laughed happily as she shook her arms free. Then, noticing Lily dressed in her grey and white housekeeper's uniform, she exclaimed, 'Why, Lily, you didn't have to dress up for me! I may have left home, but I don't consider myself a guest.'

Lily took Ruby's coat and bonnet, forcing herself to stem the torrent of words she longed to say, in deference to Daisy's presence. It wasn't her place to ask any questions. She might feel like part of the family, but she was still a servant, and it would pay her to remember that fact.

'Didn't Dr Benson tell you, Ruby? Lily is our full-time housekeeper now, I told you she was too valuable to lose, and I must say she is doing an excellent job.'

At the sound of heavy footsteps on the stairs, Ruby's face broke into a wide smile at the sight of her two brothers bounding down the stairs. Bertie was the first to reach her, and, placing his hands under her armpits, he swung her off the ground, shouting with delight, 'Welcome home, little sister! The house has been dead without your lively chatter, and although I never thought I'd admit it, I missed you. We all have. How long can you stay?'

'Yes, Ruby, how long can you stay?' Daisy asked, her voice full of hope.

Struggling to get free from Bertie's arms, Ruby answered breathlessly, 'I have to be back by six o'clock. Bertie, put me down, do, else I'll spend my entire day in the hall!'

Gently lowering her to the ground, Bertie steadied her before placing his arm firmly round her shoulders, while Daisy continued to talk. 'Lily, hang up Miss Ruby's bonnet and coat, will you? Then ask Cook to make us all some tea.' Lily bobbed her knee, then hurried off to the kitchen, casting a longing look over her shoulder, wishing she could stay and hear Ruby's news.

As the family made their way to the parlour, Daisy resumed her questioning. 'Didn't Dr Benson come in with you? No, well, I expect he is a busy man. No rest for a doctor, is there, even on a Sunday? He keeps us informed of your progress, but I want to hear all about it from you. What's this Lady Caldworthy like? Are you coping with the work? How do the servants treat you?'

'Mum, please!' Ruby pleaded. 'Let's wait until we're all sitting down having our tea, and then I'll tell you all you want to know.'

Bernard stood up as they entered the room, his face betraying nothing of the emotion he was feeling at seeing his daughter again after such a long separation. Laying his newspaper down carefully on the arm of the chair, he pulled at the bottom of his waistcoat before saying gruffly, 'Hello, Ruby. It's very pleasant to have you home with us again, even if it is only for a short while.'

Ruby looked at her father's impassive face and felt a tug at her heart. She could see past the stoic countenance to the vulnerable man that lay beneath the surface of the façade he presented to the world. 'Oh, Dad!' she cried, the two simple words catching in her throat. And then she was in his arms, her defences down, as the worry, anxiety and homesickness she had been suffering in silence were finally given release.

Daisy looked on with mixed emotions. She was happy that Ruby and her father were so close, but there was a part of her that felt resentful and jealous of their relationship. She felt her smile slipping, and quickly stretched her lips into an even wider grin. She was being silly: all daughters had a special affection for their fathers, it was a known fact, and she knew in her heart of hearts that Ruby loved them both equally. Clearing her throat loudly, she said cheerfully, 'Now that all the greetings have been dispensed with, shall we sit down? Lily will be bringing tea shortly, then we can all have a proper talk.'

Reluctantly pulling herself from Bernard's arms, Ruby settled herself into the chair next to the leather armchair. When they were all seated, she looked from one dear face to the next, all of them smiling at her, and for one wild moment she thought how lovely it would be if she didn't have to return to the house in Islington but could remain here among the people she loved. She was saved from making such a rash declaration by the arrival of Lily carrying a large silver tray.

No more words were spoken until Lily had placed the heavy tray on the table, saying, 'Would you like me to pour the tea, Mrs Chadwick?' hoping fervently that the answer would be yes, so that maybe she too would be able to listen to Ruby's account of her new life.

Her hopes were dashed when Daisy replied brightly, 'Oh, no, Lily, it's all right, I'll see to it.'

Bowing slightly, she was about to leave the room when Ruby's voice stopped her.

'Dad . . .' she began hesitantly, 'Dad, do you think we can dispense with formality for today and let Lily have her tea with us? I've such a lot to tell you all, and I'd like her to hear what I have to say.' She saw the look of disapproval cloud her father's face, and added quickly, 'Please, Dad? Just for today.'

Bernard felt the five pairs of eyes staring at him, and, anxious not to let anything spoil the pleasure of the day, inclined his head in assent.

Clapping her hands with glee, Ruby cried out gaily, 'Oh, thank you, Dad! Lily, you sit beside George, and while Mum pours the tea, I'll tell you all the details.' She waited until Lily, her cheeks pink with embarrassment and pleasure, was seated, and then she began to talk.

The next hour passed quickly, with questions being fired at her from all sides. Happier than she'd been for weeks, she answered each one with a simple truthfulness that touched them all. They listened in silence as she told them about the autocratic Lady Caldworthy, and how the old lady would treat her like an old and trusted friend one minute, and then rapidly change tack and order her around as if she were a common skivvy. These mood swings, Ruby surmised, were merely to remind her new companion that although she might enjoy a certain familiarity with her mistress, she was still only a paid servant, and the message was driven home at least once a week. The servants on the other hand, had gone out of their way to help her. She described them all in detail, starting with her favourite, Mrs Rodgers, the warm-hearted, jolly cook, before switching to Mr Masters, the elderly butler who had worked for Lady Caldworthy and her late husband for over thirty years and saw himself as master below stairs, thus showing a tendency to be aloof and condescending, when he could get away with it, especially with the two young housemaids, Agnes and Rosie. These two girls, together with Mrs Rodgers, had been the saving of Ruby. She had been in the house for only a week when she'd realized what a dreadful mistake she'd made in leaving home.

When she had told Lady Caldworthy she could manage the stairs, she hadn't envisaged having to use them frequently every day. Lady Caldworthy had a voracious appetite, and it had fallen to Ruby to make the numerous trips to the kitchen for snacks for her mistress. It was on one of these occasions when, tired and weary, her stump aching from the unusual pressure, she had stood at the top of the landing, her eyes filled with despair as she gazed down on the sweeping stairway, that she had encountered Rosie, her plump arms full of clean laundry, coming up the stairs. She had been astounded when the young girl no older than herself had, after a moment's hesitation, bobbed her knee to her. The unexpected action had saddened Ruby, for it was an action that said plainly, 'You're not one of us', and she desperately wanted to be friends with the two girls. She had hastened to reassure Rosie that she herself was a servant, and thus was not entitled to any deferential treatment. From that moment on, Rosie, together with Agnes, had taken it in turns to climb the stairs several times a day to enquire if she needed anything from below. This simple, kind action had not only made Ruby glow with happiness, but had also served to free her from the uncomfortable and often painful business of the dreaded stairs. She still had to use them, of course, since one of her duties entailed a daily visit to the kitchen to discuss with Mrs Rodgers the menus for the following day, and also to make sure everything was running smoothly. These visits had become the highlight of Ruby's day.

In the afternoons, when Lady Caldworthy was having her sleep, she would make her way at leisure down the once dreaded stairs to the warm cosy kitchen where Mrs Rodgers would stop whatever she was doing to settle Ruby into the old brown armchair by the fire that was kept burning all day, whatever the weather. There she would sit comfortably for an hour or more while the cook prepared the evening meal, listening to her reminiscing over the events that had occurred in the house over the thirty years she had been in service. Ruby was fascinated by these stories and, through them, came to see what her employer had been like as a young woman.

She in turn had overcome her natural reserve and told Mrs Rodgers about her early beginnings, her lovely face animated as she spoke about her life in the rooms above the King's Arms. Only when she'd touched lightly on her accident and the awful pain-filled months following it had her face clouded, her bright blue eyes momentarily dimmed by the memories. She had quickly skimmed through that part of her life and on to the events that had lifted her family from the East End into the beautiful house where they now lived. She had ended her tale at the evening of her eighteenth birthday party, and her decision to leave home to seek employment. When she had added that she'd made this decision not because of any discord at home, but simply because she wanted to stand on her own two feet, she had stopped in mid-sentence, her eyes and mouth wide as she realized the irony of what she'd said before bursting into a loud peal of laughter.

Mrs Rodgers had been dumbstruck that anyone in Ruby's condition could make a joke of it, and had been full of admiration for the young girl. When at last Ruby reluctantly hauled herself out of the armchair, Mrs Rodgers without fail would ask if she needed any help in climbing back to the top floor, even though Ruby had repeatedly told the anxious woman that she could easily manage the stairs. It had only been difficult when she had been encumbered with the heavy silver platter bearing Lady Caldworthy's meals.

'So, there you have the whole story,' she finished proudly. 'I can admit now that it was hard work the first week, and I was ready to waylay Dr Benson at the first opportunity and beg him to take me home. But thanks to the kindness and help I receive from the rest of the staff, I think I will be very happy in my grand position of companion, providing of course I am allowed my free time. I've missed you all dreadfully.' She clasped Daisy's hand, squeezing it gently, the gesture encompassing them all.

'Is that all the staff there are, Ruby? It doesn't seem much,' Bertie said, puzzled. 'Isn't there a coachman and stable hands? And surely there must be a gardener? Dr Benson told us that Lady Caldworthy had beautiful gardens. Unless she sees to them herself!' he added, smiling broadly.

Ruby felt the blood rush to her face and was inwardly furious with herself. Fanning herself with her hand, she exclaimed, 'Goodness, it's hot in here! Lily, would you open a window, please?'

Lily rose from her chair, her shrewd glance going to Ruby's flushed cheeks before doing as she was bid. Ruby saw the look, and fanned her face harder. 'Damn it, Lily knows it wasn't the non-existent heat that was making me blush!' Fortunately none of the others had noticed anything amiss, or if they had, it would be put down to her excitement at being home. Adopting a casual tone, she said airily, 'Oh, Lady Caldworthy doesn't have a carriage; she hasn't been out of the house for years. As for the gardener,' here she shrugged her shoulders nonchalantly, 'he retired some time ago. I believe Lady Caldworthy has instructed Mr Masters to engage somebody, but there have been no suitable applicants yet.'

Now that all the questions had been exhausted, an uneasy silence settled upon the room until George, his earnest plump face showing his concern, asked the question that was on everyone's mind. 'Are you really happy, Ruby? I mean, if you're just saying you are to make us feel easier in our minds, there's no need. We all think you've done marvellously, and we're all very proud of you. So if – if you would rather give up your job and return home, please don't feel ashamed to admit it.' He saw Ruby's body stiffen, and before she could make a reply he hurried on, his nervousness making him stumble over his words. 'What I mean is . . . Well, that is, what we would all like is for you to come back home for good. The house seems empty without you, Ruby. So, well . . . As I said, if – if you've any regrets, you know . . .' His words trailed off miserably as he hung his head, afraid to look at his beloved fiery sister for fear of what emotions he would see in her face.

The genuine love and concern in George's voice touched Ruby deeply. She felt the tension leave her body and as gently as she could, she replied, 'I'm sorry, George, really I am, but I made a promise to myself, and I intend to stand by it. It's something I have to do. Please try to understand, all of you. And yes, I am happy; you need have no worries on that score.'

'All right, Ruby, just as long as it's what you want to do,' George said, his voice resigned.

'Good! Now then,' Ruby cried briskly, 'I don't know about the rest of you, but I'm starving! What time is dinner?'

The lightness of her tone had the desired effect so that the conversation turned to different matters, as everyone, bar Lily, began to fill her in on the happenings in their own lives since she'd been away. As the talk flowed freely, Lily rose quietly and left the room. For a short time she had been a part of the family, but now she slipped effortlessly back into her role of housekeeper and made her way to the kitchen to see how the dinner was progressing.

The precious hours flew past at an alarming speed, and now Ruby stood once more dressed in her outdoor clothes, her family gathered round her while Dr Benson waited for her in his carriage.

'Goodbye, my dear. Let Dr Benson know if there's anything you need,' Daisy said tearfully, loath to let her daughter go.

'Don't let the old dragon do you out of your free time, do you hear?' Bertie said, hugging her fiercely.

George was next to say his goodbyes. Shyly he put his arms round her shoulders, saying quietly, 'Bye, Ruby. Look after yourself.'

Choked with emotion, Ruby could only bow her head, afraid to speak lest she break down and agree to stay with them, an action she would surely regret tomorrow. It was left to Bernard to walk her to the waiting carriage and Dr Benson. As he opened the front door for her, he tutted with annoyance at the sight of the teeming rain. 'Blasted weather! I thought it had stopped for the day. Lily, fetch my umbrella for Miss Ruby while I run and open the carriage door.' With a last wave to her family, Ruby stepped out on the path, her head close to Lily's as they sheltered under the large black umbrella.

'What's he like?' Lily whispered cautiously, her elbow digging the startled Ruby in the ribs.

'What's who like, Lily? I don't know what you're talking about,' Ruby stammered, her eyes darting nervously to where her father stood waiting only a few feet away.

'Never mind. You can tell me all about him on your next visit.' Then, raising her voice, she called out cheerfully, 'Good evening, Dr Benson. Dreadful weather isn't it?'

'Indeed it is, Lily,' Dr Benson replied from the comfort of his carriage, looking out at the rain.

Lily stood back as Bernard helped Ruby into the carriage. When she was safely seated, she leaned out of the window, saying, 'Bye, Dad, I'll see you soon. Bye, Lily.'

'Goodbye, Ruby. I look forward to your next visit,' Bernard said gruffly, and then for the second time that day he dispensed with formality as he hastily ducked under the umbrella with Lily and stood watching until the carriage was out of sight.

Chapter Sixteen

'For goodness' sake, Ruby, close that window before I catch my death of cold!' Lady Caldworthy sat huddled in her armchair, the lower half of her body wrapped in blankets despite the hot July sun that streamed into the room. Ruby appeared not to have heard the querulous cry as she continued to look down on the large square patch of garden and the broad figure of the man who was at that moment busily digging over the flower beds. 'Ruby, have you gone deaf, girl? Close the window; there's a terrible draught in here. What's so interesting about the gardens all of a sudden that you can't tear yourself away from the window?' The strident voice bellowed across the room, causing Ruby to start guiltily.

'I'm sorry, Lady Caldworthy, I was wool-gathering. I'll close the window immediately.'

'See that you do, girl, and shut it tightly. I can't abide fresh air, not at my time of life. What were you thinking of? You know I'm susceptible to the cold. And draw the curtains while you're about it, I wish to have my afternoon sleep.'

'Yes, Lady Caldworthy,' Ruby answered demurely, anxious to fob off any probing questions. The old lady's brain was still as sharp as a razor and she'd have to watch herself, else Lady Caldworthy would become suspicious. Pulling the window down, she leaned on the bottom sill to make sure it was shut tight. Just as she was about to draw the curtains, she caught sight of a figure entering the garden. Her eyes narrowed as she watched the tall figure of Agnes, her brown curls bouncing on her shoulders, saunter over to Michael, one hand holding a glass of lemonade, leaving the other hand free to touch his brown muscular arm. Ruby's lips settled into a grim line of jealousy as she witnessed the deliberate act before savagely drawing together the heavy curtains and plunging the room into semi-darkness.

Pausing briefly to make sure her employer was asleep, she quickly crossed the floor to her own room. Once inside, she stood against the door, her eyes closed, clenching, then unclenching, her small fists. 'You're mad, mad, mad!' she whispered to the silent room. 'He's not for you! He could have any girl he wants, so it's not likely he'll set his cap at a cripple, is it?'

Taking a long shuddering breath, she forced herself to by-pass her window without looking out, but she couldn't shut out the sound. Michael's clear voice floated up to her room as he chaffed the delighted Agnes, and the sound was so painful that she clapped her hands over her ears in a futile effort to drown out their laughter. Lying on her bed, she stared at the high ceiling, her troubled mind trying to decide what course of action to take.

It had been over six months since she had first seen Michael O'Brien as they'd sheltered together under the porch. She had returned to the house that evening to hear from an excited Agnes about the tall good-looking Irishman who had been taken on as the new gardener. Even the level-headed Rosie, who had been happily walking out with a young man from a neighbouring household for over two years, had been impressed with the new addition to the staff. Ruby could recall clearly how her heart had hammered against her ribs at the news, while at the same time she maintained a show of indifference. Remembering the tremendous physical impact the man had made on her, she had wisely kept her distance from him for nearly a month. Then one bright cold afternoon she had ventured out into the garden, determined to face this strange man to whom she had spoken only once, but with such devastating effect. She had hoped that, once she saw him again and found him to be an ordinary working-class man, the foolishness she had been harbouring would vanish, and she could then dispel him from her mind. She had even envisaged laughing at herself for behaving as she had the first time she'd met him.

She had made her way confidently across the arid winter lawn to where Michael was busily engaged on building a rockery. But the meeting hadn't gone as she'd expected, for the moment he had turned to greet her, she had been lost. What she had talked about she couldn't remember, only the dryness of her mouth and the sudden trembling of her body remained firmly etched into her memory. And when he had taken her arm and enquired solicitously if she was feeling cold, she had hurriedly pulled away and left him staring after her as she had walked across the lawn, her haste making her uneven gait more noticeable. She had tried her best to avoid him after that humiliating day, but it wasn't always easy. Some days, when Rosie and Agnes were busy, she would be forced to go to the kitchen for Lady Caldworthy's meals, and more often than not she would find him there, his sturdy hands clasped firmly round a steaming mug of strong tea as he chatted to Mrs Rodgers. On these occasions she would collect the waiting tray and leave immediately, refusing stoutly any offers of help with the climb back to the top floor. Even her precious afternoons by the fire had been sacrificed in an effort to avoid him. She knew Mrs Rodgers was hurt and puzzled by this sudden change in her attitude, but she couldn't sit in the same room as him for long, for fear that some action or expression on her part would reveal her feelings, and she must avoid that at all costs. The wisest thing she could do was to leave here now and return home, but she knew she would never willingly give up her job. Lady Caldworthy needed her, and despite the old woman's moods and tempers, Ruby had grown genuinely fond of her. Besides, painful as it was to be near someone you loved, knowing that love would never be returned, it would be infinitely more so never to see him again.

'Bye for now, Michael. I'll see you later.'

Ruby heard Agnes call out her farewell, and looked longingly at the open window. Blowing her cheeks out impatiently, she walked over to it. She knew she was torturing herself needlessly, but what of it? Sneaking a glimpse of him was the only pleasure she had. Carefully pulling back the curtain she gazed down, then jumped with fright as she saw Michael directly beneath her window staring straight into her startled eyes. She stood rooted to the spot, her heart thumping wildly as she tried to control her rapid breathing, hoping he would say something and so break this paralysing spell that seemed to be turning her very bones to water. But still he stood silently, his eyes boring into her, until with an agonizing cry she tore herself away and, leaning against the wall, she whispered urgently, 'Oh, Michael, what am I going to do? Whatever am I going to do?'

'Would you like me to read to you tonight, Lady Caldworthy? I thought perhaps we could start on Lord Chesterfield's *Letters to his Son*. It has many amusing passages you might enjoy.' Ruby stood by the bookshelf, her hand resting on a slim brown book.

'You may find them amusing. I on the other hand find them tedious in the extreme,' Lady Caldworthy said irritably. 'How the man managed to get them published is a mystery to me. In particular, the letter advocating the use of a handkerchief instead of picking one's nose. Did you know the son in question was his bastard?'

Ruby coloured slightly. 'No, ma'am, I didn't know that.'

'Well, he was.' The old lady turned in her chair. 'And, that being the case, you would have thought he would want to keep them secret, instead of showing them to the world! Now if it's interesting letters you want, you'll find plenty in the bottom drawer of my writing-desk, but it would be a brave publisher that would put them into print,' she ended with a chuckle. The sight of Ruby's face caused her to laugh louder. 'I've embarrassed you, haven't I, girl? Well, no matter, pick out one of the new books you brought from your last visit home. Better still, you can start on that Stowe woman's book. When you've finished, we can have a lively discussion on the pro's and con's of slavery.'

Ruby settled herself comfortably in her chair, determined to forget about Michael for at least a few hours, and what better way than between the pages of a good book. Turning back the cover, she began to read.

CHAPTER I

In which the reader is introduced to a Man of Humanity.

Late in the afternoon of a chilly day in February two gentlemen were sitting alone over their wine in a well-furnished dining-parlour in the town of . . .

She broke off suddenly as a knock sounded at the door.

'Now, who the devil can that be?' Laldy Caldworthy exclaimed irritably before calling out, 'Come in.'

'Begging your pardon, ma'am, I was wondering if I could be having a few words with you?' Michael O'Brien stood in the doorway, his handsome face solemn, his manner respectful.

At the sound of his voice, Ruby had started nervously, causing the book on her lap to slide to the floor. Grateful for any kind of diversion, she bent forward to retrieve it, her long hair falling forward to cover the excitement on her face.

'Well, what is it?'

The question was barked at the unexpected intruder, and Michael, focusing his attention on his employer, who at this moment was looking very angry indeed, said quickly, 'I was wondering, ma'am, if I could start a small vegetable plot at the far end of the garden. There's nothing growing there at the moment, and it would be perfect for the growing of potatoes and turnips, and maybe even cabbages . . . If you're agreeable, ma'am.'

'A vegetable plot?' The words held a note of incredulity. 'You have interrupted my evening and invaded my privacy to talk about vegetable plots? Have you taken leave of your senses, young man? Any business concerning the garden or any other duties you are required to perform is the responsibility of Mr Masters. If you have any complaints or requests, I suggest you make them to the appropriate person. Now leave me, and do not let me catch you in this part of the house again. Your place is downstairs.'

'Yes, ma'am. Sorry, ma'am.' Michael briefly touched his forehead and turned to go.

'Wait a minute, young man. While you are here, and since you have taken the liberty of bearding me in my den, I don't suppose it will hurt me to listen to what you have to say. Come over here so that I can get a better look at you.'

Michael turned round slowly and was surprised and a little disconcerted to feel the shrewd intelligent eyes appraising him. This was no doddery old woman he would be able to charm as he had charmed so many of his previous employers. He had the uncomfortable feeling that she could see right through him, and was forced to bow his head against the piercing gaze. He would have to tread warily, very warily indeed.

Michael was correct in his evaluation, for Mabel Caldworthy had met many Michael O'Briens in her day – charming, handsome men who strolled through life surviving on their wits and the susceptibility of foolish women eager to part with their money at the first sight of a good-looking man. She had nothing against these men, reserving her scorn instead for the stupid women who were so readily taken in. Her eyes raked his body. He was a handsome specimen, no doubt about that, and for a moment she felt a pang for the passing of time. Forty years ago she would have played him at his own game and enjoyed doing it, but those days were long gone. Shifting her position slightly, she snapped, 'What is your name?'

'Michael Sean O'Brien, ma'am.'

'Well, that answers my second question before I've asked it. There's not much doubt where you hail from. I've met many of your countrymen, rogues most of them, charming people blessed with a silver tongue, but rogues nevertheless. Tell me about yourself, Mr O'Brien. I'm curious to know what a man like you is doing working in such a lowly occupation.'

'Well now, ma'am,' Michael answered, his confidence returning, 'I've always been good with the soil, and there's nothing gives me greater pleasure than to work in the open air. It's a grand feeling, so it is. It's as if I'm me own master.'

'And you think that one day you will achieve that ambition? To be your own master?'

'Nothing's impossible, ma'am, if a man's prepared to work for what he wants. But for now, I'm very happy where I am, and hope to stay here for as long as I make meself useful.'

'That being the case, I see no reason why you shouldn't remain here for quite some time.' Lady Caldworthy tapped her fingers on the arm of her chair, uncomfortably aware of the magnetism of the man standing before her. His very presence was stirring feelings in her she had thought long dead, and if he could affect her tired-out old body, he must be wreaking havoc below stairs, especially with Agnes. That flighty piece would run after a broom if it was wearing trousers! Thank the Lord, Ruby was well out of his way. Casting an affectionate look at her young companion, her smile faltered, her body stiffening in alarm. Unaware she was being watched, Ruby had let her guard down momentarily, but it was long enough for Lady Caldworthy to see the look of adoration on her face.

'Dear God, no! She couldn't be falling for the man. She never had the opportunity to come across his path, had she?' Closing her eyes briefly, she shook her head as if trying to ward off an unpleasant image, and when she opened them again Ruby's face was once again impassive. But she hadn't been mistaken a moment ago. She could only hope it was mere infatuation on Ruby's part, and that the man had no inkling of her feelings. But why had he come here this evening? Certainly not to ask permission to start an allotment! She had seen through that ruse straight away, but had imagined it an excuse to introduce himself to her, maybe to ingratiate himself, taking advantage of the fact that Mr Masters was off today.

'Lady Caldworthy, are you all right? You look very pale. Shall I help you to bed?' Ruby was bending over her, her face full of concern.

So agitated was she that she slapped at Ruby's arm, pushing her away before returning her steely gaze to the man. When she saw the mocking smile on his full lips and the impudent look in his eyes, she actually cried out in dismay.

'Oh, Lady Caldworthy, what is it? Shall I send for Dr Benson?'

Ruby was once again by her side, and as she stared into the innocent face that had become so dear to her, she felt her strength return. Gently she patted Ruby's arm. 'Just a minor bout of dizziness, dear. I'm perfectly all right now.' Then, turning once again to

Michael, she said in a clear firm voice, 'I'm glad you decided to visit us, Mr O'Brien. I don't normally meet my outdoor staff so the experience has been quite a revelation.'

Michael returned her unblinking stare. Then, with a disarming smile, he lightly touched his forehead before turning his back on the two women, closing the door behind him.

No sooner was the door shut than Ruby hastily walked over to the mahogany sideboard where Lady Caldworthy's medicines were kept. Careful to avoid her employer's gaze, she began to measure out the mixture.

Lady Caldworthy looked at Ruby's stiff back and called out softly, 'Ruby, leave that for a minute. I wish to talk to you.'

'I'm preparing your evening medication, ma'am. Dr Benson was most insistent you should take it at the prescribed times.' Ruby's voice was muffled as she tried to compose herself before facing the enquiring eyes she knew were scrutinising her.

'I'll take my medicine later. At present I have more important things on my mind. Stop fussing with those bottles and come here. *Now*, Ruby.'

The last two words were issued in the form of a command, and Ruby, inhaling deeply, turned round ready to stave off the penetrating questions she knew were coming, but when she saw the wrinkled face full of pity and concern, her resolve broke, and without thinking she half ran to Lady Caldworthy's side. Dropping awkwardly to the floor she buried her face into the camphor-scented folds of the old lady's dress.

Lady Caldworthy looked down upon the bowed head, her gnarled hand resting on the crown of thick glossy auburn hair. Her faded blue eyes full of compassion, she wondered what tone to take before adopting the line she had always used: straight and to the point. Having decided on her course of action, she said without preamble, 'Is there something between you and Michael O'Brien? And, if so, how far has it gone?'

Hearing the bluntness of the words, Ruby shuddered, then, lifting her head, she said simply, 'There is nothing between us, Lady Caldworthy. We often talk when we meet in the gardens, but he has always treated me with the utmost respect. He feels nothing for me other than friendship. There has never been any attempt at impropriety on his side, on that you have my word. So, you see, you have nothing to worry about.' Her words trailed off miserably, and then, her voice breaking, she added fiercely, 'But, oh, God, how I wish there were. I love him. I know it's hopeless, but I can't help the way I feel. I love him so much that it hurts!'

The intensity of her words touched a chord in Lady Caldworthy's heart, and the part of her that was once young found empathy with Ruby's anguish. She waited until Ruby's sobs had quietened, and then, lifting up the trembling chin, she said, 'I am very sad to see you in such distress, child, and I wish I could say something to ease your pain, but I must speak the truth as I see it. Come, lay your head in my lap and listen. What I am going to say will undoubtedly hurt you, but please believe me when I tell you that I have only your best interests at heart.'

Ruby felt her body shrink but she nodded her head, too drained to make any rejoinder, telling herself that no matter what Lady Caldworthy said, nothing would change the feelings she had for Michael.

Lady Caldworthy leaned back in her chair, lost for a moment in the past, and then, stroking Ruby's hair, she began to speak. 'I'm an old woman, Ruby, past my three score years and ten, but as with many old people, the past is often clearer to me than the present. I can remember what it was like to be young, to feel the strong vitality of life coursing through my veins, and I can still recall what it was like to be in love: that glorious feeling that is part pain and part pleasure. The feeling of exquisite excitement when I saw the young man of the moment walking towards me and my heart would begin to pound. My whole being seeming to melt and dissolve at the sight of a warm smile or the touch of a hand on mine.' Her voice faltered for a moment as memories came rushing back.

The sudden movement of Ruby's body jerked her back to the present and, putting an arm round the young girl's shoulders, she pulled her closer before continuing. 'I was about your age, maybe a little older, when I first met Patrick Flynn. He was a groom at my father's stables. At first I didn't take any notice of him. He was only a groom, after all, and I was the young lady of the house. I don't even remember when I first realized I was falling in love with him. My father was delighted at my sudden interest in his beloved horses, for I'd never shown any before. He never suspected for a moment the purpose behind my daily visits to the stables. I wasn't sure myself; I only knew that I couldn't let a day pass without looking at the handsome Irishman with the laughing eyes. Patrick himself never knew of my feelings for him, for I was always very careful to remain aloof when I was in his presence. Then one day I was out riding on Hackney Marshes, and I met him returning from his day off. He walked alongside me and suddenly there was a tremendous thunderstorm. Patrick grabbed hold of the horse's bridle and led us to an old shed on the edge of the park. We were drenched to the skin and I can remember laughing and talking too loudly, conscious of the fact that we were alone in the dark shed. And then the laughing stopped . . .'

Ruby lifted her head and stared in amazement at the face above hers. The years seemed to have vanished from the old lady's face, the eyes appeared clearer and the lines softer, and for a brief moment she caught a glimpse of the beauty that had once been. Her own troubles forgotten, she asked quietly, 'What happened then?'

The wrinkled hand came out and tapped Ruby gently on the cheek. 'That, child, I will leave to your imagination,' she answered wickedly, the familiar grin lighting up her face.

Ruby felt her cheeks redden, and stuttered quickly, 'No, I mean . . . What happened to Patrick?'

The smile slipped from the old lady's face as she recalled, 'We had four glorious months together, months of loving and laughing, and I thought it would go on for ever. Then I discovered I was pregnant, a natural thing to happen under the circumstances. I was so afraid . . . afraid of what my parents would do when they found out, but more afraid that Patrick would leave me. When I told him, he insisted we go at once to my parents and tell them we wanted to get married. I was horrified at the suggestion – not that I didn't want to marry him, as it was what I wanted more than anything in life, but I knew my parents would never agree. Well-brought-up ladies did not marry below their class. It wasn't done, and it still isn't done.'

The implication wasn't lost on Ruby, but before she could interject, the old lady swept on, 'I was terrified at the prospect of facing my parents, but such was the power of Patrick's persuasion that I began to believe that everything would be all right. How naïve I was, or maybe I was simply so much in love that I believed my parents would see Patrick as I saw him. There was a terrible confrontation when my mother, bless her, fainted clean away. My father never uttered a word, but drew back his fist and hit him straight between the eyes. Patrick never had a chance to retaliate. Before he could get to his feet, my father, with the aid of his valet, grabbed him by the scruff of the neck and threw him from the room and out of the house. I was nearly hysterical by this time and ran screaming after them, proclaiming loudly that I was going to marry him and nobody was going to stop me. And there was poor Patrick sprawled on the gravel outside the house, looking bewildered and angry. I think, in retrospect, it was the loss of dignity that offended him the most. I was kept a virtual prisoner for the next few days and refused to eat or drink until I could see Patrick again. At last, fearful for my well-being, my father agreed to let me go to the house where he knew Patrick was then working. He even gave his permission for us to marry on condition that I wouldn't expect him to support us. If I was insistent on marrying a groom, then I must be prepared to live the life of a groom's wife. I was ecstatic; I didn't care about my father's money, I only wanted Patrick. I couldn't wait to get to him and tell him the good news. I was so excited that I never noticed him drawing away from me. Oh, he said all the right things, assured me that nothing mattered but being together, that the money was unimportant, and he would love me for ever – and I believed him, young impressionable fool that I was! He told me to leave the wedding arrangements to him and that as soon as we were married he would take me to a house he knew of where they needed a groom and a house-maid. I kissed him goodbye and hurried home full of plans, not giving a thought to the hurt I would be inflicting on my parents. But then, the young are often cruel. When I arrived back at the house, my father met me in the hall. He asked just one question: "Did you tell him there would be no money coming to you?", to which I replied grandly that I had, and it made no difference. He merely nodded his head and walked into his study, shutting the door. He was a very wise man, my father. Of course I never saw Patrick again. When I returned to the house where he had been working, I was told he had gone off in the night without even waiting for his wages. That was over fifty years ago, but sometimes in the middle of the night I wake up and still feel the dreadful soul-destroying hurt and ache I felt that day.'

Ruby reached out and took hold of the trembling hand, her heart full of pity for the proud elderly woman. 'I'm so very sorry that you suffered so much. He must have been a terrible man to have treated you like that.'

'No, Ruby, he wasn't. He was a charming likeable man with a strong personality that drew people to him, men and women alike. He had a presence about him that very few men have. It's not something one can emulate, it comes from within; such men are born with the gift of attracting people to them. They often are not aware of the power they possess, but having that power ensures them an easy life, for there will always be a woman to look after them. Whether as mother or lover, women will always be drawn to these men. That is what makes them weak, for they never have to strive for anything, as it comes naturally to them. It also prevents them from ever being capable of loving only one woman, when there are so many to choose from. I believe, even now, that if things had been different and I had been able to bring the money with me, he would never have been faithful. That type of man never is; they can't help themselves. In a perverse way it's part of their charm, for every woman thinks she will be the one who will finally tame him. Although, since he wasn't prepared to take me in my shift, as the saying goes, I shall never know for sure.'

She fell silent once again, and this time Ruby didn't interrupt her reverie. She felt certain there was more to come and settled herself to wait for the conclusion, and, more important, the reason for the story. The silence stretched, and Ruby found her eyelids drooping, but she was jerked awake by the sound of harsh coughing. As quickly as she could, she went over to the sideboard, where the bottle of medicine stood ready. Measuring out two spoonfuls into a small glass vial, she carried it back to her mistress.

Lady Caldworthy took the white chalky substance and swallowed it quickly, grimacing at the bitter taste. Then, wiping her mouth with a white-lace handkerchief, she motioned Ruby to resume her position beside her on the floor. 'I'm sorry, my dear. Are you comfortable sitting on the floor? I sometimes forget your disability.'

Ruby smiled warmly. 'I'm perfectly comfortable, thank you, and I'm glad you sometimes forget about my leg. It makes me feel more normal.'

Lady Caldworthy looked down on the smiling face, feeling a surge of love and affection for the young girl. If only she had been blessed with a daughter such as she! But now she must tread warily, for if she handled the situation badly she might lose her for good, and that thought was unbearable. Clearing her throat, she said briskly, 'Well, now, my sorry tale is nearly over. I was packed off to an elderly aunt in Northumberland to have the baby. It was taken from me at birth and I never saw it again. I don't even know if it was a boy or a girl. When I returned to London, my father had already arranged a marriage for me to the son of a friend. Of course everyone knew why I'd been sent away, and under normal circumstances no man of my class would have even considered marrying a girl who had let herself become pregnant by a common workman, but this particular family were in dire financial straits. My father paid them handsomely to make an honest woman of me, and the young man he chose was kind enough. In time he fell in love with me, but I could never return his love. The marriage lasted only five years, and I was happy enough, I suppose, then quite suddenly he caught a chill which turned into pneumonia, and within two weeks he was dead. I can't pretend I was prostrate with grief, but I did feel remorse that I had never been able to return his shows of affection, for, as I've already said, he was a kind man and deserved better than me.'

Ruby wanted to protest, but was firmly silenced. 'Over the last fifty years I've had four husbands and numerous lovers, but none of them ever quite measured up to my Patrick. How could they? For, as each year passed, I added more and more attributes to my Irishman than he ever possessed in real life. But I did have those glorious months with him, and despite how he treated me, some part of me still loves him, or the young man he was. My time with him was short, but I lived more in those few months than I have ever lived since. Men like Patrick are rare, a breed apart. You cannot help loving them, even though you know it will end in tears, and once you have experienced that kind of love, nothing else will ever be quite the same. When Michael O'Brien walked in here tonight, I recognized him immediately, or rather, I recognized the type of man he is. It was as if Patrick had come back into my life, and then I saw the look on your face and I knew straight away what had happened. Ruby, dear' – her hand tightened on Ruby's cold fingers – 'don't make the same mistake I did, I beg you. Nothing can come of such an alliance. Even if Michael were to return your love, you must know that your father would never allow you to marry him. One more thing I must add' – here she swallowed painfully – 'The man's an opportunist. He would quite willingly marry you if he thought that one day you would inherit some of your father's money, and, of course, it would be an added bonus for him to get himself not only a rich wife but a beautiful one into the bargain. He will speak to you soon, I'm sure, but please, Ruby, don't be taken in by his blarney, as I once was with Patrick! You can do better, much better. What you are feeling now is merely sexual attraction, and I know what I'm talking about. Don't feel, because of your disability, that you have to take the first man who asks you. You have so much to offer, and if . . .'

Ruby got clumsily to her feet, her face white with anger. 'Why don't you say what you really mean, ma'am? You're implying that Michael thinks he can marry me if he wishes and in so doing feather his nest with a tidy bit of money thrown in. All this good fortune is because I'm a cripple and, as such, can't afford to be too choosy where marriage is concerned!'

Lady Caldworthy felt her stomach lurch painfully at the sound of the bitterness in Ruby's voice. She had handled the situation badly.

She should have said nothing, and simply given Mr Masters orders to dismiss the Irishman as soon as possible. Maybe it wasn't too late. Maybe, if she spoke to the man himself, offered him a sizeable amount of money, he would leave of his own accord. If he accepted, and she was certain he would, Ruby would never know that she had played any part in his sudden departure. Comforted by her decision, she relaxed into her chair, only to jump forward at Ruby's next words.

'Do you imagine I don't know how limited my chances of marriage are? It never mattered to me until I met Michael, but now it does. If he asked me tomorrow to marry him, I'd say yes, even if I knew it was only my father's money he was interested in. If that's the only way I can get him, then I'll use it to good advantage. You said yourself that those four months with Patrick were the happiest days of your life. Well, I want my four months, and I intend to get them in any way I can!'

'But, child, your father would never agree to such a marriage; never! He dotes on you, and he would see through Michael as easily as my father saw through Patrick, with much the same results. Think, Ruby! Don't suffer the humiliation I did, please.'

At the sound of the desperate plea in the old lady's voice, the stiffness went out of Ruby's body and the colour returned to her face as she said wearily, 'All this is rather beside the point, isn't it? Michael has shown no sign of wanting to marry me. So far, he has shown friendship, nothing more. But if you are thinking of dismissing him, then know now that the day he leaves this house, I go too. If I have to follow him all over the country, I'll do it! I'll be his friend, I'll be godmother to his children, I'll be anything he wants me to be as long as I can be near him. Now, ma'am, if there's nothing else, I will go to my room. I need to think for a while, as I'm sure you do. I'll be back at ten o'clock to undress you and get you ready for bed.'

Lady Caldworthy watched in dismay as Ruby left the room, and when she heard the click of her door closing, her face crumpled slowly.

Michael walked across the darkened garden, his handsome face suffused with anger. Savagely he kicked a large stone from his path as he made his way to the two-roomed lodge where he lived. He entered the gloomy room, and moved to the table that served as a place to eat and was also where he pored over his meagre collection of books every evening. Quickly lighting the old copper lantern, he placed it on the table and sat down heavily on the only chair in the room. The clean but faded cotton curtains hung dispiritedly at the sides of the tiny cracked window, and in the hearth, the fire he had left burning brightly had gone out. Shivering slightly, for the night had turned cold, he gathered some old newspapers, which he thrust under the pile of wood in the grate and set light to them. As he sat on his haunches waiting for the fire to catch, he thought back to the interview he had just endured.

Well, he had blown his chances there, right enough. Why had he antagonized the old lady? He'd had no intention of doing so when he'd first entered the room. He had been genuine in his request for permission to start an allotment, but had used that only so that he could work his way round to asking for the coming Saturday off, because that old bugger Mr Masters would never have agreed to his taking a day off a week early. He'd had it all planned out: to charm the old dear into granting him his request and then to waylay Ruby and ask her to come with him to the fair. He could have done it, too, if he hadn't been so cocksure!

Those piercing blue eyes had seen through him, right enough, and by this time tomorrow he would likely be out on the streets looking for a new job. He watched dismally as the fire began to take hold, then walked back to the table and sat down restlessly. The room wasn't much, but he had lived in worse – oh, yes, much worse! Unable to settle, he got to his feet and began pacing the floor, then, going over to the small stove he placed the kettle of water on it. While he waited for it to boil, he opened his cupboard and took out the solitary mug and plate, upon which reposed a thick ham sandwich covered with a damp muslin cloth that Agnes had brought over earlier that evening. Thinking of the young housemaid, he felt the beginnings of a smile come to his stiff lips. If ever a woman was asking for it, she was! She'd done everything but put his hand up her skirt, but Michael preferred to do his own chasing, and so far had declined the unspoken offer. Now if it had been Ruby! But there was no chance of that happening, especially not now. Oh, God, what a fool he'd been! All his life he'd wanted to amount to something, and for years he had struggled to educate himself with the help of the books he had bought, borrowed or stolen on his many travels.

He had been only eleven when his parents had worked themselves into early graves back in his home town of Drogheda, and had then watched helplessly as his remaining two brothers and one sister had died from starvation and neglect. He himself had been rescued by the village priest, who had taken him in and given him shelter, even though the old man's stipend had barely covered the cost of his own meagre needs. It was this kind man who had first introduced Michael to the world of books, and the knowledge that could be gleaned from their pages. When he had died, Michael, by then fifteen, had stowed away on a ship bound for England, and had nearly died for his pains. Cramped into a dark stinking hold with no food or water for three days, he had eventually been found by one of the crew, who took him to the captain. He had stood before the great giant of a man, dirty, and with an overpowering stink from the rotting hold where he had been hiding.

He had worked his passage, and when the ship had finally docked at Tilbury weeks later, he had walked proudly off it with five shillings in his pockets and a set of secondhand clothes on his back. It had taken him only two days to find a job as stablehand in a grand house in Kilburn, and as soon as he'd saved enough money, he had left. His next job had been as coachman for a middle-aged woman whose husband had recently died. Within a month, Michael had moved from the top of the carriage and into her bed. At first he had been embarrassed to take the money she'd offered, but had quickly overcome his scruples. Tiring of her eventually, he had once again set off on the road, this time with two books stolen from the lady's shelves tucked safely inside his canvas bag. He had had many jobs since, but never had he felt at home until he had come here.

He was now twenty-five, and the feeling of wanting a family of his own had been growing for some time. But it would have to be with a woman with some money of her own, for although he was well aware of his charm, he knew this wasn't enough. He needed education if he wanted to make anything of himself, and in Ruby he had seen the chance of killing two birds with one stone. She would help to educate him, and her father was rich. Michael wasn't stupid enough to believe that he would be welcomed with open arms by the unknown Mr Chadwick, but he was willing to bide his time. Just let him get Ruby to marry him and by the time there were two or three grandchildren running around, the old man would relent! If that failed, well, he couldn't live for ever, and from what he'd heard in the kitchen, the old man was crazy about his only daughter. Even though the bulk of his money would go to the elder son, Ruby would surely receive a handsome inheritance. Yes, he would wait. He was a patient man, and she wanted him; he could see it in her eyes.

If only the old lady didn't dismiss him! Cursing himself once again for his stupidity, he carried his mug of strong black tea into his bedroom. This room, like the kitchen, was small, just barely large enough to accommodate the double bed, a chest of drawers and a night table. Finishing off the sandwich and the mug of tea, he began to undress, wondering where he'd be this time tomorrow night. Just as he was about to pull his shirt over his head, he heard the faint sound of a knock on the door. He stopped what he was doing, his arms raised over his head, the shirt half-covering his face, and listened intently. There it was again, louder this time. Quickly pulling his shirt back over his chest, he picked up the lantern and walked to the door. It couldn't be, could it? Surely Ruby hadn't come to him at this time of night? No, the idea was preposterous, but if not Ruby, then who? Not Mr Masters, returned from his day out, come to deliver his notice? If so, the old girl hadn't wasted much time!

The knocking became more insistent, and a soft voice whispered urgently, 'Michael, open the door before someone sees me!'

He sprang forward to draw back the bolt. The voice was muffled, but it could be only one person. When he threw back the door and saw Agnes standing there, the disappointment made him feel sick. Then the feeling turned to anger. If she wanted it that badly, then by God he wouldn't disappoint her! Without a word he grasped her arm and dragged her into the lodge. Pushing her in front of him he steered her into the bedroom, and then, still without a word, he shoved her roughly on to the bed, and threw himself down on her.

Chapter Seventeen

When a week had passed without any further word from the house, Michael began to relax. If he had been going to be dismissed, he would have heard by now. All the same, he couldn't help wondering why he had been given a reprieve. As he bent over the herbaceous border, his strong hands busily trying to pull out the stubborn weeds that had infiltrated his pride and joy, he became aware of a presence beside him. Turning his sweating face sideways, he groaned silently at the sight of Agnes standing behind him, one hand perched on her plump hip, a saucy grin on her rosy face.

'Good morning, Michael,' she said coyly. 'Cook wants to know if you're coming in for your breakfast. It's past nine and she wants to clear away the dishes. We've all had ours ages ago. Why haven't you been in?'

Turning back to his task, Michael answered brusquely, 'I haven't time for any breakfast today. I want to get the garden ready for the holiday weekend. Lady Caldworthy has friends coming over. She plans to hold a tea-party out here, and I want to make sure the garden doesn't disgrace her in front of her fine friends.'

Agnes looked down on his broad back, her uneven teeth nipping at her bottom lip. She wasn't the brightest of women, but even she knew when she was being rebuffed, and after that night they'd had as well! She'd hoped that night would have heralded the start of a firm relationship, but it seemed to have had the opposite effect, for Michael's avoidance of her since was too obvious to be ignored. An inner wisdom told her to tread warily, if she didn't want to scare him off for good. He was the best-looking man she'd ever met, and she didn't intend to give him up without a fight. Maybe he was feeling guilty about the way he had treated her. She still had the bruises from that night, small mauve and blue blemishes on her body to remind her of the rough lovemaking she had enjoyed with him. But they didn't worry her; in fact she was delighted that she'd had the power to incite him to such passion.

Michael pulled viciously at a long yellow weed, wishing the girl would go away. He wished wholeheartedly that that night had never happened, for the girl had followed him around like a lovesick cow ever since. He had tried his best to avoid her but to no avail: every chance she got she was out in the garden standing over him as she was now, hoping, he knew, for some kind word, but he had none to give. It was bad enough that he had slept with her, an action he bitterly regretted even before the loveless act had finished, but there was no way he was going to give her any further encouragement. If she'd been a virgin it would have been different, for then he would have tempered his irritation with kindness, telling himself that she must have thought highly of him indeed. For no girl or woman gives up that precious commodity unless she really cares for the man in question. But this one standing behind him had been no innocent. Begod, no, she knew what it was all about, right enough! Now he had the problem of shaking her off – if she was entertaining any thoughts about a permanent relationship, she was going to be sorely disappointed. He had definite ideas about the kind of woman he would eventually marry, and when he took his bride to bed it would be with the certain knowledge that he was the first man she had been with, someone like Ruby.

What was he thinking of? That avenue was closed to him. He had thought he meant something to her, but since that night in the old lady's room he hadn't seen hide nor hair of her. Well, he'd give it another month, and if she still hadn't made any attempt to seek him out, he would move on. But there was still Agnes to contend with. Straightening up, he stroked his chin absently with a dirt-streaked hand while he sought for the right words. He didn't want to hurt the girl, for he wasn't a cruel man, but he had to make it clear that there was no future for her with him.

Clearing his throat, he turned to face her, and as gently as possible said, 'Look, Agnes, I've been meaning to speak to you about the other night. It's heart-sorry I am that I behaved the way I did, and I can promise you that it will never happen again. A good-looking woman like yourself can do a lot better than the likes of me, so what say we forget it happened, eh?'

The girl's eyes clouded over in anger, and a mulish look came over her normally happy face. 'Forget it, you say?' Agnes stood squarely in front of him, her hands resting firmly on her ample hips. 'And suppose I don't want to forget it? Just suppose there's a result of that night – have you thought of that?' She saw the look of surprise and disbelief that crossed Michael's face and felt a surge of triumph.

Then it was her turn to stare open-mouthed in disbelief as he threw back his head in a great gust of laughter. 'Oh, no, me darlin'! You're not catching me with that old trick. I got off the boat from Ireland ten years ago, not yesterday. Go on now, get yourself back into the house and tell Cook I'll be in shortly.' As Agnes turned away dejectedly, he couldn't prevent his impulse to take a swipe at her swaying backside.

The stinging slap brought Agnes's head round sharply, but the angry words died on her lips at the sight of the engaging grin that was now spread across Michael's face. In spite of her anger and disappointment, she felt herself smiling back at him before walking back into the house.

Left alone once more, the grin slipped from Michael's face. That little scene could have turned very nasty, but once again his Irish charm had rescued him, as it had done so many times before. Whistling gaily, he returned to his work.

Ruby watched the small scenario from her bedroom window, her ears straining to hear the conversation, but the two people she was most interested in were too far away from her to hear more than a muted fusion of voices. She watched with sadness and envy as Michael playfully slapped Agnes on the bottom before sending her on her way, smiling happily to herself. Her body weighed down with unhappiness, she let the curtain drop and walked to her bed. Easing herself on to the soft feather mattress, she let her eyes close. Lady Caldworthy was resting, as was her custom after breakfast; she always maintained it helped her digestive system to rest after every meal, but Ruby suspected it was more the onset of old age that prompted these frequent naps.

Turning on to her side, she tried to take a nap herself; there was nothing else to do these days. Her work had become less and less over the past months, with Lady Caldworthy delegating her former duties to the rest of the staff. The only real work she did now was to attend the old lady, who had seemed to become more and more dependent upon her. In fact, just lately she had seemed afraid to let Ruby out of her sight. The social barriers that had existed between them were slowly crumbling and Ruby knew that the woman lying in the next room was coming to look upon her as a friend rather than a paid companion. She in turn had become very fond of her gruff employer and knew that despite her threat to leave if Michael went, she would never be able to bring herself to carry it out. And now she was trapped here in this house in much the same way as she'd been at home: trapped by her own feelings of loyalty.

Dear God! What was she to do? Nothing had worked out the way she had planned. Where was her precious independence now? Where was the pride in receiving money for a job well done? The only experience she had come across was heartache. Sighing heavily, she stared mournfully at the high whitewashed ceiling, her mind wandering aimlessly, then with a start she sat bolt upright, her hands clenching themselves into tight fists.

'What's come over you, Ruby Chadwick, moping and mooning like a half-wit!' she reproached herself sharply. 'Things don't happen just by wishing for them, you have to make them happen. So get up off your backside and start doing some positive thinking.'

Her spirits restored, she got off the bed and began to walk slowly round her room, her active mind whirling with plans for the future – *her* future. Next week was a bank holiday, and she had the Sunday off to visit her parents. She had originally intended to spend the Monday with them as well, but Lady Caldworthy had organized a garden party for a few of her old friends, friends with eligible grandsons, no doubt. She had to applaud the old woman's cunning, and she, Ruby, would go along with the plans to please the mistress she had become so very fond of. On Monday she would wear the blue dress she'd worn for her eighteenth birthday and, if necessary, flirt with any young man who attended the gathering. The practice would come in useful! Crossing to the window once more, she looked out just as Michael was gazing at her window. Waving gaily to him, she was delighted to see the genuine smile of pleasure light up his face at the sight of her. Giving one last wave, she turned and made her way across her room to check if Lady Caldworthy was awake yet, and as she opened her door, she thought cheerfully, 'Make the most of your freedom, Michael O'Brien, because I'm coming after you!'

With a sudden rush of confidence she brushed aside her anxieties over her stump and the hateful wooden leg. She was pretty and intelligent, and no more would she look upon herself as a cripple. She was as good as any woman, and once she was Mrs O'Brien, she would no longer have to prove anything to herself, and would at last be able to lay her ghosts to rest.

'Have you taken leave of your senses? You calmly tell me you're planning on marrying a common gardener, just like that? No lead-up to it?

No, what do you think I should do? You've gone mad, that's what's happened! Shut up with a senile old woman all day, it's sent you round the twist!'

'It's no use your shouting and carrying on, Lily! I've made up my mind. If Michael will have me, then I will marry him, and nothing you can do or say will make me think again.'

Lily stared aghast at her friend's set determined face, her mind in a turmoil. She didn't know whether to laugh or run for a doctor. God Almighty, if the master heard her, he'd lock her up in the attic and throw away the key, and she'd stand guard outside the door; yes, she would, if it meant saving her dearest friend from a life of hardship and misery. Yet if Ruby was determined to marry this man, she'd do it; one way or another she'd do it. Lily shook her head wildly. She couldn't allow this to happen, she wouldn't let it happen. Ruby wasn't the only one with a strong determined streak. Raising her chin, she said sarcastically, 'And what does this Michael O'Brien have to say about the forthcoming marriage, or haven't you told him yet?'

She waited for Ruby to swing round, bracing herself for an angry retort, but Ruby continued to sort through her wardrobe, picking out various dresses and putting them back again. Then, gently pushing Lily to one side, she carried the long blue evening gown over to the bed and carefully placed it across the coverlet before going to her dressing-table and opening the top drawer. 'Where are my necklace and earrings, Lily? Have they been put into the safe? I can't wear the dress without them; it's too plain on its own.'

Exasperated beyond control, Lily grabbed hold of Ruby's arm, turning her round to face her. 'Have you listened to a word I've said? Your father would never allow you to marry beneath your station. I believe he'd kill you first!' Her voice dropped to a whisper before repeating, 'He would, you know. He'd kill you before he'd let you marry a common Irishman.'

Ruby felt a jolt of fear at the ominous words, then attempted to laugh, but the effect was strained even to her own ears. 'You must stop reading those cheap novelettes you're so fond of! My dad isn't capable of killing anyone, and as for marrying beneath my station, what is my station? I was born over a pub in the East End of London and spent my childhood years running with the assorted ragamuffins of the streets – when my dad wasn't watching, of course. If my grandfather hadn't died and left Dad his money, we'd still be there.'

Lily closed her eyes wearily. Was Ruby being deliberately dense? Surely she knew that her father considered himself one of the upper class. Even when he'd stood behind the bar of the King's Arms he'd thought himself a cut above everyone else in the neighbourhood. Running her hand distractedly through her blonde hair, she thought frantically, 'Why did this have to happen?' But maybe the Irishman would take to his heels when he learned of Ruby's plans for him. If, as Ruby maintained, he had as yet no inkling of her feelings, there was a good chance he wouldn't take kindly to having his future mapped out for him. From what little Ruby had told her about him, he didn't sound the type of man who would be willing to brave the wrath of any angry father but was rather the kind who preferred an uncomplicated life. Please God that was the case, because, if not, all hell would break loose soon. Then, quite suddenly, a new thought came to her, giving her the first glimpse of hope she'd had since Ruby had dropped the bombshell in her lap.

'All right, Ruby, let's say for argument's sake that this Michael of yours agrees to marry you. Do you think he'll be prepared to wait three years until you come of age? Because no matter how much you protest that your father will come to accept the situation, we both know you're deluding yourself. And what about your mother? I can't see her being over the moon with joy either, can you?'

With shaking hands Ruby continued to fold the long dress carefully, her face, studiously calm, reflecting none of the apprehension and fear she was feeling. All of what Lily had said was true: just thinking of facing her dad with her news – providing Michael felt the same, of course – made her bowels turn to water. But that last piece of information about having to wait three years made her feel physically sick. She could see all her carefully laid plans flying out of the window, for the inner part of herself that never shied from the truth told her with sickening clarity that Michael would never wait three years for her; it was doubtful if he'd wait three months.

She knew from her conversations with him that this post as gardener was the longest he had ever held down, but if that was the case, why had he stayed so long? She'd hoped, desperately hoped, that the reason for his continuing presence was herself, but just suppose it was Agnes he was staying on for? Oh, no, it couldn't be, it couldn't! But she'd seen them together, seen the easy familiarity between them, but surely if it was Agnes he was after, he'd have spoken to her before now, and he hadn't, she was sure of that if of nothing else. If he had, the news would have been common knowledge in the house; Agnes would have seen to that, for it was obvious the girl was smitten with him – as indeed she herself was. Well, there was only one way to find out, and tomorrow at the garden party she would seek him out and ask him. It would take all the courage she possessed, but do it she would and take the consequences, however painful they might be.

Forcing a watery smile to her lips, she faced the anxious Lily and said softly, 'Don't worry, Lily, everything will be all right. Now will you help me to fold this dress so that it won't crease on the journey back to the house?'

The large immaculate garden was full of people. Lady Caldworthy had delved deep into her memory to renew old acquaintances, in particular those friends who had grandsons of marriageable age. Seated in a large wicker chair in the centre of the lush green lawn, she smiled happily at the scene before her.

'Would you care for a drink, ma'am?' Michael stood at her side dressed in the unfamiliar garb of butler, because Mr Masters had had the misfortune to sprain his ankle just hours before.

'Thank you, Michael, I'll have a glass of port,' she replied graciously, her ever-watchful eyes noticing that the black morning coat seemed to be straining across his broad shoulders. Taking the proffered glass from his white-gloved hand, she continued, 'Are you managing all right with your new duties?'

'Yes, thank you, ma'am, although I wouldn't care to make a career of it.' Bowing slightly, he moved off into the crowd, leaving Lady Caldworthy free to resume her watch on Ruby.

Taking a delicate sip of her port, she looked over to where the girl stood talking to a young fair-haired man, the eligible grandson of old friends she hadn't seen for years. He looked presentable enough, and she could only hope he hadn't inherited his parents' boring attributes. She felt ridiculously pleased that so many of her friends had responded to her invitation, particularly as she hadn't seen many of them for a very long time. It had come as a great surprise to find that the majority of them were still living, but although she was genuinely pleased to see them again, it was their grandchildren whom she was most interested in. Of the twelve couples she had invited, she had been delighted to note eight grandsons accompanying them. Surely there would be one among them who would take Ruby's fancy?

Then, out of the corner of her eye, she saw her girlhood friend Celia Simpson bearing down on her, and groaned inwardly. When she had sent out the invitations, she'd had no real hope of receiving a reply, imagining the woman to be long dead. But here she was, larger than life and even more tiresome that she'd remembered. Holding her arm was a young man young enough to be her grandson, who had been introduced earlier on as a 'very dear friend', in such a cloying manner that Lady Caldworthy had felt quite nauseated.

'Mabel, my dear, I can't tell you how lovely it's been to see you again, and all our old friends. To be honest, I thought most of them would be dead, but I've had such a marvellous time that I've decided to hold a party of my own. You will come, won't you, Mabel dear? and of course you must bring that sweet companion of yours. Such a charming girl.' Dropping her voice, she glanced round furtively before adding, 'Anne Forsythe told me that the girl has a peg-leg. I couldn't believe it at first until I caught a glimpse of the wooden tip showing below her dress, and I said to Anne, how like dear Mabel to take a cripple into her home and treat her as one of the family! You've always been so kind, my dear. She comes from a good family, so I hear. Such a tragic waste of a young life, and so pretty, too.'

Lady Caldworthy looked with distaste at the heavily made-up face peering down at her. Now she remembered why she had broken off the friendship. Celia had always been an empty-headed fool, especially where men were concerned, but in her youth she had been kind. Now it seemed that her inborn insensitivity had turned to cruelty, and this fact was borne out when she added spitefully, 'I see young Thomas Castleton is taking a good deal of interest in her, I wonder if he knows of her deformity? You really should warn her not to set her expectations too high, my dear. As I've already said, she's very pretty, but young men are very particular where women are concerned, and I really can't see any of our circle of friends welcoming a cripple into the family, can you?'

Mabel drew herself upright, her face dark with rage. How dared this raddled old woman criticize Ruby in such a manner? Her cold glance took in the frilly low-cut blue dress that would have been better suited to a girl of twenty, and then to the over-painted face. Good God, she had enough powder on to blow up the Houses of Parliament! In a voice that dripped with ice, she retorted, 'There I have to disagree with you, Celia. I would imagine that any parents would welcome a young, intelligent, loving girl like Ruby into their family. As for young men today being particular . . .' Here she broke off, her eyes going to the effeminate man standing awkwardly by the side of his elderly benefactor, then, her lips curling with distaste at the sight of the ill-matched pair she continued, 'There will always be some who aren't too fussy whom they take up with, provided, of course, that the necessary inducement is offered. Fortunately, Ruby will never have to bribe her way into a man's affections: her good breeding would never allow her to stoop to such a distasteful level.' She watched with satisfaction as the young man's face became suffused with colour before switching her attention to her one-time friend who was by now bridling with indignation. Her shot had found its mark.

'Really, Mabel, you always did have a vindictive character! What you are implying is completely untrue, and I will not stay here to be insulted in this manner! As for your precious protégée, well, I'd like to wager that before too many years have passed she'll be only to glad to drop her standards. Pretty and intelligent she may be, but she's still a cripple, and . . .' Her next words were cut off, to be replaced by a loud shriek as a pitcher of lemonade cascaded down the front of her silk dress.

'Oh Lord, ma'am, I'm terribly sorry! It was an accident, so it was. Someone pushed me from behind. Your pretty dress is ruined, so you'd best be away home to change. It would be unwise to stand around in wet clothes. You might catch a chill, and that could be dangerous . . . at your age, ma'am.' Michael stood before the enraged old woman, the look of contrition on his face unable to mask the anger in his blue eyes.

'You clumsy oaf, how dare you speak to a lady in such a fashion! You deserve to be horsewhipped!' The young man had stepped forward, his pride so much wounded by Lady Caldworthy's remark that he sought to find a way to assert his masculinity and restore his bruised ego. Celia Simpson's hand clutching protectively at his arm boosted his courage, and drawing his shoulders back, he faced the tall dark-haired servant, ready to take his humiliation out on the easiest of prey; one of the lower classes. Patting the old woman's hand tenderly, he stepped nearer to Michael, but any words he'd planned to say died on his lips as he stared into the steely eyes of the man before him.

'It's true what you say, sir. I deserve to be horsewhipped for my clumsy behaviour. If you would like to follow me round to the back of the house to mete out the punishment I deserve, I'll not argue.'

The young man licked his lips nervously, his body shrinking at the thinly-disguised threat. Searching wildly for a way out of the situation, he nearly fainted with relief when the voice of his mistress came to his rescue.

'Are you going to sit there and let a servant talk to one of his betters in a most insulting manner, Mabel?' Celia's voice had risen, causing people's heads to turn. Many of them had witnessed the incident, but had been too far away to hear the ensuing argument. Now they moved closer, eager to see the outcome. Feeling the advantage slipping away from her, Celia quickly took hold of the now perspiring young man's arm, and with as much dignity as she could muster, said, 'Lord Caldworthy would turn in his grave if he could see how you've changed, Mabel! Taking in stray dogs and letting servants insult your guests without so much as a word of reprimand. But then, your husband was born into the nobility; you simply married into it, and it shows. Now I'll bid you good day, Mabel. I'm sorry our long friendship had to end on such a sour note.'

Resisting the temptation to make a further retort, Lady Caldworthy watched as the odd couple swept through the gathering, and a small part of her could not but applaud Celia's grand exit. Turning her head slightly, she looked at Michael, his hands still clenched by his sides, his face grim as he stared after the retreating pair. She could feel his anger and the reason for it, and a feeling of pity and acute anxiety swept over her. No man acted as he had done unless he had strong feelings for the woman involved. In spite of the hot summer day, she felt a chill settle on her.

Michael noticed her shiver, and asked, 'Are you cold, ma'am? Shall I ask Rosie to fetch you a rug?'

She shook her head sadly. A rug wouldn't banish the coldness she felt. Raising her eyes to his, she held his gaze for a long moment before shifting her attention to where Ruby stood over by the ornamental fountain, her long auburn hair shining like burnished gold in the sunlight as she looked over in their direction, a questioning look on her face.

'If you're sure you don't need anything, ma'am, I'll take the jug back to the kitchen and get it refilled,' said Michael, bending down to pick it up. When it was safely back on the silver tray, he waited silently for a moment and then, his voice grave, he said, 'Don't worry, ma'am. It's not broken. It was a mistake to put me in the role of butler; I'm not cut out for the job. In fact, ma'am, I've been thinking that maybe it's time I moved on. May I talk to you later after the guests have gone?'

'That won't be necessary, O'Brien. You have my permission to leave whenever you wish, and may I add my thanks for the work you have done on my behalf. And may I also say I think you have made a wise decision. There is nothing for you here, and I'm sure you don't wish to remain a gardener all your life.'

Despite her steady tone, Michael was quick to pick up the note of relief in her voice. Bowing stiffly, he turned from her and made his way back into the house.

Lady Caldworthy watched him go with regret. There was no doubt that, despite his lowly garb, he was the best-looking man there today. And, if the truth be told, the best man there altogether. Compared to that pathetic excuse that had come with Celia, he had put the term 'gentleman' to shame with his strong overpowering character. Heaving a heavy sigh, she reflected upon the unfairness of the workings of the social order. Put a man like Michael O'Brien into fine clothes and give him money and power, and he would rise to the very pinnacle of success, while others who were born with these attributes merely wasted their time drifting from one trivial pursuit to another with nothing to show for their lives. But not all of them. No, not all of them!

Forcing a smile to her lips, she waved briefly to Ruby as she stood talking to Thomas Castleton, who seemed to be completely captivated by his companion. Yes, there was a young man who would be suitable for Ruby, if only she could arrange it. And if the Irishman was indeed leaving, it would give her more time in which to achieve her object.

Almost as if she'd conjured him up in her mind, Michael reappeared by her side, a brightly-coloured rug in his hands. 'I took the liberty of fetching a rug, ma'am, if you'll allow me to cover your legs. It's turning a bit chilly now.'

Lady Caldworthy looked into his face, where the sudden resignation caused a deep sadness to settle on her. Her voice trembled slightly as, meeting his eyes, she whispered, 'I'm sorry.'

Michael looked back at her and then, his voice weary, replied, 'So am I, ma'am. So am I.'

Chapter Eighteen

'You looked very beautiful today, dear, and young Thomas Castleton seemed to think so too. What did you think of him, Ruby? You appeared to be getting on very well.' Lady Caldworthy sat upright in her bed, her head and shoulders propped up by a mountain of pillows. The long day had taken its toll on her old body, and although it wasn't yet nine o'clock she was more than ready for her night's sleep.

Ruby, too, was tired, tired and disappointed, but she knew she wouldn't be able to escape to her own bed until she'd put the old lady's mind at rest. 'I had a marvellous day, ma'am,' she said brightly. 'I think it all went off very well. As for Thomas, he seems a nice young man and I enjoyed his company. Now, you rest and we can talk at length tomorrow.'

'But did he ask if he could call on you?' The owner of the thin high voice was determined to press for information.

Ruby heard the querulous tone, and sighed deeply. She knew only too well what Lady Caldworthy wanted to hear, but she could see no point in raising her hopes. Tucking the bedclothes tighter round the mattress, she said firmly, 'Yes, he did ask if he could call, and I know that is what you wanted, but he is too nice a person to be trifled with, so I didn't give him any encouragement.'

Seeing the look of distress that crossed the lined face, Ruby felt a pang of guilt, coupled with a strong sense of irritation. When was she going to be allowed to lead her own life, make her own choices? She knew Lady Caldworthy's concern arose out of affection for her, but at this moment it made no difference. She needed to be by herself. Patting her trembling hand, she said briskly, 'Now, no more questions. We're both tired, so if there's nothing more you want, I'll take my leave.'

Without waiting for a reply, she walked away, her leg dragging heavily at her side. Once inside her own room, she sat down at her dressing-table, then, cupping her face in her hands, she stared at the reflection in the mirror and whispered, 'Coward!'

She had been determined to confront Michael today, and had fortified herself with numerous glasses of port, but the opportunity hadn't presented itself and she had lacked the courage to seek him out. The nearest she had come to him were the occasions when he had handed her and Thomas Castleton their drinks. She had felt the excitement mounting in her while trying to maintain an air of nonchalance. Unaccustomed to the flattery of the young men present, she had turned to Michael, expecting to see the same admiration mirrored in his eyes, but he had looked at her with reproach, almost as though she'd somehow betrayed him. 'Well, what did you expect him to do?' she asked herself crossly. 'Throw down the trayful of drinks and sweep you up into his arms in front of all those people? Oh, to hell with him!'

Impatiently she pulled at the diamond earrings, nearly tearing them from her lobes, and threw them down on the dressing-table. Then, reaching round to the back of her neck, she fumbled with the clasp of the necklace before tossing it alongside them with a gesture of disgust. Damn it, why did her grandfather have to die and leave her dad all his money? After today she didn't know where she belonged any more, she likened her situation to the old saying: 'Neither fish, fowl nor good red meat.' According to Lady Caldworthy and Lily, Michael was inferior to her in class, and she knew this opinion would be violently expounded if her dad found out her feelings for Michael. But on the other hand she was inferior in class to the kind of man Lady Caldworthy and her dad would like her to marry. Oh, it was true the young men today had shown her attention, but she had seen the furtive looks of suspicion and alarm in the eyes of their parents and grandparents at their offsprings' attentions towards a companion, however grandly dressed.

She rose from the stool and began to take off her dress, wondering wistfully if she would ever have an occasion to wear it again. Folding it carefully, she laid it at the bottom of her wardrobe, and then limping back to her bed, she sat down. Her stump was hurting badly; she had hardly sat down all day, and the pressure of the wooden leg on her flesh was becoming unbearable. But before she could have the relief of removing it for the night, she must first go down to the kitchen and compliment Mrs Rodgers and the two girls on their excellent efforts. While she was there, she would get herself a cup of hot milk to help her to sleep, for although her body was tired to the bone, her thoughts were whirling so fast that she knew she would have difficulty in getting her much-needed rest.

Resisting the desire to sink on to her soft bed again, she urged herself into the small bathroom and quickly washed her face before returning to put on her navy wool dress. Then, with a quick look once more in her mirror, she nodded her approval at the change in her attire and left the room. Once out on the landing, she looked down at the circular stairway with dismay. Why was it that the stairs seemed to multiply when she was tired? Clinging to the polished banister, she began her slow descent, gritting her teeth against the sharp pains that were now coursing through her leg.

The first sight to meet her eyes as she entered the large cosy kitchen was Agnes sitting down, her head buried in her plump arms as she cried loudly, her shoulders heaving, while Rosie tried to comfort her. Hearing Ruby come into the room, Mrs Rodgers looked up, her kindly face filled with anxiety. 'Oh, Miss Ruby, I'm glad you've come down. Maybe you can talk some sense into Agnes? She'll make herself ill, carrying on like this!'

Startled and slightly embarrassed by the scene before her, Ruby walked over to Agnes's side and laid a hand on her heaving shoulder. 'What is it, Agnes? Who's upset you?' she asked gently.

The solicitous enquiry brought forth a fresh outburst of weeping from the distressed girl, and Ruby hurriedly removed her hand, looking across the room to Mrs Rodgers as if seeking an answer there, but the agitated cook merely shrugged, before saying, 'I don't know what's the matter with her, Miss Ruby. She was out in the garden tidying up, all cheerful like; then she came rushing back in here crying and wailing like somebody'd just died! Me and Rosie have been trying to get some sense out of her, but she just keeps crying.'

Wearily Ruby shook her head. Whatever ailed Agnes would have to keep until tomorrow, for she was in no mood to cope with a hysterical girl tonight. 'I think perhaps it would be wiser to leave her for a while until she calms down, Mrs Rodgers. As you said, it's impossible to get any sense out of her while she's like this. I'll come down again later to speak to her if I can, but I can't promise I won't fall asleep as soon as I reach my room. I'm very tired this evening, as I'm sure you all are,' she said, smiling. 'Lady Caldworthy has asked me to thank you all for the marvellous way you coped today. It must have been very difficult for you all to maintain the high standard you did. Her ladyship realizes that each of you had to treble your workload and she is very proud of you all. She especially asked me to convey her compliments to you, Mrs Rodgers, for the abundant supply of food. I myself heard many of the guests remarking on the excellence of your pies and pastries. I hope this won't result in your being enticed away from us by one of today's guests!'

The simple lie brought a beam of pleasure to Mrs Rodgers's homely face. Smoothing down her spotlessly white apron, she said proudly, 'Oh, there's no fear of that happening, Miss Ruby. I've been with her ladyship for nearly thirty years, so I'm not going to change mistresses now! And may I say, Miss Ruby, how lovely you looked. I said to Rosie and Agnes as how you were better dressed than some of them so-called ladies. Didn't I, Rosie?' she enquired of the girl who stood by the still wailing Agnes.

'She did, Miss Ruby, and me and Agnes agreed, you did look lovely. Were those jewels real, Miss Ruby? Oh, Agnes, give over, you'll be sick in a minute,' Rosie said sharply, her hand rocking Agnes's shoulder faster as if consoling a crying infant, with as much success.

Ruby smiled faintly at the swift change of conversation. She had done her duty, and now she was anxious to get to her bed. Turning back to Mrs Rodgers, she asked, 'May I have a cup of hot milk to take up with me? I don't mind making it myself. You've done enough for one day.'

Sniffing loudly, Mrs Rodgers said indignantly, 'You'll do no such thing, Miss Ruby! Now you sit yourself down for a minute while I heat the milk.'

'Thank you, and, Mrs Rodgers,' Ruby paused, feeling uncomfortable at the attention she was receiving while poor Agnes continued to wail loudly, 'it's very kind of you to compare me to a lady, but I think I'm best suited to what I'm wearing now. But I'll admit it was a nice change to dress up for the day.' Turning to Rosie, she added, 'As to your question, Rosie, yes, the jewels are real. They belonged to my grandmother, and today was the second time I'd had the opportunity to wear them.' And in all probability the last, she thought sadly.

'Here you are, Miss Ruby, nice and hot. Do you want Rosie to carry it upstairs for you?'

'Oh, no, no thank you, I can manage. You get yourselves off to bed, I'll see you all in the morning.' She was about to take the steaming cup from Mrs Rodgers's outstretched hand when she asked casually, 'By the way, where's Michael? Lady Caldworthy asked me to congratulate him for the excellent job he did in standing in for Mr Masters today.'

Before Ruby had finished speaking, a loud shriek erupted from Agnes, causing them all to jump. 'Where's Michael, you ask? Well,

I'll tell you where he is, the sly ungrateful bleeder! He's packing his bags, that's where he is, planning to do a moonlight flit. And if I hadn't gone over to the lodge to ask if he was coming in for supper, he would have gone off without a word to anyone, the bastard. And after all I done for him, as well!'

Ruby looked down at the red blotchy face contorted with anger, and felt her stomach lurch with fear. Her eyes darted to the kitchen door that led out into the garden. She couldn't believe it! He was leaving without a word to her. She couldn't let him go, she couldn't! The cup of hot milk slipped from her fingers, its steaming contents spilling out over the stone floor. Then the three women watched in amazement as she seemed to bound across the room, wrenching open the door before fleeing out into the dark night.

Mrs Rodgers stood silently watching the retreating figure, her mouth agape, her simple mind struggling to comprehend what had happened. Raising her startled gaze to the two girls who were also staring at the open door, she thought wildly, 'Oh, no, not Miss Ruby and him, surely not? But why else did she fly out of the room like that?' Her jumbled thoughts were interrupted by a fresh outburst from Agnes.

'There, you see, Rosie! I told you, didn't I, but you wouldn't believe me. Said I was making it up, but I knew there was something going on between them!' Agnes was on her feet now, all traces of tears gone, her chest heaving with righteous indignation. 'Her with her hoity-toity ways, and all the time making eyes at a common gardener! That's why he's going. He doesn't want to be stuck with a cripple round his neck – even if her dad has got money,' she shouted into the night, her voice dripping with scorn.

'Shut up, Agnes,' Rosie said quietly as she walked over to shut the kitchen door.

'Don't you tell me to shut up, Rosie Hawkins! I'm going to go up and tell her ladyship what's been going on behind her back, you see if I don't.'

As she started out of the room, Rosie pushed her back into the chair. Then, leaning over the irate figure, she told her, 'You're not going anywhere, Agnes. If what you say is true, then good for Miss Ruby; she deserves a bit of happiness. You're just jealous because Michael didn't want anything to do with you. We've all seen you following him around like a lapdog, not giving the poor man any peace. If it's anyone's fault he going, it's to get away from *you*! Now, you sit still while I tidy up this mess on the floor, and if you try to move out of that chair you'll find yourself alongside the spilt milk.'

Agnes stared back defiantly at her friend, her mouth working silently as she tried to find a way to retaliate, but the look in Rosie's eyes stopped her. She had to be content with an exaggerated 'humpphh' before flouncing round on her chair, staring sullenly out of the large window into the night.

Michael looked around his rooms for the last time, his face solemn. On the table stood his canvas bag already packed with his few possessions. He had been ready to leave an hour before, but something had kept him, a reluctance to leave the first real home he'd ever had. Leaning forward in his battered but comfortable armchair, he absently threw another lump of coal on the dying fire. He knew he should go now while his resolve was firm, but still he sat as though waiting.

Despite his confidence that Ruby would fall into his arms at the first opportunity, she had held herself in reserve whenever they were alone together. She was always friendly and obviously enjoyed his company, but that, it seemed now, was all she felt for him. Moodily he continued to stare into the dying embers of the fire before giving a soft derisive laugh. 'Well, me boyo, it looks as if your Irish charm has failed this time!' But, damn it, he had been so sure she felt something for him. How, knowing women as he did, could he have been so wrong?

The sight of her that afternoon decked out like a duchess had knocked him sideways. He'd always known she was pretty, but had never realised just how beautiful she was. Seeing her clothed in the long blue dress and wearing jewellery that obviously was worth a fortune had brought home to him just how far apart in class they were. It was only when he'd overheard that spiteful old harpy sneer at Ruby that he had realized he truly cared for the girl, and the shock of the discovery had almost sent him reeling. Him, Michael O'Brien in love? And if it wasn't the everlasting kind of love the poets wrote about, it was the closest he would ever come to it. That painted old floozie had been lucky that the lemonade had only gone over her ridiculous dress; it had taken all his will-power to stop himself from hurling the jugful in her face! And as for that remark about not being able to buy her way into the upper class . . . Begod, some of them hadn't a penny to call their own and would marry a hunchbacked one-eyed idiot as long as she brought a good dowry with her! At least he would have made her happy. But what was the use in staying here torturing himself; the sooner he was away, the better. Bending over, he banked down the fire, then swung his hessian bag over his shoulder. With one last fond look around the lodge he walked slowly to the door, only to stop in his tracks as a frantic hammering started on the door.

Who the hell could that be? Surely not Agnes again! Bejasus, the woman was harder to shake off than a flea on a mangy dog! Grimly he wrenched open the door, only to fall back in surprise at the sight of Ruby standing in the doorway. 'What . . . ?'

He staggered as she pushed past him, then watched in bewilderment and hope as she positioned herself in front of the dying fire. She had changed out of her finery into her more familiar attire, and for that alone he was grateful. He saw clearly the trembling of her body and longed to go forward and take her in his arms, but she must make the first move. Anything that happened now would be her choice. His own breathing became restricted as he waited for her to speak, while thinking, 'Holy Mother of Mercy, make her choice be me!'

Across the room, Ruby licked her lips nervously, her hands tightly clasped. Breathing heavily as if she'd run up a steep hill, she gazed at the tall dark-haired man, her thoughts galloping. What if he said no? What if he laughed at her? Her spirit would be crushed to the ground, but who would know? Only the two of them, and he would be gone, but she couldn't let him go without knowing how he felt.

Straightening her back, she took another deep breath and then, with all the courage she possessed, said quietly, 'Agnes tells me you are leaving.' Her eyes flickered towards the bag that lay at his feet. 'I see she was telling the truth. But before you go, there is something I have to tell you. I love you, Michael, and if you go, a part of me will die. I think you feel a certain affection for me, and so I've come to ask you if you will take me with you. I don't expect you to marry me, but feeling as I do, I'll be quite happy to live with you, if only for a short while. Please, Michael, take me with you, or stay here with me? I won't make any demands. I just . . .'

Her voice broke as the tears began to fall, and with one bound Michael was standing in front of her, his arms round her. Pulling her close, he murmured into her hair, 'Ah, Ruby, Ruby, don't! Don't demean yourself. I'd be proud to make you me wife. And I'll make you happy, Ruby, I swear by the Blessed Virgin you'll never regret this day. Oh, me darling, me darling Ruby!'

Ruby felt her body shudder with relief and joy. He wanted her. Michael O'Brien, who could have his pick of women, wanted *her*! Closing her eyes, she buried her head against his broad chest.

Chapter Nineteen

'I believe there is something you wish to tell me, Ruby. Please don't keep us in suspense; we are all anxiously waiting to hear the news.'

The thinly veiled contempt in her father's voice made Ruby's stomach contract painfully. She stared down at him as he sat behind the safety of his desk, his eyes daring her to speak the words she had rehearsed for days. Under his penetrating gaze her courage deserted her, and she looked nervously to where Dr Benson stood silently by the window, his face turned towards the street, his hands clasped firmly behind his back. Seeing the familiar figure here in the library had been a severe shock to her. When he had told her the week before that he would be unable to accompany her on her fortnightly visit due to pressure of work, she had believed him, why shouldn't she have?

All the way home in the cab she had gone over and over in her mind what she would say to her dad once she arrived. Now it appeared that she had no need to worry; it was obvious the news had already been broken to him. She wondered briefly whose idea it had been, Dr Benson's or Lady Caldworthy's, but what did it matter? The painful task had been taken out of her hands and she didn't know whether to be grateful to Dr Benson for sparing her the ordeal or angry with him for his betrayal. God, she felt sick! She could feel her head begin to jerk alarmingly and told herself to calm down. She had known the interview with her dad would be difficult and painful, but she hadn't bargained on the look of fury and something akin to distaste in his eyes. Silently she thanked God she hadn't allowed Michael to accompany her as he wanted to; his presence would only have aggravated the already tense atmosphere. Turning her head slightly, she looked to where her mother was sitting quietly, her eyes full of pain as she returned Ruby's gaze.

'Well, Ruby, I'm waiting. We are all waiting to hear this startling revelation you intended to spring upon us,' Bernard said coldly, his thin lips set into a grim line.

Ruby's attention was brought forcibly back to the man sitting behind the desk, and as she once again looked into his eyes she felt a moment of fear as she recalled Lily's words: for this man sitting so quietly looked as if he could indeed commit murder. It was as if she were looking into the face of a stranger, and her fear grew so strong that she glanced wildly to her mother for support. But Daisy's head was bowed, her hands covering her face as if she were unable to witness the scene before her. Dr Benson also remained staring resolutely out of the window as if determined not to meet her anguished gaze. Her whole body was shaking now, the only thought in her mind to flee this room and make her way back to Michael and the safety of his arms.

But before she went, she had to defend herself, and so, taking a deep trembling breath, she said shakily, 'I'm sorry, Dad, and you too, Mum. I never meant to hurt either of you, it just happened. I love Michael and he loves me. And – and we want to get married as – as soon as possible. Please don't be angry with me; I – I only want to be happy. Please try to understand . . . Please?' The sound of the placating tone of her voice sickened her, and swallowing the bile that had risen in her throat, she stood silently waiting for her father to speak, her eyes begging him to understand.

Bernard looked at his daughter, his proud beautiful daughter, the one person in his life he had tried so hard to protect from the outside world, and felt the hatred building in him for the unknown man who had taken her from him. Grinding his teeth, he said scornfully, 'An Irishman, the scum of the earth. Couldn't you do better than that, Ruby? Or had you become so desperate for a husband that you'd marry anyone so long as you had a man in your bed?'

She was going to be sick. She had to get out of this room before she vomited on the carpet! With a supreme effort she turned to leave, her voice dejected as she said, 'There's no point in my staying here. I – I'll go and pack the remainder of my belongings. Maybe – maybe when you've had time to calm down, you'll . . . you'll reconsider what you've said and how you've hurt me. I've done wrong in not telling you about Michael, but I thought . . . I really thought that once your anger had abated, you'd see how I felt and want me to be happy, but I see now I was wrong.' She wanted to say more, much more, but the lump in her throat was constricting her breathing. Casting one last pleading look in Daisy's direction, she turned to leave.

'Just a minute, Ruby. Aren't you forgetting something?' Ruby stopped abruptly, a faint glimmer of hope stirring in her breast, a hope that died instantly at the sound of her father's next words. 'Your grandmother's necklace and earrings. You have them with you, I trust?'

Wordlessly Ruby bent over her bag and delved into the interior until she found the velvet-lined case, then with trembling fingers she laid it on the desk. The sound of quiet sobbing came from where Daisy was sitting in the armchair, her body now rocking back and forth in anguish. She stared at her mother, her eyes wide with distress. 'Oh, Mum, don't! Please don't! Everything will work out. I'm sorry, I'm so sorry. I wouldn't have deliberately hurt you for the world.'

'That's enough,' Bernard snapped sharply. 'Take what you need from your room and go before I do something I'll regret.'

The hot tears blurring her vision, Ruby made one last effort to reconcile herself with her parents. Her voice thick with emotion, she cried desperately, 'I don't understand, Dad! I mean, I knew you'd be angry. I expected it, but not this ... not this contempt and hatred you've levelled at me since I came into this room. Why, why are you behaving like this? I've done nothing wrong except to fall in love. And he's a good man; he is, Dad. If you'd only agree to meet him ... you'd see the man he is ... Please, Dad, I'm begging you. Don't let me go like this ... Please!' She broke off as the deep heart-wrenching sobs tore at her body, but Bernard remained unmoved.

'That's enough!' he bellowed, banging his fist on the desk. 'You stand there asking why. It would seem that your Irishman has not only made you into a whore, he's also turned you into a consummate liar!'

The vicious words caused Ruby to stagger back in disbelief. 'What are you talking about? I ...'

'I said *that's enough*!' Bernard was on his feet now, his face only inches from her own. 'You were seen leaving the man's lodgings in the early hours of the morning, so don't bother trying to deny it. Why do you think I haven't forbidden you to marry? If, as you imply, you have done nothing to be ashamed of, why do you think I would allow you to leave here to return to your Irish tinker?' Unblinking, she stared at him in horror. There seemed to be no recognizable feature in the face before her, so suffused was it with anger. 'You thought you were clever, didn't you, eh? Get yourself pregnant and force my hand, is that what the pair of you planned? Is it? Well now, you can take yourself back to your lover and tell him the plan didn't work. If, when he finds there's no money coming with you, he still wants to marry you,

you have my permission, but only because I don't want the added shame of a bastard grandchild.'

Ruby clutched at the front of the desk. Oh, God . . . Oh dear God, so that was what they all thought. But it wasn't true. She had stayed with Michael for hours talking over their future and the pitfalls that lay ahead of them, but they hadn't . . . Oh, they hadn't! Who could have carried such a tale? But did she need to ask? Who else but Agnes? She must have been spying on them that night. But that her family could believe such a story without giving her the chance to defend herself was unforgivable.

She felt the anger and outrage rising in her and, leaning forward, shouted into Bernard's face, 'Yes, it's true, I slept with a man, and it was wonderful, do you hear? If you'd had your way I'd have remained a virgin for the rest of my life. Ever since I came into the room, you've acted more like an outraged husband than a father. Why are you so upset at the thought of my having a lover? Your behaviour goes beyond any paternal feelings. Were you planning on saving me for yourself?'

'Ruby, stop it, stop it, child! Don't make things worse.' Daisy was out of her chair, her hands stretched in front of her in supplication, the tears still raining down her face.

Bernard stood rigid, the accusation Ruby had thrown striking a chord, forcing him to realize just how near the truth she had come. The knowledge was unbearable and, raising his arm high in the air, he brought the full force of it down on Ruby, the flat of his hand crashing against her face. The blow sent her reeling backwards and, before Daisy could reach her side, she fell heavily to the floor.

Bernard looked at the prone body, his eyes wide with disbelief and horror. All these years he had tried to ignore Ruby's handicap, pushing the memories of the early days to the far corner of his mind, but now the truth was staring him in the face. As Daisy and Dr Benson rushed to help Ruby to her feet, he closed his eyes, but the image of her lying on the floor, her dress rumpled up around her hip to reveal the wooden leg and the leather straps attached to the white flesh, stayed fixed in his mind.

Within seconds of falling, Ruby had frantically pushed her dress down, but too late. Stunned with shock and humiliation, she stared up into Bernard's ashen face. His eyes open now, he flinched as if he too had been struck by the look of pure hatred that was flaring from his daughter's pain-filled eyes.

'Oh, Ruby, Ruby, dear, come on, get up! Look, put your arm round my neck. That's it, come on.' Daisy struggled to lift her from the floor, assisted by Dr Benson, the old man's normally placid face quivering with suppressed rage. When Ruby was standing once more, Daisy placed her arm tenderly round her waist before leading her from the room.

As the door closed quietly behind them, Dr Benson rounded on Bernard. 'What in God's name has come over you, man?' he thundered at the now calm figure still standing behind his desk. 'When I told you about Ruby and the gardener, I explained that it was only hearsay from one of the maids at the house. Why didn't you give the girl a chance to defend herself? When I agreed with Daisy to let you talk to Ruby without interference, we neither of us thought you would react in such a despicable way. You treated your own daughter as if she were no more than a common slut. Why, Bernard? Why did you behave in such a way? And to strike her! Dear God, that I should witness such an act.'

Shaking his head sadly, he turned on his heel, anxious now to get to Ruby and see if there was anything he could do to help the poor girl. A feeling of guilt weighed heavily on his frail shoulders. He had thought he was acting for the best, but he had badly underestimated his old friend. Pulling the door open, he paused for a moment before facing Bernard once more to say gravely, 'We have been friends for a good number of years, Bernard, and I thought I knew you. It seems I was mistaken. You sought to shame Ruby, but she walked from this room with dignity. It is you, Bernard, who has been shamed.' With those damning words he left the room.

Bernard sank slowly into his leather chair, staring sightlessly at the closed door. He had hit her; he had raised his hand and struck out at the beloved face, felling his daughter to the floor, and the sight of her lying there helpless would stay with him for ever. His head sunk low on his chest, he muttered, 'Oh, God, why? Why did I hit her? I never meant to.' But even as he whispered the words, his mind screamed the reason at him. He had lashed out at her because he felt as if she had betrayed him, and the image of her lying naked with an unknown man had sent him into such a fury he hadn't been able to control his actions. Now his rage had subsided, he recalled the words she had flung in his face and admitted to himself that there was some truth in her accusations. He had never wanted her to leave home, had never wanted her to marry. Instead, he had tried to keep her by his side so that he could watch over her and shield her from the outside world. He wanted to shield her from any more hurt, and instead it had been he himself who had hurt her the most.

The muted sounds from the hall suddenly became louder, and raising his head, he heard the familiar voice of his elder son shouting, 'He did *what*?'

The words held a note of incredulity, and were quickly followed by Daisy's pleading tone, 'No, Bertie, leave it, please. There's been enough damage done today.'

Then the door was flung open as Bertie, still clothed in his uniform, burst into the room. In three quick strides he was standing by the desk, his hands clutching at his open cloak. He stood silently, the muscles of his face working furiously, and then, his voice low and bitter he growled, 'You miserable bastard, for two pins I'd give you a taste of your own medicine! The only thing stopping me from hitting you is respect for Mother; I don't think she can take much more today. But this I will tell you. You were wrong about Ruby, she's as innocent as the day she was born, and now you've lost her. Oh, yes, Father, you've lost her for good, and that knowledge alone will cause you more pain that I could cause by striking you as you deserve. Now I'll give you some good news. You look as if you need some! I'm going upstairs now to pack my things. Oh, I know that won't cause you any distress, because you've never liked me, have you, Father?' Bertie waited for an answer, the rage in his voice unable to mask the unspoken plea in his question.

Bernard however, remained as though turned to stone. The two men stared at each other for a moment longer, then, with an exclamation of disgust, Bertie turned away from him, saying bitterly, 'At least some good has come out of today's revelations! You won't have to put up with the sight of a common policeman around your precious home after today. You'll be able to entertain your friends in comfort, without fear that I'll walk into the room and shame you. God, you make me sick!'

The contempt in his son's voice brought Bernard out of his apathetic state. Pushing his chair back sharply, he shouted after the retreating back, 'Go, then! Go back to the slums you were born in, both of you! It's where the pair of you belong! Go, get out of my house.'

Without a word or a backward glance Bertie stormed out, leaving Bernard to sink slowly back into his chair. He listened to the activity in the hall, his mind screaming at him to go after his son, tell him he loved him, was proud of him. It wasn't too late. If he could only get out of this chair and go to both of them, tell them he was sorry, beg them for forgiveness, he could save his family from being divided for ever.

But his body refused to obey his mind. When the front door banged shut, his body slumped down in the chair, his head hanging on his chest as he sat silently in misery. He had lost them both, just as surely as if they had died, and whereas one day Ruby might forgive him, he knew that Bertie never would. Covering his face with his hands he leaned over his desk, and, for the second time in his adult life, Bernard Chadwick cried.

Chapter Twenty

They were married a week before Christmas. Michael had wanted to bring the wedding forward to the end of summer, but Ruby had insisted on waiting.

It was six months since her father had thrown her from the house, the hateful words ringing in her ears, and she was determined that no child born to them would ever suffer the stigma of being conceived outside marriage. During the six-month interim, her mother had become a regular visitor at the house and had formed a strong friendship with Lady Caldworthy. Although Michael had been annoyed by having to wait, Ruby knew that the two women had been vastly relieved to hear that she wasn't planning a hasty marriage. She also knew they were both secretly hoping that Michael would tire of waiting and vanish from her life. Many anxious nights she too had suffered, wondering if she was being foolish to allow so much time to elapse, but the need to demonstrate to her father that his spiteful accusations had been totally unfounded overcame her desire to marry quickly.

She had caused further consternation by insisting on being married in a church in the East End, insisting that as she no longer belonged to the upper classes, it would be a sham to be married in a manner above her new station. The only concession she had made to the distressed Daisy was to accept the cream lace wedding dress she'd bought from Harrod's. It was indeed a beautiful gown, the tightly ruched bodice threaded with tiny seed-pearls forming a vee at the front, contrasting strongly with the plainness of the skirt. At the hem was a three-inch frill that billowed out in a wide circle to the ground, so that there was no chance of the wooden tip of her left leg showing beneath it.

The ceremony was brief. The vicar was flustered and slightly overawed by the small group of smartly dressed people not usually seen in this part of London. He was more accustomed to marrying the working-class people of his parish. When he pronounced the couple man and wife, he was quick to note the tight smiles on the faces of the people present and wondered at the story behind the scene. As the breathy sound of the ancient organ filled the church, its pedals pumped furiously by an over-enthusiastic spinster, Michael offered Ruby his arm and together they walked down the threadbare carpeted aisle.

Behind them walked Lily, in a pink silk dress, the only bridesmaid. Then came Bertie, who had taken the place of his father and given his sister away, his hand patting Daisy's arm as if consoling her. Last came George and Dr Benson, their faces solemn, as though attending a funeral rather than a wedding.

Once outside the gloomy church, they posed for the photographer that Daisy had engaged. Standing together for warmth, they waited patiently as the little man cheerfully captured them for posterity with his new Kodak.

The photos taken, the small group disbanded, each one feeling the strain of the day. Especially Daisy, who wrapped her new fox fur stole tighter around her neck as she eyed the growing band of beggars and small ragged children that had gathered around the church railings to catch a glimpse of the 'posh wedding', and maybe scrounge a few shillings into the bargain. Sensing his mother's fear, Bertie marshalled them all through the iron gates to the waiting carriages, at the same time scattering the handful of silver he had put into his pocket for just such an occasion. As the men, women, and children scrambled for the unexpected windfall, Bertie helped Daisy up into the carriage, then stood aside as Dr Benson and George followed her. Leaving the door open, he walked the few yards to where Ruby stood hand in hand with her new husband, whily Lily sobbed uncontrollably behind them.

'Best get going, Ruby. Lady Caldworthy will be waiting for us back at the house,' Bertie said, his eyes scanning her face as though memorizing it, thinking that she had never looked lovelier. Reaching up, he gently plucked one of the many dried flowers that Lily had entwined in Ruby's hair and inserted it in his buttonhole. Then, as he was about to hand her into the carriage, he felt a restraining hand on his arm.

'I can see to me wife, Mr Chadwick, thanks all the same,' said Michael.

Ruby stood between the two men she loved and felt her heart tug in her breast. She had hoped they would get on together, but from their first meeting they had taken an instant dislike to each other. Her eyes clouding over, she leant forward and kissed Bertie on his cheek, saying softly, 'I'll see you back at the house, Bertie. You will stay for the party, won't you?'

'Yes, of course I will, but I'm on duty at eight tonight, so I'll have to leave about six.' Then, turning to the still sobbing Lily, he smiled broadly. 'Come on, Lily, anyone would think this was a funeral! Cheer up!' He was rewarded by a tremulous smile, and patted her wet cheek gently before walking back to his carriage. Once inside, he looked at the grim-faced occupants. Directing his attention to his mother, he said flatly, 'Well, it's done. There's no going back now.' Then, leaning slightly out of the window he shouted, 'Drive on, coachman.'

The wedding party was a strained affair. Ruby glanced anxiously from her family to Michael as she chattered nervously. From the moment they had arrived back at the house, she had known it was a mistake to accept Lady Caldworthy's offer to hold the reception here. She wished now she had insisted on parting from her family at the church and gone straight to the newly refurbished lodge with Michael for their own private celebration. She watched with dismay as he downed another glass of whisky, his face tight with anger at the unveiled hostility that had been directed at him by her family, and prayed he wouldn't do or say something that would result in the day ending in a fight.

At the far end of the table, Bertie looked once again at his pocket watch before switching his attention to his new brother-in-law, asking himself why he should feel such animosity towards the man. It wasn't just brotherly concern, but a deep-rooted fear that Michael wasn't right for Ruby. It had nothing to do with class barriers; he prided himself on judging a man on his character, not on how much money he had in his pockets. No, it was something else, something he couldn't define, he just knew deep down that this man would bring Ruby suffering. He had tried to like him for Ruby's sake, but although he had only met him a few times, the first impression of distrust remained, and try as he might, he couldn't shake it off.

Aware that he was being watched, Michael raised his eyes to Bertie, his lips set in a tight line. 'God damn the little snot!' he thought viciously. 'And the rest of them. Looking down their long noses at me as if I were the dirt beneath their feet,' while at the same time he cried silently, 'Why? Why won't you give me a chance? I want you to like me, I want all of you to like me, to accept me into your family.'

He could never replace his own family that he had lost at such an early age, but he had hoped that one day he would become part of another when he finally married. He felt the maudlin tears come to his eyes and quickly looked away from Bertie. Well, there was no chance he would ever be a part of this particular family, but what odds? He would create his own, with plenty of sons and daughters to make him proud. Turning to Ruby, he leaned over and kissed her deeply on the lips, and felt a further rejection when she hurriedly pulled away, clearly embarrassed at such behaviour in front of company. His response to this rebuff was to call Rosie to replenish his glass, his eyes sweeping round the table, openingly daring anyone to admonish him. But when he faced Daisy's dour, accusing stare, he was forced to drop his gaze.

Bertie was the first to leave, announcing that he had to be on duty in an hour. His announcement was greeted with undisguised relief by the rest of the guests, as one by one they rose and made their farewells. Trying desperately to keep the tears from spilling over, Ruby kept the smile she had worn all day as she hugged her mother and brothers goodbye. Lily and Dr Benson stood to one side waiting for their turn, and when they too had kissed her cheek in farewell, they walked silently from the house to the waiting carriage. No words had been spoken; there was nothing left to say.

At last the carriage pulled away and Ruby walked slowly back into the dining-room, telling herself she mustn't let Michael see how upset she was, for she knew only too well how he must be feeling. When she entered, there was no sign of him, only the servants and Lady Caldworthy remained. The false smile slid from her face as she cried anxiously, 'Where's Michael?'

'Now, don't go getting yourself upset, Ruby,' Lady Caldworthy said. 'He's gone to the lodge. I would imagine the vast amounts of whisky he has consumed have finally taken their toll.'

Suddenly angry, Ruby turned on the old woman, 'And can you blame him? Considering how he's been treated today, can you really blame him for acting as he did? In his place, I would have behaved just the same way.'

As she made to leave the room, Lady Caldworthy called out, 'Child, child, what did you expect? You knew how your family felt about this marriage. Did you really imagine they would suddenly change their minds at the last minute and welcome him with open arms? I blame myself for this fiasco, I should never have coerced you into holding a wedding party when you were so clearly against it, but the damage is done now. You'd better go to him, for his pride has taken a severe beating, and, to be truthful, I feel sorry for him, for no man should be humiliated on his wedding day. Go to him, Ruby. Only you can give him back his self-esteem.'

Ruby stood for a moment torn between the desire to go to Michael and her loyalty to her employer. She looked so old and ill, she couldn't leave her like this, not after all the kindness she had shown these past six months.

When she had finally accepted that Ruby was determined to marry her Irishman, she had had the lodge fully redecorated and modernized. The place had been practically pulled down and rebuilt. It had cost her a small fortune, but she had told herself it was worth every penny if it kept Ruby from leaving her.

'I'm sorry, ma'am,' she whispered humbly. 'I shouldn't have spoken to you in such a manner. Let me see you to your room, for you must be very tired.'

Waving her hand at her, Lady Caldworthy replied waspishly, 'Rosie can help me to my room. You have a husband waiting for you. Go, child. Don't leave him alone to brood.'

Swiftly Ruby bent to kiss the frail cheek before leaving the room, and as she crossed the darkened garden she thought sadly, 'Even the servants didn't wish me good luck.'

Ruby peered into the darkness of the lodge, calling out softly, 'Michael, Michael, are you there?'

When no answer came, she closed the door, then, making her way to the table where she knew the oil-lamp stood, she fumbled until the soft light illuminated the room. Picking up the lamp, she swung it round, then gasped in surprise and relief at the sight of Michael sitting dejectedly in the chair by the cold fireplace. 'Oh Lord, you did give me a fright, Michael! Why didn't you answer? I thought for a moment you had gone off without me.'

'Maybe it would have been better if I had.'

His flat reply made her feel sympathy for him. Then, seeing how he lay slumped in the chair feeling sorry for himself, anger surged in her. He hadn't even taken the trouble to get a fire going! Shivering, she placed the lamp back on the table, then stood before him, her hands resting on her hips.

'Well, if this is how you're going to react every time life deals you a blow, then perhaps you're right. Look at yourself, sitting there wallowing in self-pity without a thought for how *I* might be feeling! I've alienated myself from my father, a father I still love deeply in spite of the way he has behaved. I've hurt my mother and brothers, and I'm asking myself if it was worth it. If their indifference offends your pride so deeply, then it would be best if you did go now, because even though I love you, I don't intend to spend the rest of my days propping up your wounded pride. You surprise me, Michael, I was led to believe that the Irish possessed a fighting spirit, but it seems I was mistaken.'

His face dark with rage, Michael bounded from the chair, his hands grabbing her shoulders, shaking her wildly. 'Don't ever speak to me like that again! I'll not stand for it, do you hear me? I'll not stand for it.'

'Let go of me! I won't be bullied, and I won't be prevented from speaking my mind.' Her calm voice held no trace of fear, while she faced him steadily until he dropped his hands from her shoulders.

The anger seeped from his face as he gazed down tenderly at her. 'Aye, you won't be bullied, will you, me darlin'? That's one of the reasons I love you, even though it makes me as mad as hell. And you're wrong when you say I don't care about what you're feeling. I know what you've given up for me, and it frightens me to think that one day you'll wake up and realize what you've done and go haring off back to your family. Oh, Ruby, I'm sorry, I'm sorry! I was half out of me mind with anger at the way they looked down their noses at me, and how I stopped meself from punching your brother, I'll never know.'

'It's just as well you did! Bertie can look after himself. You might have found yourself flat out on the floor.'

'There you go again, defending your family against me. Is it always going to be like this, Ruby? Them against me?'

Ruby hung her head, her shoulders drooping. She'd always imagined her wedding day would be the happiest of her life, but instead it had turned into a nightmare. Into her mind sprang a vision of her room at home, of Lily waiting to talk to her, and her family all gathered in the parlour after dinner, and she had a sudden wild longing to flee from this freezing depressive room. Then she lifted her eyes and saw the misery and uncertainty in Michael's face, and all the love she felt for him came flooding back. Stepping nearer to him, she whispered, 'No, Michael, not them against you; let's say them against *us*. I love you, Michael, and much as I love my family, I'd give them all up if it meant losing you.'

At the sound of her passionate words, Michael straightened his back, his confidence returning. Taking her in his arms, he exclaimed, 'Holy Mary, you're freezing! In fact the whole place is freezing. Come on, let's go to bed. We can talk more in the morning.' He felt her body stiffen, and the frown came back to his face. Lifting her chin up, he stared deeply into her eyes. 'What is it, Ruby?'

'Nothing, I . . .'

'Nothing? Don't tell me it's nothing! I felt you pull away when I mentioned going to bed. Is that the way of it? I'll be gentle, darlin', and I promise I'll not do anything unless you say so. We have the rest of our lives together, so I can wait a while longer, if that's what you want. But not too much longer,' he laughed shakily.

Ruby shook her head. She was afraid, of course she was, as any young bride would be, but it was the thought of her leg that was troubling her more than any pain or discomfort she was due to experience. 'It's not that. It's . . . I'm afraid, Michael. I'm so afraid that when you see me without my clothes you'll feel repelled. My – My s – stump isn't very pretty to look at.'

Michael reared back in surprise. Saints above, he hadn't even thought of that aspect! Looking down on her bent head, he felt a wave of love and protectiveness run through his body. Holding her tighter he whispered hoarsely, 'Ruby, darlin', I wouldn't care if you had no legs at all, and if your stump isn't pretty to look at, your face more than makes up for it. And I want to spend the rest of me days looking at it. Now, Mrs O'Brien, shall we go to bed before we freeze to death?'

Ruby raised her head, her eyes filled with apprehension before she nodded slowly. 'Yes, Michael, let's go to bed.'

Then, with her heart beating wildly, she walked with her new husband into the bedroom.

Chapter Twenty-One

Mabel Caldworthy took to her bed three days after the state funeral of her beloved sovereign Queen Victoria in 1901, but she herself did not die until two years later. It had been almost as though she no longer wanted to live in a world without the small regal figure that had been a part of her life. Ruby had sat with her dear friend until the end, taking turns with Dr Benson to keep watch, and when the frail old lady took her last breath, they had both wept unashamedly.

The sun was shining on the day of the funeral. Ruby sat stiffly on the plush leather seat in Dr. Benson's coach, her eyes wide and unblinking as she stared out of the open window at the cortège in front. When the hearse driven by four horses, their black plumage swaying in the wind, slowly came to a halt, she waited until he had alighted, then holding out her hand she allowed him to help her down, her mother following close behind. They waited silently as the light oak coffin with three sets of brass handles was lifted from the hearse on to the shoulders of the pall-bearers.

Squeezing her eyes to blot out the painful sight, she remembered the last words Mabel had said to her. 'Don't let them bury me in the rain, Ruby. Promise me, child! Don't let them bury me in the rain.'

'Can you manage, dear? The path is very uneven.' Daisy stood beside her daughter, her face etched with concern.

Unable to speak, Ruby merely nodded before linking her arm through her mother's, grateful that she had come with her. They waited a few minutes until the carriage carrying Michael and the rest of the staff had deposited its passengers before following the pall-bearers to the open grave.

Throughout the brief service, Ruby kept her eyes fixed on the tall middle-aged man who stood solemnly by the side of the parson. She had first made the acquaintance of Sir Charles Caldworthy four days earlier, when he had arrived unannounced to take over the estate of his late stepmother. Not yet over the first stages of grief at the loss of their beloved employer, the staff, including Michael and herself, had been told by the new owner that he intended to close up the house and therefore would no longer have need of their services. The news had had little effect upon Ruby, who had already decided to leave just as soon as Michael found himself another post, but Mrs Rodgers and Mr Masters, both nearing retirement age, had been devastated. She hoped with all her heart that Mabel had left them well provided for.

The sound of Mrs Rodgers's sobs broke into her reverie, and she laid her hand on the old woman's arm. Unable to bear the sight of her friend's grief, she shifted her gaze to where Michael stood at the back of the small group, a black band on the sleeve of his best grey suit, his body slumped in an attitude of deep sorrow, and fought down the wild impulse to shout out 'Hyprocrite!'

With a supreme effort she focused her attention once again on the imposing figure of Mabel's stepson. Not once since entering the cemetery had she looked at the coffin now reposing in its shallow grave, her mind still refusing to accept that her dearly loved friend was really dead. She couldn't believe that never again would the familiar voice call to her, or the bright twinkling eyes laugh at her. If she could only endure the ceremony without breaking down, if she could avoid looking at the coffin, then she would be able to keep alive the memory of the woman she'd loved so dearly. Closing her eyes, she listened with detachment as the parson finished his eulogy. Thank God she had stood out against Michael's wish for the children to be present and had insisted instead that Lily came to the house to look after them.

The sound of the first clods of earth being shovelled on to the coffin roused her, and then she was staring down into the grave. But there was something wrong, for the coffin seemed to be jumping and turning from side to side.

'Come along, dear. There's nothing more you can do for her, poor soul,' Daisy said gently as she made to turn Ruby back in the direction of the waiting carriages, but the figure beside her refused to move.

Ruby stood as if transfixed. She could feel a strange sensation in the pit of her stomach, then, as if gathering momentum, the feeling surged through her body, and when the two grave-diggers shovelled another spadeful of dirt on to the exposed coffin, she cried out piteously, 'Stop it, stop it, she won't be able to breathe! Get her out! Oh please, somebody, get her out before she suffocates!' and then she was falling, her head bursting with tiny bright lights before plunging into total blackness.

'Here you are, dear. Try and take a sip of tea, it will make you feel better,' Daisy coaxed softly, her arm round Ruby's shoulders. As the hot tea touched her lips, Ruby jerked her head back, so that the steaming liquid ran down the front of her black silk dress. 'Oh dear, I'm sorry! It was too hot. I should have checked. Let me fetch a cloth to clean your dress.'

As Daisy removed her arm, Ruby's head flopped back against the pile of pillows, the memory of the day's events crowding over her. And when the scalding tears cascaded down her cheeks, she made no effort to restrain them. After the spasm had ceased, she became aware of another presence in the room, and, turning her head to one side, she saw the stooped figure of Dr Benson watching her, his eyes full of sadness. Immediately she struggled to sit up in the bed, only to be gently pushed back by her mother.

'Lie still for a while, dear. There's nothing for you to get up for; everything's being taken care of.'

'The children?' Ruby croaked weakly. 'And the mourners? I have to see to the funeral tea.'

'The children are with Lily in the lodge, and the mourners left over two hours ago.'

Ruby stared up at her mother in bewilderment. 'Two hours ago? But . . . I mean . . . How long have I been asleep?'

Dr Benson moved to the bed and took her hand, saying kindly, 'Not so much asleep, my dear, more like collapse from complete exhaustion. As to how long . . . well, let me see.' Taking out his watch, he added, 'It's now six o'clock, so you have been . . . sleeping for over seven hours.'

'Seven hours? I can't have been!' Ruby exclaimed. Then, before either her mother or Dr Benson could stop her, she threw back the blanket that had been covering her and swung the bottom half of her body over the edge of the bed, then froze as she realized that the artificial limb that was almost a part of her had been removed. She felt a sudden rush of blood to her face as she imagined her mother and Dr Benson pulling up her heavy silk skirt to unhook the leather corset and straps that held the leg in place; but worse, much, much worse, was the knowledge that they had witnessed the sight of the mutilated, scarred stump.

Since the age of fourteen, when she had finally mastered the technique of attaching her leg, the only person who had seen her deformity was the carpenter at the Seamen's Mission Hospital. On these half-yearly visits she had made her mother wait outside the workshop while the cheerful ex-sailor had measured her for a new leg. These visits had ceased shortly after her seventeenth birthday when it was decided that she was unlikely to grow any taller. She had returned to the hospital only once during the intervening years, and that was only because the leather straps had become worn, as had the corset. On that occasion she had insisted on removing the necessary objects in the dubious privacy of the tiny storeroom behind the workshop, and had then waited while the carpenter, a man she had never seen before, had taken her measurements. When he had finished, she had thanked him politely, ignoring the amused expression in his eyes, and had quickly re-fitted the leg while he was making out the invoice. Not even Michael had ever seen her wholly undressed, she had made sure of that.

And now these two people whom she trusted most had invaded her privacy in the worst possible way. The tears of grief turned to tears of mortification, and, angrily wiping her cheeks with the back of her hand, she glared up at her mother, saying bitterly, 'How could you? Either of you? Both of you know how I feel about keeping my my handicap private. It was unforgivable to do this to me when I was in no fit state to object!'

'Listen to me, dear, please,' Daisy said, her voice filled with distress. 'William was concerned about you. You've not been off your feet for weeks, what with seeing to Mabel and looking after the house. Mrs Rodgers has told me that you've not been bothering to take the leg off even when you've gone to bed. The skin must be red raw, and despite what you say to the contrary, it must be hurting badly.'

'Your mother's right, Ruby,' Dr Benson said quietly, 'and you should know better than to keep the leg attached for long periods of time. The skin could break with the constant chafing, causing infection, and if that should happen . . . well, it would be weeks, maybe months, before you could wear the leg again.'

Ruby looked from one anxious face to the other, her mind telling her that they were right, but still she couldn't help feeling as if she'd been violated. She buried her face in the pillows, her body shuddering with a sense of shock and deep, intense shame.

Daisy and Dr Benson looked at each other, their faces mirroring their concern, but neither spoke until Ruby said in a muffled voice, 'I'm sorry . . . I know you acted for the best . . . but you shouldn't have done it . . . You shouldn't have.'

'No, we shouldn't have, and we're both deeply sorry for upsetting you so. But, Ruby, we both love you, and if you think for one moment that the sight of your . . . stump would alter that feeling in any way, then you must imagine our love for you to be very shallow.' Daisy's voice had dropped to a whisper, and Ruby, hearing her pain, gave a loud cry and threw herself into her mother's arms.

Dr Benson stood back from the bed, slightly embarrassed by the emotional scene. He waited for a few more minutes before giving a discreet cough, then said briskly, 'Ahem! This may sound insensitive, Ruby, but the reading of Mabel's will took place over an hour ago. I took the liberty of asking Sir Charles to let Mr Cox, the solicitor, proceed without you. They are both at present waiting in the study, but if you don't feel up to it at the moment, I'm sure Mr Cox can came back tomorrow.'

Daisy felt Ruby's body stiffen and pulled her closer, saying firmly, 'I don't think that now is an appropriate time, William. If you would be kind enough to go downstairs and inform them that tomorrow would be more convenient, I'd be most grateful.'

Dr Benson nodded in agreement, and was about to leave the room when Ruby stopped him. 'No, I'd rather see them now, Mum. I might feel even worse tomorrow, so it's best I get it out of the way tonight.'

'All right, dear, if that's what you want,' Daisy replied, bending over to kiss her tear-stained cheek. 'I'll wait for you at the lodge. It will give me an opportunity to spend some time with my grandchildren.'

Ruby waited until Daisy had pulled on her gloves and was preparing to leave before asking, 'Where's Michael? You said earlier that Lily was looking after the children. Why isn't Michael with them?' She was quick to note the glance that passed between her mother and Dr Benson, and felt a shrinking sensation in her stomach. 'Well, I'm waiting, Mum. Where is he?'

'He – he said he had to go out for a while, to – to visit a friend. I'm sure he'll be back shortly,' Daisy said, her eyes avoiding Ruby's.

Ruby nodded slowly, with an expression of understanding. Then, in a firm voice, she asked, 'How much did Mabel leave him?'

'Well now, I'm not sure, dear. Why don't you wait until he gets home? He . . .'

'I asked how much, Mum, and don't pretend you don't know! I can tell by your face you're keeping something from me.'

Daisy cast a desperate look at Dr Benson, then, plucking nervously at her fingers, she replied, 'Two hundred pounds.'

Ruby blinked in disbelief. Two hundred pounds! So that's why her mother was so nervous – she probably thought he wouldn't be coming back! She nearly laughed out loud at the notion. Of course he'd be back! He wouldn't leave without finding out how much his wife was now worth. As to where he was . . . the nearest pub would be the most obvious bet. Forcing a smile to her lips, she said cheerfully, 'It's all right, Mum, there's no need to look so tragic! I know where he's gone as well as you do, but he'll be back, that's one thing I am certain of. Now, I'd best get ready to go downstairs. I'll meet you at the lodge. I shouldn't be too long.'

'Very well, dear.'

'Goodnight, Ruby,' Dr Benson said gruffly, then, pointing to the dressing-table, he added, 'I've left some salve and a lint bandage. They will help to ease the chafing.'

Ruby swallowed before replying, 'Thank you, Doctor. I'm very grateful for all your help.'

After they had left the room, she hopped over to the dressing-table, picked up the bottle of salve and the small piece of linen, returned to the bed, and sat down. Pulling up her skirt, she gingerly applied the salve to the inflamed stump, then winced as the burning pain brought fresh tears to her eyes. When the pain had abated, she gritted her teeth before applying another liberal helping and then padded the stump with the soft linen bandage. She waited a few more moments until the pain had eased further then pulled the leg towards her.

When she was ready, she limped painfully over to the dressing-table and dabbed some powder over her face. At the sight of her red-rimmed eyes, she shrugged wearily: what did it matter how she looked? Collecting her wide-brimmed black bonnet, she walked over to the connecting door and opened it wide.

The sight of the large empty bed made her eyes fill with tears again. Choking down the sobs that were starting to fill her throat, she quickly closed the door, then murmured, 'Goodbye, Mabel. I'll never forget you.' Dashing her hand across her eyes, she made her way across the room that held so many memories, and ignoring the pain in her leg, made her way downstairs.

'Ah, Mrs O'Brien. Please sit down. I trust you are feeling better?'

'Much better, thank you, Sir Charles,' Ruby answered as she gratefully accepted the chair that had been placed for her. The journey down the long stairs had been a nightmare, with each step sending a searing pain through the top half of her leg.

'This is Mr Cox. I believe you've met?' Sir Charles was

saying, indicating the small, dapper man standing by the side of the writing-desk.

'Yes, indeed we have,' the solicitor replied, smiling gravely. 'Your late stepmother changed her will a number of times over the past few years, and Mrs O'Brien always saw to it that I had some refreshment before I left the house – an action that was much appreciated.'

Ruby smiled back, wishing the man would stop his chattering and get on with matters. She was tired and in pain, and she wanted to see her children.

As if sensing her impatience, Mr Cox cleared his throat, before seating himself behind the desk. 'Well, now, I'm sure you'd rather I got straight down to business, Mrs O'Brien. But before I tell you how much Lady Caldworthy bequeathed to you, I must say I expected the amount to be more substantial. I'm only telling you this beforehand to save you any disappointment.'

The tone of the solicitor's words sent a tremor of apprehension through Ruby, and it was with a supreme effort that she kept her face impassive. Her voice steady, she replied, 'Whatever the amount may be is of no consequence. The happy times I spent in her ladyship's company are payment enough. Please continue.'

Clearing his throat once more, Mr Cox looked over his moon-shaped spectacles, and said, 'Her ladyship left you the sum of three hundred pounds, Mrs O'Brien. And if I may repeat my former comments, I am deeply shocked and surprised that she should have left you such a small amount, compared with the bequests to the rest of the staff. I know how very fond of you she was, and I confess to being baffled at her decision.'

Ruby's breathing quickened as the solicitor's words sank in. It wasn't possible. Surely Mabel wouldn't have left her only marginally better off than Michael? There must be some mistake . . . There must! She had certainly had no hopes of a large bequest – indeed three hundred pounds was a great deal of money – but why had she left Michael such a large amount? She'd never trusted him. She'd liked him, yes, but never trusted him. And if she were being completely honest with herself, she would admit that she had expected a rather larger amount. Dear Lord, what was she thinking of? Poor Mabel had only been buried that morning and here she was fretting as to the whys and wherefores of who had received what.

Her head began to swim, and, taking a deep breath, she smiled at Mr Cox again and held out her hand. 'Thank you for waiting for me. It was very good of you. As to the bequest, rest assured that I am very content with my legacy. Now, if you'll excuse me, gentlemen, I'll bid you both good evening.'

Both men stood up awkwardly, and as Sir Charles led her to the door, he leaned forward and said softly, 'I realize you must be exhausted after all the work you've had to shoulder these past few weeks, but I know that the staff are anxious to see you. They were very concerned about you, and I know they'd appreciate it if you would pay them a visit before returning to the lodge.'

Ruby groaned. She was in no fit state to be sociable, even if the people in question were her friends. Bowing her head, she replied, 'Very well. I'll have a quick word with them before returning home.' Once outside the door, she resisted the temptation to ignore Sir Charles's request and make for home, but took another deep shuddering breath, and headed for the kitchen.

Half an hour later she was once more standing in the hall, her face bewildered as she recalled the news they had given her. Mrs Rodgers and Mr Masters had received five hundred pounds each, and Rosie and Agnes two hundred and fifty pounds. She didn't begrudge Mrs Rodgers or Mr Masters one penny of their legacies; they had been with Mabel for over thirty years and it was only natural that she would see them provided for. Even in their grief, the relief had shown in their faces, and could she blame them? It would be very hard for either of them to find another post at their time of life. It was different for Rosie and Agnes, who were young enough to find other positions, and yet Mabel had left them both enough to see them comfortably off for a couple of years at least. Obviously her late employer hadn't thought as much of her as she'd been led to believe. And what would Michael's reaction be when he found out? He hadn't said as much, but she knew he was expecting a small fortune to be coming his way. Well, he was in for a great disappointment, wasn't he? For not only would he have to give up his plans for a life of ease, he'd also have to find another job, and that prospect wasn't going to go down too well.

Then the study door was opened, and when she saw Sir Charles standing in the doorway, she nodded curtly and made to move on. She had heard Mabel refer to him on only one occasion, and that had been to tell her that her stepson had disapproved of his father's remarriage and had never set foot in the house since the day of his funeral. Well, he'd been quick enough about getting his foot back in the door now that his stepmother was no longer alive! she thought bitterly.

'Ah, Mrs O'Brien, I was waiting for you to emerge from the kitchen.

If you could spare me just another moment, I promise I won't keep you long. I know you must be desperate to get home.'

Ruby, numb with fatigue, limped past him back into the study, wondering as she did so if she would ever see her home or her children again. Sitting down in the chair she had only recently vacated, she felt her mouth turn dry with fright. What could he possibly want now? Perhaps to discuss her now redundant situation in the house? Surely he wasn't going to evict them from the lodge already? He couldn't! She needed time to recover her strength, to rest her aching body and weary mind, before setting about the business of finding another home. Her face showing no trace of her anguish, she prayed wildly, 'Please, God, don't let him evict us! Not just yet. We've nowhere to go, and I don't think I can take much more today.'

When Sir Charles was seated, he said, 'First of all, may I thank you for all the support and kindness you showed to my late stepmother. I've learned from the staff and Mr Cox of the close relationship that existed between you, and for that reason alone I would have thought she would have left you better provided for. However, the answer may be in this letter that was delivered by a bank messenger shortly after we returned from the funeral, with strict instructions that it should be given to you in private after the reading of the will. I sincerely hope that the contents will be to your advantage.'

Ruby gazed at the long white envelope lying on the desk, her heart thudding. Raising her head, she looked at Sir Charles, and felt her breath catch in her throat at the kindliness on his face. He looked nothing like the forbidding gentleman who had entered the house so bombastically just a short week ago. She began to relax as she waited for him to continue.

'I don't know what you have heard about my relationship with my stepmother, but it was common knowledge that we didn't get on. It was partly my fault. I didn't like the idea of my father marrying again, and being young and idealistic, I didn't hesitate to let them know my feelings. Mabel in turn told me exactly what she thought of me. "A snotty-nosed spoiled brat" is the term she used, if my memory serves me correctly. And do you know, Mrs O'Brien? She was right!' His brown eyes clouded over as the past came flooding back, then, with a wry smile, he added, 'Although we never really got to know each other, on the few occasions when I was in her company, she left a strong impression upon me. She was a remarkable woman, and will be sadly missed. As you are already aware, I intend to close the house for an indefinite period. My home is in Essex, and my wife is very happy where she is, so I can't see us taking up residence here. At the same time, I can't quite bring myself to sell the house.' He spread his arms as though asking her advice, then, pushing the envelope towards her, he said kindly, 'If you like, I shall leave you alone while you read it, or perhaps you would prefer to wait until you are at home?'

Ruby thought of her mother and Lily waiting at the lodge, ready to fuss over her the moment she walked through the door; and the children, who would be clamouring for her attention. And what if Michael, unable to bear the suspense any longer, decided to return home early? For all she knew, he might well be waiting for her this very minute. With a trembling hand she took hold of the envelope, saying shakily, 'Thank you, but I'd prefer to read it now.' He rose to leave, but she said quickly, 'Please, there is no need for you to leave, but – but I appreciate the gesture.'

Taking a paperknife from him, she carefully slit open the seal. Inside the envelope were three neatly written pages.

My dearest Ruby,

How bewildered you must be feeling at this moment. I know it's not the small amount I left to you that will be causing you so much anguish, but the belief that I saw you as merely another member of my staff. My, dear, dear friend, did you really imagine I could think of you thus? You, who have brought such love and happiness to my last years? No words will ever express how much you meant to me. I don't think I need to tell you how much I loved you, dearest Ruby, and I would like to think that the feeling was reciprocated.

I've always prided myself on not being a sentimental woman, so I shall get to the point of this letter and pray that when you have finished reading it you will understand why I have acted as I did, and harbour no ill-feeling against me.

I have instructed my bank to pay to you unconditionally the sum of three thousand pounds. It is a great deal of money, which is why I didn't want the rest of the staff to know of your true inheritance; hence the nominal sum that was stated at the reading of the will. Also, I wanted you to have the choice as to whether or not you confided to Michael the amount of money you received. You see, my dear, I still am not satisfied in my mind that he is the right man for you. Only you know that for sure, but being the loyal person you are, you would never complain if your marriage hadn't turned out as you had hoped. It was with this thought in mind that I made arrangements for you to keep your legacy secret if you wish to do so.

If I am wrong in my feelings regarding Michael, you have the option to share your good fortune with him. Please don't be angry with me for my feelings of distrust against your husband. I may not have shown it, but I had a certain fondness for your Irishman. He reminded me so much of my Patrick, which is probably the reason for my misgivings. I have only ever had your well-being at heart, and that of the children.

The decision is yours alone, Ruby. Nobody apart from Mr Bunting, the manager of my bank, knows the contents of this letter. I urge you to think long and hard before you decide what to do. Used wisely, the money will enable you to buy a house of your own, for I fear that my stepson will wish to sell this house since he has no use for it. Also it will enable you and the children to live comfortably for many years without the worry of having to seek employment.

I am very tired, Ruby: tired and dispirited. My world seems empty without the Queen. It's difficult to explain, but she was a part of my life, the rock upon which England stood, and now that she is gone I am aware of a void that no one else can fill, not even you, dear child.

I have lived longer than I expected and I am not afraid of dying. Don't grieve too long for me, Ruby, I am at peace now. You have your life to live and two wonderful children to love and care for.

Be happy, my dearest, dearest Ruby. Maybe we shall meet again if there is a hereafter.

> Goodbye child,
> Your dear friend,
> Mabel

The last words swam in front of her eyes, and her hand was still shaking when she carefully folded the pages and returned them to the envelope.

'Are you all right, Mrs O'Brien?' Sir Charles enquired, coming over to her side.

'Yes . . . thank you,' she answered tearfully, her body churning with emotion at the knowledge of the love that had gone into the writing of the letter.

She reflected on the wisdom of her friend's action, for since her death only a week ago, Michael had barely been able to contain his excitement at the prospect of the money he felt certain Ruby would inherit. And while she had mourned for her dead friend, he had been making plans for the future, a future in which he would never again have to call any man 'sir'. If she were to tell him about the money, he would immediately begin to make plans. She knew his greatest desire was to own a pub, and, if given the chance, he would use her legacy to realize his dream. Dear Lord, the idea was ludicrous! He would drink most of the profits! 'Stop it! Stop thinking like this; he's your husband!' she told herself sternly, 'and you love him still.' But loving him didn't blind her to the fact that he would never be happy until he felt he was his own master. He needed to feel superior to the ordinary man in the street, much in the same way that her father had felt, but for Michael there would be no wealthy grandfather to help him to achieve his ambitions. Even were she to hand over the entire amount to him, it would be nowhere near enough for the position in life he was aiming for.

Sighing deeply, she made to get up from her chair. Seeing her movement, Sir Charles put his hand out to steady her, and was met by an icy stare. 'I can manage to rise from a chair by myself, Sir Charles,' she said coolly, then, seeing his startled look, she felt immediately contrite. 'I'm sorry,' she murmured, 'but I cannot bear to be treated as a cripple.'

Sir Charles raised his eyebrows in surprise. 'Believe me, Mrs O'Brien, that was not my intent. I would offer my assistance to any lady who was in such obvious distress as you seem to be at the moment.'

Ruby bowed her head in shame, then, lifting her chin proudly, she placed her hand firmly on his arm and allowed him to help her from the chair. When they were standing by the now open door, she withdrew her hand and, looking up at him, said quietly, 'You haven't asked about the contents of the letter. You must be curious?'

Taking hold of her hand, Sir Charles assured her, 'The contents of the letter are your business, and your business alone, Mrs O'Brien. However, if at any time you need my help in any way, please don't hesitate to approach me.' So saying, he stood aside to let her pass, and Ruby, with a slight bow of her head, left the room.

Chapter Twenty-Two

'I don't want Auntie Mabel to go to heaven with the angels, Mum, I want her to come back home!'

Ruby looked at her seven-year-old son, full of compassion as his blue eyes filled with tears, his soft bottom lip beginning to tremble as he struggled to come to terms with the bewildering fact that the kind old lady whom he'd loved was never, ever coming back to him. Pulling him closer, she looked across to where Daisy sat, her four-year-old granddaughter Florrie fast asleep in her arms. Since her arrival back at the lodge over an hour since, Ruby had been patiently trying to console her son, but with no success. Now, her nerves frayed beyond endurance, she spoke to him harshly. 'Look, Danny, we've been over all this. I miss her too, more than you'll ever know. There's nothing more I can do, and I'm tired, son, so very, very tired. Be a good boy and let Aunt Lily take you up to bed. We'll talk more in the morning after we've all had a good night's sleep.'

'But, Mum . . .'

'I said *that's enough*! Now go to bed.'

Hearing the note of hysteria creeping into Ruby's voice, Lily quickly crossed the room and took Danny gently by the arm. 'Come along, Danny. Your mummy's tired, I'll take you up and read you a story.'

Without a word Danny allowed himself to be led away, his shoulders shaking, his head bowed, his young mind still trying to comprehend the enormity of the situation. Daisy also rose, the child in her arms still sleeping fitfully, and followed Lily from the room.

Left alone, Ruby stared into the blazing fire, her teeth chewing nervously on her bottom lip. Although it was already nine o'clock, still there was no sign of Michael. Her body tensed at the thought of the confrontation ahead. He was probably celebrating at this very moment in anticipation of his coming good fortune, but she had no intention of telling him about the letter. Nor anybody else for that matter, not even her mother. She'd decided that the wisest course would be to put the money away for the children; then, if anything happened to her or Michael, at least they would be well provided for. As soon as she was able, she intended to go to the bank and instruct the manager accordingly. The sound of footsteps on the stairs jerked her back to the present.

'Florrie's still asleep, dear, and Danny is quieter now,' Daisy said softly as she settled herself in the chair opposite Ruby. 'Is there anything else you'd like me or Lily to do for you before we return home?'

Shaking her head tiredly, Ruby answered, 'No thanks, Mum, but thank you for coming with me today. It was a great comfort.'

Daisy nodded, then, looking to where Lily stood by the door, said, 'Lily, would you fetch our coats? Mr Chadwick will be wondering where we are.' When Lily had left the room, Daisy leaned forward and said anxiously, 'Are you sure you'll be all right, dear? I mean, Lily could stay with you tonight if you wish, just in case . . .'

Her words were cut off sharply as the door burst open and Michael staggered into the lodge. 'Good evening, ladies. I'm sorry I'm late, but . . . I was un – unavoidably delayed,' he slurred drunkenly, while clutching at the edge of the table for support.

Ruby didn't even acknowledge his presence. After one brief look of disgust, she turned her gaze back to the roaring fire.

Daisy stood up slowly, her eyes taking in the spectacle of her son-in-law. Apart from the slight paunch around his middle, Michael hadn't changed much in eight years. He was still handsome in spite of his drinking habits, but at this moment all Daisy beheld was a red-faced, drunken slob who was threatening to wake her grandchildren with his raucous voice. She grabbed hold of his collar, and shook him violently. 'Be quiet! Do you hear me?' she demanded, her face filled with anger. 'You should be ashamed of yourself, coming home in this state, and on a day like today! Have you no respect for the dead?'

Michael looked down with amazement at his normally placid mother-in-law, then, pulling himself away from her grasp, he snarled, 'Thish is my house . . . madam. And I'll thank you to mind your own business. Now I'd like . . . to talk to me wife – in private.'

As he went to walk away, Daisy once more grabbed hold of his coat, and aided now by a startled Lily, proceeded to push him past the bemused Ruby and into the bedroom. With one last concerted shove they threw him on to the bed, and Daisy, breathing heavily, said angrily, 'You can stay there and sleep it off, and if you attempt to bother my daughter tonight, I – I'll take the poker to you!'

Michael lay across the bed, his mouth agape at the unexpected attack. He was about to pull himself up but seeing the wild look in Daisy's eyes, thought better of it, and with a contemptuous shrug, he flopped over on his side.

Shutting the door firmly, Daisy whispered to Lily, 'I think you'd better stay here tonight, just in case.'

Before Lily could answer, the muffled sound of laughter brought both their heads round to where Ruby was bending forward, her arms holding her stomach as she tried to stifle her merriment at the scene she'd just witnessed. Both women stood agape, then, when Daisy saw the tug at the corners of Lily's mouth, she too began to laugh.

'Oh dear,' Ruby gasped, 'I didn't think I'd ever laugh again, but the sight of you and Lily bundling Michael past me into the bedroom, well! It's the funniest thing I've seen in ages. And did you see the look on his face? He didn't know what had hit him!'

When at last they had composed themselves, Daisy picked up her hat and coat from the back of the settee where Lily had thrown them and, still smiling, said, 'Are you sure you don't want Lily to say tonight, dear?'

'I don't mind, Ruby, and I could help with the children in the morning,' Lily said, anxious to be of assistance.

'No, it's kind of you both, but I'll manage. You'd better get off home, else Dad will be wondering what's happened to you. Mr Masters will get you a cab.'

Tying the ribbons of her bonnet under her chin, Daisy said in a hesitant voice, 'You could always come home with us, dear. Your father would be overjoyed to see you, and the children.'

Ruby looked away quickly. She didn't want to go over this same topic again, not tonight. 'I've told you before, Mum. Dad knows where I live, and if he badly wants to see me, he can always come here.'

Daisy's face fell, then opening the door, she said over her shoulder, 'It works both ways, Ruby. Remember that, it works both ways.'

Ruby watched as the two women departed through the garden, then shut the door. Making her way back to the fire, she sat down wearily. She was grateful for her mother's offer, but she couldn't go back to the house she had once shared with her father – not until he asked, and knowing him as she did, that request would never be forthcoming. When tears prickled behind her eyelids, she shook herself angrily, then thought yearningly of her soft feather bed, but she was certainly not going to sleep with Michael tonight. Despite the light relief of seeing him being bundled unceremoniously out by her mother and Lily, she was still angry with him for the way he'd behaved. He should have been with her after the funeral, not off getting drunk in some pub. She hadn't been surprised, but it still hurt to think he cared so little for her that he could leave her when she so much needed him. She began to think back.

It was nearly nine years since she'd last seen her father. When Dr Benson had placed the newborn Danny in her arms, she had prayed that once her father knew he had a grandson, he would swallow his pride and come to see her, but she had waited in vain. Even the weekly visits from her mother and Lily, and the periodic visits from George and Bertie, couldn't erase her need to see her father again. If only there were some way of healing the rift between them without losing face, she would grab at it, and so would Bertie. Like her, he hadn't seen his father since the day they had both stormed out of their former home.

Fighting to keep her eyes open, she dragged herself from the comfort of the settee and opened the bedroom door. Careful not to disturb Michael, she pulled her nightdress from beneath the pillow and quietly returned to the living-room. Once undressed, she quickly unhooked the mesh corset and leather straps and sighed with relief as the wretched leg was set free from her aching stump. Pushing the whole lot out of sight, she banked down the fire and settled herself on the settee.

She could feel the comforting warmth of the fire adding to her tiredness. Before she finally closed her eyes, she thought, 'I'll go and see Bertie; see if we can find some way of making up with Dad without losing face. Oh, damn it, what difference does it make!' She cared no more about false pride: if she had to humble herself, then so be it, she was willing to take the chance of rejection. What had she to lose? She didn't know if Bertie would feel the same way; in fact she hardly saw him nowadays, not since he'd married that girl from Boots just over a year ago. She must make the effort to visit them more often, for she didn't want to lose touch with her brother as well as her father, but it was difficult, what with Michael and Bertie not getting on. 'Oh, go to sleep, woman,' she chided herself. 'Worry about getting yourself and Michael sorted out before planning how to get the family back together again.' Her eyelids were so heavy, so very, very heavy. Her last thought before sleep overtook her was the knowledge that with all the commotion with Danny and then Michael, she hadn't had the chance to tell her mother how much Mabel had left her in her will.

*

'I want to talk to you, Bernard.'

Bernard lowered his newspaper and looked at his wife, his eyebrows lifting at the sight of her flushed face, a sure sign that she was in one of her rare tempers. Folding the paper carefully, he laid it on his lap, wondering what had happened to cause her evident anger. 'I expected you back sooner than this,' he said mildly. 'I suppose you've been comforting Ruby. She must be feeling very upset at losing the old girl and . . .'

He jumped in surprise as she stormed towards him, saying loudly, 'How on earth would you know how Ruby's feeling? You haven't seen her for nine years, yet you talk about her as if she's just walked out of the room.'

Daisy stared at him for a long moment, then, turning on her heel, she whirled away from his startled gaze only to stop suddenly and face him again, her face set, as she determined to say what she should have said years ago. 'I was going to add that people change, but they don't, not really, not deep down where it matters most. Here you all are, you, Bertie and Ruby, all longing to see an end to this stupid feud, but not one of you willing to be the first to say that one simple word, "Sorry". God, but it makes me so angry! You should have gone after them that day, Bernard, but no, you were so sure they'd come back to you cap in hand, begging forgiveness, that you were content to sit back and wait, but it didn't happen like that, did it? And it never is going to happen like that because both Bertie and Ruby have too much of you in them to swallow their pride and admit that they were wrong. And why should they? You're the one who threw them out in a fit of temper, so it's up to you to shoulder the responsibility for the whole sorry business.'

Bernard tensed as he listened to Daisy's words. Throwing the paper on the floor, he stood up quickly, and his anger matching hers, replied harshly, 'What's got into you? You come back here after being absent for the best part of the day and immediately start berating me for something that happened years ago! What do you expect me to do, eh? Run out into the street and hail the first cab I see and make my way to Ruby's home and beg her to forgive me for being such a dreadful father? Or would you prefer I went to Bertie first?' he sneered.

Daisy's eyes bored into his until he was forced to drop his gaze. 'You can bluster all you like, Bernard, but you know that what I've said is true. Unless you're prepared to climb down and admit that you are in the wrong, you may never see either of your children again.' Her anger had given way to pity at the sight of the conflicting emotions passing over Bernard's flushed face, but there was nothing she could do to help him. Walking towards the door, she turned her head and said sadly, 'You spent many unhappy years because of your father's neglect and indifference. Don't you think it's ironic that you should end up doing the same to your own children?'

Bernard watched in silence as she went out, the words he wanted to say in retaliation dying in his throat. Slowly he returned to his chair and, picking up the fallen paper, he spread it on his lap, then stared down unseeingly at it.

It was a sheepish Michael who emerged from the bedroom the following morning. His eyes downcast, he sidled past the table where Ruby and the children were having breakfast and made his way to the scullery. Ten minutes later, washed and looking a bit more presentable, he came back into the room, a look of contrition on his face. 'Morning, darlin',' he said hopefully.

'Get down from the table, children, and go and play in the garden until I call you,' Ruby told the two forlorn figures on either side of her. Without a murmur they clambered down, and, Danny taking Florrie's hand, walked slowly out.

When the door had shut behind them, Ruby turned to Michael. 'So, you've finally surfaced,' she said coolly. 'Will you be wanting any breakfast? You don't normally, after a night out with your friends.'

'Ah, now, darlin', don't start,' Michael implored, his hand to his forehead, trying to elicit some sympathy, but his gesture was wasted. Looking into her cold blue eyes, he pulled out a chair and sat down heavily. Still playing for time, he put his head in his hands, saying wearily, 'It's heart-sorry I am about the way I behaved last night. I was upset. When we got back from the funeral, I felt so down, I had to get out of the house. I never realized how fond I was of the auld girl until I saw her being lowered into the grave, and . . .' He winced as Ruby scraped her chair back.

'Don't you dare give Mabel as an excuse to get drunk!' she shouted. 'You've never needed one before, and while we're on the subject of Mabel, I hope you didn't spend all the money she left you. I only got a hundred more than you did, and we're going to need every penny – unless of course you already have another job lined up.'

Michael stared up at her, his mouth agape. 'What are you saying? She must have left you more than that! She always said she'd leave you well provided for.'

Ruby glared back. The confrontation she'd been dreading was

being made easier by her anger at his stunned expression. 'Well, she must have thought that five hundred pounds between the pair of us was provision enough. And now I'll leave you to look after the children. I still work at the house, and I have a lot to see to.'

As she made to pass, he grabbed her arm. 'Just a minute! You can't drop a bombshell like that in me lap and just walk away! We need to talk. This changes everything . . . I had plans . . . I had it all worked out . . .'

'Let go of my arm, Michael, you're hurting me.'

The icy tone of her voice made him release his grip, then, bunching his hands into fists, he banged on the table. 'The mean auld bitch!' he muttered furiously. 'She must have had thousands tucked away, and all we got was a measly five hundred pounds between us. Jasus, she must have had a good laugh at our expense, and after all we did for her, the spiteful auld . . .'

'That's enough, Michael! I won't listen to another word. Mabel was my friend, a kind dear friend, and what's all this about "all we did for her"? *You* never did anything except to suck up to her, waiting for her to die. But she saw through you, Michael! Oh, yes, she might have been old, but she wasn't stupid!'

He got to his feet, his chair crashing to the floor. 'Don't you ever talk to me like that again!' he roared, his face red with outrage. 'I've never sucked up to anyone in me life! And as for you . . . Well, ye can forget about buying our own house; we'll rent somewhere when we leave here. As you've pointed out, we're going to need every penny, and I'm not going to waste any of it on a bloody house! Do you hear me, woman?'

Ruby lifted her chin high and said calmly, 'There you are mistaken, Michael. I'm not taking the children into some slum just so that you can have more drinking money in your pocket. If needs be, I'll buy a house out of my own money; I have enough. And I'll find another post to support us if you won't. But, if I do, I'll go alone. I'll work to support my children, but not you.'

Michael tried to control the workings of his face, and then began to laugh. 'Ah, that's rich, darlin'! And what do you intend to do? Will you tell me that? You've had it soft here . . . it'll be different elsewhere. And there's not that many places that'll hire one-legged help.'

When her hand came up, he grabbed at it, and pulling her close to him, added, 'Aye, the truth hurts, doesn't it? Well, remember that little fact when you think back to what you've said to me this day.'

Wrenching her hand away, she yelled, 'You cruel bugger! Well, let me tell you, Michael O'Brien, I can achieve more with one leg than you ever could with two. I'll show you I can manage with or without you . . . it's your choice.' She continued to glare at him, panting, and when she got no response, the thought that had been whirling in her mind all night burst from her stiff lips. '*And* I'm going to see my father. Tomorrow, if possible. It's – It's time the rift . . . was healed, so don't – don't try to stop me. I'm going . . . whether you like it or . . .'

She got no further before he grasped her arm again and once more was leaning over her, muttering, 'Begod you're not! You made your choice nine years ago when you married me. I'll not have you running back to him now, so you can put that idea out of your head!'

She could feel his hot breath fanning her face and turned her head away, but not before she'd seen through the bluster to the uncertainty in his wide eyes. She felt his grip on her arm loosen, and still not looking at him, said, 'You can't stop me, Michael, and don't even think of trying. You'll only come out the loser.' She limped quickly to the door and slammed out of the lodge.

Michael stared at the closed door for a long time, then, picking up the fallen chair, he sank into it wearily. God, he hadn't meant to say those things to her! What had possessed him? Yet even as he asked himself the question his mind shouted back, 'Face it man, you were banking on the auld girl's fondness of Ruby to enable you to set yerself up for life. But what's more, you wanted to show that toffee-nosed family of hers that you were a man to be reckoned with.' That's what was hurting him most, the realization that without the thousands he'd been hoping for, he could never be on an equal footing with his father-in-law. He passed a hand over his bleary eyes. And now she was going back, back to the house he had been barred from. He knew that, despite his words, she would do as she liked, and he also knew that he didn't have the strength of character to stop her. In many ways she was stronger than him, and it was this knowledge that had always made him feel inferior to her, and always would. What had she said to him? 'I can achieve more with one leg than you ever could with two!'

Suddenly he felt very alone, and very afraid.

Ruby strode purposefully up the garden path, the metal tip on her leg tapping out a staccato on the flagstones. Pausing outside the kitchen door, she waited until her breathing had returned to normal before opening it. The familiar sight of Mrs Rodgers on her knees black-leading the stove brought her back to a sense of normality.

'Why, Ruby, I didn't expect you to come over today,' the old lady said in surprise. 'Sir Charles came in here last night after you'd gone and told us you'd be having a few days' rest.'

'Well, he didn't say anything to me, so I'd best carry on working until I'm told differently,' Ruby replied lightly, then, looking round the empty kitchen, she asked, 'Where is everyone? I thought I'd find you all in here making plans for the future.'

Mrs Rodgers sat back on her heels, her sharp eyes taking in the puffiness of Ruby's eyes and the high colour in her cheeks, and thought, 'I bet there's been high jinks over in the lodge this morning!' Although Ruby hadn't told them anything last night, the solicitor, Mr Cox, had stopped off in the kitchen for a cup of tea on his way home, and with a little prompting had informed them of the small legacy Lady Caldworthy's former companion had received. Mrs Rodgers wouldn't have liked the job of telling Michael, because, as they all knew, he had been expecting much, much more. Wiping her hands carefully, she answered, 'Mr Masters is upstairs with Sir Charles, and Rosie and Agnes have gone into town to get some groceries. It's not worth having them delivered any more, not with things as they are at the moment. I thought it better to buy from day to day until Sir Charles decides exactly when he's going to close up the house. I hope I did right?' she added anxiously.

'Yes, of course. I should have thought of it myself,' Ruby hastened to reassure her.

Mrs Rodgers's homely face broke into a warm smile. 'Oh, Ruby, you've had more than enough to think about without worrying over trivial matters like food and drink! I don't know how you managed it all, really I don't. What with looking after her ladyship these past few weeks when she was really bad, and then arranging the funeral, not to mention taking care of the children . . . you must be worn out. And I'd like to bet you haven't had a decent meal for weeks, have you?'

Shaking her head, Ruby replied, 'I haven't felt hungry, Mrs Rodgers. And now, if you don't mind, I'd like to go over what has to be done in the house before we all leave.'

Heaving herself to her feet, Mrs Rodgers put down the blackened cloth and starting to wash her hands, said over her shoulder, 'There's not much left to do, Ruby. We only finished spring cleaning last month, don't you remember? It was just before her ladyship got taken bad.'

Ruby didn't answer, but merely stared down numbly.

Spring cleaning, that time of year that everyone in the house both loved and hated. Curtains and covers were taken down and washed, the carpets pulled up and carried out into the garden, where the winter dirt and grime were beaten out with wicker carpet-beaters. Then the furniture was draped with dust-sheets, while the house was cleaned from attic to cellar. When the cleaning was completed, everything was put back into place, leaving the entire house smelling of beeswax and soap. It was back-breaking work, but when it was finished there remained the satisfied feeling of a job well done. And now it really was over, for never again would she supervise and assist in the yearly ritual of this house. Ruby felt the first droplets of tears splash on to her hands, and leaning over the table, she rested her head on her arms, and wept.

'Oh, Ruby! I know, love, I know!' Mrs Rodgers was standing by her, her heavy hand stroking her long auburn hair, and Ruby, with a heart-rending cry, turned and buried her face against the warm fat body of the motherly woman at her side. 'I miss her, Mrs Rodgers! I can't believe she's dead.' The words seemed to be torn from her aching throat. 'I loved her, you know. I really loved her.' She felt the body she was clutching at begin to tremble, and tightened her hold.

Sir Charles stood quietly in the doorway, his eyes taking the scene in, then without a word he walked away, leaving the two women alone with their grief.

Chapter Twenty-Three

'I'm afraid it'll take a bit of time to get to Brixton, missus. Most people are coming 'ome from work this time of day. You in a 'urry?' the cabbie shouted through the top of the horse-drawn carriage.

Ruby looked up at the cheerful ruddy face and replied, 'No, no hurry. My time is my own.'

'Right you are, missus.'

Sinking back on the blue leather seat, Ruby faced the two small figures and smiled reassuringly at them. 'Cheer up, you two, there's no need to look so glum! We're going to see Nan and Aunt Lily. I thought you'd both be pleased of a day out.'

Danny peered at her from beneath his straw boater, his face sullen. 'What about "him"?'

Ruby's hands tightened in her lap, then, her face set, she answered, 'If you mean your grandfather, then say so. And yes, he will be there too.' When she received no response, she leaned over and took his small hand, saying, 'Listen, Danny, there's no need to be frightened. We'll just stay for an hour or so, and then we'll go home.'

'But what if Grandad doesn't like us, Mum? I wish Dad was with us. Why didn't Dad come? Is it because he doesn't like Grandad?'

Ruby gently squeezed his hand, wondering just how much he had overheard of the argument she had had with Michael that morning. The night before, for the first time in their married life he had slept on the settee, and the moment she had emerged from the bedroom he had started in on her again, rehashing the argument from the previous day. He had seemed more concerned about the visit to her parents than about the money, and had tried to prevent her from leaving the lodge with the children. First he had pleaded and cajoled, and when that hadn't worked, he had stormed off into the garden, muttering furiously.

'Look, Mummy, a monkey! Can we go and see it?' Florrie cried excitedly, at the sight of the organ-grinder and his pet monkey on the pavement.

Ruby looked affectionately at her daughter and then past her to the sight outside the window. The street was packed with stalls, the people milling around the pavement and into the road, causing problems for the many cabs and carriages that were trying to make their way through the seething throng. Following Florrie's pointing finger, she looked at the man holding the gaudily dressed monkey by a chain, while his other hand wound a wooden handle that produced a tinny musical sound. All around was noise and a sense of vitality, and although the sights and sounds were distracting Florrie, they seemed to be having little effect on her son. 'Not now, dear,' she admonished gently before returning her attention to him. There was a miserable, frightened look in his eyes, and she swallowed nervously. Maybe it hadn't been such a good idea to bring them with her; neither was it fair to use them as a barrier against her father, but she couldn't face the thought of going to the house alone. She chose her next words carefully.

'Your dad has never met your grandfather. They – They had a row a long time ago, and now I'm going to try and make it up with him. Do you understand, Danny?'

The blue eyes so like Michael's stared back at her, a well of tears forming on his black eyelashes. 'Oh, don't, Danny! You'll upset Florrie. Now come on, son, we won't stay long, I promise.'

Half an hour later they were standing on the doorstep, Ruby's hand hovering uncertainly over the brass knocker. Taking a deep breath, she quickly rapped twice on the door, then stepped back in sudden fright, grasping the children's hands. When the door swung open to reveal a startled Lily, she smiled at her old friend and said, 'Well, are you going to let us in, Lily? Or do we have to go round to the tradesmen's entrance?'

'Ruby, what are you doing here?' Lily faltered, looking over her shoulder as though fearing some unknown force would descend upon them.

'Well, I was in the neighbourhood and I thought I'd pop in for a cup of tea,' Ruby replied, the false gaiety sounding strained even to her own ears.

'I want to go home, Mum! Let's go home, please,' wailed Danny, clutching at her arm.

'Me too, Mum! I wanter go home to Dad!' Florrie echoed, her normally happy face beginning to crumple.

'There now, you two, what's all the rumpus?' Lily cried, trying to ease the tension. 'Don't you want to see your nan?'

Ruby's nerves were by now stretched to breaking-point. It would be so easy to take the children and leave, but if she did, she knew she'd never have the courage to come again. Grasping the children's hands tightly, she said, 'Will you tell them I'm here, Lily?'

Lily looked anxiously at her friend, and swallowed hard before answering, 'Yes, of course.' Then, bending down to the children, she added, 'Do you want to take your coats off?'

'No, leave them as they are, Lily. I don't know how long we'll be stopping.'

Lily, hearing the tremor in Ruby's voice, turned to walk away, then stopped. Looking over her shoulder, she asked gently, 'You're sure you know what you're doing, Ruby?'

The look of grim determination on Ruby's face was answer enough.

Shaking her head, Lily walked over to the parlour and knocked on the door. She waited a moment before entering, and then, in a voice that was far from steady, announced, 'Miss Ruby and the children, Mr Chadwick,' then moved aside to let the unexpected visitors enter.

If the king himself had been announced, the effect could not have been more startling. Daisy stared at the trio as if not believing the evidence of her own eyes. Then, throwing an anxious look in Bernard's direction, she laid down her embroidery and held out her arms. 'Danny, Florrie, come to Nan,' she cried to the children.

Their eyes darted to their nan and then to the stern-looking man who had risen from his chair and was now standing, his hands clasped behind his back, his face showing no emotion. Daisy pushed them gently, and, sidling carefully past the man they knew to be their grandfather, they made a concerted dash to the safety of their nan's outstretched arms.

'May I sit down, Father? Unless of course you would prefer us to leave.'

Ruby's words were stilted, and Bernard's heart jumped at her unfamiliar address. He saw a young woman clothed in black, with a mass of auburn hair piled high at the back of her head, and felt as if he were in the presence of a stranger. But when he saw the silent pleading in her eyes, suddenly the years were swept away. He tried to speak, and found he couldn't utter a word. Bowing his head in confusion, he gestured to a nearby chair, and when she was seated, he still stood, unsure what to do next.

'Come, children, let Nan have your coats,' Daisy said, her voice assuming a cheerful note, but the pretence did not deceive either child.

'Don't want to take our coats off. We want to go home,' Danny wailed.

His cry was suddenly cut off as Ruby said angrily, 'That's enough, both of you! Now give your nan your coats and behave yourselves.'

At the children's crying, Bernard looked to where Daisy sat, a child on either side, their wide eyes showing their fear, and felt an overwhelming sense of guilt. Completely at a loss, he walked back to his chair and, safely seated, he continued to stare at the children, his chest churning with emotion.

Nine years, nine long soul-destroying years he had been suffering the torment of the damned, and now she was back, and with her his grandchildren. How many nights had he lain awake praying for this moment? He knew he could have ended the feud at any time over those years, but he couldn't swallow his pride so easily. Now the nightmare was over, and he silently vowed that nothing and no one would ever come between them again. He was painfully aware of the tension in the room and strained to say something, but he seemed to have been deprived of the power of speech.

It was Florrie who saved the day. Her voice trembling, she pointed over at him and asked Daisy, 'Is that man my grandad, Nan?'

Daisy held her tighter, then answered shakily, 'Yes, dear, that man is your grandad.'

Florrie's tears miraculously vanished, to be replaced by a look of awe. Leaving the safety of her nan's side, she walked over to Bernard, whose body was taut as he waited for the child to speak.

'Hello, Grandad. My name's Florrie. How do you do?' she said gravely, her face now showing no sign of any fear.

Bernard stared hard at her as though trying to find some resemblance to himself. He saw the blue eyes and long shiny blonde hair that spilled out from under the straw hat, and caught his breath. How like Ruby she was at the same age! It was only the hair colouring that was different. As if in a dream, his hands came out and pulled her closer, and then she was sitting on his lap, her eyes staring trustingly up into his.

Ruby watched the small scenario and felt the tension drain from her. Thank God she had brought them today, for with the simplicity of a child, Florrie had unwittingly broken down the barricades. Even though Danny still clung to his grandmother's side, it was a start. She could feel the tears pricking behind her eyes and her nose began to tingle alarmingly. She said hoarsely, 'It's good to be home, Fa – I mean Dad.'

Bernard looked across at her, his eyes suspiciously bright as he answered awkwardly, 'It's good to have you back, Ruby. I've m – missed you . . . very much, my dear.'

Daisy looked on delightedly, and reaching for the service bell, she shook it vigorously. The last chimes had hardly died away before Lily appeared, looking anxiously from one face to the other.

'Ah, Lily, could you fetch some tea, please, and some cakes for the children, if Cook has made any today?'

'Yes, Mrs Chadwick. Right away, Mrs Chadwick,' Lily babbled happily, her face splitting into a huge grin before she hurried from the room.

When the door closed behind her, an uneasy silence settled on the room again until Ruby said nervously, 'I'm sorry, Dad.'

Bernard's head jerked as he heard the humility in his proud daughter's voice. Pulling Florrie further up on his lap, he answered gruffly, 'Sorry? You have nothing to reproach yourself for, Ruby. I have only myself to blame for the unnecessary suffering I've caused over the years. I – I never meant to hurt you . . .' He broke off as Lily reappeared, and thankfully turned his attention to the matter of refreshments.

'Thank you, Lily. Set the tray down, will you? We'll help ourselves,' Daisy said breathlessly, her voice unsteady as she rejoiced at this miracle. Gently disentangling Danny's arms from her waist, she said softly, 'Bernard, aren't you going to say hello to your grandson?'

Bernard raised his eyes warily. He had avoided looking at the boy, but now he must take courage and face the Irishman's son. He had taken to the girl child immediately, but the boy? Nobody knew that Bernard had ever seen Michael, but he had been there on the day they had married, hiding behind a broken wall like a common thief as he'd watched his beloved daughter come from the church, her face radiant as she looked up at her dark-haired husband. And now his son was in this room, a miniature replica of the man he had hated for nine years! He looked at the small sturdy boy, dressed in a navy and white sailor suit, regarding him fearfully from beneath his straw boater, and drew a deep breath. If he were going to make his peace with Ruby, he must rid himself of this unreasonable hatred he felt for her husband. He must remember also that the child was Ruby's son, too. Let him think of the boy in that way: Danny was his daughter's son. He extended his hand, saying, 'Come, Danny. Come and stand by me.'

But the child turned and buried his face further into the folds of Daisy's skirt, and he felt a stab of guilt run through his body. Shamefaced, he stared at Daisy, his eyes mirroring his silent pain. It was disturbingly obvious that the boy knew something about the situation that existed between the two families. He had probably heard his parents talking when he should have been elsewhere. Still, some children were naturally shy with strangers. Easing himself out of the chair, he set Florrie down and, ignoring her protests, walked over to Daisy. Squatting down on his haunches, he tentatively put a hand on the boy's unyielding shoulder. When he didn't pull away, he carefully moved it on to his plump arm, and turned the child round to face him.

After a long moment, Danny, his face still swollen from crying, said in a high voice, 'My dad doesn't like you.'

The words were like a slap in the face for Bernard, and he heard Ruby gasp in horror and sensed Daisy's body stiffen in alarm. Bowing his head, he thought desperately, 'I must go very carefully here; very carefully.' Clearing his throat noisily, he said, 'I'm sorry your father feels like that, but your mother likes me, and so does your grandmother. Do you think you could learn to like me too?'

Danny appraised Bernard for another heart-stopping moment, then, with a small lift of his chin, he replied shakily, 'I suppose so.' Extending his hand, he took hold of Bernard's and began to pump it vigorously, as he'd been taught to do when meeting a strange gentleman. The feel of the tiny hand engulfed in his own caused the final pieces of ice to melt around Bernard's heart, and with a loud laugh he lifted Danny under the armpits and threw him high in the air.

Florrie, seeing her brother receive so much attention, moved quickly away from her mother, and pulling at the bottom of Bernard's jacket, cried out, 'Me too! Me too!'

Ruby looked at the trio and felt her eyes begin to blur, but when her father attempted to lift Florrie, she cried, 'Be careful, Dad! They'll have you over in a minute.'

Still laughing, Bernard said ruefully, 'You're right, I'm not as young as I used to be.' Then, looking from Danny to Florrie, he added, 'How would you like it if we took our tea in the garden? I'm sure your mother and grandmother would like the chance to have a talk.'

'Oh, yes, please, Grandad,' Florrie squealed delightedly.

'That's settled, then,' Bernard said as he rang the bell. Once again Lily appeared in the room within seconds. 'Ah, Lily, the children and

I are going to take our tea in the garden. Would you carry the tray for us, please?'

Daisy and Ruby watched wordlessly as the three of them left the room. Lily quickly moved away from the door to let them pass, then she picked up the plate of cakes and the jug of lemonade, and with a quick bob in Daisy's direction, hurried after the trio, the grin still wide on her face.

Left alone, the two women looked at each other, then as if at a given signal they both burst into tears. When the paroxysm finally abated, Ruby wiped her eyes, and hiccupping loudly said, 'If I'd known it would be so easy, I would have come back years ago. It's as though I'd never been away. He seems to have wiped from his mind all that's happened, but I don't mind. I've been dreading having to cover all the old ground and reopen old wounds, but if Dad would rather not talk about the past, that's fine by me. Did you see how he took to the children?' She beamed, her face blotchy from crying.

Daisy smiled happily. 'He looks ten years younger! Oh, Ruby, I can't tell you what this means to me . . . to both of us. I've been dreaming of this day for so long: to have my grandchildren around me in my own home. Oh dear . . .' Her voice dropped, but quickly recovering herself she went on, 'Dear me, this is one of the happiest days of my life, yet I can't seem to stop crying! It's the relief, I suppose. But tell me, did you have any trouble with Michael about coming here today?'

Ruby's feeling of happiness vanished as she thought back to that morning and the repetition of an argument that had been going on for years. She sighed deeply. 'He didn't want me to come. We had words, and from what Danny said to Dad, he must have been listening in his bedroom. Oh, Mum, what am I going to do? It was bad enough before, because, as you know, Michael has never forgiven Dad for condemning him without a hearing. But now I've come back, how is he going to react when I come visiting, knowing that he is still barred from the house. Unless . . .' She leaned forward, her eyes asking the question, but Daisy shook her head.

'Give him time, Ruby. I know it's unreasonable, this feeling of antagonism your father has against Michael, but be patient. Who knows but he may change his mind . . .' Her words trailed off miserably as she saw the look of hopelessness on Ruby's face. In an effort to change the painful subject, she pulled herself upright, and exclaimed, 'I nearly forgot! With all the excitement of seeing you and the children, I didn't ask you about the will. Would it be too nosy of me to ask how much Mabel left you?'

For a wild moment Ruby was tempted to tell her the truth, but just as quickly the feeling vanished. The fewer people who knew about the money, the better. Besides, it wasn't hers, it was for the children, and once she'd been to see the bank manager and settled the matter, she intended to forget all about it. 'Three hundred pounds.' The words came out breathlessly, and when she saw the look of stunned surprise on Daisy's face, she quickly averted her eyes. This was the first time she had ever lied to her mother, and an uncomfortable feeling of guilt settled heavily upon her.

'Three hundred pounds?' Daisy echoed, her eyes and mouth stretched wide in disbelief. 'But that's impossible! Mabel told me not long ago that she intended to see that you were provided for. There must be some mistake, dear.'

'There's been no mistake, Mum. Anyway, as I told Michael, five hundred pounds between the two of us is more than enough to give us a new start.' The words came tumbling out in confusion.

Daisy, still staring at her daughter, noted the high colour that had sprung to her cheeks, and frowned. 'Is there something you're not telling me, Ruby?'

Ruby's head snapped up, and with a supreme effort she returned her mother's shrewd gaze. 'Of course not!' she replied indignantly, all the while thinking, 'I'm not lying, not really. I don't intend to use the money for myself. And if I tell her, then she'll tell Dad, and he'll insist on investing it for me, and I don't want it invested; I just want a nest-egg for the children. Oh dear, how does that old saying from Shakespeare go? "Oh what a tangled web we weave when first we practise to deceive."' Forcing a smile to her stiff lips, she said firmly, 'Let's forget about the money, Mum. As I've already said, it's enough to see us through until Michael gets himself another post, and I might try to get a job myself once Florrie starts school.'

'But what would you do, dear? There's not many places that would take you on with two young children, and you're not trained for anything else.'

'Look, forget about my problems for today, will you, Mum? I'll think of something,' Ruby said impatiently. 'I might even start a small business of my own. I'll have to wait until we're settled and see how much money is left after buying a house.'

Daisy's mouth dropped in alarm. 'Start your own business? Oh, Ruby, you can't be serious! Look, if you need help, your father would be only too . . .'

'No.' The word sounded like the crack of a whip, and Daisy flinched

as though she'd been struck. Ruby saw the stricken look, and cried,
Oh, Mum, I'm sorry! I didn't mean to shout, but you must try to
understand that I need to make my own way in life. Although I'm
grateful for your offer, I couldn't possibly accept. I'm quite capable of
working, even with my handicap, but if ever I needed help I would
come to you. My pride isn't so great that I would let the children
starve rather than admit defeat.'

Daisy surveyed her daughter, wondering why she was so surprised
at what she'd said. She had always known that Ruby would never sit
idle when she could be doing something productive, and although she
still felt worried about her future, secretly she was proud of her
daughter's indomitable spirit. If only her husband possessed the same
quality! And yet, despite knowing the kind of man Michael was, she
couldn't help liking him. He was always courteous to her, and often
made her laugh out loud with his humorous stories about the 'auld
country', as he referred to Ireland, even though he could only have
been a boy when he'd left his native land. But beneath his cheerful
countenance Daisy sensed a restless man, a man who wanted things
from life that he was, and always would be, unable to achieve for himself. She had watched them together over the years, and was as sure as
she could be that he loved her daughter, and he idolized his children.
Just seeing them together frolicking in the large garden of Mabel's
home had been proof enough of that. But the suspicion that he had
married Ruby in the hope of being taken into the family and lining his
pockets in some humdrum job alongside Bernard and George still remained firmly rooted in her mind. It was a fear she shared silently
with Bernard, and while she might possibly give him the benefit of the
doubt, she knew that Bernard would always be distrustful of his son-
in-law, no matter what.

Hearing the children returning, she said quickly, 'Will you bring
them again, dear? Next week for tea, perhaps? Sunday would be best,
as George will be at home and I know he'd love to see them. He's out
with some friends at the moment, but if I tell him you're coming next
week, I know he'll make a point of being home.'

Ruby looked into her mother's pleading eyes and fought down the
panic that suddenly assailed her. She would have to be very careful
how she told Michael. He was going to be put out, and when he was in
one of his resentful moods, the tension in the small lodge was unbearable. It would be even worse now that there was no Mabel to go to
for comfort.

She was about to answer, when her father walked into the room with Florrie tucked securely under his arm and Danny sitting astride his neck, both of them squealing with delight. He must have caught the tail-end of the conversation, and was waiting for an answer. When she saw the look of hope in his eyes, she bent her head and said, 'Of course I will! Next Sunday, it is then?'

The look of joy on her parents' faces was reward enough for the price she would have to pay when she returned home.

Michael watched as the three of them crossed the garden, heading for the lodge. It was obvious from the happy expressions on the children's faces that the visit had gone well. Dropping the net curtain, he went into the bedroom to give himself time to compose himself before they came through the door. His mind was in a turmoil: half of him had been hoping that they would return within the hour, having found the door shut in their faces, but the other side of him – the side that still desperately wanted to belong to Ruby's family, to be welcomed into the large villa in Brixton and to mingle with important men from the City – was overriding the deep resentment he felt towards the man who, to his mind, had treated him so shabbily.

When the door burst open and Danny shouted, 'Dad, Dad, where are you? We've been playing with Grandad, and we're going back for tea next week,' he felt his heart leap. She'd done it! She'd made it up with the auld fellow, and in doing so had opened up a whole new world to him. And it couldn't have come at a better time, for he didn't fancy the idea of spending the rest of his life slaving away in someone else's garden for a pittance. He thought again of the measly amount the old girl had left to Ruby, and grimaced. Spite, pure spite, it must have been, and yet he still couldn't believe her capable of such a deed.

'Michael? Are you in there?' Ruby called from the door.

'Aye. I'll be out in a moment!' he called back as he straightened his jacket, then stretching his neck within his starched collar, he thought grimly, 'Next Sunday for tea, was it? Well now, he wasn't going to appear too eager. No, begod!' He was no puppy that could be treated badly one minute and be expected to lick the hand that had meted out the punishment the next. Smoothing down his trousers, he assumed a nonchalant expression, then, taking a deep breath, he sauntered into the sitting-room.

'Ah, there you are! I thought for a moment you had gone out,' Ruby said over her shoulder as she helped the children off with their coats.

Before he could say anything, he was nearly bowled over as the children rushed headlong into his arms. 'Dad, Dad, I want to tell you bout Grandad's house! It's lovely, Dad, and we saw Nan and Aunt Lily, and Uncle George will be there next week, but not Uncle Bertie. Uncle Bertie doesn't go there any more, does he, Dad? Doesn't Grandad like him either?'

The innocent question posed by his son brought Michael's head up swiftly as he looked sharply at Ruby, standing with her hand to her throat. 'Danny, that's enough now,' she said crossly, 'It's getting late, and you've both had a long day. Take your sister upstairs. You can play for a bit while I talk to your dad. Go on, I'll be up shortly.'

'Oh, Mum!'

The plea came from both of them, and gritting her teeth, she snapped, 'Do as you're told, both of you!' Her head was beginning to ache in anticipation of the argument that was going to ensue as soon as the children were out of earshot.

Seeing the look on their mother's face, the two forlorn figures began to make their way towards the stairs.

When she heard their bedroom door close loudly, she turned reluctantly to Michael. Rubbing her throbbing temple with both hands, she said, 'Well, aren't you going to ask me how the visit went?'

Michael was standing in front of the blazing fire, his hands clasped firmly behind his back, a stance he often assumed when he was about to lay down the law. Rocking backwards on his heels, he gave a 'Huh' of a laugh before answering. 'Begod, you ask me that? You've been gone for nearly four hours, and you come back looking the picture of happiness. Well, the children looked happy enough. And all this talk about "Grandad" now, and him never setting his foot over the doorstep since the day they were born. Jasus, a blind man could see how the visit went! Did you not spare a thought to how *I* might be feeling, left alone for the best part of the day with no one to talk to but the four walls?'

Fighting back an angry retort, Ruby answered wearily, 'Michael, I haven't seen my dad for nearly nine years. Surely you didn't expect me to walk out on him after a few minutes? Yes, I know, I know.' She held up her hand to forestall the usual reply. 'He knows where we live, but he's a proud man, Michael. I understand him, more than even my mother does. He's been suffering all these years for what he did to me that night, but it's over now. And I'll be going back again, as – as often as I can. So if that's going to be a problem for you, we'd better talk it out now, because I don't think I can bear the thought of having to endure an argument every time I wish to visit my parents.'

As the import of her words sank in, Michael began to feel very apprehensive, and he swallowed twice before asking, 'This invitation for tea next Sunday; is it for all of us, or am I to be left at home again?' He held his breath as he waited for Ruby's reply, then, seeing her bowed head, he felt the familiar anger and disappointment. Bending over her he roared angrily, 'So that's the way of it, is it? I'm still not good enough for your precious father! Well, let me tell you, if I had been invited, I would have said no. Do ye think I'd sit with a man who's treated me worse than a mangy dog you'd find by the roadside? Do you?'

'Michael, please!' Ruby pleaded, as the pain in her temple worsened. 'Give him time! And it's not only you. Bertie hasn't crossed the doorstep since that night, and he's his own son! I – I'm going to work on him, to try to bring him round, be – because I know in my heart that he misses Bertie, but he's afraid to make the first move in case he's rebuffed. Leave it for a few more weeks, please? Maybe . . .'

'Shut up! Do ye hear me? Shut up! What do I care about Bertie? He's as bad as his father, always looking down his nose at me whenever he comes round here, and him a lousy peeler.' He leaned closer until his face was only inches from her own, a fine spray of spittle on his lips. Ruby drew back in alarm as the violent anger contorted his features. 'Now I'll tell you something else, and you'll listen! I've never hated a man in me life before, but I hate your father, and that snooty upstart of a brother. And if the pair of them died the morrow, I'd dance on their graves! While I'm on the subject, you'll not be going visiting any more, because if I'm not good enough for your miserable bastard of a father, then neither are me children.'

Ruby stared unflinchingly into his wild eyes, and then whispered 'I'll take my children wherever I wish, and nothing you say will stop me. And don't you ever speak about my father in that fashion again. I won't tolerate it, I won't!'

When she saw his hand coming out towards her, she cried out sharply, 'You lay one finger on me, Michael, and I'll leave you and take the children with me! I'm warning you. I'd do it, so don't put it to the test!'

Slowly Michael lowered his arm, then standing upright, his fists clenched by his side, he stared at her, his eyes filled with loathing. 'Don't worry! I'll not bring meself down to his level. I've never hit a woman in me life, and I'll not start now.' He flung himself away from her and, grabbing his coat, made for the door. Wrenching it open, he gazed out into the garden, then declared, 'Damn your family! Damn the whole rotten bunch of them! And damn you too for putting them afore me!'

Ruby watched through pain-filled eyes as the door slammed behind him. It was too much! She was still grieving for Mabel, and Michael knew how upset she was, and yet he had still gone for her, putting his own feelings first as he had always done. Was it merely insensitivity, or deliberate cruelty?

'Mum, what's happening? Why are you and Dad shouting?' Danny's frightened voice floated down the stairs. 'Me and Florrie are scared!'

Limping heavily, she walked towards the stairs. 'Nothing's wrong, son. Go back to your room, I'm coming up.'

Chapter Twenty-Four

Along the one mile of Whitechapel Road from Commercial Street to Stepney Green there were no less than forty-eight drinking places, and it fell to the Metropolitan Police Force to patrol these areas, day and night.

On this Friday evening, Sergeant Bertie Chadwick and a new constable named Charlie Smithers were making their rounds down Whitechapel Road when they spotted a man very much the worse for drink staggering in their direction, proclaiming at the top of his thick fuddled voice his love for a certain 'Molly Malone'. Left to himself, Bertie would have bypassed the man, for it was nearly the end of his shift and he was anxious to get home, but not so the newly recruited constable.

'Looks like 'e's 'ad a skinful, Sarge. Best get him back to the station before he causes any trouble,' Charlie Smithers said eagerly.

Bertie glanced at the young constable with annoyance. If they took the man in, he would be stuck at the station for who knew how long, and that was the last thing he wanted, especially tonight. Walking on briskly, he came to a firm decision. 'The man's not doing any harm, Smithers, and while I admire your enthusiasm, you'd be better off learning to curb it. If we were to run in every man found drunk on these streets, the cells would be bulging night and day.'

'All right, Sarge,' the constable answered sulkily, still eyeing the swaying man who was now leaning against the door of a tenement.

They had gone only a few steps when the man started up his rendition again, this time accompanied by a frantic hammering on the dilapidated door. The man's voice made Bertie falter for a moment, then, his eyes like steel, he marched on. 'The drunken bastard!' he thought furiously. Why in God's name had Ruby married the man? Even as he asked himself the question, he knew the answer. When Michael O'Brien was sober, he was a charming, witty person, and his powerful personality had at times even broken through his own dislike

222

of the man. He had known for a long time that his brother-in-law liked a drink, but this was the first occasion he had encountered him in such a state. He wondered briefly what had sparked off this drunken spree, and then hot on the heels of this thought came another. Was Michael the type of man who turned violent when drunk? And, if so, would Ruby and the children be in danger if he found his way home? He stopped suddenly in his tracks. Looking back to where Michael now lay half slumped in the doorway, he doubted if he would, but he couldn't afford to take that chance, not with Ruby's safety at risk. Turning back, he said to the surprised Smithers, 'You may be right, Constable. Get him to his feet if you can and we'll take him in, just to be on the safe side.' Charlie Smithers stared at the hard face of his sergeant for a moment, wondering what had brought about this sudden change of mind. 'Now, Constable!' Bertie snapped.

'Right away, Sarge,' Smithers cried, as he walked quickly back to where Michael lay. 'Come on, mate, on yer feet! We've got a nice warm cell for you. Come along, we don't want no trouble.'

Michael looked up into the young fresh face and shook his head, trying to clear his fuddled brain. He couldn't remember where he was or how he'd got here, he just wanted to get home. Rising unsteadily to his feet, he was about to answer the policeman as civilly as he could when he noticed the other officer behind him. Bertie stood under the street-lamp, his features clearly visible, and at the sight of the hated face Michael lunged forward, shouting wildly, 'Bastard, lousy scum of the earth! It's all your fault, you and yer high-and-mighty father. Who do you think you are, eh? Bloody peeler, that's all you are, looking down your nose at me. I'll teach yer! I'll show yer who's the better man!' Swaying drunkenly, he advanced upon the impassive Bertie, swinging his fists wildly.

Bertie watched him coming, his face full of distaste, then scornfully he stepped slowly aside so that Michael sprawled head-first in the gutter. 'And that's where you belong!' Bertie whispered between clenched teeth.

Constable Smithers watched the scene with a startled expression. He had never seen the sergeant look so fierce. There was something odd going on here, and he was at a loss as to how to cope with the unexpected situation.

'Get up, you drunken scum!' Bertie said harshly, the tip of his heavy black boot only inches away from Michael's head.

''Old on, Sarge! What's going on? Do yer know 'im?'

'Mind your own business, Constable, and help me get him on his feet.' The two men bent down and with some difficulty managed to get Michael standing. Then, to Bertie's further disgust, his brother-in-law started to cry.

'Never gave me a chance, none of you, never even gave me a chance. And the auld bitch spoiled all me plans, she did, all of you against me! S'not fair. S'not fair!'

Bertie heard the maudlin self-pity in Michael's voice and felt anger rise in him again. Whom was he referring to when he spoke of the 'auld bitch'? Surely it wasn't his mother, for she had always gone out of her way to show kindness to her unwelcome son-in-law. And then he realized: Lady Caldworthy must have died. Oh Lord, if that was the case, then Ruby would be feeling very low, because she'd been very fond of her employer. He watched with detachment as Michael, helped by Smithers, struggled to his feet, then staggered back as the Irishman threw himself against his shoulder, sobbing uncontrollably. Fighting down his revulsion, he came to a quick decision.

If it were up to him, he would have no compunction in throwing Michael into a cell for the night, but if he did that, he would have to inform Ruby of what he had done. Knowing her, she would insist on coming down to bail her husband out. He dismissed the idea. He thought too much of his wilful sister to put her through such an ordeal, so, holding on to the limp form, he turned to his constable.

'I'll deal with this, Smithers. My watch is nearly at an end, so you go on ahead to meet Sergeant Burrows. He'll be waiting at the Flying Horse in the Commercial Road. Tell him . . . Tell him I've had to deal with a family emergency.'

'Very well, Sarge. You sure you can manage 'im on yer own?'

'Yes. Yes, of course. This man is my – my brother-in-law. I'll see him safely home. Go on now. Sergeant Burrows will be waiting.' When the reluctant constable had moved on, he hoisted Michael to his feet, wrapped his arm round his shoulder and began walking.

'Amy? Amy, are you there?' Bertie called out hopefully as he entered the dark house. When no answer came, he sighed, then, half dragging, half carrying the semi-conscious Michael, he pulled him across the room before depositing him on the settee. Leaving the man sprawling, he hurried into the bedroom, where he prayed he would find his wife asleep, although even before he threw open the door he knew she would not be there. Making his way to the bedside table, he turned the lamp up, then slowly, as if fearing to look, he turned round to see the empty double bed and the half-empty wardrobe, its doors hanging open as though it had been cleared in a hurry. Chewing worriedly on his bottom lip, he carried the lamp into the other room, and after a brief glance at the still figure on the settee, he walked past him and into the tiny kitchen.

With his elbows on the table, he stared bleakly into space. So she had done it! After all the months of threatening to leave, she had finally kept her word. Where had he gone wrong? He had tried to be a good husband, had given her everything he could, within his power, but it hadn't been enough. Bunching his hand into a fist he crashed it down heavily on the table. God damn it! She could have tried harder to make it work, but no, she had become bored with married life very quickly, and like the child she was had thrown their lives together away as easily as a discarded toy.

A retching sound from the next room brought his head up sharply. Damn it all to hell, that was all he needed! He should have left the drunken bastard in the gutter. Blowing out his cheeks impatiently he quickly walked into the sitting-room. 'Here, not on the carpet! Oh, blast it! Come on, get on your feet. I'm getting you a cab, that is if I can find one willing to take you home in your state.' Satisfied that Michael was in no fit state to harm Ruby, Bertie pulled at his limp arm to heave him from the settee, but it was hopeless.

'Sorry, Bertie. Didn't mean it to be like this,' Michael muttered thickly, his sodden features contorted with pain and shame. 'Just wanted to be friends, that's all. Just friends . . . Never even tried to like me . . . did you? Had a down on me as soon . . . as soon as you clapped eyes on me. And your father . . . treated me like I was scum . . . only your mother made an effort . . . But even she doesn't really like me. Why? What did I ever do, except . . . except to fall in love with Ruby?' Screwing up his eyes, he glared at Bertie, then, with a tremendous effort, he added, 'Did you know that Ruby went to the house the day? Came back like a – a dog with two tails, she did. Made it up with the auld fella . . . Invited back to tea next Sunday. But not me . . . Oh no, not Michael O'Brien. I've to stay where I belong . . . in the background, like – like a bad smell. You'll be back next . . . all you have to do is knock . . . Knock on the door, and you'll be welcomed back with open arms. Now, won't . . . won't that be grand? All one big happy family again, and where will that leave me, eh? I'll tell ye where! Out on me arse, that's where . . . That's where I'll be, out on me – me arse.' His head rolled back as he sank once more into a stupor.

Bertie stared at the prone figure with a look of stunned disbelief. Ruby and his father together again after all this time? What could have brought that about? Well, whatever the reason, he was glad of it. If only . . . No, get that idea out of your head, he told himself sternly. He'd tried to make amends by sending his father an invitation to his wedding, only to receive a stilted letter saying that as they were on strained terms he thought it prudent not to attend the ceremony for fear of causing any unpleasantness. And now Ruby had been taken back into the fold . . . Maybe . . .? He shook his head sadly, then, as the smell of vomit assailed his nostrils, he wrinkled his nose in distaste before hurrying from the room to find a cloth to clean up the mess.

An hour later he was still waiting, watching the front door as if by the power of thought he could conjure up his wife, but it remained firmly closed. He couldn't believe that she had really left him. She was probably trying to give him a fright, but for what purpose he didn't know. She'd soon be back, dragging with her the large suitcase she'd packed a dozen times during their short marriage, but what then? He didn't know what she wanted from him. He didn't think she knew herself.

How proud he'd been a year ago when he'd carried his new bride over the threshold into this house, a house he'd bought outright, not rented like those of his colleagues. They hadn't had the good fortune to have acquired savings, as he had done. It had taken every penny he had to purchase the house, a modest little two-bedroomed terrace in the more salubrious part of Mile End, an action he had never regretted. There was something about owning one's own home that gave a man a feeling of importance, and this at least was one thing he had in common with his father.

Closing his eyes wearily, he thought back to the first time he'd seen Amy. It had been his day off, a Saturday. George had called round and asked if he would like a walk over to Victoria Park. He'd gladly consented and the pair of them had set off happily, a wicker hamper tucked under George's arm. After they'd eaten the sandwiches and drunk the flask of lemonade, Bertie had stretched out on the warm grass while George had run off to play football with some children. He had laughed at the sight of George running around after the tatty ball while a dozen or more small boys had tried unsuccessfully to retrieve their prized possession. Turning on to his stomach, he had first noticed the small blonde girl sitting under a large oak, her green eyes studiously reading a gaudy magazine. Without stopping to think, he'd called out to her and had been rewarded by a shy fleeting smile. Emboldened by the girl's response, he had moved nearer and struck up a conversation. She'd told him her name was Amy White, and that she worked as a counter assistant at Boots in Stepney. He had been captivated by her gentle demeanour and before he'd left the park they had made arrangements to meet the following Saturday. They had married a year later. The first six months had been wonderful, and then she had begun to change in her attitude to him. He tried to pinpoint the exact date the subtle change had begun, but found it impossible. All he knew now was that they had slowly begun to drift apart. She no longer wanted to hear about his work; in fact the mere mention of yet another arrest seemed to bore her utterly, and she hadn't tried to hide the fact. Then had come the turning away from him in bed. At first he had been sympathetic, but very soon the flimsy excuses had worn thin. Now she jumped whenever he tried to touch her and endeavoured to keep out of his way as much as possible. Then had followed the threats of leaving, but when he had tried to find out the reason, she would merely shrug her shoulders and walk away, saying she hadn't meant it.

'Oh, Amy! Amy, come back! We'll work it out. Whatever is troubling you, we can work something out.' The time was now two-thirty. Where could she have gone? To his knowledge, she didn't have any close friends she could be with at this hour, but then what did he really know about her acquaintances? With the hours he worked, nights as well as days, she could have a dozen friends he knew nothing about, especially if she wanted to keep him in the dark. Pushing the nagging thought of another man to the back of his mind, he closed his eyes.

'Just for a few minutes,' he whispered wearily. 'Then I'll go and look for her. She's probably changed her mind and is frightened to come home. Just a few minutes' rest, that's all I need.' Stifling an enormous yawn, he settled himself down more comfortably in the soft armchair.

The bright sunlight streaming in through the net curtains made Michael screw up his gritty eyes in discomfort. With a supreme effort he opened them and stared around, wondering where on earth he had landed himself. Groaning out loud, he pulled himself to a sitting position, then winced as a sharp pain tore across his head. Gingerly now he swung his legs to the floor and held his aching head in his hands, staying motionless for a few minutes as he tried to get his brain in working order. He could remember clearly walking out of the lodge and making his way down to the Whitechapel Road – after that, everything was a blur. Then looking across the room, he jumped with surprise at the sight of Bertie, still dressed in his uniform, slumped in the armchair opposite. Dear God in heaven, what was he doing here? And where was 'here' anyway? Vague memories of the night before began to return, and he groaned aloud. The neat sitting-room with its cheerful flowered wallpaper and the orderly furniture must mean that he was in Bertie's home. But why? Well, whatever the reason, he wasn't going to stay. He'd best be moving before his nibs woke up. Standing up carefully, he checked his pockets to make sure he had the price of a cab, then walked on tip-toe across to the front door and let himself out.

Bertie heard the door bang, and quickly jumped to his feet. 'Amy? Amy, is that you?' he called hopefully to the empty room before sinking back in his chair, a look of resignation on his stubbly cheeks. His eyes flickered to the empty settee and then back to the front door. Rubbing his face, he got up and walked into the scullery.

Chapter Twenty-Five

D anny stood on a chair, his anxious face pressed against the cool window pane as he waited for his dad to come home. Suddenly his face broke into a huge grin of relief as he came walking across the lawn towards the lodge. 'Mum, Mum, Dad's home!' he cried as he jumped down to open the door.

In the bedroom, Ruby heard the high-pitched voice and felt her stomach muscles tighten.

'Mummy, hurry up, I want to go and see Dad,' Florrie said impatiently as she waited for Ruby to finish buttoning the back of her dress.

The simple task completed, Ruby propelled her daughter gently out of the room. Going over to the dressing-table mirror, she surveyed her face critically, making sure that the night of crying had left no trace. The past forty-eight hours were at last beginning to tell. She felt drained, completely worn out with tiredness and emotion, but with all that had happened during the past two days, it was the remark Michael had made about 'one-legged help' that remained firmly embedded in her mind. Although she knew he had spoken in anger and would be full of apologies as soon as she went to meet him, the words had cut deep, and she was more determined than ever to show that she was as good as the next woman. Stepping back, she smoothed down the front of her purple dress, then pushed a stray tendril back into the tight chignon at the back of her head. Lastly she picked up a black band and fastened it securely to the top of her sleeve. Then, taking in a great mouthful of air, she raised her head and opened the bedroom door.

Ignoring the painful churning in her stomach, she walked past Michael, who was rolling on the floor with the children, and into the kitchen. Taking the steaming pot of porridge from the stove, she carefully made her way back into the sitting-room, depositing the heavy pot on the table at the far end of the room. 'Breakfast's ready!' she called, making her voice cheerful for the sake of the children.

Michael eyed her warily as she calmly set the plates and bowls out, only a slight trembling of her hands betraying her agitation. Still holding the children, he walked to the table, quickly settling them in their chairs before sitting down himself.

'Oh, Mum, not porridge again. I hate porridge!' Danny cried in dismay.

'So do I,' echoed Florrie, banging her spoon on the table.

'Now then, behave yourselves,' Michael said sternly, 'Don't be upsetting your mother.'

Banging down a large bowlful of porridge in front of him, Ruby answered sharply. 'I'm quite capable of dealing with my children, thank you.'

Sensing their mother's mood, the children made a face at each other before applying themselves to their food. Michael too thought it wiser to keep silent, and picking up his spoon he began to shovel the porridge into his mouth, praying that he would be able to keep the sticky substance down. When the silent meal was over and the children were happily playing in their bedroom, Ruby began to stack the dirty dishes, her face composed as she studiously ignored the figure by her side.

Michael watched her set face and sought desperately for a way to break the strained silence. He'd have to say something soon. More importantly, he'd have to think up a suitable peace-offering. Unbidden, the solution sprang to his mind. It would bring the smile back to her face, but could he himself bear it? When his mug, still half full of strong hot tea, was whisked out from under his nose, he made up his mind. Before he could give himself time to reconsider, he blurted out, 'Are you not going to ask where I've been all night?'

'Where you've been or whom you've been with is no concern of mine,' Ruby replied.

Michael's eyes widened in surprise. Jasus, she thought he'd been with another woman! The knowledge that she still cared enough for him to be angry made his body slump with relief. He had the strong desire to laugh out loud, but curbed it, for he knew that if he gave rein to his mirth, his mug of tea that she was still holding would end up in his lap. Composing his face into a mask of contrition, he said humbly, 'I'm heart-sorry for the way I behaved last night, sweetheart. I didn't mean half of what I said, and as for what I said about . . . Well, you know, about you not being able to . . .'

'You mean about not many places wanting to hire one-legged help?'

she finished the sentence for him.

'Ruby, I'm sorry! It was a terrible thing to say. Will you not forget it?' The tight look on her face was answer enough, and quickly averting his eyes he hurried on. 'It was me Irish temper talking, and, talking about the Irish, I had the luck of it last night. If Bertie hadn't found me walking the streets, I'd probably be locked up in a polis station this minute, or lying with a knife in me back down some dark alley.'

Ruby's grim look vanished, to be replaced by astonishment, and when she pulled out a chair and sat down, he breathed a silent sigh of relief. He had crossed the first hurdle; now he had to go one step further and produce the peace-offering. He knew he'd regret it the minute the words had passed his lips, but if it made Ruby happy and was the means of bringing them closer again, he was willing to make the sacrifice. 'Aye, you can look surprised; I was meself. This was the way of it. I'd had a skinful . . . Well, that'll come as no surprise to you. Anyhow, the next thing I remember is waking up on a sofa with Bertie sprawled out on a chair opposite me. He must have found me and brought me home with him. Why, I don't know, 'cos there's never been any love lost atween the pair of us. But there you are, I'm grateful to him for looking after me as he did, not that he did it out of any feelings for meself. Still, in all, it was good of him. I was going to wake him to say thanks but thought better of it, so I left him asleep.'

Pushing the bowls away from her, Ruby asked, 'You were with Bertie last night?'

'Aye, aren't I after telling you so? And I was thinking, there are some nice houses round that area. What would you say to looking at some of them?'

Ruby looked suspiciously at the unshaven face, searching for some sign of mockery hidden behind the question, but found none. God, he must be feeling guilty about last night, and not without good reason! Well, if that was the case, she'd make good use of it, as long as he didn't change his mind tomorrow and try and wriggle out of it. She swallowed hard before replying, 'You're not just saying that to placate me? I mean you'd really be willing to live near Bertie and Amy?'

Michael looked deeply into her large blue eyes. Well, he'd done it now! The very thought of living close to his brother-in-law caused him to groan silently with dismay, but there was no turning back. Forcing a wide grin to his lips, he said, 'Haven't I just said so? We'll have to work out what we're going to do when we leave here. I was thinking . . .' He paused . . . 'If we put our money together, I could maybe get a stall down one of the markets. I know a lot of fellows who . . .'

But Ruby stood up quickly, sending her chair scraping along the floor. 'No, Michael. I've thought a lot about it, and I've finally decided. I'm going to start a business of my own. And I'm not just saying it out of spite; it's something I want to do. Anyway, two hundred pounds is more than enough to buy a stall, or is it the thought of my being independent that worries you?'

'Begod, Ruby, setting up in business is man's work. What would you do, will you tell me that?'

Drawing a number of circles with her fingers on the table, she waited a while before replying, 'I'm going to start a dressmaking business and aim for the working women who normally buy their clothes down the markets. I could make them dresses for the same price, but twice the quality. I plan to buy some advertising space in the daily papers, but of course I can't do that until we're settled. I've made my own clothes for years, so I'm qualified for the job. I'll need to buy a new sewing machine, but I'll soon recoup the money I spend once I get some customers.'

Michael fought to control his rising panic. The way things were at present, with her being welcomed back into the family fold and therefore once again under her father's protection, the last thing he wanted was for her to achieve independence. He wanted her to depend on him for security, he needed that feeling of importance, no matter how misplaced. Joining his hands together, he said carefully, 'And why did you learn to make your own clothes? I'll tell you, in case you've forgotten. It's because you didn't like going into shops to buy any, wasn't it? The last time you went was to buy your wedding dress, and you came back nearly in tears because of the stares you had to put up with; do you remember?' When she remained staring fixedly at her hands, he exclaimed, 'Ruby, from when you were a young girl you've been protected from the outside world. First with your parents, then when you came here, the auld girl took over where they'd left off. Whenever you've been out, there's always been someone with you, either meself or your mother and Lily, and now you're talking about going to the newspapers to put advertisements in, and having hordes of strange women come to you for their clothes. Think, woman! Think of what you're planning to do. If you still want to go ahead, then I'll not stand in your way, but if you do, then you'll have to develop a thick skin, 'cos people are cruel, Ruby, in the main. People are cruel.'

She thought for a long moment before answering softly, 'Oh I know that, Michael. I know that to my cost.'

He looked at her set face, at the pain in her eyes, and dropped his head. God Almighty, if he could only take back what he'd said last night! But he couldn't, just as he couldn't stop her from going her own way. He left the table and walked unsteadily into the bedroom.

Hardcastle Street, situated in a quiet position just off the Mile End Road, consisted of a neat row of terraced houses on both sides of the street. The majority of its tenants were made up of bank clerks and office workers, those people in the enviable position of being able to afford to rent or buy their own home. It was a different world from the tenements that occupied most of Mile End just a short way away. The people behind the lace curtains would do without food and clothing rather than give up their hard-earned status of respectability.

Ruby got off the tram at the corner of the road, her face aflame with embarrassment. In an effort to show Michael that she could cope on her own, she had insisted on coming by herself to view the house they'd picked out the week before to measure up for the curtains. Putting her head down against the cold, she hurried along, the familiar clicking of her leg echoing as she walked. Keeping her eyes studiously down, she didn't stop until she'd reached the safety of number eleven. Quickly inserting the key in the lock, she hurried inside. Her body was shivering, but her face was still warm from her experience on the tram. How mortified she'd felt when that man had tripped over her outstretched leg, and even worse when he'd started to shout at her, only to stop as he realized her handicap. His flustered apologies had brought the attention of the other passengers to her, and two elderly women sitting opposite had kindly warned other passengers of the obstruction in the confined carriage. She had fought down the strong impulse to alight and hail a cab, but had resisted, knowing that from now on this would have to be her form of transport. But, oh, the shame she'd felt as the kindly but prying eyes had stared! Slowly she crossed to an old wooden chair, the only piece of furniture in the house. Sinking down gratefully, she looked around the cold empty room, feeling tears begin to form.

Now, then, there's no time for self-pity, she reproached herself. As Michael had so forcefully pointed out, she'd have to get used to the stares. And he had been right in all that he'd said. She had imagined herself so brave and self-sufficient when she'd first left home to go out into the big wide world, but what had she really achieved? She'd simply gone for one cosseted household to another. In all the time she'd spent with Mabel, she had hardly ever left the house except when she had company, and then the journeys had always been by hansom cab. But no more. From this day on she would use public transport, for it was the only way she would ever learn to steel herself against the sympathetic looks. Giving herself a mental shake, she stood up, briskly determined that she would conquer the shame she felt. It was a case of learning endurance or spending the rest of her life hiding behind the door of her home, and she wasn't going to do that. Swallowing the lump in her throat, she took out her measuring tape and began to size up the windows.

When she was finished, she wandered round the rooms, chiding herself for playing for time. The journey back had to be faced, and not only that one, but many more. She had to find a new school for Danny, and enrol Florrie, who was fast approaching school age. Moreover, she had to find time to visit the bank and arrange for the money Mabel had left to be legally transferred to the children. The bequests had been handed out by Sir Charles, much to her relief. She'd been terrified she would have to go to the bank for it, and, if so, Michael quite naturally would have wanted to accompany her to collect his own inheritance, and what if the bank manager had mentioned the three thousand? Shuddering, she closed her eyes at the dreadful thought. What explanation could she have given to Michael then? Still, it hadn't happened like that , thank God, and in two weeks they would all be living here in a house that would herald a new start for them all, and in particular for herself. She's already marked the storeroom for her sewing machine and writing-desk, and despite Michael's scornful words she was determined to make a success of her venture. As to what he intended to do, she'd have to wait and see, because apart from that one mention of a stall, the subject of a job for him hadn't arisen and she'd been wise enough not to push it – for now.

It was a pity that both Bertie and Amy would be at work at this time of day, for she would have liked to visit them. She only hoped that her sister-in-law wouldn't object to the idea of their being neighbours. Realizing that she was wool-gathering simply to postpone the moment of going out once more into the street, she took a deep breath, then, pulling on her gloves, she straightened her wide-brimmed hat and sallied forth on her journey home.

'Goodbye, Ruby, I'll miss you and the children,' Mrs Rodgers sobbed, wiping her overflowing eyes with a large white handkerchief.

They were in the kitchen waiting for the cab Sir Charles had hired to take them to their new home. He had been so kind to Ruby these past few weeks, even going so far as to offer her the furniture from the lodge. She only wished he'd offered sooner, for it would have saved her a great deal of money. The purchase of the house, plus contents, had all come out of her own money; Michael was keeping his safely tucked away, an action that was causing Ruby deep resentment. Even so, she would have liked him to be with her today, but he had hurried out early that morning, saying something about a friend knowing of a shop going cheap down Aldgate way. He hadn't even looked back; the knowledge that he would never again set foot in the place that had been his home for nine years had not made him sentimental. Not so herself, who had said goodbye to each and every room with a lump in her throat. Even the knowledge that her new home, completely furnished, was waiting had brought no comfort.

'Will you write and let me know how you're getting on, Ruby? I can't bear the thought of never seeing or hearing from you again,' Mrs Rodgers was saying.

'Of course I'll keep in touch. I have your sister's address, and I can't tell you how happy I am at knowing your future is so settled.'

Mrs Rodgers's face creased into a quivering smile. 'Well now, Ruby, my sister's been on at me for years to go and live with her, I've always liked Kent, but I had her ladyship to see to. I would never have left while she was alive, and also, I couldn't have gone empty-handed; I wouldn't have felt right.'

The sound of the knocker interrupted them, and looking at each other, they rose to their feet. 'I'd better get the children,' Ruby said breathlessly. Walking unsteadily to the window, she tapped on it sharply to summon them in from their last romp in the garden.

'Oh, Mum, is it time to go already?' Danny said sadly.

'Yes, I'm afraid it is, son. Now say goodbye to Mrs Rodgers. You too, Florrie. The cab driver is waiting.'

Both the children were gathered to the kindly woman's ample bosom for so long that she was afraid her old friend would smother them both. Watching the poignant scene reminded Ruby once again of the morning she had spent saying goodbye to the people she had spent the last nine years with. It had been an emotional experience. Mr Masters had retained his usual stiff composure until Danny had held out his hand to say goodbye. Then Florrie had put her arms out for a hug, and the old man's stern face had crumbled, and gruffly bidding them all good luck he had turned away, but not before Ruby had seen the tears in his pale eyes. Rosie too had been tearful, and Ruby had had trouble prising the children away from her. Only Agnes had

235

remained unmoved by the highly charged atmosphere, too full of her own plans to be concerned about anyone else. They had all gone now. Only herself and Mrs Rodgers were left.

'Mrs Rodgers, we'll have to go. The cabbie is waiting, come along now,' she said gently, trying to keep her voice steady. The memories of the house were crowding in on her, causing her to feel unbearably sad. She could feel the presence of Lady Caldworthy everywhere and could almost hear the quavering voice saying, 'Be happy, Ruby. Be happy.' Taking Florrie's hand, she stumbled to the front door, and only Mrs Rodgers's stout arm prevented her from falling.

Seeing the small group emerge from the house, the cab-driver jumped down and helped Ruby and the children into the coach.

Her eyes brimming with tears, Ruby leaned out of the window and clasped Mrs Rodgers's hand, glad now that Michael wasn't here to witness her grief. As the cabbie clicked his whip, she cried in a choked voice, 'Goodbye, dear friend! I'll never forget you.'

'Nor I you, Ruby. May God watch over you and the little ones. Goodbye, my dear. Goodbye!'

Ruby was forced to relinquish her hand as the coach began to move off. Taking a last anguished look at the older woman's face awash with tears, she pulled away from the window and sank back on the leather seat. Then, covering her face with her hands, she wept unashamedly while the children tried to console her.

Chapter Twenty-Six

They had been in their new home for nearly three months, but it wasn't until Ruby had seen Florrie off to school with Danny a week earlier that she had finally called at the office of one of the daily papers and asked for her advertisement to be inserted in the next edition. Now she sat waiting for her first customer to knock at the front door.

For the tenth time that morning she looked at the clock, wondering if she dare leave her post to go and see Bertie, then shook her head sadly. Since Amy had left him, he had changed into a person she no longer knew. When she first heard the news, she'd hardly been off his doorstep, but his silences and sudden bursts of self-pity had left her at a loss as to how she could help him. She knew it would take a higher authority than herself to break through the hard, morose shell her brother had built round himself, and she was determined to speak to her father on Sunday, to try to make him see just how much Bertie needed him, now more than ever.

The clock chimed the half-hour: twelve-thirty, and still no sign of a potential client. Nipping her bottom lip, she stood up and went into the bedroom to have another look at herself in her new outfit. Skirting around the brass double bed and mahogany wardrobe, she opened the top drawer of the tallboy and took out a clean handkerchief before turning back to face the full-sized mirror that stood in the far corner. Her fingers picking nervously at the tiny pearl buttons, she studied her reflection, uncomfortably aware that the red dress with its high-necked collar and leg-o'mutton sleeves was about five years out of date. According to Lily, she should throw out her entire wardrobe and make herself some new clothes more in keeping with the latest fashion. Turning away, she tutted impatiently. It was all very well for Lily to talk; she didn't have a handicap to conceal. Although the new mode of simpler, straighter skirts and tailor-made costumes were giving women more freedom of movement, she still preferred the wide heavy layers of petticoats and skirts that successfully hid the void on the right side of her body. Lily was right, as usual. She couldn't go on wearing the same clothes for ever, and besides, it wasn't a very good advertisement for her new business to be seen in old-fashioned garments.

She went next door into her workshop, her eyes resting briefly on the new Singer sewing machine on top of a sturdy table. Going to a chest of drawers, she opened one and pulled out a length of blue cotton, nodding to herself. She'd start this evening. What she'd do would be to make a blouse out of the bale of white lace in the top drawer and use this blue cotton for a skirt. But she wouldn't make it too narrow – oh no, she wasn't yet ready to change her mode of dress overnight; she'd take it one stage at a time. Humming gently, she put the fabric back in its place and went back into the sitting-room to wait. She was just about to sit down when the knocker sounded at the front door, making her start nervously. Wetting her lips, she smoothed down the front of her dress and, head held high, opened the door, 'Oh, it's you!' she exclaimed, her voice heavy with disappointment.

'Ah, now that's a nice way to welcome your husband!' Michael stood on the doorstep, twisting his bowler hat in his hands. 'I thought I'd better knock in case you had a room full of half-dressed women in here.'

Clicking her tongue in annoyance, she threw the door open wide. 'Don't be so stupid! And what are you doing home from work at this time of day anyway?'

Michael raised his eyebrows in mock surprise as he shut the door behind him. He was dressed smartly in a pair of narrow black trousers and grey morning jacket, underneath which was a crisp white shirt topped by a black cravat. He had used his money to buy a haberdasher's in the middle of a row of shops in Aldgate. A former assistant there, by the name of Mr Midson, had come with the shop and as he knew all there was to know about running the place, Michael had been only too pleased to keep the grateful old man on. Michael spent most of his time talking to the women customers, charming them into buying articles they didn't really need and standing in the doorway exchanging snippets of conversation with the other owners, who, like him, were content to let their assistants carry on with the hard work. Then of course there was always the pub to go to if he became bored, and Michael became bored very easily.

Whistling under his breath, he eyed her warily before saying, 'I thought I'd come home and see how you were getting on. But if you want me to go, just say the word.'

'Oh . . . take no notice of me. I've a lot on my mind at the moment. Are you home for the day, or is this your dinner hour?'

'Well, I could manage a bite if you're going to cook . . .' He saw the look on her face, and hastily added, 'But don't trouble yourself on my account. I can get something at the pub.'

'I was just about to make a cup of tea, if you want one. Then, if no one turns up within the next hour, I thought I'd pop down to see if Bertie's in. I'm worried about him; he seems to be getting worse.'

Michael sat down, his eyebrows drawing together in annoyance. 'And what will you say if he is in, eh? The last time you went down there, you came back in tears. Now, I'm telling you for your own good, Ruby, leave well enough alone. I know he's your brother, but to my mind he doesn't want to be helped. Why, he even turned on George last week, didn't he? Told him to get out and not interfere . . . No, there's nothing else you can do. Leave him. He'll come round in his own good time. Now . . . promise me you'll not go down there?' He bounced his head at her, his face solemn. 'You know I hate to see you upset. I'm only thinking of you, darlin'.'

Ruby looked away, unable to stand his hypocrisy. He had no concern for Bertie, and would be more than pleased to keep the relationship between them strained, but she'd be damned if she would! Placing her hands on her hips, she faced him angrily. 'You're not thinking of me. You're thinking of yourself, as usual! I should have known better than to confide in you. But you've made me realize that I can't stand by any longer and see him suffer. I was going to wait until Sunday, but now I've decided to go and see my dad tonight. I know George and Mum have tried to get him to go round to see Bertie, and now it's my turn. I'll make him see sense if I have to drag him down here myself!' Her stomach lurched at the prospect of facing her dad, for since they had resumed their old relationship she had gone out of her way to keep the peace between them, even to the point of backing down on occasions, but no longer.

'What do you mean – you're going round tonight? You were there only a few days ago, and I can't look after the children, I have someone to meet later on. No, Ruby, I don't mind you going there once a week, but I'm not having you traipsing off there whenever the fancy takes you! I'm telling you . . .' He was on his feet now, his eyes glittering with anger.

'Don't you dare tell me when I can visit my parents! I'll go whenever I choose. As for the children, I'll ask Mrs Williams from next door to look after them.'

'Aye, at a shilling a time. And how do you propose to get there? You can't travel by tram at night, and we can't afford a cab. It would be different if you were earning, but . . .' he indicated the room, 'it doesn't look like your bright idea is going to work, does it? I told you it was a stupid idea, but no, you wouldn't listen, you always think you know best . . . Now for the last time . . .' He broke off as the knocker sounded loudly at the front door.

Ruby was across the room in moments, and when she saw the young woman standing nervously on the doorstep she smiled broadly.

'Excuse me, are you Mrs Ruby O'Brien? I – I've come about the advertisement.'

'Yes, I'm Mrs O'Brien. Please come in.' She stood aside to let the woman enter, then quickly moved out of the way as Michael stormed past her.

Gripping the door, he hissed at her, 'Remember what I said, and don't wait up for me. I don't know what time I'll be home.'

Ruby nodded curtly before turning to her first customer. 'Would you like a cup of tea, Miss . . . ?'

'Oh, me name's Ada, and I would like a cuppa! I've come in me dinner-time so I can't stop long.'

As Ruby walked towards the kitchen, she could sense the woman's eyes on her, and thought, 'I'm going to have to get used to this, and the best form of defence is attack!' When she emerged a few minutes later with a tray, she set it down on the table and said cheerfully, 'I see you've noticed my leg. I had an accident when I was a child, but I don't suppose you're interested in my past history. Now, Ada, how can I help you?'

'Ruby, I am pleased to see you!' an agitated George said with relief as he opened the door to his sister. Almost tearing the coat from her back, he hopped from one leg to the other, his eyes darting furtively towards the closed parlour door before adding urgently, 'I was just on my way round to Bertie's, I'm really worried about him. I stopped off on my way home yesterday, even though he went for me the last time I went round. Anyway, the door was wide open, and at first I thought the place had been burgled. Then I saw him. Oh, Ruby, I hardly recognized him. He was slumped across the settee reeking of drink. I couldn't rouse him, hard as I tried, and the house, my God, it was filthy. When I think of how proud he was of his home, and how fastidious he's always been about his appearance, I thought for a moment 'd stumbled into the wrong house. I was going to come down to you, but . . . well, I know how Michael feels about us all . . . and . . .' Gulping twice, he ran a finger round his collar and added, 'I tried to talk to Father. I really did, Ruby, but the moment I mentioned Bertie's name, his eyes clouded over and – and I was too afraid to push the subject. I'm not strong enough to tackle him on my own; he still . . . frightens me at times. I feel so ashamed for being the way I am, but I can't tell Mother. If she knew the awful state he was in she'd go round, and God knows what the effect would be on her if she were to see him as he was yesterday. But she was saying at dinner that she planned to visit him this week-end. Will you talk to Father, Ruby? You're . . . you're stronger than I am, and he'll be more likely to listen to you. He respects you. Please, Ruby? I'm so afraid for Bertie. If he goes on like this, he'll end up killing himself.'

Ruby looked at his round chubby face and thought sadly that despite his twenty-five years he was still a young boy and would likely remain so to the end of his days.

Unnoticed by them, Lily had entered the hall, her normally happy face grave. 'George told me about Bertie, Ruby. Will you . . . ?'

'All right, all right,' Ruby answered sharply, 'That's the reason I came round. I'm as concerned about Bertie as you are. He is my brother, after all.' Handing Lily her hat and coat, she walked stiffly to the parlour.

'Why, Ruby, this is a lovely surprise,' Daisy cried happily, then, her face dropping, she said, 'There's nothing wrong, is there? Has something happened to the children?'

'No, there's nothing wrong. I just felt like a visit without them for a change. I never get the chance to talk in peace when they're around.' Scanning the cosy room, she asked, 'Where's Dad? Is he still at work?'

'No, of course not! He's in the library; there's some paperwork he has to catch up with. Why do you ask?'

'No reason; I just wondered where he was,' Ruby answered defensively.

Daisy looked at her daughter for a moment, then, putting down her needlework, she pulled herself to the edge of her chair and said firmly, 'What's wrong, Ruby?' She held up her hand to ward off any interruption. 'Don't tell me this visit is merely social; I know you too well, my girl! Is it something to do with Michael? Are you two in trouble of any kind?'

Ruby rubbed her forehead wearily. She should have known better than to try and deceive her mother. Resting her hands in her lap, she said softly, 'It's Bertie, Mum. He's not getting any better. What I mean is, he's not making any effort to pull himself together, so I thought I'd try and talk to Dad, to see if I can persuade him to go to see him. I've tried to snap him out of his depression and so has George but he won't listen to us. And, Mum, he's – he's a lot worse since you last saw him. As for me, I'm afraid I've stopped going. I thought if he was left alone he might come round on his own, but George saw him yesterday. He was drunk, Mum, and not just tipsy, but dead to the world. I didn't know how bad he was until just now. I only came round tonight because I was feeling guilty about not doing enough, but now I'm glad I did.' She stopped as she saw the look of alarm cross her mother's face. 'Oh, Mum, I'm sorry, I didn't mean to upset you! But listen, I've just had an idea. Do you think Dr Benson would go and see him? Bertie always respected him, and he might be able to give him something. What do you think?'

Daisy shook her head despairingly. 'I'm afraid poor William is past caring for the sick. He's been ill himself for a number of months and is planning to leave London and take up residence in the country. No, it's up to your father now, and if he still refuses to make his peace with Bertie, then I'll go myself. I'll stay by his side until he's well again.'

Ruby stood up, her body trembling, 'Give me a chance to talk to Dad, Mum? If I don't have any luck, we'll have to get Bertie well ourselves.' Bending over the still figure, she said gently, 'Don't worry, Mum. We'll sort something out, you'll see.' With a final reassuring pat on her mother's hand, she walked to the library door and knocked before entering.

'Ruby, what are you doing here?' Bernard said in surprise, then repeating what Daisy had said earlier, he asked anxiously, 'There's nothing wrong, is there? Are the children all right?'

'That's nearly exactly what Mum said when she saw me,' Ruby said shakily. 'May I sit down, Dad? I have something I need to talk to you about.'

At her words Bernard stiffened, then nodding curtly, he said, 'If it's about your brother, you're wasting your time. George has already tried to intercede on his behalf. He's a grown man and should be able to sort out his own affairs without any help from me. So if that's all you came for, I'm afraid your journey has been wasted.'

Ruby stared at the stern figure and for a moment imagined herself transported back to the days when he had had the power to frighten her, but no longer. 'It's no use your looking at me like that, Dad. I'm not a child any longer, so I can't be scared into silence by a steely look.

I don't know what George told you, but I'm telling you now that if Bertie carries on as he has been for much longer, he will almost certainly lose his job. That alone would be the finish of him, because you know how much it means to him. But that's not the worst of it. He doesn't wash or shave any more and his home is like a pigsty. I wouldn't have believed that Amy's going would have affected him so badly, but it has, and I'm afraid that if he doesn't come to his senses soon, it will be too late. Please, Dad, won't you swallow your pride and help him?'

Bernard quelled the rising turmoil within him. Bertie ill? Why had no one told him? He knew of course about his wife leaving him, and knew also that he was having a bad time coming to terms with what had happened, but he'd had no idea that his elder son had sunk to such depths of despair. Placing his fingers on his lips, he gazed thoughtfully into space. The desire to go to him this very minute was overwhelming, but the fear of having the door slammed in his face kept him firmly seated in his chair.

Mistaking his attitude for complacency, Ruby heaved herself up, her face nearly white with anger. 'How can you sit there with that indifferent look on your face? Bertie could be lying dead in a pool of vomit while you sit there deliberating as to whether to stir yourself or not!' She was standing by the desk now, her hands gripping the edge tightly. 'Good God, what kind of a father are you? If I hadn't come crawling back you would never have taken the trouble to seek me out, and by the same token you would never have seen your grandchildren – the same grandchildren who have grown to love you. I loved you enough to humiliate myself, not knowing if you would welcome me or throw me out, and now it's your turn to take the same risk.' When he still didn't answer, she leaned over the desk until their faces were nearly touching, and said bitterly, 'Even when we were children, you never had time for us! I had to lose a leg before you showed me any warmth, and I'll tell you something else, shall I? Bertie once told me that he thought I was lucky, can you imagine that? He thought I was lucky! He was only thirteen at the time, but he said that he wished it had been he who'd had the accident, then maybe you might have shown him some affection.'

'*Stop it!*' Bernard had risen from his chair. 'I won't have you speaking to me in this manner! Now get out before I . . .'

Near to tears, Ruby banged her fist on the desk, shouting, 'Damn it, Dad, he's your son!'

So engrossed were they that Daisy was able to slip into the room, and they were unaware of her presence until she spoke. 'Go to him, Bernard,' she said tearfully, 'before it's too late. Make your peace with him and bring our son home.'

Bernard looked at both of the women, then, without a word, he strode past them and out of the house, slamming the door.

The tap-room was packed to bursting as Michael pushed his way through the throng. God, he needed a drink! He had gone home straight after the shop had closed and found Ruby on her way out. He'd only been in the house five minutes when they'd been at each other's throats again. All because of that brother of hers. What in God's name did she expect him to do if the man's own father wouldn't lift a finger to help his son? Jasus, but he was a hard-hearted man, that one. When he thought of his own dear father, God rest his soul, a man who would have given his last farthing to a stranger if need be, he could find it in his heart to feel pity for Bertie. His tankard clasped tightly in his hand, he looked around in the hope of spotting a familiar face, then shrugged, and leaned against the bar, his foot on the brass rail. As he sipped his beer, he wondered why this particular pub held such a fascination for him. He had come here originally to see the place where Ruby had been born, and had imagined that once his curiosity was satisfied, he would no longer have any interest in the place, but he always seemed to be drawn back. Draining his tankard, he leaned across the counter waiting for the landlord to return and re-plenish it. While he waited, he tried to imagine Bernard Chadwick, that high-and-mighty man of the City, working behind a bar, but found it impossible. Giving a short laugh, he reasoned with himself that as he'd never clapped eyes on the man, it wasn't surprising. His tankard full once more, he moved away from the bar to find a seat in the densely-packed room. Brushing past one of the three-legged tables, he stopped to apologize to the man he had accidentally shoved in the back, then froze in his tracks.

God preserve and protect us, it couldn't be! Moving swiftly away, he positioned himself in the far corner and stared in stunned amaze-ment at the sight of Bertie Chadwick, looking no better than a com-mon tramp, seated morosely over his half-empty mug of beer. Taking another long mouthful of his drink, he continued to stare at the dis-hevelled form of his brother-in-law. He had listened without interest to Ruby's fears concerning Bertie; now, seeing him here like this, he was overcome with confusion. His first impulse was to try to help the man, but would his help be welcomed? To hell with him, it was no business of his! He'd best finish his drink and move on to another pub; but he remained staring at the hunched form. Wiping his mouth with the back of his hand, he returned to the bar, his thoughts whirling. This could be a golden opportunity to make friends with the man he'd envied and despised for years. If he could persuade Bertie to come along home with him, it would smooth things out with Ruby. When he'd taken a long swig from his third mug of beer, he nodded his head. He'd do it – he'd try to talk to the man. What had he to lose? Squaring his shoulders he strode purposefully back to the table, then once again his footsteps faltered as the pub door swung open and a tall distinguished man stepped hesitantly into the smoky crowded room. Michael felt his mouth turn dry. Even though he'd never seen Bernard Chadwick he knew, deep down in his bones, that here was Ruby's father, and when the stranger, after scanning the room, walked slowly over to Bertie, he knew for certain. For a moment Michael experienced a terrible feeling of loss, as though he had been deprived of something precious. He felt a sudden pang of sadness as he turned and walked back to the bar.

Bernard stopped outside the King's Arms, his face weary. He had been in almost every public house this side of the water, and so far without success. Taking off his high hat, he rubbed his eyes tiredly. If he wasn't in here, he would have to give up for the day and try to reach him at his home again tomorrow. Pushing open the heavy door, he stepped into the place that had once been his home, and shuddered slightly; the pub held no fond memories for him, it was just another crowded smoky pub. Worn out with fatigue, he looked into the faces, and was about to leave when he stopped and slowly turned back. His eyes focusing on the bent figure of the man seated in the middle of the room, he walked heavily towards him, his heart thumping. When he was near enough for the man to hear him, he said tentatively, 'Bertie! Dear God, Bertie, is it you?'

Bertie lifted his red-rimmed eyes and blinked twice at the tall figure standing before him. The man's face seemed blurred to his drink-fuddled brain.

Bernard felt the room sway beneath his feet. 'Oh, dear God, forgive me,' he prayed silently as he looked down at the unkempt drunkard that was his son, and touching Bertie's arm, he said, 'Bertie, it's me . . . Father.'

Bertie angrily pushed his hand away, then, as if recognizing the voice from the past, he looked up again, his mind trying to focus. A look of hope passed over his face, and then in a voice filled with incredulity, he mumbled thickly, 'Father?'

Fighting to keep control, Bernard took hold of Bertie's arm and, using all the strength he possessed, raised him to his feet, his son's limp arm round his shoulder. 'Yes, it's me, son,' he said. 'Let's go home. Your mother is waiting for us.' Holding his son tightly against his side, Bernard led Bertie from the pub.

Chapter Twenty-Seven

'**H**appy birthday, Mummy!'

'Happy birthday, Mum!'

'Oh, this is a nice surprise! Thank you,' Ruby cried delightedly as she undid the gaily wrapped parcel.

'Me and Florrie bought it ourselves, Mum, out of our pocket money,' Danny said earnestly, anxious that his sacrifice would not go unnoticed. 'But we couldn't go to the shops by ourselves, so Aunt Lily took us yesterday while you were out.'

'Well, I'm very grateful to you both. Oh . . . what a lovely scarf! It's just what I wanted.' She smiled as she looked down at the bright orange and purple monstrosity.

'We picked it out ourselves,' Florrie chipped in. 'We wouldn't let Aunt Lily do it.'

Ruby smiled at them fondly. 'I'm sure you did, and I'm very proud of you both. Now, off the bed and let me get up. I still have to make the breakfast, even if it is my birthday.'

Reluctantly the children left the room, knowing that they weren't allowed to watch their mother get dressed. They had sometimes tried to catch a glimpse of her attaching the wooden leg, but without success. They had both learned very early that she guarded her privacy, and although they yearned to discover how the wooden leg got from the wall to beneath her skirt, that secret was still a mystery.

Ruby didn't get up immediately, but started to think about the empty place in the bed beside her. It no longer worried her when Michael didn't come home after a night's drinking, but it was sad to realize that even the children were becoming so used to his absences that they no longer asked where he was. Thinking of the way he had changed brought on the familiar feeling of guilt, and she threw the bedcovers back, and got up. Washed and dressed, she went to the kitchen to prepare breakfast, the feeling of guilt still niggling.

It had been over a year since she'd started her dressmaking business and already had enough steady customers to warrant taking someone on to help. Rene Blanks, a young cheerful red-headed girl, had been with her for only three weeks, but was already making herself indispensable. For a long time Ruby had toyed with the idea of visiting those women who wanted items of clothing but were too busy to come to her. News of her new venture had quickly spread, and she already had a number of potential clients to call on. All in all, her future looked set, unlike that of Michael, who had been forced to sell his shop through lack of business.

'It's not my fault he didn't make it work,' she whispered to herself as she turned the sizzling bacon in the iron frying-pan. 'He should have tried harder; I would have done.' But no, as soon as the going had got tough, he had given in without a fight. He had come to her for help, asking her to borrow three hundred pounds from her father so that he might get the business back on its feet. When she'd refused, he'd flung himself out of the house, blustering and shouting. On that occasion he hadn't come home for four days. She sighed at the memory of that day, and the knowledge that she could have given him the money from the children's trust fund weighed heavily.

'Mum, is breakfast ready yet? We'll be late for school!' Danny called from the sitting-room. Brought back to the present day, Ruby quickly dished up the bacon and eggs and carried them through to the waiting children. Half an hour later when they were dressed and ready to leave, the front door opened slowly to reveal a dishevelled Michael clutching a bunch of flowers in one hand and a large box of chocolates in the other.

'Morning, sweetheart! Happy birthday,' he said sheepishly.

'Daddy, Daddy!' the children shouted, rushing towards him, but they stopped suddenly as he backed away.

'Not now, kids. I don't feel very well. I'll play with you when you get home from school.'

Ruby's lips tightened. She had become used to being pushed away, but for him to treat the children in the same manner was unforgivable.

'Come along, both of you, else we'll be late,' she said as she made to move past Michael.

'Morning, Mrs O'Brien!'

Ruby turned quickly to see Rene about to enter the house, smiling broadly. Forcing a smile to her own lips, she said, 'Rene, do you think you could take the children to school for me, just for today? I – I have some paperwork I'd like to see to before going out. If you don't mind, that is?'

Rene looked at the woman who had saved her from a life of working fourteen hours a day in a sweatshop. Would she mind? Lord, she'd do anything for Mrs O'Brien, she only had to ask! 'Course I don't mind! Come on, kids,' she cried gaily. 'We'll 'ave a game of 'opsctotch on the way. I've got me key to get back in if you want to go out, Mrs O'Brien. I'll make a start on that green dress just as soon as I've got these two settled.'

'That'll be fine, Rene. As a matter of fact I think I'll go to see that woman in Hackney. You know, the one who wrote to me yesterday.'

'Mrs O'Brien, don't you worry abaht nuffink; I'll look after fings 'ere. You take your time.'

When the door had closed after them, Ruby rounded on Michael. 'What the hell do you think you're doing? How long is this going to go on? Coming home when you feel like it, pushing your children away because you're too drunk to give them any attention . . .' Looking at the presents he had laid on the table, she added scornfully, 'And don't think you can bribe me with a few flowers and a box of chocolates. It won't wash any more! You've got to pull yourself together, Michael. I'm not putting up with it for much longer.'

'Ruby, Ruby, don't start! It's all right for you, you've a good business going,' he answered, his hand holding his brow. 'I'm trying, honest I am, but it's not easy to get a job at my age.'

'Rubbish!' Ruby shouted, her body quivering with anger. 'You haven't even tried! Even since you lost the shop, you've been walking round as though somebody had died. You haven't even tried to get a job, but then you don't want a job, do you? You think such menial work is beneath you now that you've had a taste of being your own boss. Well, I'm giving you fair warning, I'm not prepared to put up with your behaviour any more. No self-respecting man would be content to let his wife support him; not when he was quite capable of work himself.'

'That's enough, woman! I'm sick of your preaching. I don't have a wealthy father to finance me, and don't tell me he hasn't been helping you, 'cos I don't believe it.'

Ruby was unable to believe what she was hearing. She had made her business work without help from her father or anyone else, and Michael certainly knew it. Still . . . if it made him feel better to think so, then let him; she was past caring. Walking towards the door, she said over her shoulder, 'I don't know what time I'll be back, but in case you're not here when I return, you'd better know that I've arranged to go out with my parents on Saturday night. They're taking me out for dinner, to celebrate my birthday. I don't suppose you'll be home, so I've asked Lily to look after the children while I'm out.'

Michael lowered his head; he didn't want her to see the hurt in his eyes. She could have said no to her parents, could have said she'd rather spend her birthday celebration with her husband, but no; and who could blame her? They'd probably take her to a fancy restaurant up the West End, and what could he himself offer? At best, a few drinks in the local pub. In a voice filled with pain, he said, 'You're a hard woman, Ruby. I was always proud of your strength, but now I see it for what it really is. You're hard; you always have been.'

Ruby watched him shamble away, pursing her lips. She wasn't hard. She wasn't! She was just trying to survive in the only way she knew. Her eyes pricking with tears, she stumbled from the house.

As she made her way down the road, her eyes firmly looking out for any hidden potholes, a cab passed her, and it took all her will-power to stop herself from hailing it. How lovely it would be to sink into the soft leather seats and be driven straight to the door of her destination, but she mustn't get soft again. It had taken her months to get used to riding on trams, and although she still didn't like them, she had become accustomed to them. She would always stand during her journey, to cut out the chance of tripping any unsuspecting passenger. The only problem now was the persistence of gentlemen who insisted on offering her their seat. It was a great pity that no one had thought of inventing an artificial leg that bent at the knee, but she was one of a minority and inventors needed a mass market.

While Ruby waited for the tram, she took out the letter that had arrived the day before. It was from a woman in Hackney who wanted some new uniforms for her women staff. Reading it through once more, she felt a moment's apprehension. Was she biting off more than she could chew? If she made a good job of the order, however, it was more than likely that the woman would recommend her to her friends. Taking one last look at the address, she returned the letter to its envelope, her mind immediately returning to Michael and what he had said to her.

It wasn't fair! She had worked damned hard, and if he had shown the slightest inclination to knuckle down and work to save the shop, she would have fought alongside him; she would even have gone so far as to get him the money he needed. But Michael didn't want help. He wanted someone to do all the work for him, to shoulder the responsibility, and, in short, to be allowed to live a worry-free existence. She had known for a long time that she had married a weak man, but never had the knowledge been so painfully evident as it had been this past year. Shaking her head sadly, her thoughts turned to Bertie and his complete recovery from his mental disorder of the previous year. He had stayed at the house in Brixton for nearly six months while her mother and father, not to mention Lily, had fussed over him and nursed him back to health. Bernard had even gone down to the police station and spoken with Bertie's Inspector, the result being three months' compassionate leave with no reprimand for his previous behaviour. He'd returned to duty over two months ago and was now back home, a quieter, more serious Bertie, but nevertheless a sober one. A sudden shove from behind made her look up, and seeing the tram coming, she concentrated on the business of getting on, as it was already nearly full.

An hour later she was standing outside the address in Hackney, her mouth dry as she looked at the imposing house before her. The stone pillars flanking the porch reminded her of Mabel's home, and, with it, memories of another life. Giving herself a mental shake, she drew a deep breath and mounted the stone steps leading up to the front door. Pulling the iron bell, she stepped back and waited for a long agonizing moment before the door was opened by a young girl in a grey dress with a stiff white frilled apron and a starched frilly cap.

'Yes? Can I help you?' the girl enquired.

'I hope so. My name is Mrs O'Brien, and I'm expected by Mrs Chiddy.'

'Oh, yes. Come in. May I take your coat?'

Ruby allowed herself to be helped off with her coat, glad now that she had taken extra care with her appearance. She was wearing a white lace blouse with a full black skirt. Although the extra layers of petticoats didn't hide her handicap, they gave her a feeling of security. Following the maid, she entered a large room and was dismayed to find not one woman but three, all watching her as she came towards them.

'Ah, Mrs O'Brien, so good of you to come! Please take a seat.' A small woman, elegantly dressed, extended her hand towards a nearby chair.

Ruby could feel her face beginning to burn as she felt the eyes of the women upon her. Carefully lowering herself into the chair, she self-consciously pulled at the hem of her skirt in an effort to stop the tip of her leg from showing, but to no avail.

'I'm so glad you were able to come, Mrs O'Brien, I've heard such a lot about you. Doris – that's the maid that let you in – well, her mother was one of your clients, and she was so impressed by your work that she's been telling everyone she meets. When I mentioned to my house-keeper about needing new uniforms for the staff, Doris mentioned your name, and, well, here you are.'

Ruby smiled weakly, the uncomfortable feeling she'd experienced when she'd entered the room growing stronger by the minute. 'Thank you for the compliment,' she told Mrs Chiddy. 'I try to please my clients, and I hope I can be of service. May I ask exactly what you re-quire? You see, I only have one assistant and we do have a lot of orders to finish.'

'Of course, of course, but first let me offer you some refreshment. Then you can tell us all about yourself.'

Before Ruby could protest, Mrs Chiddy had rung the bell, and while they waited for Doris to appear, she could feel the women's con-tinuing scrutiny. She jumped slightly as a younger woman leaned for-ward in her chair.

'Tell me, Mrs O'Brien, how do you manage to visit your clientèle? It must be so awkward for you to travel by public conveyance that I suppose you use cabs for your journeys.'

Swallowing nervously, Ruby looked from one to another of the faces, all of which displayed an avid eagerness, and felt the first stir-rings of anger rise inside her. The bloody nerve of the woman . . . of all of them! They were surveying her as though she were on display in a cattle market! Lifting her head, she answered firmly, 'As a matter of fact I do use trams. I find them a much quicker form of travel than hansom cabs.'

'But, my dear, wouldn't it be easier and more convenient for you to travel by cab? After all, with your . . . disability it must be uncomfort-able travelling among a crowd of people.'

Ruby eyed the woman with distaste. It was becoming increasingly obvious that she had been summoned as an object of curiosity rather than as a *bona fide* business proposition. A sick feeling settled in her chest, and with a slight tremor in her voice, she answered, 'It's very kind of you to be concerned, but I didn't come all this way to discuss my travelling arrangements, so I'd be grateful if you'd tell me what it is you require. I'm a very busy woman, as I'm sure you all are.'

The women looked at each other, and Ruby was quick to see the knowing glances that passed between them. The sickness was now moving up to her throat, but before she could speak, the woman she knew as Mrs Chiddy put her hand to her throat, and with a sym-pathetic look, said earnestly, 'But, my dear, we didn't mean to pry!